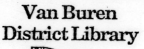

"A strong sense of the city of Santa Fe and its environs and the appeal of the two well-developed main characters show why this mystery was the first winner of the Tony Hillerman Prize for the best debut mystery set in the Southwest."
                                                    —*Booklist*

"Barber's first novel is full of exquisite New Mexico scenery."
                                        —*Publishers Weekly*

"Isn't it great when a new writer comes along and makes you sit up and take notice? Christine Barber does just that with *The Replacement Child*. Don't miss it."
                    —Michael McGarrity, author of *Nothing But Trouble*

"In this excellent debut, newcomer Christine Barber weaves a heartbreaking mystery with the assured hand of an old pro. *The Replacement Child* has many charms: It's a riveting procedural, a compassionate and perceptive study of human nature, and a wonderfully labyrinthine whodunit. But it's the heart of this story that is the real charmer: the fascinating landscape of northern New Mexico and the tangle of cultures, old and new, that populate it. I guarantee that if you let Christine Barber take you there once, you'll want to go back with her again."
                    —William Kent Krueger, author of *Thunder Bay*

"*The Replacement Child* is a gripping story set against the deceptive calm of an ancient land in modern times. In northern New Mexico, lives and events are interconnected, and Christine Barber weaves a tale where nothing is irrelevant and no one is unimportant. Barber is a wonderful storyteller and her characters invite us into their hidden places, compelling us to turn the page."
                    —David Sundstrand, author of *Shadow of the Raven*

"Barber writes with charm and gusto, having a special talent for depicting her main characters."
                    —*I Love a Mystery* (highly recommended)

THE BONE FIRE

THE BONE FIRE

Christine Barber

MINOTAUR BOOKS

A Thomas Dunne Book

New York

This is a work of fiction. All of the characters,
organizations, and events portrayed in this novel are either
products of the author's imagination or are used fictitiously.

A THOMAS DUNNE BOOK FOR MINOTAUR BOOKS.
An imprint of St. Martin's Publishing Group.

Book design by Rich Arnold

www.thomasdunnebooks.com
www.minotaurbooks.com

Library of Congress Cataloging-in-Publication Data

Barber, Christine.
    The bone fire / Christine Barber.—1st ed.
        p. cm.
    "A Thomas Dunne book."
    ISBN 978-0-312-59350-6
    1. Police—New Mexico—Fiction.   2. Women
journalists—Fiction.   3. Murder—Invetstigation—
Fiction.   4. Santa Fe (N.M.)—Fiction.   I. Title.
    PS3602.A7595B66 2010
    813'.6—dc22

                                        2010012841

First Edition: July 2010

P   1

To my mom—I miss you.
To the cancer that took her—you suck.

AUTHOR'S NOTE

The Spanish words used in this book reflect New Mexico's unique Spanish dialect and, as such, do not share all of the characteristics of the better-known, modern-day Spanish. For instance, most Spanish speakers today would say "mi hijo" when referring to their son, while Spanish speakers from Northern New Mexico would say "mi hito."

Additionally, in the book the term "Hispanic" is used instead of "Latino" when referring to someone from Northern New Mexico who is of Spanish decent. While "Latino" is the term most used in the rest of the country, "Hispanic" is the commonly used local term.

CHAPTER ONE

Thursday Night

The lights flashed off, and a few people screamed.

A couple of teenagers nearby held up lighters as if they were at a rock concert. Someone yelled, "Freebird," which got a slight swell of laughter from the crowd standing in the dark, open field.

Lucy Newroe looked at the family of four standing next to her. The dad had his arm around the mom. Two kids—both girls—stood in front, their eyes shining. The younger girl, who looked all of eight with brown hair down to her shoulders and big eyes, suddenly screamed, "Burn him!" into the night.

The parents laughed. The older sister playfully jostled the younger one before yelling, "Burn him!" The parents smiled. The two girls started to yell together, and the parents joined in; the dad cupped his hands around his mouth so his voice would carry, and the family chanted together, "Burn him! Burn him!"

The group of teenagers behind Lucy took up the cry and yelled, "Burn him!" even louder. Then more people behind her joined in. "Burn him!" Within seconds, the entire crowd of thirty thousand seemed to be screaming the words together. Lucy turned back toward the still-dark stage they were all facing. Lucy checked her watch: 9:02 P.M. It should start any minute now.

The crowd was still shouting, "Burn him! Burn him!" when the boom of fireworks broke out high above them. Everyone cheered. A bouquet of colored lights flashed on, illuminating a large effigy that stood on a dais in the front of the crowd. The puppet—or more correctly the marionette—was fifty feet tall, taller than a four-story building. Santa Fe schoolchildren had spent the last week constructing him of chicken wire, paper, and muslin. He was all white, except for a shock of blue hair and a black tie, which went nicely with the long white skirt he was wearing. He had pizza pans for eyes, huge ears that stuck out at least six feet, and big, full lips. He looked like a cross between Ted Koppel and Frankenstein.

The puppet had a name, Zozobra, and a nickname, Old Man Gloom. In a few minutes, they were going to burn him to death. This was an execution. He stood on a hill, arms outstretched on a cross made of metal. The monster must die for our sins.

Somewhere, a gong began to strike.

Zozobra started to move his huge arms in a floating resemblance of a Martha Graham dancer. His mouth opened and closed as he faced the crowd. Zozobra started to growl. It was like the deep noise an old man makes when woken from a good nap. It was like the sound of an engine revving on a Dodge Charger. The growling didn't stop.

Lucy shifted from foot to foot in the dark, not sure what to expect next. She had to admit she was a little bit anxious. She had never been to Zozobra before, but then she'd only lived in Santa Fe for a year and a half. Her boss, Harold Richards, who had been city editor at the *Capital Tribune* for the past twenty years, described it as "a bunch of people standing around while they torch a big puppet." She hadn't believed him at first. It had sounded so silly—and so pagan in a city as Catholic as Santa Fe, whose very name means "Holy Faith."

Still, Zozobra had been a Santa Fe tradition for more than eighty

years. It was the opening salvo in the fiesta party arsenal. The actual
Fiesta de Santa Fe didn't begin until tomorrow. Like any good Catholic celebration, the weekend started with the fires of salvation and
ended in acts of sin. Tonight was about redemption. Tomorrow was
about partying your ass off. In a wholesome, family way, of course.
Because fiesta was about faith, plain and simple. It was about the faith
of one man—Don Diego de Vargas—who more than three hundred
years ago said a prayer while encamped with his army outside Santa
Fe. It was the eve of battle, so of course he prayed hard. He needed to
retake the city, which the Spanish had lost to the Pueblo Indians more
than a decade earlier. He prayed that he could do so without bloodshed. He said this prayer to La Conquistadora, a wooden statue of the
Virgin Mary, and he made her a promise. More of a bargain, really. If
she would deliver the city to him without loss of life, he'd throw her a
big party every year in thanksgiving. She delivered and he succeeded,
and so Fiesta de Santa Fe was born. Fiesta nowadays consisted mostly
of parades and sitting around the Plaza eating Navajo tacos and bur-
ritos. There also was a procession honoring the statue of La Conquistadora, which was carried on a handmade wooden litter though
downtown.

Zozobra was a newfangled event, comparatively. It was started
mainly as a fund-raiser for college scholarships, but one that would
have put the fear of God into Edgar Allan Poe.

Zozobra's look and size had changed over the years. During
World War II, he'd been only eight feet tall and made to look like a
combination of Hitler, Mussolini, and Emperor Hirohito. Now he
looked more like an old man in a nightgown. Even so, Zozobra was
as hip as any teenager—he had his own Web site, and his fans could
follow him on Twitter.

Lucy heard far-off music start to play and could barely make out
a performer slinking across the stage in front of the puppet. Zozobra started to groan more loudly in anticipation. If a guy had made
a noise like that in bed, Lucy would have checked to see if he'd broken something. The yelling of the crowd was constant now. Too loud
to distinguish between words.

She tried to keep an eye on the dancer—who was only ankle-high to Zozobra—but the people in front of her blocked the view. At only five feet tall, she felt like a mushroom in a forest of sequoias. She jumped up to see what was going on, but she only caught a glimpse of the stage. She got jostled by the dad in front of her and could only see the chest of the man behind. On either side, there were just elbows and shoulders. She was in her own private cell with four walls of people. Her foot got stepped on. Her hair caught on someone's jacket.

She needed to move to see better—and so that she wouldn't be black and blue tomorrow. She made her way through the crowd, which was surprisingly easy. Most of the people were so intent on the figure ahead they didn't even notice her passing by. She decided to get to the edge of the field and then figure out where to relocate.

The lights of the stage flashed blue, red, and green on the faces in the crowd. Occasionally, she heard another group start the "Burn him! Burn him!" chant. Every once in a while someone yelled "Que viva!" or "Que viva la fiesta!"

Lucy found the edge of the field, which was lined with booths selling soft drinks and Zozobra merchandise. The image of Zozobra adorned everything from T-shirts to temporary tattoos, shot glasses to earrings. She considered a Zozobra beer mug before her attention was diverted back to the stage by Zozobra's growl getting louder.

She felt the current of the crowd change from relaxed to anxious. The tension became skintight as the pop, pop, fizz, fizz of fireworks faded into the background. She noticed a patch of short-looking people near the middle of the field and thought it best to join her own kind. She made her way to them, only to realize when she was a few feet away that they were in wheelchairs. Still, she could easily see over their heads.

The stage was now filled with people whirling and whipping torches. Another dancer in red and yellow started a complicated performance near Zozobra's feet. The monster growled louder. A bunch of little bonfires flared up on the stage as careening fireworks started to go off again and the field boomed with their echoes. Tracers of red, green, and white sizzled into the sky. The crowd was going crazy, but they were drowned out by the fireworks, the music, and the growling, which was almost a scream by now. Lucy wasn't sure how long she could take the noise and tension without some release.

It almost surprised her when Zozobra's execution was delivered by a single flare launched directly into his open mouth. His head caught fire first, his face melting quickly away, while his eyes and mouth became hauntingly backlit by the orange flames. His skull spit sparks up into the night sky as his arms twisted and writhed uselessly at his sides. He was a demon caught in the flames of hell.

The rest of his body caught next as ash showered down onto his dress and fountains of massive sparklers came to life nearby. The brilliant strobes of light bounced off the faces in the crowd like a million camera flashes. Lucy could feel the heat from the flames that licked their way down his body. Zozobra snapped and crackled as the terrorizing flames scorched his dress.

Zozobra kept growling, the crowd kept screaming, and Lucy closed her eyes in a prayer of sorts. She tried to let the anxiety she'd been holding on to for months flow out of her.

Zozobra was a monster, but first and foremost, he represented a new beginning. He was burned every year so the problems of the past would go up in flames with him. He was Old Man Gloom, and the people in the crowd were the victors, the conquistadores. They would triumph over their troubles by burning their past mistakes. Zozobra was one big cleansing fire.

Lucy hoped it was true. She hoped the memory of the last few months would be wiped away in the white-hot fire. She opened her eyes again. Zozobra was a metal skeleton now devoid of his paper flesh. He still hung on his stand, a small bonfire burning at his feet. Fireworks burst into the night; the crowd laughed around her. She heard one of the teenagers behind her say, "That was a good burn." Lucy hoped it was.

Part of the Zozobra tradition was for people to write letters that were put in the base of Zozobra before he was burned. They threw in old photos, divorce papers, police reports—any worry they wanted to be rid of. She had written a note that had been burned in the fire, as so many other people had.

Her note had been simple: *Release me.*

CHAPTER TWO

Friday Morning

Detective Sergeant Gilbert Montoya of the Special Investigations Team stood on a hill, looking out over the baseball field littered with trash—plastic cups, paper plates, food wrappers. The sun was still coming up, yet he could make out almost everything in the navy blue morning, the faintest trace of crispness in the newly autumn air.

He glanced up at the Sangre de Cristo Mountains to see if any of the aspen had started to turn yet, but there was no flash of yellow. The hillsides still had their swatches of green. Then again, it was only the second week of September. In another month, the color would be there. He turned his attention back to the hill he stood on, which last night had served as a stage.

He walked back over to the pile of ash that had been Zozobra only eight hours ago and looked up at the metal pole that was permanently cemented into the hilltop. It had served as Zozobra's backbone during all the burnings. The fifty-foot-tall pole, scarred and pitted with years of fire, still held tightly to the chicken-wire mesh of Zozobra's skeleton from the night before.

Gil looked down at the huge pile of ash, as did the four other people standing next to him.

The four men were all members of the Protectores de la Fiesta, a group whose job for almost three hundred years has been to guard the fiesta's tradition and symbols. Gil's grandfather and dad had both been members before they died. It was an elite group, allowing in only male descendents from one of the forty or so Spanish families that founded Santa Fe.

Growing up, Gil always knew it was fiesta weekend by two things: his mother making tray after tray of carne adovada and his dad and grandfather dressing in the uniform of the Protectores—black pants and a yellow satin shirt with a red sash. The colors of the New Mexico flag.

The four Protectores who had been watching the remains of Zozobra all night were there to make sure no sparks got free and nothing got rekindled. They had been the ones who had prompted Gil's wake-up call. As the sky had started to lighten, something strange in the ashes had caught their attention. They had raked and pushed the cinders around until they finally figured out what they were looking at—a human skull.

Gil had been woken up from a sound sleep. He had gone to bed early—just after 10:00 P.M. He and his family hadn't gone to Zozobra. In fact, they had never gone together. The year his daughter Therese was born, there had been a gang shooting on the Plaza just after Zozobra burned. Susan had refused to bring their daughters since. Gil had thought about insisting they go this year. The girls were old enough—Joy was twelve; Therese was ten. The girls themselves had pestered Susan every day for the last week, but his wife never budged.

He glanced at his watch again, wondering when the field deputy for the Office of the Medical Investigator might arrive. Gil had called the OMI on his way to the scene and gotten assurances that someone would be there soon. He had already called his boss, Chief Bill Kline, to tell him the news: that thirty thousand people might have watched while someone burned to death. Kline's only response was "I'm on my way." Gil glanced again at the mountains, which were starting to glow with sunshine, then looked back at the ashes.

The skull had been bleached white by the fire.

It was a small skull. The skull of a child.

Gil looked away again.

Lucy woke up with a start from a dead sleep, her fire department pager screeching next to her on the nightstand. She grabbed it, cranked down the volume, and jumped out of bed, stumbling out of the room before she could wake up the man next to her.

Behind the closed bathroom door, she turned the pager volume up to barely audible and heard the dispatcher call out a car fire in an arroyo. She sighed and rubbed her eyes, debating. She wasn't a firefighter, so she didn't need to go. Hell, she was only a volunteer medic at the department, so she really didn't need to ever go. She could just slip back into bed. On the other hand, the bed held its own problems she didn't want to deal with. Plus, they might need a medic at the fire to run rehab for the firefighters. Should she stay or should she go? Honestly, Lucy would rather deal with a deadly fire than any man in her bed.

"Okay," she said to herself, the decision made. She turned on the bathroom light and opened the top bathroom drawer. She pushed aside some tampons and pulled out her Breathalyzer. She knew from experience that if she drank a six-pack and then slept for at least five hours, the machine would register a .02. Last night, though, she'd done the unusual. She'd had tangy shots and sweet mixed drinks. Who knew what that'd do to her blood alcohol level?

She pulled out the device, which was about the shape and size of a cell phone, and blew into the mouthpiece. She had ordered the Breathalyzer a month or so ago after seeing too many DWI crashes. Now, if she did decide to have a beer or two, she could be sure the morning after that she was okay to drive. She considered it the ultimate act of responsibility.

She waited a minute, then looked at the digital readout on the machine. It flashed .07. The legal in New Mexico was .08, so she was good.

She walked back into her dark room, where she stubbed her toe on something in the middle of the floor, yelling out "Oww" before she could stop herself.

"What the hell are you doing out there?" came a voice from the bed.

"You left your shoes in the middle of the floor."

"Only because you wanted to get my pants off so bad," he said, chuckling.

The sound made her nauseous and annoyed. She was having day-after remorse, regretting that she'd ever brought him home. It had seemed like such a good idea last night. The alcohol was probably to blame for that.

She'd gone to the Cowgirl after Zozobra, looking for a drink and wanting to hold on to the frenzy of the crowd. She needed to be some-place loud and raucous, but the Cowgirl was quiet. She stood alone at the bar for a moment, looking over the few diners who were finishing up their meals. She had decided to leave when the bartender asked her what she wanted to drink.

She glanced up at him absently. He was studly, in that he was covered in studs. On his dog collar, in his ears, through his nose. She wondered where else.

"Umm, I guess I'll just have a shot of something," she said. As he turned to grab an amber bottle, she noticed a tattoo on the back of his shaved head. He poured her a generous shot of who-knows-what and set it in front of her. Lucy downed it in one swallow. It was sweet with a hard edge of alcohol.

"Is that the best you got?" she asked, running a little flirtation up the flagpole to see what happened. She was still geared up from Zo-zobra and needed to keep the spark going. She was all tension, and, as usual, it came out of her in naughty ways.

"Honey, I got a whole lot better than that," he said with a smile. He took a clear bottle full of viscous liquid off the shelf, and she watched him mix her a drink. His arms were covered in tattoos.

He smiled, and she noticed he had on mascara and a sweep of purple eye shadow. Which was more makeup then she was wearing at the moment. Interesting. Maybe he was gay or bi? Lucy decided there was only one way to be sure.

"I've never slept with a man wearing makeup before," she said. Might as well get an answer to the gay question before she got too far along in her flirting.

"What makes you think we're going to sleep together?"

"What makes you think we're not?"

Gil had been on scene for only a few minutes when Liz Hahn pulled up in the medical investigator van. Liz, from Ocean Grove, New Jersey, had moved to Santa Fe with her partner, Shelly. They had two kids, one of whom was in the same grade as Therese.

Liz called, "Hey," over to Gil by way of a greeting. She stopped short of approaching the ashes and instead looked around. She flipped open a notebook and scribbled a few quick notes about the initial scene. She took a camera out of the duffle bag she was carrying and snapped a picture of the mountains as they became tinged with pink, then wrote down the time: 7:10 A.M. "Shelly is a sucker for sunrise shots," she said before turning the camera to the ashes, clicking away for a good minute.

She went closer to the ashes, carefully crouching down next to the skull. She stared and wrote in her pad, then stared and wrote some more before taking another round of photos. She went back to her truck and got out a small hand rake, which she used gingerly on the ashes for a few minutes, before getting up and going over to the Protectores. Gil heard her ask them how they found the skull and when. They told her the same thing they told Gil—that they had been there all night, they stopped raking the ashes as soon as they saw it, and no one had touched anything since.

Liz looked over to Gil for confirmation, and he gave a nod of his head. She went back to the ashes. This time Gil joined her with his notebook, knowing that this was how Liz liked to work: first, get a clear idea of the scene; second, get as much information about the scene as possible; then lastly grab the nearest detective and formulate a theory. Gil liked the method. He always left with a good idea of what Liz was thinking. Not all investigators were so polite. A few actually forbade all people on the scene from talking and left without revealing a thing.

Liz gently poked at the skull with the tip of her capped pen before saying, "Obviously it's a child. My guess is somewhere around one or two years old. I'll have a better idea when we look at the skull in the lab."

"Cause of death?" he said, scribbling in his notebook in his own shorthand.

"It's hard to say, but let me show you this." She tipped the skull over slightly to reveal something stuck on the bottom. It was a mass of swirled red, green, and blue gunk with wire and metal pieces frozen in it. "This stuff covers the whole back side. It looks like melted plastic. We'll have to get that off before we can get a good look."

"So you can't even say it's a homicide?"

"No. It could just be nothing more than improper disposal of a body. Who knows?"

"Boy or girl?"

"No idea," she said, letting the skull fall back into place.

"I'm guessing the kid didn't die in the fire."

"I don't think so. I haven't seen any other bones that would indicate the whole body was here. Also, I don't see any organic material here," she said as she poked at the ash with her pen. "So the decomposition took place somewhere else and just the skull was dumped here."

Gil nodded and asked, "Any way to know how long the kid's been dead?"

She made a noise that could have meant yes or no. "The skull doesn't look very brittle," Liz said. "So my initial guess is, not that old, but the fire . . ." She looked up at the metal frame that had been Zozobra before saying, "I don't know what the fire would have done to the bones."

Liz stood up and called over to the Protectores, "Hey, how hot would the fire have been last night?" They looked at her blankly and didn't answer. She shrugged and whispered to Gil, "Big fricking help."

"It's not their fault," Gil said. "Those guys actually have nothing to do with Zozobra. The whole thing is run by the Kiwanis Club as a fund-raiser. The only thing the Protectores do is sit around the fire all night to make sure there aren't any sparks. Then in the morning they clean the trash up. They consider it a way of protecting the sanctity of fiesta, which is what they are all about."

"You know a lot about this," Liz said.

"Too much," Gil said.

Liz sighed, sat back on her heels, and said, "All right, so Zozobra is mostly made of paper and wood, so the fire wouldn't have been that hot. Maybe like a thousand degrees. It would have had to be about fifteen hundred degrees to melt off flesh." She stopped for a minute before saying, "Look, all I can tell you is the skull was probably dry when it ended up here, but where it was before that . . . I just can't narrow the time of death down more right now. This kid could have died yesterday or fifty years ago."

She stood up and dusted off her pants before saying, "This is Santa Fe. Cars don't rust and bodies don't rot."

"Hey, you. It's time to go," Lucy said to the lump in her bed, as she pulled on her combat boots and laced them up. She tucked her navy blue fire department T-shirt into her black pants and clipped her pager on her belt.

The man turned over and smiled at her, saying, "I bet you don't even remember my name."

Lucy sighed. She just wanted him gone, so she said in one breath, "Your name is Nathan. You moved here five years ago from Pennsylvania. Your mom's a Realtor. You haven't talked to your dad in ten years, and your only sister is coming to visit in two weeks. The best job you ever had was working one summer as a heavy equipment operator for the Forest Service. And, oh yeah, you work at the Cowgirl to make ends meet, but your true passion is art because you like the creative process. Now get the hell up."

"How did you remember all that?"

"I'm a reporter. I pretty much just interview everybody when I meet them. It's a habit," she said.

"Wait. I thought you were a waitress, and you worked at some-place downtown . . . or something. The only thing I know about you is that your name is Tina."

Lucy had forgotten she'd used her one-night-stand cover ID with him. "You know, Nathan, I'm really boring, so that about covers it," she said. "Now, you have to go."

"Why are you wearing an EMT uniform?"

"Nathan," she yelled. "Get up and get out. I have to go. Lives are at stake. Or at least the life of a car is at stake."

She pulled him off the bed and rummaged around for his shoes and shirt, which she threw at him. He started to put on his pants, but she said, "There's no time for that." She pushed him outside in front of her as he pulled his T-shirt on.

She locked her door in the faint twilight as he struggled with his pants, saying, "At least let me . . ."

"Sorry. Good-bye."

She jumped in her car and pulled out of her drive while calling herself into service on her EMS radio that was bolted onto her dash-board. She popped a mint into her mouth. She had to stop herself from looking back at Nathan and checking him out in his state of undress.

She wanted to speed through her neighborhood of old adobe houses and cottonwood trees, but the roads here were old—too old to accommodate more than one car. That made getting to and from her house a constant lesson in patience as other drivers stopped and started in the narrow lanes. This morning was quiet, so she quickly made it out into the world of real streets that had proper crosswalks and bike lanes.

She was at the fire station a few minutes later, having broken many a speeding law. She opened the passenger door of the ambulance, which had PIÑON VOLUNTEER FIRE DEPARTMENT written in reflective paint on its side, and jumped in.

Paramedic Gerald Trujillo, in the driver's seat, didn't say good morning. The daily niceties between them had fallen away a while ago. They were partners, each knowing what the other required.

Gerald drove the ambulance out of the bay and into the street.

She picked up the radio, saying to Dispatch, "Santa Fe, Piñon Medic One en route to car fire."

As Gerald flipped on the lights and sirens, Lucy smiled. She hadn't lied to Nathan when she told him she was boring. She was—most of the time. A couple of times a week, though, right when the sirens started to blare, she became a true blue action hero.

"God, I hope it's not her," Gil heard one of the Protectores say as he stared at the ashes.

"I kind of hope it is in a way," another answered. "You know, to help the family deal with it."

"Yeah, but at least before they had hope," the first one said.

"There was never any hope," a third man said, before making the sign of the cross, kissing his thumb, and glancing up at the sky.

"I hope it's not her," the first one said again.

Gil knew whom they were talking about: Brianna Rodriguez.

While Gil had been waiting for Liz, he had called Santa Fe dispatch to see if any children had been reported missing in the past twenty-four hours. The answer had been negative, which he knew it would be. A missing child in Santa Fe was so rare, he would have known about it the moment it happened. Then the dispatcher had added, "There's always Brianna."

Two-year-old Brianna Rodriguez had gone missing during a family barbecue more than a year ago. The unofficial theory was that Brianna had been swept away by a monsoon-fueled flash flood. The family's backyard was unfenced and backed up to an arroyo, like many Santa Fe homes. It had started to rain when they noticed she was gone, and within minutes an intense flash flood from a summer monsoon had filled the arroyo to the top, washing away any trace of Brianna. They had done ground searches and dog searches and interviewed everyone and anyone who had ever seen the girl. The Protectores, like Gil, had probably helped with the search, volunteering their free time to comb the neighborhood.

The only other possibility was that it had been a stranger abduction, which had been mostly discounted—until now.

"Is this kid big enough to be her?" one of the Protectores asked.

"Brianna was thirty-one and a half inches tall and twenty-two pounds," Gil heard someone say next to him. He turned and saw Detective Joe Phillips, who had somehow walked up to Gil's side without him noticing. Of course, Joe had served in the military, so he had been trained to be invisible. "She was a preemie, so she was a small kid," Joe added as he watched Liz sweep ashes into a plastic evidence bag. Phillips was in his late twenties and had become a detective only a few months ago. He had been with the department for two and a half years following a stint with the Pennsylvania state police. Gil didn't know much about Phillips's life before he came to New Mexico, other than that he had gone into the army after high school and done a tour in Iraq. Gil had heard that Phillips had gotten married and divorced at some point, even though the man seemed too young to have an ex-wife. Phillips looked even younger than usual this morning. His red hair and goatee needed a trim, and he was dressed in T-shirt and jeans, as if he had just rolled out of bed. Gil knew he had worked Zozobra the night before—like most Santa Fe police officers—and wondered who had called him.

Phillips turned away from the ashes and looked at the rising sun, rubbing his eyes. He had been the first officer on scene when Brianna was reported missing. He had set up the initial search perimeter and set up a command center until a detective could arrive. That detective had been Brian Fisher, who committed suicide six months ago using his service weapon. A few months before Fisher died, the Rodriguez family had filed a lawsuit for police harassment against the department, Fisher, and Chief Kline.

Gil walked over to Phillips but said nothing, waiting for the other man to speak.

"It's her" was how Phillips started. Gil still said nothing. "I thought we'd find her alive. Fisher—that goddamn moron—always knew she was dead."

Phillips turned to face Gil. "I bet Fisher a hundred bucks that we'd find her alive. If that stupid bastard hadn't killed himself, he would have enough money right now to buy us all breakfast."

He turned back toward the sunrise and wiped his eyes again. Even though Fisher hadn't been killed on the job, Phillips had worn a black band around his badge during the funeral. To him, it was Brianna's case that had killed Fisher, and that made it a line-of-duty death.

"Fisher knew she was dead," Phillips said, more to himself than Gil, before adding, "but who put her here?"

Liz, who had stopped working to listen to them, said, "Look, I can't tell you if it's her . . ."

"Liz," Phillips said in a tired voice, "why don't you shut the hell up? Of course it's her. Who else could it be?"

"Joe," she said, annoyed, her New Jersey accent becoming more pronounced, "there's always the chance it's just a skull from some archaeological dig. We've got a million of those going on all the time. Hell, every time anyone builds anything around here they find bones."

Phillips shook his head and started to pace. Liz muttered something under her breath and went back to work.

Before Brianna, there had been no missing kid cases in Santa Fe since 2000. The last had been Robbie Romero, a seven-year-old who had walked out of his house one night to go visit his friend three doors down and was never seen again. These bones were too small to be from anyone over the age of five. Before Robbie, there had been no cases Gil could remember.

Phillips reached into his back pocket and pulled out a worn brown wallet. He opened it, taking out a small photo that was tucked behind his driver's license. It was of Brianna. It showed her face and part of her shoulders, her chin resting sweetly on her hand. Her hair was short, not yet grown out from its baby wispiness. Tiny pink rhinestones sparkled in her pierced ears, matching her pink T-shirt with roses. Her big, dark eyes smiled. It was the same photo Gil had seen a thousand times—on posters at every convenience store around town and in the newspaper accompanying each story about Brianna's disappearance. Phillips stared at the photo for a moment and seemed about to give it to Gil, but he put it back in his wallet, which he shoved into his pocket with force.

"I hate this," Joe said. "What does this mean, finding her now? It's been a year since she disappeared. Does this mean someone killed her last year and kept her body this whole time, doing who knows what with it? Or does this mean that he kept her alive and then just killed her, like, last week? . . . Oh, God."

Joe walked off toward the bushes looking like he might throw up. Gil considered going over to check on him, but then realized that was probably a bad idea. As cold as it sounded, Gil couldn't allow himself to get too caught up in emotion and speculation. No matter how horrible the crime seemed at the moment, he would still have to build a solid case, one brick at a time, just like any other investigation. He couldn't head off into the scary places just yet. Or, like Joe, he would end up being sick.

An old Ford truck pulled up near the crime scene tape, and a man with a shaved head jumped out. Gil recognized him instantly. It was Mike Vigil, the director of Zozobra for the Kiwanis Club. Mike and Gil had played basketball together at St. Michael's High School almost fifteen years ago. Gil walked toward him, and the two men shook hands. Gil assumed one of the Protectores had called him.

"What can you tell me?" Mike asked.

"Basically, all I can say is that we found a skull in Zozobra," Gil said.

"I heard it was a kid's skull," Mike said.

"I can't tell you anything more about it, sorry," Gil said. He knew this had to be tough for Mike. He was in charge of the burning, which was a family event that usually went off without a hitch.

"Okay, but you've got to tell me this," Mike said, his eyes tearing up slightly. "Did I burn a kid alive last night?"

"No, Mike," Gil said, putting a hand on his shoulder. "No. Whoever the skull belongs to was long dead." Mike nodded, taking a big breath of relief. Gil said to him, "Look, can I get your business card? I'm sure I'm going to have to call to get more information once the investigation gets started."

Mike pulled a card out of his wallet and handed it to Gil, saying, "Thanks." He stopped to shake the hands of the Protectores before getting in his truck and speeding off.

Gil went back over to Liz, who was packing up her gear. "How's Shelly?" he asked, just to make small talk, hoping the normalcy of it would quiet his worms of worry.

"She was fine until she got a bug up her butt about moving out to Eldorado after your wife told her how good the schools are," Liz said. "Have you and Susan found a place up there yet?"

"We have to wait until we sell our house in town."

"Did you do the upside-down statue of St. Joseph?" Liz asked. "My cousin did that and he didn't even have to list his house. Some guy out of the blue comes up to him wanting to buy it."

"Yeah, we did that."

"Did you bury it in the backyard, not the front?"

"Yeah, it's just the market," Gil said. "Susan wants us to buy a place in Eldorado even if it doesn't sell."

"And leave you with two mortgages? Hell no."

Gil was helping Liz load her equipment back into her van when Santa Fe police chief Bill Kline pulled up in his black SUV. Kline got out, along with Captain Paul Garcia, who was the department spokesman.

He heard Liz say, "The big boys are here," as the men came walking over.

Kline said, "Liz," as a way of greeting. Gil told the men all that he knew: It was the skull of a small child who did not die in the fire.

Kline nodded, saying, "How long will it take to get an ID?"

"I don't know," Liz said. "It's an hour drive down to Albuquerque, and then I'll have to call in our skeletal specialist . . . it'll be at least two hours or probably closer to three before I can tell you anything. An ID is probably going to take a lot longer, until at least next week. We could end up with inconclusive results because the bone sample was too weathered or damaged in the fire. Who knows. This is going to be a mess no matter how we slice it."

"If it's her . . ." Garcia said, trailing off.

If it was her, all hell would break loose.

CHAPTER THREE

Friday Morning

Santa Fe Municipal Court Judge Victor Otero pulled yet another paper from the stack and firmly, without flourish, signed his name. He flipped the paper smoothly over onto a pile laid neatly next to his elbow. He checked his watch. It was 7:55 A.M. Time to head into court. He was starting court early today because of fiesta. Most city workers had the day off. Since he was one of the Protectores de la Fiesta, he had been at Zozobra until almost 2:00 A.M., but he didn't feel tired.

He stood, sliding his chair neatly under the huge oak desk, which had been used by every municipal judge since 1902. It had been his since 1994. He would move it to his office at home when he retired.

He took his robe off the coat hanger and zipped it up. He headed to the bathroom off his office to check his reflection. He looked intently at himself in the mirror. He straightened his red tie, just visible under this robe. His hair was less than a quarter inch from touching his ears. He would need to get it trimmed within the next week. He always went to Earl's Barbershop, as his father and grandfather had before him. The Earl in charge now was Earl Junior. Earl charged him seven dollars for a trim and sold some of the best green chile in town, but the judge went there mainly for information, as did state senators, the police chief, and the mayor. Or used to. In the past twenty years, things had changed. Only the old-timers still went to Earl's.

He glanced at his watch. Precisely eight o'clock. He took one last look in the mirror, then one last look at his office, making sure everything was in its place before going out into the courtroom.

Lucy stared down at the ground. Tiny rocks of every hue pockmarked the pink-beige earth. Periwinkle blue, dark chocolate, butterscotch. They were like a scattering of jelly beans from a knocked-over box. Bite-sized and smooth. She bent down and picked up a smooth black rock. It had a stripe of white through its licorice black center.

She heard a loud pop and looked up. The car on fire across the road groaned as the metal warped from the heat. Two firefighters on the hose directed a stream of water onto the fire. With a few sweeps of the nozzle—and a sizzle and a vent of steam—the fire was out.

She stood next to the ambulance, waiting like she always did for someone to get hurt or exhausted so she could spring into action. Her job on fire scenes was to be everyone's Jewish grandmother. She was constantly asking, "Are you tired? Are you hungry? Are you thirsty? Sit, sit, while I get you something." She made sure everyone stayed refreshed and renewed. Because if one firefighter got too tired, then all their safety was at risk.

This had been drilled into her head by Gerald, who, at the moment, was handling the hose as other firefighters popped the hood of the car with a crowbar to make sure the battery—or was it the carburetor—wasn't on fire. She wasn't a firefighter and had little concept of what they did.

She dropped the black rock into her pocket. She would add it to her collection at home, which included rocks she'd picked up during other calls in this same place. For some reason this isolated spot—ringed with piñon pine and juniper—was a popular area for car fires.

Why the car thieves, or whoever, kept dumping cars out here was a mystery. Why in their fire district? Why not a mile or so away, where La Cienega's district started? Then they could get up at 6:00 A.M. to put out a car fire.

The area, with its remoteness, made for a fun secret getaway the whole family could enjoy—just not together. Here teenagers would gather to drink around late-night fires. Here parents would dump washing machines and mattresses that had finished serving their purpose. Lucy kicked at pieces of plastic and china embedded in the dirt. The desert was where household goods went to die. People seemed to think they could throw away everything unwanted and expect the desert to eventually cover it with sand.

Back east, especially in Florida, where Lucy grew up, plants and decaying foliage quickly reclaim the discarded junk of our lives. They pull it down into a warm, moist grave where it will stay forever hidden.

The desert can't be trusted, though. It has two faces. On its surface, it can hide nothing. Everything is exposed and vulnerable. Underneath and underfoot, it can hide whole civilizations. Ancient bones and long-forgotten ruins.

The desert is always coy in what it hides and what it reveals. If what the sands reveal is a body, it will either be ripped apart by coyotes and vultures or mummified by the incinerating heat.

A few years ago, a woman walking her dog in the outskirts of Albuquerque found a bone. Most locals would have thought little of it. It actually happens all the time. The bone could have been from a prehistoric site. A wayward inmate from one of the thousands of archaeological digs in the state. It wasn't. After bringing in backhoes and shovels, the police found eleven bodies. They were not ancient bones but the remains of women dead only a few years. Likely it was the work of a serial killer who thought, like so many New Mexicans, that if you dumped your trash in the desert, no one would ever find it.

Gil sat at his desk, waiting. Chief Kline had called in most of the other detectives for a meeting that was supposed to start ten minutes ago. Gil stared at the posters about rape and domestic violence that lined the walls of the station. The flags waving out front cast rippling shadows that passed over the windows, like a soft strobe light. Gil glanced at the book open on his desk. It was a criminal behavior analysis textbook. Next to that was a piece of paper where he had written the words *fire*, *skull*, *child*, and *audience*, followed by a line of question marks.

Joe came over to Gil's desk and sat in the chair next to it, saying, "Can we get going already?"

"Relax," Gil said.

Gil saw Kline go into the conference room, and he and Joe got up to follow. Inside was a group of a half-dozen detectives and a few officers who had hung back after the morning report to help with the new case. One of them was Officer Kristen Valdez, who had worked Zozobra last night but was back here this morning to help out. She must be exhausted, Gil thought, as he sat down at the long brown table with Kline at the head.

"Okay, first I want to thank all of you who have volunteered to work a double shift this morning to lend a hand," Kline said. "We've got ourselves a case that is going to take some doing. Gil, why don't you get us started?"

Gil pulled out his incident report and notebook. "At approximately six forty-four this morning we received a phone call from an individual who said he had found a skull at Fort Marcy Park. I was dispatched at six forty-seven and arrived on scene at seven oh two." Gil told the rest of the story as the officers and detectives took their own notes—except for Joe, who stood in the back of the room, bouncing his leg. Gil's report was over within less than five minutes.

"Thanks, Gil," Kline said. "Now, I know we are all thinking that this could be Brianna, but we just can't assume that—"

"Chief, I don't—" Joe started to say as everyone turned to look at him.

"Hang on. Just a second. We need to look at this case two ways—like it isn't Brianna and like it is. So, for those of us tracking the idea that it isn't her, we'll look at all national missing kids cases and see if there is any way this could be one of them. Like do any of the suspects have ties to New Mexico? You know the drill. The rest of us will treat this like it is Brianna until we find out otherwise."

Kline took a deep breath, knowing the next part would be hard to say and harder to hear. "With Fisher gone, we need to start at the beginning of the investigation—" Joe started to talk again, but Kline said, "Hold on. I am in no way saying that Fisher did a bad job, but he's gone, and we need to have new eyes on this now that there might be a body. Even if this isn't Brianna, we need to have a new detective take over her case. I've been putting that off for too long. So that'll be Gil." Gil nodded.

Kline continued, "We have to pull all the police reports from the afternoon she went missing, both city and county. Look for anything out of the ordinary; traffic stops where someone acted strange, any break-ins in the area. Do the sex offender checks. The usual."

Kline went on to hand out individual assignments and dismissed everyone from the room, with the exception of Joe and Gil.

"Now for the tricky part," Kline said. "We have to notify the family. We can't wait until we get a positive ID. This is going to be all over the news in just a few hours, and the public is going to assume it's Brianna no matter how much we say that we can't be sure. If we don't tell the family now, they'll get blindsided. Let me call Robert here and see what we need to do." Robert Sandoval was the police lawyer and the man who stood between the department and the Rodriguez family attorney.

The department had been four weeks into the investigation of Brianna's disappearance when the family had finally decided they'd had enough and filed a harassment lawsuit. Looking at it from their perspective, Gil wasn't sure he could blame them. For the first few weeks, there had been a police officer on duty at all times in the house and a car stationed across the street. All the family's phones were hooked up to recording devices, and every single one of their movements was detailed. By the fourth week, the police, after considering every lead, unofficially decided that Brianna probably died in an accidental drowning.

That didn't stop public pressure about the case. So the department kept pushing so they could tell the media that they had exhausted every possible lead. It was when the family was approached about taking polygraphs and the FBI showed up to take forensic samples from everyone that they decided to file the harassment suit. The family released a statement through their lawyer saying that they believed as the police did—that Brianna had drowned. Now they just wanted to get back to their lives and grieve for their little girl out of the public spotlight. A judge agreed that the family was under undue stress and ordered the officers to cut back on their intrusions. The case had already cost the department hundreds of thousands of dollars, and without any new leads, the police agreed.

All but Fisher, who continued to visit the family's home about half a dozen times, despite the warning, to check out new evidence, use the latest tracking gear, or just clarify a point in his mind. He was eventually suspended with pay for a week, which was the department's way of saying loudly, "This is a reprimand," then adding in a whisper, "But not really." Fisher could have just considered it a vacation due to attitude. Instead he shot himself.

Fisher's suicide gave the department yet another reason—like the lawsuit and the lack of evidence—to put the investigation on a shelf until they got a new lead. Gil only wished that lead had been finding a new suspect instead of a body.

Kline clicked his phone shut and said, "Okay, so Robert says I can't talk to the family because I'm individually named in the lawsuit, but you two can go as long as we can justify it as necessary contact. Gil, why don't you go over there and just let them know the circumstances. Joe, I need you there for continuity, plus it'll give you a little on-the-job training. When you get back here we'll get more of a game plan going."

"Am I allowed to interview them?" Gil asked.

"Not without their attorney present. We can only do the notification. Nothing else. Keep it very informal. Just tell them we found something that might pertain to Brianna."

Lucy stood by the ambulance as the guys finished up with the fire. Even though they were only twenty feet away, she couldn't just walk over to them. She was in the safety zone, and they were in the incident zone. She wasn't in protective clothing, only her regular uniform, while the guys in the incident zone were in full gear—helmets, face masks, breathing equipment, protective gloves, boots, coats, and pants. Because a car fire, even though it might seem like no big deal, releases toxins as it burns through plastic, gasoline, and rubber. Enough carcinogens to make a grown man die, if he gets too close.

So Lucy stayed where she was, daydreaming about sleep, until the radio on her hip squawked.

"Piñon 373, this is Attack," Gerald said. He was hard to hear through his face mask and over the rush of air from his breathing equipment.

"This is Piñon 373. Go ahead," she said.

"Are you ready to take down the VIN?"

"Copy that." She grabbed a pen and a fresh incident report. "Go ahead."

He rattled off the number as she wrote it quickly in the space provided on the report and then repeated it back to him. He then gave her the make and model of the car and a guess on its age. "Also, could you put a note on the form that there is some red spray paint on the side of the car? It could be graffiti, like it's been tagged. There might have been letters, but it was hard to tell. Maybe we should notify the gang task force."

He signed off, and she started filling in other blanks on the page. The date. The time. Personnel on scene. She then got into the passenger seat of the ambulance and pulled out a large, overflowing binder. Its cover was red and had the word BACKROADS on it, handwritten on masking tape. This was a collection of all the streets, roads, highways, and interstates in their fire district. If a lost hiker called 911 from his cell phone and only knew his general location, this binder showed all the tiny side roads and untrampled trails that he might be near. Or when a person called to say there was a brush fire by Dead Dog Well, the pages could tell them the topography of the area and whether it was dominated by grasses or trees.

Sure, the county provided them with newly printed map books, which they used daily, but for the problematic places—the locations that didn't appear on official maps—they had the binder. Yes, it was falling apart, but no matter how worn the exterior might get, the binder would never be thrown out. Because it contained something precious—thirty years of the fire department's history. Every chief in the past three decades had added his wealth of information to the pages. The history wasn't written down like a fully formed story. Firefighters have no time for that. The maps and the notes on them were the history. On the corner of one page was written the gate code to the ranch on Highway 599. On another were black X's that showed the locations of caves and climbing cliffs. Even the attack patterns that the wildland firefighting crews had used during the huge Cerro Grande fire of 2000 were drawn in red marker across a map of Los Alamos.

Lucy opened the binder now to get a general description of their location. She actually had little idea of how they had gotten to the fire; there had just been one dirt road after another bringing them deeper into national forest land. She used her pinkie and some creative mapping to guesstimate the driving distance from town. She then filled that information in on its proper place on the form.

When she was done, she went in search of the sheriff's deputy who had been on scene with them. He was sitting in his cruiser, with the passenger door open, talking on his cell phone. Lucy stood off a discreet distance while he chatted, not wanting to be impolite but hoping he would hurry up. He was a portly man with dark hair. She thought his last name was Segura. He finally noticed her, but instead of getting off his phone, he just covered up the earpiece and said, "What do you need?"

"I just wanted to give you the VIN," she said, "and I was hoping you could give me the owner's name for our records."

"No problem." He placed the phone on the seat next to him, not hanging it up, and got on the computer sitting over the middle console of his car. She told him the VIN, and he typed it in.

"Okay," he said, looking at the screen. "The first name is Beto and the last name is Escobar. My God, that is such a Mexican name."

"And the address?" she asked, not really wanting to get into a conversation with him.

"Hang on," he said. A few more keystrokes and he said, "It looks like it's 162 Airport Road."

She was busy writing it down when he said, "Huh. That's weird. We've had three burned vehicles come back to that same address this year. All different names, and we don't have stolen vehicle reports for any of them. Must be some Mexican insurance scam."

Lucy didn't comment on the unlikelihood of that. She was trying to keep good relations between their respective departments. So she said instead, "We also just wanted you to know that the car has some graffiti on it, like it's been tagged. In case the gang task force wants to know."

"Thanks. I'll write it down," he said, smiling. She noticed the phone still open on the seat next to him. It bugged her for some reason. Who was this person that would stay on hold this long? His mother? His kid? As far as she could tell, the guy really didn't deserve "on-hold" devotion.

She was about to step away when he said, "Hey, I've got a joke for you. What do you call a Mexican shooting a Chinese outside a Starbucks? . . . A cap-a-chino." He started laughing.

"That doesn't even make sense," she said, in her best you-are-a-moron tone. "So now you've told me two things about yourself. One, you're racist, and, two, you can't tell a joke."

She walked away as he started to sputter out some swear words and went back to the ambulance just as Gerald came over, pulling off his helmet and fire-retardant hood.

She handed him a bottle of water before he could ask for it, and he downed it in one gulp.

"Man, that fire was hot," he said, wiping the sweat off his face. He took off his heavy bunker jacket.

"Do you need anything else?" she asked him.

"Just some food," he said.

"Hey, so stupid racist cop over there says that the guy who owns this car lives at the same address as two other owners whose cars got burned," she said.

"Sounds like someone really doesn't like the people at that house."

"Oh, and none of the owners have ever filed stolen car reports."

"Really? That seems odd. How else are they going to get them back or get paid by their insurance company?"

"Maybe they know who's doing it and don't want to get them in trouble."

"What, like a teenage relative?"

"Could be. Or maybe the Mafia. Or it's part of a voodoo ritual. And let's not rule out aliens . . ."

"Only an idiot would rule out aliens," Gerald said, laughing. "Can we please just go get breakfast?"

Gil stood outside the station next to his unmarked dark blue Crown Victoria. While he waited for Joe, he speed-dialed his phone.

A woman answered saying, "Hello?" She sounded almost as if she'd been woken up.

"Hi, Mom. How are you?"

"Hi, hito. I'm fine."

"Bueno, you sound tired today," Gil said, automatically lapsing back into the local mishmash of Old Spanish and English. A sort of colonial Spanglish.

"Ah, I didn't sleep very good last night. The neighbors had a fiesta party."

"You should have called me."

"Oh, hito, it was late. I didn't want to wake you."

"Mom, I could have taken care of it," he said. His mom was always like this, never wanting to trouble him with anything until it was a problem. When it wouldn't have even become a problem if she had just told him about it in the first place. Gil wondered if she had been like this when she was married to his father. Or maybe he just noticed it more now that his father was gone.

It had been more than ten years since his father died. A heart attack when Gil was only twenty-three. Gil dropped out of law school and found himself taking a crash course in property taxes, insurance bills, and mortgages. He was suddenly in charge of it all, but it wasn't something he and his mom talked about. It was just expected that he would take up the reins. So his younger sister, Elena, stayed in college and got her law degree while Gil did what was required. Now, more than a decade later, he still did.

"When is Aunt Yolanda coming to get you for fiesta Mass?" Gil asked. His mother was a former fiesta queen and was expected to go down to the Plaza to be part of the official ceremonies. His father had played the part of Don Diego de Vargas, the man who three hundred years ago had reconquered Santa Fe. It was how the two of them had met more than thirty-five years ago. When Gil was growing up, he always imagined that he would meet his wife the same way. Instead, he met Susan in college.

"She should be here by ten thirty or so," she said.

"Okay, well, I'll call you later, then," he said, as Joe came out of the station and made his way over to the car. "Don't forget to check your blood sugar."

"Okay, hito. Have a good day."

Gil hung up. "You set?" Joe said and got into the passenger seat, holding a palm-sized spiral notebook and a manila file folder.

"What have you got there?" Gil asked, nodding toward what Joe was carrying.

"Fisher's original case notes," Joe said. "I've been going over them since this morning. You know, to freshen up."

"Good thinking," Gil said as he backed the car out of the station and headed into town. "So what can you tell me about the family?"

"Well, you have Ashley, who is Brianna's mom. She's twenty now. She's been on disability since this happened," Joe said.

"She doesn't work?"

"No. Then there's Rose, Brianna's grandma. That's whose house we're going to."

"That's where Brianna went missing?" Gil knew these details. His main goal in going over them was to cement them into his mind and see if there were any inconsistencies along the way.

"Right. Rose and Ashley live in the house with Ashley's boyfriend."

"What do you know about him?"

"His name is Alex Stevens, and he owns his own tow truck company."

"They were all home when Brianna disappeared?"

"Yeah, and there were also two kids hanging out with them that day. One was Justin. He's a cousin, who's about fifteen. His house is just like a block away from the Rodriguezes', so he is pretty much over all the time. Ashley babysits him after school. Then the other kid was Laura. I think she's thirteen now. She's Justin's girlfriend."

"So we have Ashley, Rose, Alex, Justin, and Laura who were there?"

"Yeah."

"You keep referring to Alex Stevens as Ashley's boyfriend and not Brianna's dad."

"Nothing gets by you," Joe said, not sarcastically. "Brianna's real dad has spent most of his time in jail since Ashley was pregnant. The guy pretty much has never been in the picture."

"Okay, so five people were at the house the day Brianna went missing, and none of them have died or moved away since then."

"Right, and as far as I know, Ashley is still dating Alex and Justin is still with Laura."

"Everybody alibis each other?" Gil asked.

"Yep. They were all in the backyard together."

"How many times have they been interviewed?"

"Before the lawsuit, probably around a dozen times each."

"And the story never changed?"

"Never." Meaning the family probably wasn't involved. Cracks in the timeline would have shown up by now. Or they all had too much to lose.

"Fisher did all the interrogations?"

"Yeah, and he went after them every which way—soft, hard, alone, together. At the station. At home. Everything."

Gil didn't say it, but this was what he had feared—contamination so deep that the truth might never come out. Gil had known Fisher, of course. He had been a good guy who tried hard, but his interview skills were heavy-handed—and sloppy.

"Did anyone in the family take a polygraph?"

"By the time we got to that, there was the lawsuit."

"Okay, so the family is out as an information source. What about suspects? Were there any?"

"No. We checked all known sex offenders, everything. There was never a viable suspect. That's why we thought she drowned in the arroyo and her body just hadn't been found yet."

"Tell me about the evidence."

"There wasn't any. I mean, nothing. She was just gone."

"What about fingerprints or footprints?"

"The only fingerprints were the family's. As for footprints, it was monsoon season. It rained five inches in one hour. When I got there the arroyo was flooded and the backyard was soup."

"All right. So tell me about what you did when you first arrived."

"All right," Joe said, shifting in his seat. "Umm . . . I got there a little after 2:00 P.M. Ashley, the mom, answered the door."

"How did she seem?"

"Freaked out. She said they were all in the backyard grilling when it started to rain. One second Brianna was there, the next she was gone. She said she looked for Brianna for about fifteen minutes before she called 911."

"Then what?"

"I searched the house."

"You didn't call it in?"

"No, I was thinking about the JonBenét case where she was inside the house the whole time but they spent hours looking for her."

"How long did it take you?"

Joe was agitated, shifting in his seat. "Too long. I don't know. Maybe ten minutes."

"What was Ashley doing?"

"Helping me."

"Where was everyone else?"

"Umm . . . the two kids—the cousin, Justin, and his girlfriend, Laura—were out walking around looking for her. I heard them yelling for Brianna across the arroyo. Rose, Ashley's mom, was talking to neighbors, I guess, knocking on doors."

"Is that everyone?"

"Alex, Ashley's boyfriend, was driving around looking for her."

"What did you see when you searched the house?"

"Nothing weird. In the kitchen they had food out for the barbe-cue. A few empty beer bottles. That's it."

"What about out back?"

"The grill was open and there was some food still out, soaked. I walked to the arroyo and it was overflowing, going a mile a minute."

"When did you call for backup?"

"I called Garcia—he was the officer on duty that day—and ev-erybody was there in just a few minutes. Fisher was the detective on call. So between all of us we started a ground search within about a half hour of her going missing. Turn here," Joe said, pointing to the right. "It's the third house on the left . . . That's pretty much it," he said as Gil pulled up.

Lucy sat at a booth in Denny's and tried to listen to Gerald and the firefighters across from her talk about hoses, as they had been doing for ten minutes, but her mind drifted as she gazed unfocused out the restaurant windows.

She looked down at her T-shirt, which read PIÑON VOLUNTEER FIRE DEPARTMENT with an emblem over her left chest. Their depart-ment was a ragtag of volunteers, some who were firefighters only, some who were medics only, and some, like Gerald, who were both. Lucy felt bad that people might assume from her shirt that she was a firefighter when she was only a first responder. The lowest of the low on the totem pole of medics, with paramedics—referred to mockingly as para-gods behind their backs—at the top.

Since Gerald, sitting across from her and discussing hoses with zeal, was the paramedic in charge at her department, she guessed that made him her para-god. Lucy smiled to herself. Praise and glory to Gerald in the highest.

Lucy hoped her pager would go off again. She was exhausted but wired, and wanted something more interesting before she went into work.

She yawned and glanced around. Denny's at 9:00 A.M. was its

regular combination of elderly couples that didn't look at each other and men in trucker hats who didn't talk to each other.

Out the window, the Motel 6 on the other side of Cerrillos Road fluoresced in the morning light. The Quality Inn and the Floor Mart looked like they were just waking up.

Lines of cars drove along Cerrillos Road, avoiding the construction barrels that seemed to serve no purpose.

Cerrillos Road, the most cursed road in Santa Fe, was always under construction. It flooded like a river during the summer monsoons and cracked mercilessly after the winter snow. It seemed to be a giant five-mile-long strip mall of car dealerships and cheap motels.

It was an ugly road in a beautiful town. A scar on a perfect cheek.

When Lucy had first moved to Santa Fe a year and a half ago, she had no idea how to properly say words like "Cerrillos," with all its double letters mocking her. During her first month in town, she had been laughed at by co-workers for pronouncing Acoma Pueblo like a combination of "a" and "coma," and Pojoaque Pueblo like "po-jock" and "kay." Her solution was to become a master eavesdropper. She data-mined conversations overheard at gas stations and grocery stores for the right way to pronounce the names of towns, streets, and mountains. She also picked up the walking-around Spanish words you had to know in order to have a conversation in English. She had learned that a porch was called a portal—with the accent on the second syllable—and that an exposed wooden ceiling beam was a viga. A santuario was a kind of church, and an arroyo was a dry riverbed. Now, she could almost whip out the right Spanish and Native American words like a local.

She took a final swig of her coffee and considered taking another bite of her breakfast. She had ordered Moons Over My Hammy based solely on the name, but the eggs had gone cold and the cheese looked pale. She poked at it with her fork, then decided to let it rest in peace.

She yawned again and shook her head to wake up, but she knew it was time to go. She had to be at the newspaper early today so she could go over her yearly review with her boss. She was not looking forward to it. She stood up and told the boys she was leaving. They had started to say their good-byes when Gerald said to her surprise, "I'm going to take off, too."

Suddenly, she was wide-awake—and curious.

The Rodriguez house was set in an open area marked with a few small juniper trees and cut by the arroyo going past the backyard. It was in one of those Santa Fe neighborhoods where there is no structure to the streets or property. The roads were dirt, and the houses and trailers seemed to be in no particular order. In fact, there was a reason why some of the city's streets were not precise in their design. Many local families had followed the colonial property inheritance rules. Traditionally, a father would equally divide the property between his sons. Then the sons would divide it between their sons, so that generations later, extended family members lived in tight family clusters, minus the pieces that were sold off to developers over the years. Gil guessed that was what happened here.

The Rodriguez house itself was simple. It was small and boxlike with its flat Santa Fe roof. They had chosen a pale shade of beige exterior paint many years ago that had never been refreshed, but the paved pathway leading to the front door was free of weeds, and there were a few flowers near the porch.

Gil knocked on the door, which was opened by a young woman with big eyes and long dark hair who was hugely pregnant. This had to be Ashley.

"Hi, I'm Gil Montoya, and you might remember Joe Phillips, with the Santa Fe police," Gil said as Joe gave a little wave. Gil purposely didn't use their detective titles so as to keep her at ease. As it was, she frowned at them, but Gil said, "I was hoping we could come in."

He could tell she was about to refuse, so he said quickly, "It is important that we talk, and I think it might be easier for you if we sat down."

She opened the door, and they followed her into the kitchen, where she eased herself down on a chair. A woman washing dishes turned to look at them and said harshly, "Ashley, why are the police in my house?" The woman might have been in her forties, but her heavily lined face made it hard to tell. Her hair was dyed a hard black, and she looked at them with suspicion. This had to be Rose, Ashley's mother.

Gil introduced himself to Rose and asked her to join him at the table. She looked like she might say no but took a seat. Once the three of them were sitting, with Joe standing restlessly to the side, Gil turned to Ashley and said, "Look, I know you've a rocky history with us, and I'm not here to pretend that you haven't, but we both want the same thing: to find out what happened. I know all of this has been incredibly hard on you all, but whatever has happened in the past is in the past. You and me are starting from a clean slate. Okay?"

"Okay," Ashley said slowly, warily.

"Thank you," Gil said. He took a deep breath and said evenly, "There have been some new developments today that we think could be related to Brianna's case. I just wanted to come sit with you in person and talk about them, okay?"

"Okay," she said again, less wary. Gil nodded. By repeatedly asking her permission to talk about the subject, he was trying to get her to feel like she was in control of the conversation. He knew she needed that control right now.

"Now, you're going to hear things over the next few days, and those things may or may not be true, but I will always tell you the truth. I may not be able to tell you everything, but I will tell you as much as I can. Does that sound all right?"

She nodded.

"So, all of this means you're going to have to trust me just a little bit. Do you think you can do that?"

She nodded again, looking scared. Gil took a deep breath to collect his thoughts. He could see Joe standing behind Ashley. His face was surprisingly tight with anger.

Gil turned his attention back to Ashley and watched her closely as he said, "This morning, we found a skull."

He watched her for a moment as she tried to hold it together, looking anxious but okay, considering the situation, so he continued, "Now, it was in the ashes from Zozobra, and it was the skull of a child." She nodded her head as she started to cry quietly, but she didn't fidget. Mrs. Rodriguez looked down at her hands. Gil couldn't tell them everything. The newspapers would be calling the family shortly, looking for a comment. He would only reveal to them the basic facts that the newspaper would already know: that they found a skull in Zozobra. Period. End of story.

"You think it's Brianna?" Ashley said, biting her lip to keep from crying.

"It's possible," Gil said. A few tears fell on Ashley's cheek. "We won't know until we can do a DNA—"

"But she drowned in the arroyo. How did she get there?" Ashley asked, clearly fighting to keep composed.

"I don't—"

"Where's the rest of her?" Ashley asked, looking at her mom, who got up from her chair with tears in her own eyes and went to hold her daughter. As they twined their arms around each other, Gil noticed a few faint scars on Ashley's wrists.

"Did she get burned alive?" Ashley asked, as her tears, now freed, started to overwhelm her.

"No, we don't think—"

"Oh my God, oh my God . . ." she said, looking wildly at her mom.

"Ashley—" Gil said.

"Who would put her there? Oh my baby, oh my sweet baby." Her face was pressed hard into her mom's shoulder, and she started to sob as if she were gasping for air. She popped her head up suddenly and said, "I think I'm going to be sick." Gil jumped up to help pull her and her pregnant belly off the chair. Her mom escorted her to the bathroom down the hall.

As soon as the two men were left alone, Joe turned to face Gil and said, "What the fuck was that—"

The sounds of retching come from down the hall. Then running water.

"Okay, that's gross," Joe said, before turning back to Gil and saying, without lowering his voice, "What was all that shit about 'whatever the cops did in the past I'm better than that'?"

"That's not what I said."

"That's sure as hell what I heard," Joe said.

"Joe, I never meant to insult you or Detective Fisher—"

"That's a load of crap—"

"I was just trying to establish a rapport with her."

Mrs. Rodriguez came back in the room, saying, "I think she needs to lie down."

"I understand," Gil said just as the front door open and someone yelled, "Tía, we're here."

"That's my nephew, my sister's son," she said, looking stricken. "I forgot, Ashley's babysitting them. They don't have school because of fiesta."

A boy and a girl came into the kitchen and immediately looked at Gil with disdain.

The boy had blond Chia Pet hair, sticking straight out from his head in a round fuzzy ball. It was a crew cut gone wrong on a boy who shouldn't have had one. In Northern New Mexico slang, he would have been called a coyote—a person who is half white, half Hispanic. It wasn't a racial slur, only a locally used description, like Anglo or Pueblo Indian.

Next to him, holding his hand, was his girlfriend. She didn't look nervous, more like ready for a fight, but then she was used to this, too. The excitement of being interviewed by the police had probably worn off months ago. She had dark eyes and a distinctive nose that Gil's father would have said made the girl a Southern Colorado Hispanic. Long ago, two enclaves of conquistador descendents separated—one group stayed in Northern New Mexico and the other went to Southern Colorado. His father insisted that the passage of time had given each group defining physical characteristics. In the north, they tended to be taller and thinner and have bigger noses. In the south, they were stouter and had flatter faces. This, his dad would say proudly, was where Gil's height came from. Their northern relatives.

The girl wore the typical heavy black eyeliner sweeping on top of the lid. It had been a popular look for Northern New Mexico girls since he had been a teenager. His wife said it made the eyes look more almond shaped. He thought it just made them all look sinister.

"Are you Justin and Laura?" Gil asked. Neither one of them answered, but the girl said mockingly, "More cops, great."

"They found something," Mrs. Rodriguez said, trying to pacify them.

"Where's Ashley?" Justin asked.

"She's not feeling good," Gil said.

"Is she all right—" Justin started to ask, before Laura interrupted. "She's supposed to be taking us to the Plaza for fiesta." Laura was wearing a short-cropped pink tank top and running pants with sneakers, looking like one of the Bratz dolls Gil's daughter Joy used to like so much. She had the attitude to match.

"I don't think she's up to it," Mrs. Rodriguez said.

"Fine," Laura said.

"Can I talk to you guys for a second?" Gil asked.

"No," Justin said sharply.

"C'mon, dude, it's about Brianna," Joe said.

Justin rolled his eyes—and in that expression, Gil saw how tired the boy was. Not just of the questions, or of the police, but of all of it. Of death, or the possibility of it.

Lucy left her money on the table and waited for Gerald to catch up with her by the front door. He was taking his time, shaking and re-shaking hands and smacking a few backs. She looked down at the racks of newspapers. Her newspaper was there, the *Capital Tribune,* along with the competition, the *Santa Fe Times.* There were also at least three weeklies there called things like *Light Source,* which sounded like it should be about proper lighting techniques for your home, or *Heart Spirit,* which sounded more like a name of a Kentucky Derby winner. Actually both newspapers were about the same thing—alternative healing. Santa Fe's million-dollar industry. The weeklies advertised tarot readings, energy work, past life regressions, and somatic polarity. Lucy had lived in Santa Fe for a year and a half, but she had yet to get used to the Weird White People Syndrome—an illness afflicting only the entitled rich who came to town to experience the "magical healing" of the area.

They all came from the same cookie cutter. They were well-off, in their fifties or sixties, from back east; they drove huge SUVs and moved to Santa Fe for "the wide-open vistas." They shopped at organic food stores. Went to art gallery openings. Sipped wine and talked about holistic bodywork.

Lucy turned her attention to a nearby bulletin board covered in a collage of the same kind of advertisements. There were flyers for yoga classes and various types of massage using crystals, Reiki, and organic honey. There was one for communicating with pets, including those who "had passed." Lucy couldn't imagine any reason someone might want to contact a dead pet. Unless Fluffy had learned how to talk, what the hell good would it do?

Laura had pulled Justin's hand onto her lap. She was definitely the one in charge of the relationship.

They sat in the living room, the two teenagers on the couch with Gil across from them in an easy chair. Joe stood nearby, restless as usual, while Mrs. Rodriguez went to check on Ashley.

Justin was fidgeting, tapping his foot, which was in contrast to his casual posture as he leaned back into the couch. Nervous but trying to hide it.

"It's possible we found Brianna," Gil said. Maybe, he thought wistfully, if he had been allowed to interview them properly, he could have saved that information to be used as needed, to get a response—but the chief had been clear.

"Yeah, we guessed that," Justin said.

"You don't seem too broken up," Joe said.

"Whatever. This time, just check to make sure it's human," Justin said. Joe, perpetually pissed off, snorted in disgust.

Gil knew what Justin was referring to. A month after Brianna went missing and a week before the family filed the lawsuit, forensic teams were digging in the backyard of the Rodriguez house. They were using heat-sensing technology that could locate decaying flesh. The equipment and the tech were on loan from the FBI. Someone had gotten too excited by a heat signature coming from a few feet underground—or maybe because of the FBI presence. The family had been corralled in the house and kept there, being questioned on and off, while forensic techs dug carefully for over twenty-four hours, finally uncovering the family dog, which had been buried a year earlier.

"This isn't no dog," Joe said.

"But it's not Brianna," Laura said with a cock of her head.

"What makes you say that?" Gil asked as the phone in his pocket started to vibrate. He ignored it.

"Because of your track record," she said, annoyed.

"Besides, Brianna drowned in the arroyo," Justin added.

Gil looked over at Joe, who looked out the window. Gil wasn't sure what else they would get out of the visit. He wasn't even sure what they had hoped to get. He felt like he had just opened a book in the middle and started reading, with no sense of plot, characters, or back story. He felt his phone vibrate again in his pocket but continued to ignore it. He wanted to finish.

"What we found points to a small child—" Gil said before the girlfriend jumped in.

"Yeah, well, come talk to us when you know for sure," she said.

Gil decided that he was pushing the limits of what Chief Kline had wanted him to do. He was taking down all their new contact information when his phone vibrated again.

"Thank you for your time," Gil said automatically as he headed out the door. Once outside he popped open his cell phone just in time to catch it before it went to voice mail.

"Gil," his chief said before Gil could even get out a "hello." "Get to the Santuario de Guadalupe. Now."

Gerald, finally finished with his good-byes, met up with Lucy in the foyer of the restaurant, and the two walked outside together, the new morning starting to cast its shadows.

"We need to talk," he said.

Lucy groaned. No good conversation in the history of humankind had ever started that way. It was a line used all over the world, a thousand times a day, to break up with boyfriends, to fire employees, and to order assassinations. She waited for Gerald to say something.

He considered his words carefully before saying, "So, what's going on with you?" He stared her so dead in the eye that she had to turn away.

"What do you mean?" she asked in what she hoped was a calm voice as she looked at her combat boots.

"I mean like on the fire call you seemed . . . out of it."

"How so?" she said, her voice sounding high to her own ears. She could keep up these deflecting answers for days. She hadn't even used the classic "Am I?" response yet.

"Have you been drinking?" The question almost made her take a step back. She thought she had been so careful. She had taken every precaution. She had the Breathalyzer. She had popped a mint. She had masked her dark circles with big sunglasses.

Without thinking she gave the lie she'd personally heard a hundred times. It inevitably was uttered by guys who caused DWI crashes and men who'd beaten their girlfriends in an alcoholic haze. She said, "I had a couple of beers."

"When was that?

"Last night, but I'm totally sober now," she said. Legally, she knew that at least was true.

"How much are you drinking?"

"I told you, a couple of beers."

"How often?"

"I dunno. A few times a week. It's no big deal."

"Do you think that's a good idea?" They stood in the parking lot as Gerald watched her and waited for an answer.

"I don't know, I'm just . . . I'm tired," Lucy said.

"Tired?" Gerald asked.

Lucy didn't say anything more. She only felt honestly, truly tired.

"Have you ever treated patients when you've been drunk?" he asked.

"No," she said. When he didn't look convinced, she said again, more strongly, "No. Never. I swear."

"What about driving? Have you driven drunk?" he asked, his voice starting to edge into judgmental territory. Lucy was about to insist that of course she would never drink and drive when she thought about last night. How had she gotten home? She couldn't quite remember. Surely Nathan had driven her. Although in the morning her car had been at her house, as had Nathan's. She must have driven home from the Cowgirl. She couldn't remember. Oh, God. She looked up at Gerald, knowing she had to lie but not wanting to. She did anyway. "No. I'm really careful," she said firmly.

"Look, I don't know what's going on with you . . ." he said without finishing the thought, then sighed. "Just . . . take care of yourself."

"Yeah. Thanks," she said hesitantly as he turned to leave.

Take care of yourself? That's what you said to a person you hope to never see again.

CHAPTER FOUR

Friday Morning

Gil was driving lights and sirens while Joe sat in the passenger seat checking out the neighboring cars as they zipped by them.

"Hey, slow down, dude, that girl in the Toyota back there had a killer chest," Joe said, turning around to gawk.

Gil ignored him and instead said, "Look, what I said back at the house, I didn't mean to—"

"Dude," Joe said with a laugh, "it's no biggie. You just gotta ignore me when I get mad. I'm a total jackass, but I get over it fast. If I'm ever really mad, you'll know."

"How will I know?"

"By my fist punching through your chest."

Gil wondered if Joe had been as volatile before he joined the army. He maneuvered the Crown Vic around the stopped cars in front of them and through the intersection of Cerrillos Road and St. Francis Drive.

"What did you think of the family?" Joe asked.

"They were about what I expected."

"Really? Did you know what I noticed most? Laura's Nike Air Force 1s. That girl's got style. Those were some killer kicks. I bet you she's the most popular girl in school."

"What are you talking about? Her shoes?" Gil asked, negotiating his way around a city bus.

"Those aren't just shoes. I bet they were a special release. Easily cost a hundred and eighty bucks."

"For tennis shoes?"

"What? You've never heard of sneakerheads? Sneaker collecting is like the new thing. Dude, do you go out into the world at all?"

"Really?" Gil wasn't sure if Joe was joking.

"An original Nike Air Force 2 high-top from 1982 just sold for like fifteen thousand dollars," Joe said. "God, if I owned those, I'd jerk off to them I'd love them so much."

"How many do you have in your collection?" Gil asked, joking.

"I just have a couple pair of old Air Jordans. They'd sell for like maybe a hundred bucks each. Man, you should be all over this. You used to play basketball."

"Yeah, but I'd throw my shoes away when they got old. I didn't hang on to them to show to company."

"Dude, you almost made a joke," Joe said, feigning surprise.

"I did notice that Ashley had cutting marks," Gil said, trying to get them back on track.

"Really? I didn't see that," Joe said, tapping his foot on the floor. Then he asked again, as he had three times since leaving the Rodriguez house, "So the chief didn't say anything at all about where we're going?"

"I already told you, no," Gil said. Working with Joe was like being with a seven-year-old hyped up on sugar.

Gil pulled up to the Santuario de Guadalupe. He parked on the street and kept his emergency lights on. Another car raced to a stop, pulling up next to them. It was Kline with Garcia.

"Hey," Gil said to them as they got out. "What's going on?"

All Kline said was "Let's go see."

———

Gil and Joe walked up to the crowd of people gathered around the perimeter of a crime scene tape line that encircled a huge bronze statute of Our Lady of Guadalupe. She stood on the wide, cobbled sidewalk between the street and the church dedicated to her—the Santuario de Nuestra Señora de Guadalupe. The church had an old mission spire, rough-hewn doors, and small, barred windows that would have guarded against Indian attack. The Santuario, which had been built in 1777, was the oldest shrine to the Virgin Mary in the United States.

Unlike the Santuario, however, the statue of Mary was new. It had been put up in 2008 and stood fifteen feet tall. It showed Mary with her head bowed in prayer, her sky blue robes rippling with stars. Flames of gold shot out from her body; a cherub below held her aloft. This statue had been made with the faithful in mind—beneath it were cubbyholes for believers to leave flowers and other offerings. This was likely why no one had noticed earlier the bulky necklace that was placed around Mary's neck. Passersby likely thought it was a memento from one of her devoted fans.

It was a podiatrist visiting from Texas, stopping to take a picture, who finally noticed what the necklace was made of.

Gil and the other men crossed the crime scene tape and went closer to the statue.

"Lord in heaven," Gil heard Kline say next to him as Garcia crossed himself. Joe, as expected, started swearing loudly.

Gil said nothing as he went back to the uniformed officer who was keeping an eye on the crowd.

He leaned over to the officer and said quietly, "Get some crowd pictures. As soon as that's done, get this place sealed up tight. One-block radius with no line of sight. No street access, and nobody crosses the line until you radio me." The officer nodded and, without acknowledging what Gil said, turned the volume down on his radio before requesting a nonuniformed officer snap some pictures.

Kline and Garcia immediately got on their cell phones and walked out of earshot, likely calling higher-ups who needed to know. Joe was busy pacing the perimeter, which was lined with stepping-stones that made up a walking rosary—a meditation for the faithful.

He noticed Joe would have been standing on an Our Father stone. Behind Joe on the railing were glass-covered pictures that the church had put up showing the different incarnations of Mary. He counted seven images—Our Lady of Peace, Our Lady of the Miraculous Medal, Our Lady of Lourdes. The shrine took its devotion to Mary very seriously.

Gil went to stand alone in front of the statue of the Virgin and looked up at her face. Her eyes were closed as if she were too horrified to look at what was around her throat. Her necklace was heavy, loaded down with old plastic doll heads and yellow silk sunflowers. Between them, almost as spacers, were tiny bones. The finger and toe bones of a child fashioned into delicate crosses.

Mai Bhago Kaur had been up since 3:00 A.M. Before the dawn. At the time when the soul could best hear its own thoughts. Now she sat with the children. She was reading to them from a book called *Sikh Traditions for Children.* She knew they were trying to listen to the stories about the ten gurus. She could see it in their eager faces.

Mai Bhago breathed deeply and lengthened her spine as she sat in sukasana pose, her legs crossed and her buttocks firmly on the ground. She could hold the pose for hours if necessary. Or all day. Her first yoga teacher had been strict, forcing her to keep a pose for a half hour at least. That teacher hadn't understood the holy nature of yoga or that it wasn't about being harsh, but that had been almost thirty-five years ago. Back when she was still in Los Angeles. Back when she was still poisoning her body with cocaine, alcohol, and red meat. She used to love the feel of cocaine, the way it made her feel energized and so intellectual. The high never lasted, though. Now it was the hours of meditation she did every morning that gave her that high and more.

Mai Bhago wondered if cocaine had changed much in the intervening years. Maybe it was no longer the drug of choice for movie stars and TV personalities. It was a movie producer who had introduced her to it. He was casting for *The Outlaw Josey Wales,* and she was dying to work with Clint Eastwood. So she tried a little line of powder when he asked her to. She found out one week later—after spending her days and nights with the man and his friends—that he wasn't a movie producer and he'd never even seen a Clint Eastwood movie. He was simply a person taking advantage of her. She left him without drama, but it would be another five years and tens of thousands of dollars gone before she left the cocaine.

She shifted slightly as she tried to concentrate again on what she was reading. A few of the children started to giggle and she stared at them purposely until they quieted down again. She turned the page and read outloud, "Guru Gobind Singh was the tenth guru . . ."

The line officer radioed Gil, asking permission for the crime scene tech to access the area. Gil agreed and waited until Adam Granger's white van pulled up on the now empty street. The officers had done their job well—Gil could see no one in the area other than a few cops.

Adam got out of his van holding his work case. He adjusted his tall white turban, which must have been jostled in the process of getting out. Adam was a Sikh, one of the thousand or so that lived in the area. Most resided in the Hacienda de Guru Ram Das Ashram in Española, about thirty miles to the north, but some, including Adam, lived in Santa Fe.

Gil had known Granger for years. Their daughters were on the same soccer team. Adam had left the ashram when he was sixteen, dropping his Sikh name and the religion's ways. He had been tired of being known as a White Sikh—which was what some India-born Sikhs called the Anglo Westerners who lived in the ashram. Those Sikhs considered everyone at the ashram pretenders. Over the years, however, Adam softened his rebellion and decided to wear a turban again to show his faith. His parents didn't seem to mind either way. Gil had met them once at a state soccer championship. They stood out in their white clothes and turbans, watching their granddaughter with beatific smiles on their faces.

The men shook hands, and Adam said, "Let me see it." They walked over together to the statue, where Adam let out a low whistle, saying, "Now this is messed up."

"How fast can you do this?" Gil said, knowing that they were running out of time. They couldn't keep the street closed for much more than a half hour before arousing suspicion from the public and the press.

"It's pretty straightforward," Adam said, taking his camera out of his case. "There's no use processing the area because of cross-contamination. It's really just a fingerprints and photo job. I can do the paperwork later. Maybe about fifteen minutes."

Gil left Adam to do his work. He wandered into the quiet enclosed courtyard of the Santuario and sat on an old wooden bench. Yet another statue of Mary—this one of her image at Lourdes—was in a niche in front of him. A few late-summer roses were still blooming on the dozens of bushes that ringed the cool courtyard. Gil closed his eyes and said a vicious prayer. It was one of pure vengeance, tempered only by his request for justice. Gil had grown up expressing his most primal emotions through prayer. He remembered as a teenager confessing to God the usual things on a boy's mind, their conversations rife with lust and longings. Gil had never understood those people who said that prayers must be pure and clean. He saw God as the only one who would understand his deepest, darkest, and most disturbing emotions. It was God who created them.

Gil made the sign of the cross. Then he took a deep breath. He had used the prayer as an outlet for his rage, but he couldn't allow himself that luxury again. Now he needed to be persistent, controlled, and methodical. That was his advantage. That was how he had solved every case in his ten-year career. It would work in this case as well.

He dug his cell phone out of his pants pocket. He looked at the time—10:20 A.M.—before he speed-dialed his mom at home.

"Hello?" she said.

"Hi, Mom. I was just calling to see if you checked your blood sugar yet."

"Hi, hito. Oh, no, I haven't had time."

"De veras?" Gil said, exasperated. "Mom, you're going to be sitting through Mass at the cathedral for at least an hour. If your blood sugar isn't high enough you could pass out."

"Okay, okay, hito," she said. "I'll go find the machine . . ."

Joe walked into the courtyard, oblivious that Gil was on the phone. He started to pace in circles around the perimeter of the courtyard.

"I want this guy, Gil."

"Joe, I'm on the—"

"I mean I want this guy. I want to stomp on his head and cut his balls off. No, wait. First I want to cut his balls off, then—"

"I'm on the phone," Gil said again, then, into the phone, "Mom, I've got to go, I'll call you back."

"I think your Aunt Yolanda is here," she said.

"Mom, okay, so I—"

"Goddamn asshole," Joe yelled.

"Who's that yelling?" Gil's mom asked.

"Just a crazy man," Gil said. "I have to go. I'll call you later." He hung up and turned to face Joe.

"Did you have to yell every swear word you know while I was on the phone?" Gil asked.

"It wasn't every swear word," Joe said, his rant over. "I think I left out 'hell'."

"Do you feel better?" Gil asked.

"No," Joe said. "I feel like I want to kill the guy."

Gil sighed. He felt the same way, but he couldn't afford to. He had to keep whatever he was feeling tamped down because one of them needed a level head. Clearly that was not Joe's forte.

"Okay," Gil said. "Let's just talk this through and throw some ideas out there."

"Okay," Joe said. "Give me what you got."

"First off, I think these new bones clearly belong to the same body as the skull."

"I'm with you there—"

"If this is Brianna—"

"It is—"

"And she was killed last year—"

"Which I hope to God she was because the alternative creeps me the hell out—"

"Then she's been dead for a while. Why do this now? Was there some stressor on the killer? Maybe something set him off."

"Like what?"

"A divorce or a loved one dying . . . I don't know," Gil said.

"That sounds about right. But why put her bones on display with all the weird doll heads?"

Gil looked over at the small statue of Our Lady of Lourdes, considering. "All right, well, I know it's going to sound strange, but I think this might be an act of remorse."

"Dude, this is straight-up evil. The son of a bitch is taunting us. I'm thinking pedophile serial killer."

"Maybe . . . but I don't think so," Gil said. "I think this is someone who feels guilty for killing Brianna. Why put the skull in Zozobra, which is burned to ward off evil? Why put bones in this holy place, in front of Mary? She's the mother of Jesus, the protector of children."

"If he's remorseful, why make it all so creepy? I think he did this for us, for the police."

"I just don't see that," Gil said, shaking his head. "I think it's more likely that he's mentally ill and he made the display as part of some elaborate delusion. Like he knew killing Brianna was wrong and he is presenting her to Mary as a way to make amends. This display took time and skill. It isn't for us, it's for God. It's an offering."

It was Joe's turn to shake his head. "I'm not buying the guilty conscience thing. This is just fucked up beyond belief. To me that means a serial killer."

"Okay, so let's look at that," Gil said, trying to allow Joe to have his say, not wanting to shut him down completely. They were supposed to be acting as partners, after all. "If it is a serial killer, he's a guy who plans his kill in advance and then disposes of the body in a very thought-out way. That would make him a hedonist killer, who just kills for pleasure."

"Yeah, that totally fits with this," Joe said.

"We need to keep something in mind, though," Gil said. "This is Santa Fe. We only have seventy thousand people. A hedonist serial killer would really need a bigger population to hunt in."

"Come on," Joe said. "It's the only thing that makes sense."

"I feel like we're talking in circles," Gil said, frustrated.

"Yeah, me, too."

Gil rubbed his eyes and said, "Adam should be done now. Let's go check with him, and then get out of here and get some breakfast. It might make more sense after we eat."

CHAPTER FIVE

Friday Morning

Joe and Gil sat in Tecolote Café waiting to order. Adam had promised to call as soon as he made it to Albuquerque, where they would compare the new bones to the skull. Gil had called Liz on their way to the restaurant but got no answer, so he left a message. Then he called Ashley's cell phone, but Rose answered instead, her voice worried. Gil could hear a loudspeaker in the background.

"Mrs. Rodriguez, this is Detective Montoya. Is everything all right?" Gil asked.

"It's Ashley," she said. "She kept throwing up after you left, so I drove her to the hospital. I was worried about the baby."

"What are the doctors saying?" Gil asked.

"I don't know, they're talking about giving her an IV," she said, her voice muddled in concern.

"You know, I'm sure it's just a precaution," Gil said. "I'll call back later to check on you."

As soon as he hung up, Joe started ranting and

speculating about Brianna. Gil's head was aching, and he needed some quiet to figure out their next step.

"Joe, please, let's just stop talking about it for five minutes."

Joe looked at his watch. "Okay, five minutes starts . . . now. In the meantime, check out the chest on that girl over there. Do you think they're real?"

"I don't know," Gil said, amazed that Joe'd had time to even notice the woman in the few minutes they'd been in the restaurant.

"Oh, come on. Just make a guess."

"Fine . . . yeah, I think they're real," Gil said absentmindedly, looking over the menu, trying to decide between the breakfast burrito and huevos rancheros.

"Are you nuts? Look how perky they are. You haven't even looked at her."

Gil sighed and turned to look, knowing that was what it would take to get Joe to cease and desist. He saw a dark-haired woman of about twenty in a tank top and jeans sitting with a man in a baseball cap. The two looked happy, smiling at each other over coffee.

"I still think they're real," Gil said, going back to his menu.

"Are you nuts?"

"I just don't see a girl from Santa Fe getting breast implants," Gil said. "That's an L.A. thing."

"Oh, man, where have you been? Like, statistically, half a million women a year get boob jobs. That's like five million in ten years. Not all those women live in L.A."

"If you say so," Gil said quietly as the waitress came over to give them their coffee and get their order. Joe had decided on pancakes. As soon as the waitress left, he started up again. "Personally, I'm not against fake boobs. I know some guys think they're too hard, but I'm all about image, you know what I mean?"

"No," Gil said, taking a sip of coffee.

"Geez, Gil, we're just talking here. Lighten up."

"Joe, I just don't think I have enough personal knowledge about fake breasts to make an informed decision," Gil said with a smile. His attempt to lighten up.

"Well, I can tell you anything you want to know. I've done a lot of research on the subject. For instance, if you have an experienced doc, they won't let you go too huge, like some of the porn stars."

"Okay."

"Dude, you have to know what I'm talking about. Don't you ever watch porn?"

"I've been meaning to get around to that."

"You're telling me you don't watch porn?"

"I have a wife and two daughters."

"Every man watches porn. I don't care if you're married, single, gay, or straight," Joe said. Gil didn't answer, hoping Joe would let it drop. He should have known better. "You've never looked at porn?" Joe asked. "Never?"

"When I was a teenager . . ."

"So you were normal once? Thank God. I was worried," he said, taking a large sip of his coffee. "Now I want to point out two things. One, it's been five minutes, and two, the take-home message from this conversation is that you have, in fact, seen porn."

Gil chuckled as his phone rang. It was Dispatch telling him to get to the cathedral.

Gladys Soliz Portilla looked at the green liquid on the bathroom counter. It was a small amount, but she had no idea what it might be. Toothpaste? A spilled energy drink? She sighed and wiped it up, wondering yet again why the hotel didn't provide them with latex gloves for protection, not only from unknown substances they found in the guests' rooms but also from the toxic chemicals they used for cleaning. Not that she would ever complain. Her only goal at the moment was to keep out of sight. Maybe after she became a citizen, she would join the hotel workers' union.

She sprayed the mirror with the cleaner and wiped, ignoring her own reflection. Even so, she could make out the uniform she was wearing. A green polo shirt and black pants. Her long hair tied carefully back. The green shirt made her skin look strange, but their uniform was still better than the ones at other hotels, where they had to dress in silly gray maid uniforms with white collars.

She looked over the small bathroom to make sure she was done and then surveyed the rest of the room to see what else needed to be cleaned. In the closet, she saw hanger after hanger of little-boy clothes. She smiled as she touched them. They would look so cute on her son. As she made the bed, she saw that the boy had thrown his toys all around the room, so she picked them up and put them in a careful circle in the corner as if they were playing a game, thinking he would like that when he came back.

She locked the door of the room and pushed her cart to the next room. She knocked and called out, "Housekeeping," in a loud voice. No one answered, so she let herself in. She started at the front of the room and quickly vacuumed the floor, watching the cord and making sure she didn't run over the many clothes that were thrown around. She went out and got her dusting spray and her cloth. When she got to the desk, she began to wipe one corner, just visible under more clothes. She stopped the second she saw that her hand was right next to a stack of money. She froze, holding her breath, worried that any minute someone would come in and catch her staring at the pile of hundred-dollar bills. It was a big stack. Maybe about three thousand dollars' worth. Her take-home pay at the end of the month was only about eleven hundred dollars, and her rent alone was seven hundred.

She quickly stopped dusting and went right to the bathroom, wiping vigorously. She felt the need to leave the room as soon as possible.

In a few minutes, she was done. As she locked the door behind her, she wistfully hoped that a person with that much money would leave her a tip. Guests never left her tips. She wasn't even sure she would know what to do if she got one.

It had been a hotel worker who noticed the bones this time. He had been rushing to get to his front-desk shift on time and decided to cut through the church gardens. He stopped when something caught his eye. One of the statues—Our Lady of the Rosary—seemed to be cluttered with something colorful, but he was too far away to tell what it was. He debated going over to check on it. He was already late for work, but curiosity got the better of him. As he went closer, he saw Christmas lights twining around the statue of Mary and over green vines clutching an arched trellis that formed a half circle over the statue. Hanging off the shoulders of the statue was a cape made of broken digital and old-fashioned watches, stitched together by thin silver wire. He thought it was a prank or some kind of weird art.

A mobile hanging from the arch swung in the breeze and clinked together, catching his attention. It had a white rod from which dangled more white pieces that looked ceramic.

He was the son of a Wisconsin hunter, who had helped his father dress many deer before he was old enough to shoot his own. He remembered his father once telling him that one of the only ways to tell a human femur from that of a deer was to look at the bone's core. He wondered why that had occurred to him as he stared at the display. It took a moment for it to register—the white rod of the mobile swinging merrily in the wind was a tiny femur.

Gil and Joe arrived at the scene within minutes of the call. They had taken their food to go. While Gil drove to the cathedral, Joe ate his pancakes with his bare hands. Gil just left his food in the car. On the way to the church, Gil had called the officer on scene and told him to shut the area down, giving him the same instructions as he had the officer at the Santuario crime scene.

Gil and Joe were silent as they walked around to the side of the cathedral, into a cool, green alcove that smelled of earth and flowers. There was no crowd here, only two police personnel looking tense, holding a makeshift curtain to protect the scene from the public eyes. The cathedral, in the heart of downtown, would be much harder to secure than the Santuario. Here all the buildings were squished together, forcing locals and tourists alike to walk everywhere. When they shut down the streets, someone would notice. Then the media would notice.

Gil suddenly got an idea. He walked over to one of the officers and said, "Have the guys on the crime scene line tell people who ask that the road is being shut down for fiesta Mass." That should stall questions for a while. Gil looked at his watch: 10:50 A.M. It didn't give them much time before noon Mass, when the mayor, the city council, and other fiesta attendants, including his mother and Aunt Yolanda, would be arriving.

Gil walked over to the statue of Mary and stood in front of her. She was stark white and small, standing about three feet tall and set on a brick pedestal. This statue, unlike the huge, overwhelming one of Our Lady of Guadalupe, was elegant and refined. Under the cape of watches Gil could see the careful detail of her ornate robes, almost lost in the white-on-white stone. Mary's face was not downcast this time but looking straight forward. She wore a large crown and held a rosary dangling in her hands. The flowered vines that covered the trellis hung sweetly over her head, but the Christmas lights twisting around the statue covered her beauty. The killer had tied Mary up with the green wires and dead lightbulbs of the holiday season.

Joe looked at a gold plaque placed by the church at Mary's feet, then started to read aloud: "Mother of Life, intercede before your Divine Son for the victims of abortion, euthanasia, domestic violence, murder, capital punishment, abuse, genocide, warfare, and other manifestations of the culture of death." He shook his head. "I think that's what you call ironical."

Gil wondered if Joe knew how true that statement was, because this statue of Mary was not only called Our Lady of the Rosary but had another name—La Conquistadora. Our Lady of the Conquest.

The statue was a stone version of a four-hundred-year-old wooden figure that had her own ornate chapel inside the cathedral. Her history was the history of Santa Fe. The history of fiesta. It was she who had conquered New Mexico for the Spanish.

The wooden statue of La Conquistadora, made of willow wood from Spain, had come to New Mexico with the first waves of colonists who settled the area four hundred years ago, and she escaped with them to Mexico, a hundred years later, during the Pueblo Revolt. When the colonists, led by Don Diego de Vargas, came back to try to resettle the land, she was there again, and it was to her that Don Diego prayed, asking that he be able to take back the city without bloodshed. Since that day, all Santa Feans have honored his prayer to La Conquistadora by holding fiesta. Gil wondered if it was a coincidence that someone had put Brianna's bones in front of a statue of La Conquistadora during fiesta weekend.

Gil clicked open his phone and called Officer Kristen Valdez, who had been at the office earlier for the meeting. "I need every available officer to check all religious sites in the city," he said, "especially ones dedicated to Mary. Is that something you can coordinate from there? We'll need someone with a map making sure we hit all the spots."

"No problem," she said. "What are they looking for?"

Gil gave her a description of what they had found so far and said, "Joe and I will check the rest of the cathedral property since we're already here."

Just as Gil was hanging up, Kline and Garcia showed up together again. Gil, with Joe tagging along, went to join them, and the four men walked away from the scene, making sure no one was in earshot. Gil told them about Valdez organizing the search and about the precautions they had taken at the scene.

"Sounds good," Kline said. "Any ideas about what we're dealing with here?"

"I think it's a serial killer," Joe said. "He's playing with us."

"A serial killer? In Santa Fe?" Garcia said. "That's a new one."

"Maybe someone who moved into the area recently?" Joe said. "Or maybe somebody who hates Catholics."

"Maybe," Kline said. "What do you think, Gil?"

Joe answered for him. "He thinks it's a killer with a guilty conscience."

"What do you mean?" Garcia asked, turning to Gil.

"Well, assuming these bones are Brianna's, I think we can all agree that whoever killed her and set up this display is not your run-of-the-mill suspect," Gil said. "I think he has a mental disorder and he's feeling guilty for killing Brianna. He knows it was wrong and makes these displays to show God that he's sorry. Mary is the main saint who intercedes with God on a sinner's behalf."

Garcia nodded, then recited a line from the Hail Mary, "Holy Mary, mother of God, pray for us sinners . . ."

"Exactly," Gil said.

"Dude, all I know about the Virgin Mary is that she sometimes shows up on cheese sandwiches and tortillas," Joe said to no one.

"So you're thinking that the elaborate display is part of his disease presentation?" Kline asked, ignoring Joe.

"It might be," Gil said.

"Just because the guy is nuts, that doesn't mean he's not a serial killer," Joe said.

Gil sighed, tiring of this back-and-forth with him. "That's true, but statistically serial killers make up only a fraction of all homicides. I think it's more likely that Brianna's killer is local and mentally ill and that this was his first kill. There was some recent stressor that made him do all this," Gil said, gesturing to the statue.

"Could it be something to do with fiesta?" Joe asked, finally releasing his death grip on the serial killer idea. "It seems strange that it's this weekend."

"The whole fiesta thing is really about Mary," Gil said, thoughtful.

"What about a cult?" Garcia asked. "We've a fair number of weird religious groups around here."

"It's something to consider until we have any other ideas," Kline said, then added calmly, "I know we don't have much experience with this kind of case. So if this is too much and we need more manpower, we can always call in the state police or the FBI."

Lucy pulled up to her house and saw Nathan sitting on her front porch, going through her mail.

She rested her head on the steering wheel for a moment before getting out of the car.

"What are you doing here?" she said to him, annoyed. "Why are you opening my mail? Can you say federal offense?"

"Did you know they're going to disconnect your electricity on Monday unless you pay nine dollars and five cents? Why wouldn't you just pay that? Maybe if it was like two hundred, but nine dollars?"

Lucy grabbed the mail from him. "What are you still doing here?"

"I can't find my keys. I must have dropped them inside."

Lucy rolled her eyes and opened her front door.

He clumped in after her, saying, "I thought about trying to get in one of the windows, but I already have two B&Es and I don't need a third strike, you know."

"That's the exact same problem I have with my prostitution charges," Lucy said, throwing the mail down on a side table.

"Really?"

Of course she would pick up a felon with no sense of humor, who in broad daylight had really bad tattoos and some disturbing scars on his neck. She fished the licorice black rock out of her pocket and dropped it into a bowl by the front door. In the bowl were other candy-colored rocks and a few pottery shards. Lucy had taken to picking up pieces of the mishmash she saw on the desert floor, thinking they made an organic kind of potpourri.

They went into the bedroom to search for his keys, throwing aside dirty clothes. After fifteen minutes, they still hadn't found them.

Lucy looked at her watch. It was 10:00 A.M. She worked the night shift at the newspaper—usually getting in by around 2:00 P.M. and getting done by 11:00 P.M.—but today she needed to be in by 11:00 A.M. so she could meet her boss for her first yearly review.

"Look, Nathan, I have to be at work in an hour. Do you have an extra set of keys or anything? I don't think we're going to find them here."

"Yeah, back at my place. We can go over there to get them."

"I can't really do that. I have to get to work. How about I just call you a cab?"

He shrugged.

As they waited for the taxi, he sat on her bed. She needed a shower, but didn't want any nakedness to happen until after Nathan left, so she put on her makeup. She would just have to avoid getting her face wet while washing her hair. She watched Nathan's reflection in the mirror as she put on some cover-up. He was studying her bedroom in all its Goodwill furniture glory.

"Why do you have all these chairs in here?" he asked.

She looked at the walls lined with five wooden chairs that once matched a table, long since gone.

"It's for when I play musical chairs with myself."

"Really?"

She sighed. "No. I was trying to make a joke."

As she patted on face powder, she realized the chairs were from a game of sorts. One she had played with her ex-boyfriend, Del Matteucci. The game had been called Let's Move a Thousand Miles Away and Then Break Up. It wasn't a very fun game, and she was definitely the loser. She had come to Santa Fe a year and a half ago to be with Del. She had wanted to stay in Florida, but he got offered a photography job at the *Santa Fe Times*. She had hoped to get a reporting job, but in the end, she took the only job she could find—night editor at the *Capital Tribune*. Six months later, they split up. The chairs, along with the rest of their joint possessions, became the playing pieces in the Break Up game. He won the coffeemaker and silverware, and she got the chairs.

She had half of her makeup done—so the left and right sides of her face looked like before and after makeover pictures—when she heard a honk of a horn.

"Nat, the cab's here," she said.

"Okay, sure." He didn't move.

"So, let's all go out to the cab now. Come on. It'll be fun." She made shooing motions with her hands at him.

He finally got up, and they went to the door. He hesitated in the door frame. It was only at that moment she realized he might try to kiss her good-bye.

"I'll just see you out to the cab," she said to forestall any such thing.

She walked the few feet outside to the cab door, opened it, and said a sunny "Bye-bye. See you later."

"Umm . . . you know . . ." Nathan started to say, not getting into the cab.

"Look, I really need to go," Lucy said.

"Yeah, I know. It's just that, you know, I don't have any cash."

"You work at a bar. Don't you have money from tips?"

"Not really. Last night was really slow. Plus I owed this guy some money . . ."

He tried to do his best cute-dog eyes, which worked since he was still wearing his spiked dog collar.

"Fine. Whatever." She went back inside and got her wallet. Outside, she said to the cabdriver, "How much to take this guy home?"

"About fifteen dollars."

"Swell," she said. "Do you have change for a twenty?"

"You know, I just realized," she heard Nathan say from the backseat of the cab, "I'm going to have to take a taxi back here to get my car."

Lucy leaned her head against the roof of the cab and started laughing. What was supposed to have been a free and easy one-night stand was going to end up costing her thirty dollars in consequences. She pulled another ten out of her wallet and gave it to Nathan as he said, "I really appreciate it. I'll call you—"

"Take care."

"But how will I pay you back—"

"See you later."

"If you—"

She walked away, shaking her head. God, but she was a moron. She had just paid a man to go away.

Joe followed Gil as they entered the cathedral to check for any additional signs the killer might have left inside. Joe stood back a ways, looking uncomfortable.

Gil crossed himself with the cool holy water as he went though the doors. The church was just over a hundred years old, young by Santa Fe standards, and had been built in the French-Romanesque style. The interior was bright with sunlight, and tall ceilings were crisscrossed with flying arches. The locals had added their own touches, too. The Stations of the Cross were made in the santero style, and the huge altar screen featured Native American and Mexican saints.

Gil walked over to the front of the altar and genuflected, crossing himself and kissing his thumb.

"What am I supposed to do?" Joe whispered. "Bow or something?"

"Just keep walking," Gil said.

"Man, I hate churches. When can we go investigate something in a bar? Now that's my scene."

They went over to the chapel of La Conquistadora, which was to the left of the altar. This was the only part that remained of the adobe church that had stood here since the 1700s.

The back wall of the chapel was completely taken up by a huge, ornate altar screen, painted in gold, rose, and green. The star of the screen was the two-foot-tall La Conquistadora statue. She was perched on her own special balcony, with a spotlight on her stoic face. She held baby Jesus in her arms and a rosary in her hands. Her long brown hair was made of real human strands and flowed out from under a crown made of gold and gemstones—and this was only her replacement crown. Her original crown was too valuable to be left out in the open, so it was safely stored in the vault of a local bank. The statue had its own collection of 150 dresses and $200,000 worth of jewels, including emerald earrings, silver bracelets, and a turquoise squash-blossom necklace. Today she was wearing a gown of black velvet with tiny red roses embroidered on it and a mantilla of white lace surrounding her.

Between the adoring public and the altar screen was a tall wrought-iron fence to keep the worshippers from getting too close to the four-hundred-year-old statue. A line of votive candleholders, some with flames winking red in the semidark, stood in front of the fence.

"So that's La Conquistadora?" Joe said. "She looks kind of pissed."

"Actually, I'm not sure if this is her or if this is the traveling La Conquistadora. They switch the two of them around sometimes." He stood back and looked more closely at the statue's face. "No, I think this is the real one."

"What are you saying? This statue has a body double?" Joe said.

"Pretty much. The other one is over at the chapel in Rosario Cemetery. That's the one that gets used for processions out of town and other things that might be too hard on the original one."

"Sounds like overkill to me," Joe said.

"She's the oldest statue of Mary in the U.S.," Gil said. "You have no idea what a big deal that is to Catholics."

"What, are they afraid someone is going to take her?"

"Actually, yeah," Gil said. "She was kidnapped in the seventies."

"No way," Joe said.

"It was huge news," Gil said. "The governor and everybody was involved. There was a ransom note, and a priest was told to ring the cathedral bells to make the exchange. It ended up just being a couple of teenagers who stashed her in an old mine."

Joe seemed to look a little more respectfully at the statue as Gil put a dollar into the collection box and used a small stick to light one of the red votive candles. Then he crossed himself, saying a quick prayer for Brianna.

They left the chapel and did a quick sweep of the rest of the building but found no other displays. They were leaving when Joe asked, "Why did your Don Diego de Vargas dude haul the statue all the way up here from Mexico? I gotta say, it's kind of weird that a grown man carries around a statute of a lady. I guess they didn't have blow-up dolls back then—"

"Knock it off," Gil said sternly, the way he did when he was telling one of his daughters not to back-talk. "Show some respect."

"Sorry. It's just that I don't get all this stuff. I mean, you guys build this whole church for her and she's not even here all the time . . . Come to think of it, my ex-wife was a lot like that."

Outside in the sunshine, they watched the crime scene tech finish up her work. She was packing the cape made of watches into an evidence bag, causing Gil to look at his own watch. It was 11:10 A.M. Just under a hour until fiesta Mass started, when hundreds of people would swarm the area on their way into church. They had to get this cleaned up soon.

His head started aching again as he thought through the case so far. Every turn they had taken today had offered nothing more than frustration. They still didn't even know if this was a murder case, or if the bones were Brianna's. Until they got either of those facts, they had little to do, except constantly slam their heads up against a wall of theories. Which seemed to be Joe's method, and probably why Gil had a headache. To distract himself, he put a call in to Officer Valdez.

"Kristen, how is the search going?" he asked. "Anything so far?"

"Nothing yet," she said, sounding a little stressed. "I had to let a couple officers respond to an accident on Cerrillos Road, so I lost some staff."

"The cathedral is empty," Gil said. "How are we doing checking other places with a Mary connection?"

"Well, we cleared the Immaculate Heart of Mary Church, and I have someone going to Santa Maria de la Paz. Do you think we need to expand it to other places? How strong is the Mary connection?"

"Pretty strong."

"How likely is it that there are more of these displays out there?" she asked.

"I don't know," Gil said, considering the question for the first time. "If he decides to use all of the bones in displays, that could be a few more. So far, we've only collected a head, a femur, and toe and finger bones, and about a dozen other bones I couldn't identify. How many bones are there in the human body?"

"The adult human has two hundred and six bones, but kids have more than that," he heard Joe say behind him.

"Really?" Gil asked him, wondering how Joe ever had reason to know that information. "Okay. That leaves more than a hundred and eighty or so bones for him to keep putting around town." He hadn't considered the possible enormity of their situation yet. There was no way they could keep a lid on so many crime scenes. "Okay, Kristen," he said, trying to get his head back in the game. "Let's check that mural of Mary over on Alto Street. And I think there's a cottonwood stump on Alameda that's been carved into a statue."

"Jesus, Gil," she said. "If we start looking at all the images of Mary in town we could be at this for days."

That was his new fear.

Gil had volunteered to check out the Rosario Chapel near downtown. It was only a mile or so away and situated back from the road, within the Rosario Cemetery.

"Let's go lights and sirens," Joe said as they got in the Crown Vic.

"No," Gil said, starting to lose his patience. "You know the protocol. We can't do that unless someone's life is in danger."

"You did it before when we went to the cathedral," Joe said.

"That was under orders from the chief when we knew we were going to a crime scene."

"There is going to be a crime scene right up here in this car if you don't put the siren on."

Gil ignored him, instead listening to the scanner to see if there was any chatter about other sites.

"You are such a safety dog, Gil," Joe said, not letting the issue go.

"A what?" Gil asked, not sure what he was talking about.

"A safety dog. Like the guy who gets dressed up in a dog costume and goes to schools to tell kids to not play with matches or whatever."

"I think that's Smokey the Bear."

"In my school it was the safety dog," Joe said with conviction, "and that is so you, man. You always gotta follow the rules."

Joe and Gil drove down a pine-tree-lined drive into the heart of the Rosario Cemetery. The gravestones were unmatched and uneven. Some were only hand-chiseled on a piece of rock, while others were full marble vaults. A few were written in Spanish from the early 1800s, and there was a scattering of brand-new ones. The names on the graves were from old Santa Fe families—Vigil, Gurule, Pacheco, Baca, and Ortega. In the middle of the graves was the Capilla de Nuestra Señora del Rosario, a small chapel dedicated to the Virgin Mary. To La Conquistadora, specifically.

The capilla had two small circular windows above an arched door, making the front of the church look like a surprised face. There were buttresses on either side of the front door, and a silver bell in the mission-style roof.

The church was built precisely on the spot where Don Diego de Vargas made his famous prayer. The chapel was permanent proof that Santa Feans kept their promise to honor La Conquistadora if she delivered the city to the Spanish. Gil knew the capilla would be closed. It was only opened during the fiesta procession that would take place on Sunday.

It wasn't the capilla they were coming to see, though. They were coming to check the outdoor altar to Mary.

Gil parked the Crown Vic in the empty parking lot. He and Joe took a minute to steel themselves before getting out. Because they saw what awaited them.

They walked in silence over to the front of a permanent altar that had been erected by the church for open-air Masses. The chest-high altar, made of white marble, was on a dais up four brick steps. Behind the altar, a freestanding beige stucco wall rose up at least two stories. Nestled in a large cutout in the wall was a five-foot-tall white marble statue of the Virgin Mary. Where the other statues of Mary had been ornate, this one was unadorned. She was sculpted in simple flowing robes of white. Her hands were folded in prayer. Her beautiful face, looking down and etched in sorrow and grief, could have been reacting to the display on the altar below her.

This time the killer had been more intricate. Safely away from the prying eyes of the cars that passed by the gated cemetery, he had spent more time here. There was an array of glass containers, some empty and some with red liquid in them. Gil counted fourteen jars in all placed on the edges of the altar. As Gil got closer, he saw that some of the empty jars actually had bones in them. Placed next to each jar was a piece of heavy ivory paper, carefully cut out into a rectangle the size of a playing card and folded in half, like a seating marker at a fancy dinner. On each paper was written one sentence: *I was dead and buried.*

CHAPTER SIX

Friday Morning

Gil stood with his back to the crime scene, looking at a gravestone in front of him. The tombstone was of speckled marble. It was the final resting place of Henry, who had been born in 1909 and died in 1978. Next to his name was a space left for Virginia, who had been born in 1906. There was no final date for her. She had decided not to join Henry here in death. Gil wondered if Henry had forgiven her for that.

He heard Chief Kline calling his name behind him and turned around. The quiet cemetery had turned into a sparsely attended freak show, with a crime scene tech taking photo after photo as Kline, Garcia, and a few other officers peered curiously through the glass jars. Since the cemetery was off the main road, containment of this scene was fairly easily. It simply took one police cruiser parked in front of the main entrance.

Gil walked over to Kline and saw Joe coming from the other direction, doing the same. As the two of them approached each other, Joe said, "Hey, there's a guy buried over here named Montoya. It looks like he was a senator. Are you guys related?"

Gil shrugged. "Probably."

"Dude, you are like royalty around here."

They met up with Kline and Garcia in the middle of the parking lot.

"Well," Kline said, looking tense, "I don't know what else to do but to call in the FBI. This is getting pretty far out of our league."

"I think this is pretty far out of everyone's league," Gil said. He didn't see calling in the FBI as a failure on his part but as a chance to get more manpower. In the past, he had worked well with the agents, who were always helpful and well informed. There might be a problem with Brianna's family, though. The FBI had been called in on her case before, and their presence led directly to the family filing the lawsuit. If they were to call the FBI in again, what little help the Rodriguezes were giving might dry up.

Gil said as much to Kline, who said, "I agree. At the same time, we are seriously overwhelmed here."

They all stood in silence until the chief said, "Let me think about it some more. Meanwhile, I'm calling in all off-duty and retired officers for manpower. So let me know what you need."

"Actually, I have one more thing," Gil said, turning to Garcia, who was the department spokesman. "I was wondering about our media plan with all of this."

"There has to be some kind of statement," Garcia said.

"I think we locked down the crime scenes at the statues quickly enough that we shouldn't have too much firsthand exposure," Gil said. "It should make it pretty easy for us to ignore questions about those. The only people who got a good look were the ones who called it in."

"They were already informed that it would not be in their best interest to speak to the media," Garcia said.

"Okay," Gil said. "Then what would you think if we did a statement, not a press conference, and mentioned the skull only? Our exposure at the Zozobra scene is too big. We know those Protectores have already been talking to people. Let's only mention what we have to. Once all of this gets out, we are going to have more than we can handle in this investigation."

"What if the other scenes come up or if the press asks if the skull is related to Brianna?" Garcia asked.

"I think 'no comment' about covers it," Kline said, settling the matter.

Judge Otero sat on the bench, listening to a middle-aged local woman. The case was another domestic abuse. The woman was explaining why she had thrown a plate at her boyfriend.

He straightened his class ring on his finger. It was starting to look worn at the base. He rubbed it with his fingertip to see if that would improve the polish. The stone was blue and on the sides was etched "1971" and "UNM." He had gotten his degree in engineering from the University of New Mexico. That was ages ago. Before his nineteen years on the bench and his five reelections.

He looked up as the woman stopped talking, saying, "I'll send you to anger management yoga and meditation class. My clerk will give you the information." He heard a few snickers in the audience. Before the woman could thank him, he said, "Next case."

Judge Otero had started sending offenders to yoga and meditation classes after getting tired of seeing the same suspects over and over. Clearly, the usual methods other judges used didn't work. So he decided to be creative and try something new. Only he didn't expect the amount of publicity it generated. He had reporters all the way from New York calling him for interviews, and one of the cable news networks had scheduled him to talk about criminal sentences. They had canceled after the Judicial Standards Commission started its investigation a year ago, but he fully expected that they would call again once that was dealt with.

His clerk read the charges of the next case: racing on the streets, no license, no seat belt, and no registration. A young man came forward. He looked to be no more than sixteen, and his mother was with him.

"Son," Judge Otero said, "do you realize that the punishment for this is ninety days in jail and three hundred dollars? It is an extremely serious offense."

"Yes, sir," he said. "I do, sir, but I want to plead guilty with explanation."

Judge Otero leaned back in his leather chair and surveyed the boy, who looked like he might pass out from nervousness. The judge felt this pause was necessary—especially in juvenile cases—to make the defendant realize the power of the court. Often, this was the first and last time that a citizen would step into a courtroom, so the judge felt it was his duty to show his authority. Here, in this chamber, was a rare world—a place where only one person made the rules, and not following those rules had serious consequences.

Judge Otero nodded slightly and said, "Go ahead."

"I was just getting done eating and it was my birthday and I was only two blocks away—"

"Stop," the judge said. "I'll dismiss because it was your birthday, not because it was two blocks. Always wear your seat belt."

The next case was called as the judge looked at his watch and then over the courtroom. He had only a half hour left of hearing cases until he had to head off to the Plaza for the main fiesta celebration. He watched a redhead in boots play with her hair as his clerk called up a man with a suspended driver's license charge. Before the clerk finished reading the case particulars, Judge Otero interrupted with "You have a suspended license. How did you get here?"

"I walked," the man said.

"You better keep walking," the judge said as the courtroom laughed.

Chief Kline and Garcia drove off, leaving Gil and Joe standing in front of the crime scene. Near them, a goldfinch sang happily in a blue spruce tree. Gil felt like he'd been put into a pot of boiling water and left to drown. He was drifting, being pushed wherever the current took him. The chaos of the crime scenes and the implied violence were hard to wrap his head around. He needed to regain control.

"We are getting nowhere," Gil said. "All we've been doing is rushing from one scene to the next and never having a chance to formulate a real theory."

"Yeah, exactly," Joe said. "We need to step back and regroup."

A half hour later, Joe and Gil were set up in the office conference room with a few stacks of papers that represented Fisher's case files, evidence logs, and crime scene photos.

They sat before a whiteboard. On it, in green dry-erase marker, Joe had written four headings—SUSPECT TYPE, PROFILE, MOTIVE, and LOCATIONS.

"All right, so our goal here is not to get locked down on specifics," Gil said, hoping that it might forestall any disagreements. "Let's just talk in generalities."

Joe added, "I think we have to, since we still don't have any information."

Liz and Adam had yet to return any of Gil's phone calls. Kristen Valdez hadn't discovered any new crime scenes.

Under SUSPECT TYPE, Joe had already listed "serial killer," "pedophile," and "mentally ill."

"Okay," Gil said, looking at the list. "What do all these kinds of suspects have in common?"

"All of them would have committed stranger abduction," Joe said.

"Good thinking," Gil said. "So, if it is Brianna, she was snatched by a stranger. That at least gives us a broad profile to start with." He started to pace a little in front of the whiteboard, feeling the need for movement to get his brain working.

As he began to talk, he thought back to all the research he had read about offenders who committed abductions. "Okay, well . . . killers tend to be in the same racial and social categories as their victims. That means he is a white or Hispanic male, working class. He probably has a history of violence against kids, but this is the first time he's done anything like this around here or we would have heard about it. That makes him in his early to mid twenties but with a few minor prior arrests. He would need isolation, so that would mean he's unmarried, lives alone."

Joe wrote quickly on the board to keep up with Gil. The PROFILE list now had more than a half-dozen items on it.

Gil stopped pacing and looked up at the board, nodding. "That's a good start," he said. "Okay, let's move on to motive."

"Are we talking about motive for the killing or for making the displays or for abducting her?" Joe asked.

"That's a good question," Gil said. "I don't know. Are they all one and the same? Did he take her with the intent of making displays with her bones, or did that idea come later?"

Joe looked at the board for another moment before he said, "I don't think we know enough about the guy to say for a hundred percent sure why he took her or killed her." He hesitated before saying the next part. "I mean, I know this is your area of expertise with all that behavior analysis crap, but I feel we should concentrate on why he made the displays. I think they tell us a lot about him."

"How so?" Gil asked, already knowing the answer but trying to use it as a teaching moment.

"Well . . . he didn't hide her body," Joe said. It was now his turn to pace around the room. "He wanted her to be seen. Not only seen, he wanted her bones to make a statement. He put time into making that necklace and putting all that stuff into the jars, and then writing those notes. This took a lot of thought, a lot of planning."

"So he's organized," Gil said, almost smiling. Joe was finally starting to think like a detective.

"He's creative, too," Joe said. "I mean, to him he made something beautiful, something to look at."

"He thinks it's art," Gil said, picking up on Joe's train of thought, "and an artist tries to convey emotion."

"What emotion is he trying to show with this?" Joe asked.

"I think it's guilt," Gil said.

"I think it's pleasure," Joe said. Gil shook his head. Despite all their theorizing, they were right back where they had been all day. Going over the same territory, still at odds.

Gil was tired of it.

Ashley Rodriguez felt the muscles in her stomach tightening in another contraction. The nurse said they weren't real contractions, but they felt real to Ashley. She was alone in the exam room of the ER, waiting for the doctor to check her. The nurse had told her to wait on the table, but lying on her back was impossible. Her heavy belly cut off her breathing, as if someone were choking her. She had tried to lie on her side, but within a few minutes, her hip and thigh started throbbing.

She decided just to stand up and walk around the room a little, pulling the IV stand behind her. Her pregnancy with Brianna had been so different, so easy. There had been no false contractions. She had been getting a prenatal checkup when the doctor said something about taking her over to the hospital for some tests. She was quickly taken to an ultrasound room. Blood was drawn. Exams were done. Then the doctor said, "Are you ready to have your baby?" It had taken Ashley by surprise. She was only at thirty-three weeks. She had almost seven weeks left to go until her due date, and she wasn't in labor, but the doctors seemed so sure. So they gave her something to block the pain, and she had a C-section while she was still wide-awake. As soon as it was over, the nurse asked Ashley if she wanted to breastfeed, but Ashley said that she was too groggy. She really didn't want the nurse to get mad at her, but she didn't want to nurse Brianna. Just like she didn't want to nurse the new baby. She had seen what nursing does to a woman's breasts, and she didn't want hers to end up sagging and loose. Plus, if she breastfed, she'd have to pump her breast milk if she wanted to leave the baby with her mom. A bottle was so much easier.

She had been in the hospital for a few days, but Brianna had to stay longer because she came too early and the doctors said her lungs needed some extra help. Ashley spent all day in the hospital, sitting next to Brianna, holding her tiny hand, but at night, she had to go home. Even during those few hours apart, Ashley missed her little girl.

The marker Joe was using on the whiteboard made squeaking noises as he wrote. He was adding items under a heading that now read MO-TIVES FOR DISPLAYS. He had already put down "guilt" and "pleasure." They had agreed not to debate the finer points behind each of their pet motives and instead just concentrate on getting all the possible ideas down.

"I guess if he used her bones like this because of his religious beliefs we should also add 'faith' as a motive," Gil said, "and we should probably think about what Garcia said about a cult."

"What kind of cult would do this?" Joe asked as he added the new items to the board. "Like Satan worshippers? Or a death cult?"

"I have no idea," Gil said. The two men looked at the board for a moment before Gil said, "What are we missing?"

"What about a revenge motive?" Joe asked. "I would think if someone wanted Ashley or anyone else in the family to suffer, this would be a great way to do it."

"That's an interesting thought," Gil said as Joe wrote it down, "and that means we should add 'retaliation killer' to the suspect list. Did Fisher ever mention anyone in the family who had enemies?"

"Beats the hell out of me," Joe said, "but I'll go through his notes again as soon as we're done here." The two men stared at the motive list a little longer until they were out of ideas.

"All right, let's move on to locations," Gil said. "I guess you can write where we found all the bones."

Joe wrote the list quickly: Zozobra, Mary, Mary, and Mary.

Gil smiled a little. "That's not incredibly helpful, but it'll work for the moment."

"Okay," Joe said. "What do all these locations have in common besides the Mary thing? . . . I guess they're all downtown, and they all have significance to people from Santa Fe. A couple of the places are a little hard to find."

"Good, good," Gil said. "We can add that to the profile, that he's probably a local."

Joe stared at the board some more, then said, "I feel like we're missing something about Zozobra."

"How so?"

"Well, at all the other crime scenes, the bones were left at Catholic sites . . ."

"All with a statue of Mary . . ."

"Right," Joe said. "Except Zozobra. Why put her in there?"

"Well, in a way Zozobra is about making amends and forgiveness of sorts. It's a good point, though," Gil said. "Zozobra really has nothing to do with Mary or the Catholic Church."

"Maybe the better question is how the skull got there," Joe said. "Access to Zozobra was tight, I mean really tight. I was there, remember? They had security out the ying yang."

"Where were you stationed?"

"I was with the crowd."

"So how did he get it into Zozobra?" Gil said.

"I can only think of one way," Joe said. "He would have had to be standing next to Zozobra at some point before it burned."

"I know another way," Gil said, pulling a white business card out of his wallet and dialing Mike Vigil's number. Vigil answered right away.

"Hey, Mike," Gil said. "I need a couple of things from you. First, can I get a list of all the people who could have gotten close enough to toss something in the fire last night?"

"You got it."

"I also need the name of the guy who picked up the public boxes and dumped them into the fire," Gil said.

"I can give you that now," Mike said. "His name is George Quintana. Actually, he could tell you about who was near the fire last night, too." Mike then rattled off George's phone number.

"What the hell was that all about?" Joe said as soon as Gil hung up.

"Every year for Zozobra," Gil said, "they put a few public boxes around town so people who have something they want to forget about, like photos of an old girlfriend or a mortgage, can put it in the box. Then the box is dumped into Zozobra right before he burns."

"So you're thinking that maybe the killer put the skull in one of the public boxes, which was then dumped in the fire," Joe said, nodding. "Good idea."

Gil called George Quintana and explained who he was.

"So what do you need?" Quintana asked, sounding confused.

"What can you tell me about how you disposed of the public boxes?" Gil asked, trying to keep the question open-ended.

"There's nothing too complicated about it," Quintana said. "I just throw the whole thing into the fire, cardboard and all."

"Did you toss them in before the fire was set or after?"

"Right after it's set."

That sounded strange to Gil. "You're allowed to go up to the burning fire and throw it in?"

"Yeah, but I'm a retired firefighter for the city, so I handle all the action near Zozobra as soon as he is lit, you know, keeping everyone away from the area," he said.

That was good news for Gil, who needed that exact information. "So do you check Zozobra before the fire is set to make sure everything is okay?"

"Yep, I'm the one who goes up under his skirt, so to speak, and makes sure everything is good to go."

"Did you see anything out of the ordinary last night?"

"No. It was a pretty typical burn."

"Who is allowed access to Zozobra after he is set up and before he is burned?"

"Nobody but me and my two sons," he said. "We're really clear on that. They're firefighters, too. One's out in the county; the other is up at Los Alamos. We're careful not to let people get close ever since a couple of kids thought it would be funny to try to throw each other in. After that, I said no way does anyone get near Zozobra. So from the time he is set up until after the burn, he is off-limits. We set up a fence around him that no one can cross except me and my boys."

"So in your opinion, no one could have snuck something into Zozobra before he was burned?"

"I don't see how."

That skull was definitely in the fire and not put in afterward, into the ashes. The melted material on the back of the skull proved that. If Quintana and his sons were the only ones who had access to the fire, that meant Gil had to ask the next question. "Do you or your sons know Ashley or Brianna Rodriguez?"

"Who?"

Gil repeated the question, but Quintana had never heard of any of the Rodriguez family members. Gil knew it was unlikely the Quintanas were involved in Brianna's disappearance, and since it seemed almost impossible for someone to have thrown the skull into the fire just before Zozobra burned, then it must have been put in one of the public boxes.

"So, getting back to the public boxes, do you look in them before you toss them in?" Gil asked.

"Well, usually, but . . . okay, I'm supposed to look in the boxes, but I thought I told one of my sons to do it . . ."

"And it didn't get done," Gil said.

"Right. So I ended up throwing them in without ever opening them," Quintana said. "Which was a stupid thing to do. You never know what's going to be in the boxes." *Right*, thought Gil. *You never know.*

"So how many boxes were there?" Gil asked.

"I put out only one box this year," Quintana said. "I think interest in the whole public box thing is waning. I picked that one up right around five o'clock yesterday, and it was in my car until I put it in the fire."

"Where did you pick up that box from?"

"It was over in the lobby of the *Capital Tribune*."

Lucy sat in the flowered courtyard of La Casa Sena, watching people eat colorful food, artfully arranged. A blond waitress went by with a plate that held a piece of pie lined with raspberries, drizzled with chocolate, and sprinkled with rose petals. Lucy couldn't help but gawk since most of her meals came wrapped in paper and warmed under heating lamps.

Even though this was her first yearly review since working at the *Capital Tribune*, she decided that the best part of it was going to be the food, followed only by the free aspect of that food. All that was required to get the free meal was to sit through an agonizing hour of talk about her work performance with her big boss, managing editor John Lopez.

She had had yearly reviews at all her previous jobs. No matter the workplace, the conversation always followed the same script: It would begin with an hors d'oeuvre of small talk and move into an entrée about job expectations. For a salad, there was discussion of what the future might hold—a promise of a bigger title and better projects. As for the dessert, it was five minutes of "constructive criticism" that was disappointing in its lack of sweetness.

Her reviews were never that bad, but for some reason she saw them as humiliating. Maybe it was the idea of the boss's telling you that there was a dark spot on the X-ray he'd taken of your career when you'd thought it was healthy as a horse.

Lucy sat in her metal patio chair, trying not to fidget. Lopez finished ordering his salmon and carefully put the cloth napkin in his lap. Lucy quickly did the same, smiling nervously.

"So how do you think your first year at the newspaper went?" he asked, taking a sip of his water. She had actually been there for a year and a half, but Lopez ran perpetually behind on the yearly reviews. She thought it best not to point that out at the moment.

"Umm . . . great?" she said, not sure if that was the correct answer.

"Are you getting used to Santa Fe? It's a big change from Florida."

"Yeah, no, it's great here," she said, wishing she sounded like she meant it. Which she did. New Mexico was like a big present she was constantly unwrapping, finding a fabulous gift under every layer.

"How are things at the fire station?" he asked.

Lucy had been very up-front about her work as a first responder at Piñon Fire and Rescue, mainly in the hope that they would let her go to calls when things were slow at work. Which they surprisingly did. Since she was an unpaid medic and helping the public, Lopez said, he saw it as an indirect way of giving back to the readers. She didn't question his logic, if there was any logic there to question.

"Everything at the station is great," she said, realizing that she needed to find a descriptive word other than "great."

"I heard there was a car fire this morning," Lopez said.

"Yeah, there was," she said hesitantly. How did he know that?

Lopez must have seen her confusion and said, "Harold heard you on the scanner."

"Oh, okay," she said. Thanks to the police scanner that sat on a shelf over her desk, all of her co-workers could hear when she used her EMS radio on a call.

"What are you going to say in the brief about it?"

"What? What do you mean?"

"I was just thinking we need a page two brief about the car fire. Since you were there, it should make it easy for you to write it up."

"Wait. I'm sorry, I'm not sure I get it. You want me to write a brief about a call I was on?" Lucy asked. Something shifted horribly in her as she asked, "Is this part of my review?"

Lopez smiled. "I just feel it's time for us to take advantage of your hobby."

"My hobby? You want me to report on 911 calls?"

"Yes. That's actually one of the goals we have written down for you for the next year," Lopez said, taking a printed paper out of his briefcase. Sure enough, at the top was written, LUCY NEWROE. SPECIFIC GOALS TO ACCOMPLISH.

Lucy could only nod, cursing herself for not anticipating this. It was common practice at some bigger newspapers to pay people to listen to the police scanner and write up briefs on what they heard. Lopez basically was asking her to do the same thing, but in her case, she would be one of the people talking on that scanner as well. Since anyone could hear what was said over a scanner, it made every emergency call public purview. She could technically and legally write a story on all radio communications or public police and EMS reports, as long as it didn't violate patient confidentiality laws. She knew Gerald would think it was unethical. As for herself, she didn't know what to think.

"I . . . I don't know if I can do that," she said.

Lopez's phone began to ring. He said a quick "Sorry" and answered it. He listened to the person on the other end and then said, "I'll be right there." He hung up. "I actually have to get back to the office. Something's come up. We'll finish this soon."

Then she was sitting by herself in the middle of the sunny courtyard, where she was left to explain to the waitress that they needed to cancel their orders and to wonder if she would have to quit her job.

Gil sat in the lobby of the *Capital Tribune,* waiting. Joe was next to him, texting on his phone to who knows who. He was finally quiet except for the clicking of the keys.

Gil looked up at the two security cameras pointed into the lobby, a room no bigger than a two-car garage. A glass door off to the left led to the newsroom, while the door they were waiting next to had the words MANAGING EDITOR stenciled in gold.

The receptionist, an older Anglo woman with white hair and round glasses, had been helpful at first when they asked where the Zozobra box had stood. She had gotten up from her desk to stand in the exact spot. Which just happened to be in the direct line of sight of one of the cameras. When Gil asked if anyone who dropped off items in the box stood out, she seemed hesitant, but eventually said no. When Gil asked for the videotapes of the lobby for the last few weeks, the receptionist lost any will to help. She had called the managing editor and told them to wait.

As Gil sat, he looked at walls painted in a watery green and accented by badly framed newspapers from big news days gone by. There was one from the end of World War II and another from the moon landing. The building itself had a damp feel, a strange occurrence in the desert. Of course, it had probably been built in the 1800s, and at least parts of it were still adobe.

Gil looked at his watch again as the door opened and the managing editor came in, saying, "I am so sorry, gentlemen. I got here as soon as I could."

He was a trim man with lightly graying hair, wearing a white dress shirt and bolo tie. They left the outer office and went into Lopez's, where they all sat down at a heavy conference table.

"How can I help you?" Lopez asked.

"Well, we spoke with your receptionist, who said we had to talk with you about getting copies of your tapes from the security cameras in the lobby," Gil said. "We think they might have some information we need on them."

"Information that pertains to the skull you found in Zozobra?" Lopez asked. Gil wasn't surprised he already knew about the skull. It was Lopez's job, after all, to get the news.

"We can't say, sir," Gil said, though he was unsure why he added the "sir" at the end, except that Lopez seemed to be the type of man who was addressed as "sir" regularly. He wondered if Lopez was ex-military.

"Of course," Lopez said. "Unfortunately, I'm afraid I can't help you without a court order."

"Oh come on," Joe said, exasperated. "It's not like we're asking you for any state secrets. We just need to look at the tapes."

Lopez smiled sympathetically. "I realize your frustration, but this is I something I am required to do according to our code of ethics. I hope you understand. I am happy to give you the name of our attorney, if it would speed the process up."

"Dude, we can make copies of the tapes ourselves and have the originals back to you tomorrow," Joe said.

"Again, that's not the issue," Lopez said. "Like you, we serve the public, but we each have different goals. Yours is about justice, while mine is about truth."

"Our goal is always the truth," Gil said coolly.

"Yes, but it's not your main goal," Lopez said, still smiling. "We serve the public by giving them facts and being a watchdog, and one of the main institutions we scrutinize is the police. We can do nothing that might undermine our reputation in the eyes of the public."

"What the hell—" Joe said, before Gil interrupted him by saying, "There's nothing we can say to change your mind, or maybe someone else we can talk to? These are security tapes, not interviews done by reporters."

"I'm sorry," Lopez said again. "The publisher is out of town, but she would absolutely agree with me. This is standard practice, really. Of course, as soon as you get the court order, I will do everything I can to help."

"I bet," said Joe as he and Gil got up to leave. They walked past the receptionist before Joe started swearing.

Gil interrupted him. "I'm going to head into the newsroom for a second. I'll meet you back at the car." He went through the glass door before the receptionist or Joe could protest.

CHAPTER SEVEN

Friday Afternoon

Lucy walked into the newsroom and instantly knew something was up. It wasn't that people were rushing around. There was just a certain anticipation. Newsrooms were a great barometer of the importance of a news story. For people who live and breathe news, the real deal—not just a story about county taxes—gets them excited. Bad news was their best friend.

Lucy went to her desk and had just turned her computer on when she heard someone say to her, "Hi, boss."

"Hi, Tommy," she said without looking. Tommy Martinez was the cops reporter; his charm gave him access to news sources that made him indispensable in the newsroom. "What's going on? Everyone seems hyper."

"A skull was found in the ashes of Zozobra," he said.

"Seriously?" Lucy said, getting excited when any normal person would be horrified. It was the nature of their work. "Are we doing this as the front page spread?"

"I don't know," Tommy said. "We haven't talked about it yet. I've been too busy chasing the story."

"We have to be," she said. She got up and walked to the photo desk to find a printout of their daily news budget or someone who could tell her the scoop, but there was no one around. *Maybe copydesk would know,* she thought as she walked toward their warren of cubicles near the front of the windowless building.

She noticed that one of the lights overhead near the entrance to the newsroom was burnt out. The pocket of dark it left meant she could only make out hard shadows as a man came through the door, but she didn't need extra illumination to make her brain fizz in recognition. She knew who it was.

Gil Montoya. She hadn't seen him since January, and she wasn't prepared to see him again. If she had been able to run and hide, she would have, but the only place to go was copydesk's cubicle corral.

So she stood and stared as Gil walked toward her. She had forgotten how tall he was. How his dark eyelashes made his eyes seem ringed in eyeliner.

He stopped in front of her. "Hi."

"Hi."

He said nothing more as she nodded, her brain racing, trying to pin down an appropriate subject for small talk as the silence stretched out. They weren't good enough friends or unfamiliar enough acquaintances to stand in comfortable silence. Lucy felt the need to make a joke, but then that was how she always felt around him. So she said, "On a scale of one to ten, with ten being in the fires of hell, how uncomfortable do you feel right now? Personally, I'd say I'm about an eight-point-two, but I could be talked into a nine."

He smiled and said, "I'm going to go with five."

"Bastard," she said to him with a laugh. "You just have to show me up."

"How have you been?" he said.

She considered the question. If she were honest, she would have to say not good. She lied. "Fine," she said with a smile. "And you?"

Before he could answer, Peter Littlefield, one of the arts reporters, came up, saying, "Gil, it's good to see you." The two did the male back-patting hug.

"How's Susan?" Peter asked. Lucy didn't hear Gil's reply. She had forgotten there was a wife. There were kids, too, if she remembered correctly. She let out the breath she had been holding. Why did she feel guilty? Not that she and Gil had ever done or said anything even remotely inappropriate. They really barely knew each other. All their conversations had been business, always business. But . . . but she felt closer to him than to anyone else she had ever known? That was true, but that closeness was simply because he knew her secrets. He had been a spectator to her sins. He knew what she had done and still didn't shun her. As she would have shunned herself.

Nine months ago, Lucy had met Gil while checking a tip about two cops who were overheard talking about a body. By the time the dust settled, four people were dead, and Lucy was indirectly to blame for at least one of the deaths.

That was what her note in Zozobra had been about. *Release me.* There were so many things she needed to be released from; she wasn't even sure which of them she had meant in the note. Release her from her sins, from the past, from the memory? No matter; those were all the same thing. What she really needed to be released from was the stranglehold of guilt that wrapped around her. Guilt for something she knew she wasn't really to blame for. She felt the guilt, nonetheless. Because what she had said in an offhand remark led to a woman being killed. It was not her fault, but it was her burden.

Lucy kept a smile on her face as Peter and Gil talked. Peter said something about showing a Gil a picture of his new baby on his computer. As the men turned to walk off, Lucy said brightly, "Okay, great. It was good to see you again." Gil smiled at her and walked away, leaving her feeling cheap and unimportant. She was having a day of feeling cheap. That made her wonder if Nathan had picked up his car yet.

Mai Bhago Kaur was in Natural Foods, looking for vegetables for tonight's dinner. She watched a young mother next to her grab a handful of garlic and then some peppers as her baby gurgled in the shopping cart seat. Mai Bhago had to stop herself from telling the mother that she was poisoning herself and her baby with such pungent vegetables. Even worse, the woman was wearing down her feminine energies with food that was deeply rooted in heat and anger due to its masculine tendencies.

Mai Bhago reminded herself that the woman probably knew nothing of a sattvic diet. The woman was like most people, who tended to ignore the inherent energies in their foods and then wonder why they had chronic illnesses. What mattered was a food's prana, or life force. Her own diet of brown rice and mild vegetables might seem too bland to other people, when to her it was rich in subtle flavors.

She found the zucchini that she was looking for and added it to her large assortment of fruit, then pushed her cart toward the front of the store. She mostly ate fruit, often going on fruit fasts. As a result, she was in the Natural Foods store almost daily buying bananas, mango, grapes, and kiwi.

As she passed by the bread aisle, she thought back to a therapist who once advocated the wholesomeness of bread buying.

Back before she had taken the name Mai Bhago Kaur, when she still was called Donna Henshaw and had just become famous, she thought it was the ultimate luxury to hire a cook and a maid. No more food shopping, no more cleaning. Then, after a year on her television show, when she was starting to feel the first grips of depression, her therapist asked her how often she shopped for bread. The woman tried to explain that food is life and it doesn't just magically appear, it comes from somewhere. Mai Bhago knew that she was supposed to find some deep meaning in this, but she never understood what she was supposed to get out of it until much later, after years of yoga and meditation.

The cashier, a man in his fifties, smiled as she walked up. Mai Bhago knew that smile. The smile of recognition. The cashier would have been about eighteen when her show was on, right in her demographic, although they didn't call it that back then. She smiled graciously as she started to put her food on the conveyer belt and readied herself for his compliments.

"Hey, it's the Fruit Lady," he said merrily and loudly. He had probably meant to be funny, as a conversation starter, but it caused a gut reaction in Mai Bhago.

Her face became plastic, a method her acting coach had taught her after the first time she didn't win an Emmy. *Don't move the muscles in your face*, he would say. *Smile but don't show teeth. You are disappointed you didn't win but happy for the actress who did.* She had spent hours practicing it. At the next Emmy show, when Joyce DeWitt, sitting two rows in front of her, got up to go to the stage instead, Mai Bhago went plastic without a thought. The camera flashed to her and she was plastic. When Joyce breathlessly gave her acceptance speech, Mai Bhago smiled along with the rest of the crowd. Plastic. Stay plastic. She had done it years ago, but she couldn't do it now.

Mai Bhago took the money out of her wallet and handed it to the stupid, stupid cashier. She grabbed her bag, almost knocking over the person in line behind her. She didn't apologize. She got out to her car and did some calming stone breaths to center herself, but it was only when she reminded herself that he was just a man, and an impure one at that, that she finally felt calm.

Gil walked back to Joe and the car, wondering why he hadn't asked Lucy what she knew about the videotapes. That had been why he had gone to see her. When they were face-to-face, it didn't seem so easy.

He got into the car and pulled out of the parking lot. After a moment, he said to Joe, "Let's get back to the office and write up our report summaries. Something might jump out at us. At the very least, we'll have all our ducks in a row in case the FBI shows up. Then we have to get that court order from the police for the tapes."

They walked into the station and were inundated by questions and offers of help, which Gil was glad of. Gil asked two officers to go through local police reports where a suspect, victim, or patient—or anybody—had expressed delusions, especially about Mary or the Catholic Church. He asked a few other officers to call local churches to see if any had gotten threatening phone calls or letters, or had disgruntled parishioners.

Gil and Joe were just sitting down in front of the whiteboard again when Joe's phone rang, a personalized ringtone of "Pour Some Sugar on Me."

He answered, "What's up?" Followed by "Uh uh . . . uh uh . . . damn. I thought we had something there. Thanks." He hung up and said, "So there aren't any national serial killer profiles that even come close to matching this. Could this be a new one? You read all that profile crap, Gil. What do you think?"

Gil tried not to smile as he said, "Well, by definition, a suspect has to kill more than one person to be considered a serial killer. As far as we know, he hasn't."

"Damn, I thought we were really onto something . . . I guess it could be a serial killer from, like, Sri Lanka," Joe said as he looked over the suspect list.

"We still haven't really thought about the notes he left us," Gil said. "I think that's significant. He's making a statement."

"Yeah, but what does 'I was dead and buried' mean? . . . Wait a minute," Joe said, as he popped open his phone and started typing. "Okay, so no real hits on the Web with that phrase."

"Well, let's just write it on the board for now," Gil said. "I don't really have any better ideas of what to do with that. I guess we could have one of the other detectives do more research on it."

Joe went up to the board and wrote in large block letters *I was dead and buried*. He then crossed "serial killer" off the suspect type list. Gil wasn't sorry to see that theory go. That left the suspect list with four items: "pedophile," "mentally ill," "cult," and "retaliation killer."

Gil was asking yet another officer to find out about getting a court order for the security tapes when his phone interrupted him. It was Liz Hahn, finally returning his calls.

"Sorry that I'm just getting back to you," she said. "I wanted to have some actual information to pass along. Are you ready?"

Gil went over to his desk and grabbed a blank piece of paper in front of him, saying, "Go ahead."

"Okay. Before I get started, I just want to remind you that all of this is still preliminary, you know the drill," she said. "Let's start with the bones. The ones we have so far appear to match the age and decay rate of the skull."

"So the general consensus is that the skull and the bones are from the same person?"

"Yes. Next, the bones and the skull performed well under stress tests, meaning that they were exposed to the environment for no more than two years. Also, given the desiccation, the bones were free of flesh for at least six months."

"So they've been dead at least six months, but not more than two years," Gil said, repeating it back to her. "We can't do any better with time of death?"

"Nope. Sorry. Next thing is the age and sex of the victim. Now this part is actually straightforward because kids' bones aren't fully developed, especially toddlers'. That makes it easier to determine age."

"Right," Gil said, remembering how his daughters had the soft spot on their heads—where their skull was still forming—until they were almost two. Gil wondered if Liz ever thought of her own daughter while she did this work.

"Now, the posterior fontanelle in the skull was fully ossified, as was the anterior fontanelle, but the anterior cranial sutures weren't. In fact, we're lucky the fire wasn't hot enough to separate the skull at the sutures, which weren't very strong yet. Then, of course, as another age indicator, we have the epiphyseal plate's growth zone."

"Of course," Gil said. He knew Liz would eventually spell it out in laymen's terms, but she liked to use her clinical-speak to ease herself into the eventual normal, everyday language.

"All of this all puts the age right around one and a half to two years old," she said finally.

"Consistent with Brianna's age, although she was over two," Gil said as Joe came over to eavesdrop.

"Yes, but according to medical records she was a preemie, so she would have delayed development," Liz said. "Then we get to gender. Usually, we determine the sex by the pelvic bone, but that remodeling comes during puberty. So in kids, there isn't really any sexual dimorphism, which means it's unlikely we'll ever be able to tell you the gender."

"Okay," Gil said. He had been hoping to get a slam-dunk with the forensics, having it point either exactly to Brianna or exactly away.

"Last but not least, the identification," Liz said, sighing. "We're checking dental records in the national missing kids registry, but Brianna never went to the dentist, so we have nothing to compare in her case. That leaves DNA. We don't have any DNA from Brianna, but both of her parents gave us blood and DNA samples last year. So we can use them to verify that the bones are Brianna's. I'm supposed to tell you that DNA will take a minimum of a week to run, but I can get it done by Tuesday, I think."

"Thank you, Liz," Gil said.

"That leaves cause of death," she continued. "Again, all of this is preliminary. The rest of the bones didn't show anything unusual, but once we got the melted plastic off the skull, there were three distinct knife strikes through it."

"Let me make sure I got all this," Gil said. "We have a one-and-a-half- or two-year-old child of indeterminate sex who was killed in the last year or so." Gil looked over at Joe before he added, "And was murdered." As expected, Joe swore loudly.

Gladys Soliz Portilla sat in the hotel break room with the other maids and a few of the janitors. She was waiting for one of the cooks, who had promised to help her buy a Social Security number. He had said it would cost a hundred dollars, but she wanted to talk to him more before she made up her mind.

She already had her driver's license—which in New Mexico anyone could get as long as they had other ID, even from Mexico—and she had gotten a tax ID number, so she could pay her taxes as an undocumented worker, and a bank account at one of the credit unions. She didn't necessarily need the Social Security number. She could get along here without it. She was going to try to take some classes at the community college and get her GED, though, and while the college didn't care if she was documented, she was worried that at any moment someone would ask her for it. To prove that she belonged.

The women she sat with were mostly from Chihuahua, like

Gladys, and they were a loud, laughing bunch. She told them about the green spill she found in the room, but they only smiled. One of the women said, "You'll get used to that. Soon, you won't even care."

Another of the women started to talk about a couple she knew who had been killed by bandits while trying to walk across the border through the desert near Nogales in Arizona.

Gladys had no horrible border-crossing story, as so many people did. She hadn't had to battle the intense heat or days without food. She hadn't been forced to pay a coyote, then be packed into a truck with dozens of others. She simply walked across the border to Columbus, New Mexico, as she had every day for six years when she was a child. Palomas and Columbus were two small, neighboring towns, and, as such, they shared a school. The school just so happened to be built on the U.S. side of the border. Gladys had gone to Columbus Elementary until she was in the sixth grade, but then she had to drop out to help out her mother at home. She had liked school, especially when she got to write poetry or paint. Now, she wished she had paid more attention in English class, so she could get a job as a cashier or maybe a waitress.

When Gladys went over the border for the last time three months ago, she told the guards that today she was crossing because she needed to register her son for school. They looked at him but didn't mention that he was too young. Instead, they waved her across. She met her friend who was waiting for her a block away, who then drove her the six hours to Santa Fe.

She knew why the guards let her pass. They had known her husband and her father-in-law. Both had been police officers in Palomas, and both had been killed along with five others when the Juárez Cartel ambushed them as they drove in a convoy. After the funeral, there was talk of whether it also could be the work of the Sinaloa and Gulf cartels. To Gladys, it hardly mattered. Half of what mattered to her was now down in the cold ground, and she was left to protect her son.

She saw the cook come in and motion to her. She went over to him and smiled, saying quickly, "I've changed my mind, but thank you." She didn't wait for him to talk before she walked back to her table of loud friends. She was doing okay here without a Social Security number. If she had such a number, it might help her, but also make her more visible—and she had to remain invisible. For her son. She had already made herself too visible over the car problem.

Lucy, back at her desk, tried to concentrate on editing the water surcharge story that was on the computer screen. She corrected a few typos and some bad paragraph transitions. She still didn't know what was going on with the skull story, since the newsroom was doing its best impression of a beehive and no one had time to talk. Work. Work. Work. Tommy was at his desk, laughing on the phone. She wanted to go ask him what he'd found out, but it was better not to interrupt him in precoital interview mode. He was all about phone foreplay. His voice was sweet; you could almost hear him calling you baby as he asked for your phone number. That was if you were, say, a female district attorney. If you were a male police officer, it was all about guns and what could be shot with them.

There were no other stories for Lucy to read in the editing queue, so she checked her e-mail, then decided to do a quick search for stories about car fires in Santa Fe. If what that racist cop said was true, they could have something newsworthy going on at that house.

She typed the street address of 162 Airport Road into Google and was given a map and directions to Hacienda Linda Apartments. So it wasn't a house. It was an apartment complex. Weird. That probably meant the victims weren't related and might actually be strangers. They'd all had their cars burned? Definitely weird. Next, she went to their news archives and typed in "car fire" as keywords. Hundreds of entries popped up, so she narrowed the search by date. That left about twenty different police notes and crime stories for her to look through for some kind of mention of other fires.

She was about ten minutes into the process when a police note from three months ago caught her attention.

"The Santa Fe Police Department is investigating the following reports: Firefighters were called to 1608 Calle Capitan on Saturday to extinguish a vehicle fire. The vehicle was beige in color and was a

Ford Taurus 2003 with red graffiti markings on its rear passenger side."

Lucy thought about the red spray paint Gerald had seen on the burned-out car that morning. She wished now that she'd thought to take a look at it herself. It might have told her who was responsible for this.

Joe had papers spread out on the conference room table, searching Fisher's notes to see if there was a reference to any enemies. The only clean area on the table was where Gil sat, trying to finish up report summaries in between getting interrupted by his ringing phone.

One call was from Adam Granger, who was helping to process the evidence from the scenes. He had little to offer, except that, as expected, they were still working through the many sets of fingerprints on the Our Lady of Guadalupe statue, as well as lip prints where the faithful had kissed Mary's cloak. They had gotten no usable prints at the cathedral or Rosario Chapel crime scenes, but they did find out that the red liquid in the jars was colored water, not blood.

As Gil was hanging up his phone, Kristen Valdez came into the conference room with a map filled with green X's.

"So, okay," she said, sitting down and spreading the map out in front of her, over Joe's mess. "I think we've finally hit almost every religious site in the city that has an image of Mary, which, in case you were wondering, is about seventy-eight places. Now we've moved on to other churches and temples, just to cover our bases."

"How many officers are out there doing this?" Gil asked.

"We have six of our people and then about another five retired guys," she said.

"What are you saying to the churches when they ask what we're doing?"

"We tell them it's an ongoing case and just to call me if there is anything suspicious or they know of anyone who has a particular interest in the Virgin Mary," she said, snapping her gum.

"Thanks, Kristen, and good job."

"Yeah, good job, Valdez," Joe said with a sideways smile. She smiled back as she folded up the map and turned to leave, but stopped in the doorway. "Oh, one more thing I was supposed to pass along," she said. "We checked priors on the family, but there's nothing new. Just old traffic violations against the mom, Ashley. Also, of course, the dad is still in jail."

Joe jumped up. "Thank you, God, I completely forgot." He yelled, "Thank you, Kristen," as she went out the door.

When he saw Gil's blank look he said, "The dad is still in jail, dude. It's a gang thing." Joe went up to the white board and added "gang" next to "retaliation killer" under the SUSPECT TYPE list. Just when they had started to narrow it down.

"What are you talking about? What gang would kidnap a little girl and kill her?" Gil asked.

"The Company," Joe said with certainty. "That's what the Feds are now calling the Gulf Cartel. I kind of like it."

"The Gulf Cartel?" Gil asked. "Seriously? Why would they do this?"

"It's a turf war," Joe said, looking satisfied, as if he had finally won a long, hard argument. "Brianna's dad is with the West Side Locos. That's why he's in jail. He was dealing heroin for them."

"The West Side's biggest rivals are South Side, and they're a local gang," Gil said. "I can't see them doing something this extreme."

"Yeah, but lately West Side and Sureño 13 have been going at it hard," Joe said. "I have a buddy in the gang task force who says that Sureño 13 is making a play to be the area's exclusive heroin distributor. They're trying to push out West Side. And the Company supplies Sureño 13 with all its guns and drugs."

"You're saying the Gulf Cartel killed Brianna to help Sureño 13 get more territory?" Gil asked. "That sounds pretty weak. Besides, most of those guys have a tattoo of the Virgin on their backs. They revere her. They wouldn't desecrate a church dedicated to her."

"They only have her tattoo so when they get raped in prison the guy porking them from behind has to look at Mary while he's doing it," Joe said. "Those guys decapitate people left and right. They are crazy-ass killers."

Gil had to admit Joe was right about that. The drug war across the border in Mexico had been tearing its way north for years and was starting to take pieces of New Mexico with it. Albuquerque, sixty miles to the south, was already beginning to get caught up in its random and astounding violence. The Gulf Cartel was just one of three that were fighting over routes to rich customers in the United States. The Mexican government was even offering a $2.5 million reward for tips leading to the capture of any of the Gulf leadership.

"I guess it's possible," Gil said. "Was Brianna's dad that high up in the gang?" Normally, only lieutenants or higher would be subject to a retribution killing.

"I don't know," Joe said. "Let's go ask him."

Lucy still hadn't seen a news story budget by the time she went into the afternoon meeting. Her boss, Harold Richards, who was just one rank below John Lopez, slid her a copy across the long wooden table. The conference room was more of a conference closet, which meant representatives from the various departments who attended the meeting spilled into the hallway. Lopez came in and took his seat at the head of the table.

He said, "So what have we got on the skull story?"

Richards answered, "We're still chasing it. We have interviews from a couple of the Protectores who found it in the ashes, and we're trying to get the cops to confirm that the skull belonged to a kid."

"Do they think it's Brianna?" asked one of the copy editors.

"No one is saying, so what we have right now is just two guys who saw the skull telling us it looked small," Richards said.

"What do we have as far as photos?" Lopez asked.

The photo editor, Shaun Kirkpatrick, said, "Of course, we have photos of Zozobra burning, but we're still trying to find a main photo."

"Has anyone started a memorial yet at the site where they found the skull, with candles and stuff?" Richards asked. "There has to be one there by now. We could shoot that."

"Maybe," Kirkpatrick said, not sounding like he thought much of the idea.

"Let's just keep chasing it and see what happens," Lopez said. "What else do we have for the front page?"

"We have another case of bubonic plague in the county," Richards said. "The fourth this year."

"That's about normal," Kirkpatrick said.

"Anything else?" Lopez said.

Lucy zoned out while they talked, thinking about what she was going to get for dinner. She hadn't eaten since that morning and hadn't even gotten a free meal during her truncated review. The others around the table began to make rustling noises, which she took as the sign that the meeting was about to end, but just as they started to stand up, Lopez said, "There's one more thing." He waited for them to retake their seats before saying, "The police were here earlier asking for our security camera tapes."

"What?" Kirkpatrick said. "Why?"

"They were looking into ways the skull could have gotten in Zozobra," Lopez said.

Lucy finished the thought for him. "It could have been put into the offering box that was in our lobby."

"Right," he said. "As per our policy, they have to give us a court order, so if any other officer shows up asking for the tapes, just call me."

"Wait a second," Lucy said, confused and hesitant. "I thought the cameras were broken? Didn't some repairman accidentally cut the wires to them a while ago?"

"That's right," Lopez said. "I checked with the security company before I talked with the police. The cameras won't be fixed until the end of the month."

"So there are no tapes," Kirkpatrick said, disappointed. He had probably been hoping that he could use a still picture from the security camera feed to solve his lead photo problem.

"No, there aren't," Lopez said. "Of course, we couldn't tell the police that. We need to be above reproach."

"How does just telling them that there are no tapes make us below reproach?" Lucy asked. That's why Gil had been here. He had come to the newspaper with his hat in his hand asking for the tapes.

Tapes that didn't exist. When Gil saw Lucy, though, he didn't even tell her about it. He didn't ask her for help. He just stopped by to say hi. For some reason that made her furious.

"This is the way it is done at all newspapers," Lopez said with a fatherly smile. "You know that."

"In the meantime, we're jerking the cops around and making them think we have evidence," she said.

"Oh, come on," Kirkpatrick said to her. "Look at the big picture. The police can never think we'd bend over for them. We're the watchdog. We have to be completely separate from them."

"I agree with that," she said, "but in this case—"

"It can't be a case-by-case issue," Richards said. Lucy was starting to feel ganged up on. "It has to be across the board. We cannot, under any circumstances, be seen as in the pocket of the police."

"Wouldn't we best serve the public by being honest—" she said.

"We are being honest—" Richards said.

"Lucy, you're just saying this because you're in bed with them," Kirkpatrick said, causing Lucy to jump in surprise.

"What?" she asked.

"I just saw you talking to a detective in the newsroom—"

"I believe we're done here," Lopez said in his perfectly modulated, infinitely calm tone.

CHAPTER EIGHT

Friday Afternoon

The Santa Fe County Adult Detention Center, located in the grassy plains beyond the outskirts of town, housed 682 inmates from nineteen jurisdictions. The front of the building was typical of many Santa Fe government facilities. It had big square pillars supporting a square roof over a porch while faux vigas jutted out from the sides of the building. The sliding double doors were even painted turquoise, New Mexico's most-used color for trim. Gil and Joe went inside and signed in on the visitor's log, then locked their sidearms as well as their BUGs—backup guns—in the gun locker. They were escorted to a small beige room with a metal table connected to metal chairs and then connected to the floor. In case of a riot, the table and chairs wouldn't go anywhere. A few minutes later, Tony Herrera came in, wearing an orange jumpsuit. He was of slight build with a shaved head and a goatee. His arms were covered in blue prison tattoos of naked women and guns. On the back of his neck was tattooed ASHLEY in fancy script.

He was considered only a medium security prisoner, so no handcuffs were necessary.

"Hey," Phillips said to Herrera as the two men shook hands.

"Ah, dude, you're back," Herrera said. "What's up?"

Gil wondered at their familiarity. Maybe Joe had come here with Fisher during the original investigation.

Joe introduced Gil, and the three of them sat down.

"You here about Brianna?" Herrera asked.

"Yeah," Joe said. "Look, we found some bones . . ."

"Damn," Herrera said, shaking his head. "I mean, I knew she was dead, but hell . . ." He trailed off, staring into space.

"You don't seem too upset." Gil said as Joe took a small pad of paper out of his shirt pocket to take interview notes.

"I'm crying on the inside, Holmes," he said with a flash of a cruel smile.

"We're talking about your daughter," Gil said matter-of-factly, careful not to put any inflection or judgment in the sentence. He let it hang there in the air.

Herrera snorted lightly. It was a small noise, accompanied by an even smaller movement—a tightening around the eyes. It was derisive, dismissive.

"Have you talked to Ashley at all?" Joe asked, as Gil kept his eyes on Herrera's face, studying him.

Men who have been incarcerated for years develop a strong ability to mask their facial expressions. This makes it hard to interview them because there is no truth. Everything they say and everything said to them is treated as a lie. Their only emotion is suspicion. Their faces are one-note, whereas the facial expressions of the people in the general public are a symphony. Gil was hoping that with a little careful observation, he could get beneath the one-note that was Herrera's face and see down to the orchestra pit.

Herrera said he hadn't heard from Ashley in years. "How's she doing?" he asked.

"She's pretty broken up," Joe said. "You ever talk to anyone in here about Brianna?"

"In here?" he said. "No, man, nobody in here knows my business."

Gil let them forget he was there. He faded as much as he could away from the conversation.

"So how's your time going?" Joe asked.

"It's going, man. You don't do the time. The time does you, you know."

"Are you doing that work release program?"

"Yeah, out picking up trash in my little orange jumpsuit."

"What about the gang? Are you still in it?"

Herrera cocked his head. "Why do you have to go ask me that for? You know I can't tell you that."

"Look, Tony, we think that Brianna's death might be gang related," Joe said intently.

"No way, man. Who would do that? Nobody I know would go after a kid," Herrera said.

"You don't know anyone who has a beef with you?" Joe asked.

"Nah, man, I got no problems," he said.

"How about Sureño 13?" Joe asked. "Your West Side boys have been having some problems with them."

"Yeah, I heard about that," Herrera said, "but that's got nothing to do with me."

"How can you be so sure?" Joe asked.

"I ain't doing that shit no more," Herrera said. "I got out."

"Why?" Joe asked.

"I got tired of the life, you know?" Herrera said, his eyes tightening again.

Gil knew that Herrera likely was scared straight by the inherent violence. Of the reasons members left gangs, the fear of death was the one most often cited, next to starting a family.

"How do we know you're telling the truth?" Joe asked.

Gil was about to interrupt, to tell Joe that no gang member would lie about his affiliation or lack of one, when Herrera rolled up the sleeve of his orange jumpsuit. His upper right bicep was sliced with scars where someone had clearly cut through the skin several times. The effort was made to stamp out the tattoo below, which was still slightly visible. It was a w.s. for West Side Locos.

"I did this myself," Herrera said, proud of the scars he had inflicted.

Joe was about to ask another question, but Gil knew he had the opening he had been waiting for.

"Where's your tattoo for Brianna?" Gil asked. In New Mexico, where almost two thirds of people under twenty-five had tattoos, it was considered common to get inscriptions of your children's names. Especially if you were in jail. Especially if the child had died. "Every guy in here has his kids' names tattooed somewhere. Where's yours?"

"I've been meaning to get one of those," Herrera said with a flash of teeth.

"You know what else is strange? You didn't ask how Brianna died," Gil said, again without inflection. Perfectly modulated.

Herrera shrugged. "Whatever, it don't matter. It is what is. Dead is dead." Herrera's eyes tightened again. That was what Gil had been watching for. He had finally seen beneath Herrera's one-note emotion of suspicion, and what he had seen was something more sinister—a lie.

"You're not her father," Gil said. He felt Joe tighten up next to him.

Herrera started, "That's not—" but he had paused too long before jumping in with the denial.

"Who's the dad? Do you know?" Gil asked.

Herrera leaned back on his stool, his arms crossed in front of him, the blue tattoos on his arms indecipherable in their squiggles and turns. Gil saw those crossed arms and knew he needed a different tack.

He turned to Joe and said, "Why do you think he kept saying that Brianna was his kid when he knew she wasn't?"

"I totally would have done it," Joe said, catching on. "In a heartbeat. Ashley told everybody he was the dad. After Brianna went missing, all these people came in here to visit, the cops, family, you know. I bet he felt like a celebrity. Like even that cute blond TV reporter came here. She did like, what, two jailhouse interviews with you?" Joe said, turning to Herrera.

"More like three," Herrera said with a sly smile.

"Exactly," Joe said. "I would have said I was the dad of Rudolph the red-nosed reindeer if it meant I could spend a few minutes alone with her."

"When did you find out that Brianna wasn't your kid?" Gil asked.

"A year or so after she was born," he said.

"I thought you guys were dating when Ashley got pregnant," Joe said. "How do you know you're not the dad?"

"You gotta stick it in to get a baby to come out," Herrera said with a laugh.

"You never had sex?" Gil asked.

"Just one time," he said. "I totally had to force her to do it, and I know she didn't get pregnant."

"How do you know?" Gil asked.

" 'Cause I ain't stupid," Herrera said. "Brianna was born exactly nine months after Ashley and I had sex."

"But Brianna was born premature," Joe said.

"Exactly," Herrera said with a snort. "I can do the math. Ash got pregnant way after we had sex."

"It must have made you angry that Ashley lied," Gil said.

"Hell, no," Herrera said, shaking his head and looking at the wall. "I was relieved. This way I didn't have to pay no child support or nothing."

"Where were you when Brianna went missing?" Gil asked, already knowing the answer thanks to Fisher's notes. Still, it didn't hurt to ask.

"I was in here," he said, crossing his arms again.

"Did she ever tell you who the dad was?" Gil asked. This was the question he really cared about. The one he had to get answered.

"Nah. I never asked. She would have just lied anyway," Herrera said. "The whole thing would have been just one more of Ashley's games."

"Were there any guys at the time paying special attention to her?" Gil asked.

"She had boobs, man. Every guy I knew paid special attention to her," he said.

"But she was uptight about sex?" Joe asked.

"The one time she agreed to do it, she just freaked, crying and stuff," Herrera said.

"Sounds frustrating," Joe said.

"That was Ash, man," Herrera said. "She would talk about giving her dad a blow job so he would let her use the car or something, but I never got anything like that."

"She said that?" Gil asked. "That she had sex with her dad?"

"Not sex, man, just a blow job. But you know how girls talk," he said, gesturing to Joe. "They're always saying shit like that."

"Yeah, not so much, dude," Joe said. "That's messed up."

"Well, Ashley's one messed-up chick."

Lucy had to get out of the office to calm herself after the budget meeting, so she told Richards she'd be back in a half hour. She walked away from the building fast, hoping that with distance she would gain composure.

Fortunately, the newspaper building was in the heart of downtown, so she only had to go two blocks to reach the cathedral, which was her first stop. The late afternoon sun cast lemon yellow tones over the trees and the streets. She walked over to the church, but she didn't go inside. What she was interested in was outside, right under her feet, really—a labyrinth.

When Lucy first heard about the labyrinth, she got excited. Thinking it would be like one of those English garden hedge mazes. Like something out of *The Shining*. Instead, it was just a flat wheel of footstones that wound in a tight little crop-circle pattern. It was like one of those puzzles that children do with a paper and pencil, helping the mouse to find its way to the cheese. The idea was to meditate your way through the bends and loops.

The center of the labyrinth was a brick clover, which mimicked the rose window above the door of the cathedral a few feet away. The actual path of the labyrinth was paved in rose stepping-stones, while the out-of-bounds were in gray-green granite. There was nothing preventing a walker from stepping on the gray-green stones. One misstep and the person would be in the world of gray. Lucy smiled. The world of gray was where she lived all the time now.

She walked the labyrinth several times a week, the turns and twists giving her a comfort that made no sense. She started the flat maze, trying to concentrate on the plodding forward of her feet, but her mind and eyes wandered, as usual. She could hear the sounds of a mariachi band coming from the Plaza, where fiesta celebrations were in full swing.

Here at the cathedral, only a few blocks away from the party, the final tourist holdouts of the season quietly went about their exploration. She watched an enamored visitor across the street take a picture of an ivy-strewn building of wood and faux adobe. The woman said to her friend, "It's so pretty," as she snapped another shot. Lucy wondered if the woman would still think that if she knew it was just a parking garage. Other tourists took pictures of the life-sized statues of the saints in front of the church.

Lucy realized she was halfway though the labyrinth. She spent the next few steps worrying that she had somehow gotten lost. But how do you get lost when the only walls are pretend and the path leads only one way? She could simply walk to the center of the maze instead of continuing to follow the brick pathway. It was just three steps away. It would be so easy. She sighed as the cobblestones twisted her away from the center yet again.

"What do you think?" Gil asked as he clipped his paddle holster back on his belt and snapped his ankle holster in place. They stood in the lobby of the detention center, the huge windows looking out over the endless grassy plain, giving incoming prisoners one last glimpse of the big, beautiful outside world. It was cruel, in a way. It would almost be kinder if the windows overlooked an industrial site.

"I think the gang idea just got shot pretty much to hell," Joe said.

"Yeah, I agree," Gil said.

"Okay, where does that leave us?" Joe asked.

"I think we have to go back to the family," Gil said. "There's a lot of questions I need to ask them."

"That sounds good," Joe said, getting into the car. "I'd like to know about this stuff with Ashley's dad. And, oh yeah, ask her why the hell she lied about who Brianna's father was."

Gil headed the Crown Vic back toward town and dialed Mrs.

Rodriguez's cell phone. She answered and told him they were all still at the hospital. Gil said he would meet her there.

As they drove along Interstate 25 and then took the downtown exit, Gil asked Joe to look over Fisher's notes for any mention of Ashley's dad. Joe flipped through a few pages before saying, "Okay, here it is. Ashley's dad is named Rudy. He and Ashley's mom split right before Brianna disappeared, but they aren't divorced. Umm . . . it looks like he works for one of the pueblo casinos."

"How involved was he in the initial investigation?" Gil asked.

"I'm not sure," Joe said scanning the pages. "It looks like Fisher talked to him but that it was just a notification. We could check for any prior arrests, but Rudy Rodriguez is a pretty common name around here. Without his age or address, I'm not sure it would do much good."

"We can get that from Mrs. Rodriguez," Gil said without pointing out that this was information Fisher should have written down.

A few minutes later, Gil parked the car at Christus St. Vincent Hospital. They went up to the labor and delivery floor and were walking down the hallway to the patient rooms when someone said behind them, "Excuse me, officers."

They turned around.

"Hi," said an Anglo man who looked to be about twenty-five, with light brown spiky hair. "Rose wanted me to wait out here until you came. She'll be out in a minute."

This had to be Alex Stevens, Ashley's boyfriend and the father of the current baby—or soon to be baby. Gil introduced himself, noticing that Stevens's hands were rough and had deeply cut scars. Then he remembered he was a tow truck driver. Joe just nodded a hello to the man. The two of them probably hadn't seen each other since the family filed the lawsuit.

"How's Ashley doing?" Gil asked.

"Who knows," Stevens said. "I haven't got a clue about all this stuff."

"Well, good luck," Gil said, trying to think of a polite way to ask Stevens if he knew the identity of Brianna's father. He couldn't think of a way around the awkwardness of the question, so he let Stevens leave to go relieve Mrs. Rodriguez. Instead, he would try to find out from Mrs. Rodriguez, who came out a few minutes later.

"How's Ashley?" Gil asked, thinking she would have a better idea than Stevens.

"They have her hooked up to all kinds of machines and tubes," she said. "She's not even due for another month. I'm worried the baby will be early like Brianna."

"We just have a few questions for you and then you can get back in there," Joe said. They went to an empty waiting area and sat down. Joe sat next to Gil and studiously took out his notebook so he could write down the important facts of the conversation. He was supposed to be unobtrusive about it, but Gil noticed Mrs. Rodriguez looking for any movement of Joe's pen.

"We're making progress in the investigation," Gil said, to distract her, "and we just needed to check in with you about a few things, okay?"

She nodded.

"So, first of all, our investigation seems to be pointing toward someone who has some mental problems," he said. "Do you know anyone like that?"

She shook her head and said, "No. Not at all."

"No neighbors or cousins?" Joe asked.

She shook her head again.

"Okay," Gil said. "That's fine. The next thing we need to check with you about is Brianna's father. We just got done talking to Tony Herrera, and he says he's not her dad. Do you know anything about that?"

"No," she said, her forehead tightening into rows of confused wrinkles. "As far as I know Tony is Brianna's father."

"There is no one else who could be the father?" Gil asked.

"No. Ashley only has ever dated Tony and Alex, and she didn't even meet Alex until Brianna was two years old."

"Okay," Gil said gently. "Now, the last thing we wanted to talk to you about was Ashley's father. We're probably going to be talking to him later, and we wanted to get your thoughts about him and his relationship with Ashley."

"Like what do you mean?" she said.

"Were he and Ashley close?" Gil asked, forcing himself to become an observer of both the conversation and Mrs. Rodriguez.

"Oh yeah, they spent a lot of time together."

"Did you ever think that he and Ashley might be a little too close?" Gil asked. He kept the words as innocuous as possible, hoping she would fill in the blanks.

"Well . . . I don't . . . no, I don't think so," Rose said, looking away from Gil, considering, not really understanding his implication. Gil had been hoping that if Ashley had been abused by her dad, it had been something the family had already acknowledged, even if slightly. Gil had hoped that the father no longer lived at home because Rose had sent him packing after discovering the abuse.

That would have made the interview easy—he could ask Rose up front about it and get her thoughts. This would be harder. It was clear from her answer that Rose suspected something had happened, but it was also clear that she would never admit it freely. She was trapped, probably unconsciously, within her own guilt and inaction.

"Has Ashley ever had problems with her dad?"

"Only when she was mad, like any teenager."

"What kind of things did she say?"

"Oh, you know—" She stopped and smiled weakly. "The usual things, like 'I hate you' and how she wanted to kill herself."

"She said that?" Joe asked, too sharply, breaking the flow of the interview with just three words. Rose looked over at Joe and away from Gil. At that moment, Gil had never been angrier with Joe. This was not the annoyance over Joe's endless conversations about breast size or his rants that reverberated with repetitive swear words. It was pure in its intensity. Gil forced himself to smile and spoke calmly to Rose. "How often would she say things like that?"

"Oh," Rose said, her openness clearly faltering for a brief second, before her eyes went back to Gil and she said, "for a while there it seemed like every day it was about one thing or another." She laughed. Gil smiled in response, mimicking her emotions.

"So she acted up a lot?" Gil asked. An abused girl would. It was classic behavior.

"Hijole, yes," Rose said, shaking her head, smiling, remembering the bad times and rewriting them into funny little stories in her head. "She was drinking and smoking. And lying all the time. She got speeding tickets. I was at the courthouse so much they knew me by sight."

"She took a lot of it out on her dad?" Gil asked.

"It was to the point that he couldn't even look at Ashley without her screaming at him," Rose said with a pitying look. Pity for her husband.

"How was Ashley after her father moved out?"

"She seemed the same," Rose said. "Maybe a little less angry."

"Is it possible that maybe she was more relaxed because her dad was no longer around?" Gil asked gently.

"Maybe," Rose said. She seemed almost surprised she gave the answer with so little hesitation.

"It sounds like Ashley and her dad weren't all that close," Gil said.

"I think they were too much alike," Rose said, agreeing. Contradicting herself. She seemed not to realize that the carefully constructed life that she presented to the world was falling apart under scrutiny. Gil did not point this out. It wouldn't serve any purpose other than to humiliate her.

Gil took a deep breath to steel himself for the rest of the conversation. "Did you ever think that maybe as Ashley started to mature it was harder for her dad to relate to her?" Gil said. "Maybe that's why they stopped getting along."

Rose shook her head, but it seemed less of a negative answer to his question and more of a way to protect herself against what he was saying.

"You know," Gil said, leaning forward, "it can be very hard for a father when his daughter starts to mature. She was this little girl, and now she's this beautiful woman that all the boys are looking at."

Joe started nodding in agreement, slightly redeeming himself from his earlier gaffe. She nodded as well. Gil leaned closer and said, "Rose, is it possible he did more than look?"

She nodded again. Gil felt some of the tension he had been holding on to leave him. "What makes you think that? Did something happen?"

"I don't know . . . when Ashley was little, he would always tell her to pose sexy when he took her picture," she said.

"And that bothered you," Gil said. "That would bother any mother."

"Then when she was older, he would buy her these tight shirts," Rose said.

"Were there any other times?" Gil said. He was waiting for more, because he knew from experience there had to be.

"This other time, I came home and he was in the living room pulling his pants up and Ashley was sitting next to him," she said. "He said he was just adjusting his belt, but you don't pull your pants down to do that." She looked up sharply, realizing that she had just described an awful scene in an almost nonchalant way. It was likely she had never told anyone that story. Certainly she had gone over it again and again in her head, cataloguing excuses for her husband and supplying logical explanations of how it was just innocent behavior. Now that she had told the story out loud, she could no longer pretend there was anything innocent about it.

Gil had one last question that he needed to ask before he could free himself from the conversation. "Rose, do you think your husband could have gotten Ashley pregnant?"

Lucy finished the labyrinth and then headed toward the sound of the music. She took the long way around, wondering why the street names downtown were so different than in the rest of Santa Fe. Here, there were no avenidas, calles, or caminos. It seemed strange that the oldest part of town was the one with the most Anglo-sounding streets. She dodged down Washington Street, trying to figure out what its original name had been. The road had already been in existence for a hundred years by the time Washington became president. Some long-dead conquistador captain was probably wondering what had happened to his street.

Lucy loved this part of town. When you stared at it, the history seeped out where the cracked edge of a building showed the adobe underneath. Every building was connected to the next with mismatched roofs and walls, and all of them were built in different architectural styles that were called things like "Territorial" or "Pueblo Revival."

As she got closer to the Plaza, the music and noise from the crowd got louder, making Lucy hurry up a step. She had never been to fiesta. It held the title of oldest continual celebration in the country, but it was really about a people who made a promise three centuries ago to throw a party if they were given back Santa Fe. And party they have. Every year since.

Lucy suddenly found herself in the throng. This wasn't like Mardi Gras or Carnival. There was no raucous celebration or purposeful nakedness. This was nice fun. Family fun. That's probably why the party had continued all these years. Because it was about family, and what was the native Hispanic population of Santa Fe but one big, genetically isolated family? This was the biggest family reunion in the world.

Mrs. Rodriguez went back into the room to see Ashley while Gil and Joe went to find a doctor. It was time to question Ashley. Beyond time, really. Clearly she had never been interviewed properly, but it wasn't as simple as just going into her hospital room.

Gil had been there when both of his daughters were born and knew the drill. There were two stages of labor before it was time to push the baby out: the early stage, when the contractions last about thirty seconds and come every twenty minutes, and the active stage, when the contractions are longer and come every few minutes. If Ashley was in early labor, she could hold a conversation, but, if she was anything like Susan, during the active stage she'd be screaming out the pain. Gil needed to know what stage Ashley was in, and for that he needed a doctor.

They found one standing at the nurses' station. She introduced herself as Dr. Mariana Santiago. Gil explained the situation as best he could to the doctor, then said, "It's very important that I talk to her."

Dr. Santiago smiled and said, "I'm sorry. That's not a good idea. Ashley has a history of premature birth, and right now, we are trying very hard for this baby not to be premature. I'm afraid that any stress could be very detrimental to her and the baby."

"I really only have a few questions," Gil said.

"Is it possible that those questions will upset her?" Dr. Santiago asked.

Gil didn't answer. The questions he had to ask Ashley were probably some of the most stressful she would ever have to answer.

Dr. Santiago smiled again. "I just can't allow it right now. Check back with me later. When she's out of the woods, you can ask her whatever you want."

As she walked away, Joe said softly, "If we just go into Ashley's room, who is going to stop us?"

Gil shook his head. "Legally, her doctor has to okay it. We could get fired if we ignore her, and we could face civil charges if something happened to the baby. It's just not worth the risk. Look, Ashley will probably be delivering in the next twelve hours or so. We can wait."

Just as they were about to leave, Gil saw a nurse come through the door at the back of the nurses' station. He saw her and smiled. She did the same. They both leaned over the counter and hugged each other.

"How are you?" she asked. She was Gil's cousin Suzanne, the daughter of Aunt Yolanda.

"I'm good," Gil said. "I'm here on a case. Are you working up here now?"

"Oh, no," she said. "I just came up here to get a chart. I'm still down in the psych ward."

"Really?" Gil asked, getting an idea. She was exactly who he needed to talk to. He explained what he could about the case and then asked for a favor. When he was done she said, "Gil, what you're asking me . . ."

"I know . . ."

"I'll think about it," she said.

CHAPTER NINE

Friday Afternoon

Lucy was nearing the Plaza, which was only a block wide and another long, but it was filled with people, sitting and standing, who blotted out the green grass underneath. An all-girl mariachi band was playing a fast polka in the center of the Plaza, while the outside perimeter was ringed with food booths.

Lucy's only goal was to find something to eat and get in some people-watching. Everyone else's goal was different. It was to meet up with those long-lost friends, schoolmates, and relatives or to meet those new to the family tree—spouses and babies. As she wandered through the crowd, she saw every type of greeting. Handshakes. Hugs. Exclamations. Tears.

Lucy could think of no one from her past that she would get that excited to see again. Sure, it would be nice to have a visit with her mom and her two brothers, but she couldn't think of the last time she saw someone that would make her cry in happiness.

She walked over to the Palace of the Governors,

which was decked out for the occasion. The four-hundred-year-old building, now a museum, was made of four-foot-thick adobe covered by white plaster. The walls had strange bulges and dents, like a car involved in one too many fender benders. It was the main viga, hanging low over the front of the portal, that Lucy was interested in. On it were the crests of the founding families of Santa Fe and the shields representing the pueblo tribes, all put up especially for fiesta. Dozens of crests lined the lengths of the portal. She found the Trujillo family crest, which showed a field of red punctuated by blue dots and yellow Xs. No noble lions or mythical griffins. It looked more like a tic-tac-toe game. She was definitely going to have to tease Gerald about that. Next, she looked for the Martinez crest, thinking she could make fun of Tommy about it. It was near the end of the portal, but it was much more regal than Gerald's. Two fields split it diagonally—one half had bold black-and-white stripes, the other red fleur-de-lis. Very majestic. Lastly, she looked for the Montoya crest. She found it on the other end of the portal. It showed eight white hearts on a blue field. She was not quite sure what to make of it but was certain she would never make fun of it to Gil.

The mariachi band stopped, and the emcee said, "Now, get ready to greet La Reina and Don Diego de Vargas." The crowd clapped and hooted as a young man wearing a conquistador costume took the stage. He had on fabulous thigh-high leather boots, pantaloons, and a black velvet cape. The effect was surprisingly masculine. The man was playing the role of Don Diego de Vargas, the Spanish captain who made the fateful prayer for peace to La Conquistadora.

Next on the stage was La Reina, the queen. She was dressed in a strapless white gown, looking like a bride, with a long blue velvet cape edged in fur. The selection of La Reina had evolved into something of a beauty pageant. Every year the fiesta council chose a new Don Diego and La Reina. The couple would then visit nursing homes and football games throughout the year and march in the procession during fiesta.

Lucy watched the crowd a little longer, then went over to one of the food booths and ordered a Frito pie. She went to sit on the grass and started to eat her pie quickly so the Fritos wouldn't lose their crunch under the heaping of red chile, lettuce, and cheese.

She was finishing up when she felt the urge to call her mom. She dialed the phone, but it went to voice mail. She didn't leave a message. What she had really wanted was for someone to be happy that she had called, not an answering machine that could care less.

Mrs. Rodriguez had given them her husband's last known address, which they confirmed with the MVD records. His lived out near Tesuque Pueblo, about a twenty-minute drive from town.

The Crown Victoria complained its way up Opera Hill as the highway flattened out over the top of the hill and the valley stretched out green below.

"So maybe the dad snatched Brianna to get back at Ashley," Joe said as they took the exit into Tesuque. "Or, I mean, Brianna might be his own daughter, so he might have some really messed-up ideas about ownership of her."

"It's possible," Gil said, "but putting her in Zozobra and then putting the bones on an altar . . ." He realized he didn't want to finish the sentence.

"Maybe the guy is crazy."

"He would have to be," Gil said. The road dropped down into the Tesuque Valley, with its huge cottonwood trees and tiny river. It was easy to see why there had been a pueblo here since the 1200s. Apple trees, heavy with fruit, lined the road, like happy spectators at a parade. The pueblo was one of six in the state that spoke Tewa, a mostly unwritten language that is used by fewer than two thousand people. The other fourteen Pueblo tribes in New Mexico spoke Tiwa, Keres, Towa, or Zuni. Gil wondered what the Spanish first thought about the Pueblo Indians, some of whom had made towering cities of adobe. The Pueblo tribes were so unlike the Plains Indians, who traveled long distances with the buffalo herds. In New Mexico, the majority of the twenty-two tribes, including the Navajo, had a tendency to stay put.

Gil pulled into a dirt road that dead-ended by the river in a circle of mobile homes. Rudy Rodriguez's house was the second from the end. Gil and Joe got out of the car and headed up to the front door. Before they could even knock, a man was there, peering at them through the screen door.

"Hi," he said. "Can I help you?"

Gil introduced himself and Joe, then said, "We were hoping to talk to you about Brianna."

Rodriguez let them into the trailer, which was cramped but clean. A blow-up mattress was on the living room floor. Six empty beer bottles sat on the kitchen counter. The men sat down around the kitchen table, and Gil said, "I'm afraid we have some bad news. We believe we found Brianna's remains."

Rodriguez put his head in his hands and buried his face. Gil noticed a tattoo on the side of his neck that read MY L'IL ANGEL. Gil wondered if that was for Ashley or Brianna. Either idea was disturbing.

"My poor, poor baby," Rodriguez said as he started crying. "My sweet, sweet child. My beautiful sweet angel. What happened?" he asked, looking up. His eyes were red. "Who did this to her?"

The front door opened suddenly, and a woman walked in, followed by a man. "Rudy, what's going on?" the woman said as she walked over to them. She looked about forty, and Gil guessed the man who came in with her was her husband.

"They're here about Brianna," Rodriguez said, his eyes tearing up again.

"Oh no . . ." she said.

"It's bad," he said to the woman, who came over to hug Rodriguez as he sat.

"I'm his sister, Anna Maria," she said, looking up at Gil and Joe. "We're just up from Albuquerque to go to fiesta."

"They needed a place to sleep tonight," Rodriguez said. That explained the air mattress on the floor. "They're heading home in the morning."

"So what is going on . . ." Gil heard Anna Maria ask.

He didn't catch the rest of what she was saying, as the door swung open again and two little girls came in carrying groceries.

———————

Judge Otero was on the Plaza, the center of a small group of people, which included his family and about a dozen well-wishers. The noise from the crowd was loud, but not overwhelming. The judge was dressed in his yellow satin Protectores shirt and black pants, which his wife had ironed well. Around his circle of people, the crowd moved and twisted, but he stood still in the heart of it all.

The judge was talking to a former city councilor when the current city attorney came over. The councilor said his good-byes quickly, sensing that Judge Otero and the attorney needed to talk. The two men started out slowly, asking about each other's wife and children while shaking hands with most of the people who walked by.

Judge Otero looked over at his wife and eldest daughter next to him, his newest grandson in her arms. He kissed his wife on her cheek. She smiled and then walked off with his daughter and grandson so he could get down to business.

The city attorney watched them go before saying, "I hear the Judicial Standards Commission will be coming back with a ruling soon."

Judge Otero said nothing.

"Are you still sending people to that driving school?" the attorney asked.

"Of course not," Judge Otero said. "I haven't done that in months." The Safe Streets Driving School was why the judge was being investigated by the commission. He hadn't realized it would cause such uproar. It really wasn't anything they needed to be concerned about. The school was owned by his court clerk, but it was the only driving school in town, unless you counted the ones operated by that chain company that had schools all over the Southwest. Judge Otero had sent people to the Safe Streets school—and would continue sending them there until well after this all blew over—because he knew the defendants would get the best education. The fact that his clerk owned the school had nothing to do with his decision. He was doing what was needed to keep the drivers safe.

"Judge," the city attorney said, "just keep your hands clean."

Judge Otero looked at the man. He didn't like him. The city

attorney had been trying to oust him from office for years, all because the judge didn't have a law degree.

"When you've got celebrity status, people want a piece of you," the judge said. "Just keep that in mind."

Gil watched the girls put the groceries down on the kitchen counter as best they could given their height. The younger looked to be about four, and the older couldn't be more than six. The same number of years apart as Joy and Therese.

There must have been something in Gil's expression that caused Joe to say, "Mr. Rodriguez, could we continue this outside? I think this conversation might be too much for the children."

They all got up and went out into the early night, but Rodriguez made a pit stop at the fridge to grab another beer.

Gil walked quickly away from the trailer, leaving Joe and Rodriguez standing in front. Gil went to the car and pretended he needed something inside. He couldn't let Rodriguez see that he was upset. It would be too harmful when it came time to get a confession.

Rodriguez wasn't Gil's first child molester, not by a long shot, but the little girls running through the door all smiles—something inside him clicked. The second Gil saw the girls come in the house, he went from police detective to father.

He heard Joe and Rodriguez walking toward him, their feet making shuffling sounds in dirt.

Joe was saying to Rodriguez, "I think it might be a good idea to go down to the station—"

"Can we do this later? I'm really tired," Rodriguez said.

"We just want to talk a little—" Joe said.

"Can I just meet you there tomorrow?"

They couldn't force him to come with them because they didn't have sufficient information to arrest him on any abuse charges. If only Ashley had been well enough to talk. All they did have was guesses. Normally, having him come down to the station tomorrow would be fine. They would arrest him then if he confessed, but with those little girls in the house . . . if something happened to them tonight after leaving Rodriguez there with them . . . Gil couldn't finish that thought.

Legally they didn't have reasonable grounds, but ethically . . .

"Actually, I think it's best if you come with us," Gil said. His tone must have been too tough, because Rodriguez puffed up his chest.

"You can't arrest me," Rodriguez said defiantly, swaying a bit from the alcohol.

Gil started to grab his handcuffs from their holder on his belt. Joe, noticing the movement, said quickly, "You aren't under arrest. It's called protective custody. It's just a way for us to take care of you right now, at this difficult time." His voice was all concern and caring.

"I don't know . . ."

"Look, Rudy," Joe said, putting his arm around the man. "You told me that you feel really sad right now. Why don't you just come with us until you're feeling better? Then you can come back home and be at your best around your family."

Joe coaxed Rodriguez into the backseat as his sister came out of the house.

"What's going on?" Anna Maria asked.

"Ma'am, we're sorry," Joe said. "We feel like your brother is really broken up over the news about Brianna, and that, combined with the drinking, we just think it would be better for him to come with us tonight."

"He's not under arrest?" she asked.

"No, ma'am," Joe said. "Under the Detoxification Reform Act all that happens is that he comes with us and he stays in a special cell until he's more himself. He never gets charged or arrested."

Gil said nothing as he got into the driver's seat. He drove back out to the highway and took the bypass around the city, glad to be leaving the family safely behind them.

CHAPTER TEN

Friday Night

The night at work was beginning to slow down for Lucy. She had edited Tommy's skull story, which was mostly right on the mark except for a lengthy lead she had to edit down. In the fifth graph, Tommy deftly mentioned the possibility that the skull was Brianna's—along with the "no comment" answer from police about the likelihood of that. She had hit a few keys on her computer and sent it on its merry way along the editing chain.

Now she just needed an okay from copydesk that the story was good. She also wanted to check the front page proofs, which wasn't necessary, but she decided to let her OCD perfectionism guide her tonight. Because this story was important. The article would definitely be run up by all state news agencies and the Associated Press, which would send it out to newspapers across the country. More than likely it would get picked up by CNN and the other cable news shows, meaning that for a few bright moments tomorrow, tiny Santa Fe, New Mexico, would be on the map—and here she was, the final check, before it was read by millions. Tommy was still there for the same reason, making sure there were no questions.

She was mindlessly reading over wire copy when Tommy came over.

"Wanna hear something weird?" he asked.

"Always," she said.

"So I was checking out the road closures downtown today, and one guy I talked to said he'd heard that someone had put some bones in front of Our Lady of Guadalupe Church."

"Human bones?"

"That's what he said."

"There is no way that's true," Lucy said dismissively. "That's like Florida or Texas level weird. New Mexico's level of weird is some dude who blames his cat for downloading child porn. We do stupid weird."

"He said it was this whole display thing with art and dolls' heads and stuff," Tommy said, smiling broadly. A cat-eating-canary smile. He knew a great news story when he heard one. "And he said he heard there were more of them around town."

"Seriously?" she said, wondering how the story could get any more creepy. The amount of creepy in a story was directly proportional to the rate of newspaper sales. "Where are we at with it? I can call people in to help."

"The problem is his information is thirdhand at best."

"Nobody else will confirm it?" she asked, her excitement quickly deflating.

"No, and I can't even get anyone else to say that they heard the rumor."

"Really? That seems odd. How good's your source?"

"Pretty solid. I don't think he's lying,"

"But he has no direct knowledge."

"Nope," Tommy said, shaking his head.

"Was your source thinking this was related to the skull in Zozobra?"

"Yep."

"Damn it. Well, what do you want to do?"

"I'll chase it tomorrow. We might never be able to confirm it, but my gut tells me that it's true."

"Yeah, mine, too. Well, good luck tomorrow. I'm only sorry I won't be here to help you. I guess this means you won't be getting to this other story idea I had for you." She told him about the burned-out cars, the red graffiti, and how they all led back to the same apartment complex.

"That's going to take some intense investigative work," he said. Which was why Lucy had thought of him. He loved deep research and slowly cultivating sources. The boy might have grown up on a Northern New Mexico farm, but he was a natural when it came to working the city folk. She could tell he was thinking it over.

"And the reporter has to know Spanish since most of the victims seem to be Mexican," she said in a singsong voice, trying to tempt him further.

"I would love to do it," he said, "but I can't until this skull thing has cooled down."

Lucy sighed. "Yeah, I know. I'm just teasing. We'll wait until next week to get going on it. It'll hold until then."

"What about Andrea?"

"The copydesk intern?" Lucy had only bumped into her in the ladies' room, so all Lucy could say about her was that she was a thorough hand washer.

"Yeah," he said. "She's from Puerto Rico, and she's dying to do a news story."

"Tommy, come on. We both know this isn't a story for a newbie."

"She could just go over there and get the ball rolling. See what the deal is."

Lucy thought about it. It might not be such a bad idea. Andrea could serve as an initial undercover reporter, then hand it off to Tommy later.

"I guess I'll go see if she's interested," Lucy said. She walked toward the copydesk corral with Tommy following close behind her.

Andrea looked up brightly and expectantly from her computer. She had yet to learn that anyone who came over to your desk probably wanted you to do something that you didn't want to do.

"Hi," Andrea said, smiling. "What do you guys need?"

Tommy quickly explained the situation. Andrea actually clapped her hands in joy. Lucy was starting to regret her decision.

"I just need someone who can ask questions," Lucy said, trying to temper the girl's enthusiasm. "I was thinking you could go by there tomorrow."

"Are you going to be there?" Andrea asked Lucy.

"What? No," Lucy said. She had never been asked by a reporter to act as babysitter.

"Please," Andrea said imploringly. "I don't even know what questions to ask."

"How would it work if I came?" Lucy asked, annoyed. "I'd ask the questions and you'd translate? That'll go over great. An Anglo chick telling a Hispanic chick what to do."

"But I don't think I can do this myself . . ."

Lucy sighed heavily. She had no use for helpless women. "Fine. I'll come with you, but I'm staying in the car. Okay?"

She went back to her desk and sat down heavily just as her cell phone started to vibrate. It was her mom. Lucy's desire to talk to her was over, replaced by the reality that talking to her mom could be exhausting. She let it go to voice mail.

Gil drove back to the Santa Fe County Adult Detention Center and had Rodriguez booked into one of the special protective custody cells. They would bring him over to the station in the morning when he was sober. Hopefully, if they found no more bone displays, Gil might have time to question him further about Ashley's abuse.

Gil waited until he and Joe were back in the car before saying, "I think that guy's a dead end. I just don't see him taking Brianna and then setting up the crime scenes that way."

"Yeah, I agree," Joe said, sighing heavily. "He's a molesting son of a bitch, but honestly, he couldn't kill his way out of a box."

"Let's just go back to the office and go at it again."

"Copy that, good buddy," Joe said.

"And, Joe," Gil said, "I just wanted to thank you for before, back at the house with handling everything."

"Hey, you always hold it together for me, dude, so I can return the favor one time, no problem." Joe leaned his head against the passenger-side window and went to sleep for the rest of the ten-minute drive.

Gil was back at the office, making corrections on his last report, when his phone rang. It was his cousin Suzanne.

"I'm sorry I'm just calling now, but I had to wait until I left work," she said. "Don't you dare tell my mom that I'm helping you like this." Gil knew she was actually breaking the law in helping him.

"What's up?" he asked.

"We had a patient in the ward a few months ago who was schizo-phrenic and his delusions revolved around the Freemasons and the Catholic Church," she said. "Hang on . . ." He heard her talking to her four-year-old in the background. "Sweetheart, you need to go lie down." He heard a little voice respond to her but couldn't make out the words.

"Devon's not in bed yet?" Gil asked, remembering the sleep sched-ule of toddlers.

"No, he's in bed, he just can't seem to stay there," Suzanne said in the typical harried voice of a mother. "I might have to go in a min-ute. Anyway, the patient was brought in by the sheriff's department after he threatened them with a sword."

"Really?" Gil said, feeling that they finally might have gotten a break.

"Yeah, and according to his chart he was approached by police after his neighbor said the man threatened his kids."

"What happened?"

"I don't know," Suzanne said. "I never treated him."

"What's the name?"

"David Geisler," she said and gave him the address.

"That's just a few blocks from Brianna's house," Gil said.

"I know," Suzanne said. He thanked her, and they hung up.

Gil looked up the sheriff's arrest report online. On May 24, Santa Fe County sheriff's officer Jackson Yazzie approached a white male about suspicious activity. A 911 caller reported that the man, who was acting strangely, walked near some children playing outside in the street and reportedly said something about blood on a head. The arresting officer went to the suspect's house. When he opened the door, the man was holding a samurai sword. The officer called for backup, and the man was taken to the hospital for a mental evaluation.

Gil got Yazzie's cell phone number from Dispatch. Yazzie confirmed the contents of the report and added, "We've been over to the house a couple more times since then just to calm things down. The neighbors are really spooked by the guy."

"When you picked him up in May, do you remember him saying anything in particular?" Gil asked.

"He was hard to follow, but he talked a lot about religion and how God was eating our innocence," Yazzie said. "It didn't make much sense."

"Do you have his fingerprint card?" Gil asked. If so, they might finally have something to match against the prints found at the scenes.

"Yeah," Yazzie said, "but I never entered his prints on the system since he wasn't charged with anything. I can e-mail them to you."

Gil thanked him. After they hung up, Gil grabbed his keys and said, "Joe, how would you like to go on a field trip?"

On the way, Gil called Liz, who was still in the office, and asked her if the stab marks in the skull could have been made by a samurai sword. She didn't hesitate in her response. "Yes, that would fit," she said. "The wounds aren't actually that unique. I was thinking maybe a strong kitchen knife, but any thin sword would fit."

"Thanks," Gil asked, "and later on I'm going to be e-mailing you some fingerprints to check against the ones from the scenes."

"Do you have a suspect?" she asked.

"Not quite yet," he said.

Gil pulled up in front of David Geisler's house and cut the engine, but neither he nor Joe got out of the car. Dusk was coming, and some neighbors already had their porch lights on. Geisler's house was dark brown and flat-roofed, with large cracks in some of the stucco. The yard was overgrown.

No lights were on in the home, but it wasn't full dark yet.

"What do you want to do?" Joe asked.

"I don't know," Gil said. "We need to talk to him and get access to the house."

"At least he left us plenty of evidence at all the crime scenes to compare to if we can get inside," Joe said.

"We don't really have enough probable cause to arrest him."

"I think that means we go knock on the door and see what's what," Joe said, getting out of the car.

They walked up the brick path, which was heavy with weeds, and up to the porch. Joe knocked loudly on the screen door. After several more minutes and two more knocking sessions, the front door finally opened. The man inside was thin, with a chaotic brown beard.

"Are you Mr. David Geisler?" Gil asked after introducing himself.

The man said nothing. He just stared at the floor.

"Sir, we're here about some problems in the neighborhood," Joe said.

"The child . . . child . . . they got to admit they can't do that much," Geisler said, covering his mouth as he giggled.

"Are you talking about Brianna Rodriguez?" Gil asked.

"An advanced being . . . a kind of . . . a certain . . . hands of motherness, that's right . . ." he said and then giggled again.

"What do you know about her disappearance?" Gil asked.

"My sins never hope . . . that's why they want me, I think," he said. He looked up at the sky and grinned.

"Is he laughing about Brianna?" Joe asked.

"I don't know," Gil said to Joe. Then he asked Geisler, "Can we come in?"

The man said nothing; he just stared off with a slight smile on his face.

"I'm taking that as a yes," Joe said, opening the door. Geisler made no move to stop them. Inside was the normal living room, but the couch had pillows and blankets on it. It appeared to be where

Geisler slept. Two closed doors led out of the living room, but one was blocked by an ironing board and the other by a large chair.

"I was wondering, Mr. Geisler," Gil said, realizing that the man's mental illness was making him nervous enough that he kept using the formal title. "How do you feel about the Catholic Church?"

"What was said by the priests, they can hear my thoughts. It's just . . . it's just . . . the energy coming out of me . . . and I put it together . . . this means something," he said, nodding.

"So the priests can hear what you are thinking," Gil said. "That must be scary."

Geisler put his hand over his mouth and giggled. "I am a superpower . . . anyone who puts together a creative understanding . . . it's like *1984*."

"Did you know Brianna Rodriguez?" Joe asked as he looked around the room, which had beige carpet and paneled walls, making the room dark. It was made bleaker by the lack of pictures on the wall.

"They don't . . . they don't . . . God goes to penetrate the subconscious . . . and the prayer . . . it's like rats," he said. "That's why they want me . . . and I put it together and let it go . . . and if I let it go . . . Jesus is bankrupt."

Joe shot Gil a look. They weren't going to get anywhere questioning him. They should go talk to the neighbors and maybe his family to see if he'd ever been violent. Gil was about to turn to leave when Joe pushed aside the ironing board blocking one of the doors and opened it.

The room was carpeted in the same beige color and had the same paneling. It had no furniture, but over in one corner some bedsheets were taped by their edges to the ceiling and hung down in a wall of white. Making a separate room inside the room. Gil's daughters used to make forts like that when they would stay home from school on snow days. Gil pushed his way past the soft white fabric, holding the panel back for Joe. On the other side was a kitchen table lined with newspapers. In its center lay a silver samurai sword, its black handle embedded with silver triangles.

The curved tip of the sword reflected the dim light of the room.

As Gil moved closer to the sword, he noticed that rust had started to form on the blade's edge. It took him a moment to realize that the rust was more the color of dried blood.

Gladys Soliz Portilla stood at the bus stop and looked again at the time on her cell phone. She needed to pick her son up in fifteen minutes, and the bus was ten minutes late. She had called her babysitter, who had said she wouldn't wait. Now she was trying to get in touch with one of the neighbors to see if they could go get him.

She missed her car. It had been more than ten years old when she bought it from a nice man who lived near downtown Santa Fe, but it was reliable. And it was hers. Back when she was married, whenever she and her husband went anywhere together, he always drove. They had fought about it a little. She told him he was too traditional. He said she was too liberal. She missed him, too.

They had been married for only three years, but she had known him much longer. When he told her he was entering the new police academy that the state of Chihuahua was creating in order to combat the drug cartels, she didn't try to talk him out of it. She knew what might happen, though. As did he. She also knew that he would take the worst job out there, if it meant providing for her and her son. Plus, it was more interesting work than what she did at the factory.

Her father-in-law had followed his son into the academy, seeing that it was the best way to make an income. She wondered about her mother-in-law for a moment, about how she was doing. The two of them had never really gotten along. Even so, she should send a card, just to let her know that her grandson was doing all right here. That Gladys was doing all right, too.

Well, mostly doing all right. Except for the car problem. The bus came up, puffing out a little black exhaust from its backside. Gladys got on quickly, thinking she might still make it in time to get her son.

Gil and Joe waited outside the house, watching David Geisler through the open windows as the man puttered around in the near dark. Gil had called Kline to get an arrest warrant more than twenty minutes ago. Joe paced back and forth next to the cruiser while Gil stood considering. He knew he would have to get inside Geisler's mind in order to get a confession during the interrogation, and right now what was worrying Gil was that Geisler's mind was none too intact. Gil might have to accept that even if they got a confession, their case would ultimately rest with the evidence, and that meant the sword, the blood on it, Geisler's previous behavior toward neighbor children, and his match to the profile.

Joe stopped near Gil. "I know it's not scientific, but that laughing thing he was doing makes me think we've got our guy."

Gil felt the same way. For the first time all day, he had hope that they might actually solve the case. Then the brutality of the crime scenes would be washed away. At least from his conscious mind. His unconscious would never forget.

A car sped down the street and pulled up. Chief Kline got out of the driver's seat and handed Gil a piece of paper, saying, "Here's the warrant. Go get the bastard."

"Yeah, let's do this," Joe said.

He and Gil went back to the front door and knocked again. This time Geisler didn't answer. They were forced to go in, hands on holstered guns. Geisler quietly sat in the living room as they entered. Gil read Geisler his Miranda rights while Joe cuffed him.

Geisler didn't resist as they put his hands behind his back. He only said, "They're trying to kill me for my sins."

"What sins are those?" Joe asked.

"I'm so scared that the table has a stomachache," Geisler said, looking at his coffee table, as Joe pulled him up to a standing position.

"That's always a big concern of mine, too," Joe said.

As they were walking out the front door, the crime scene techs arrived at the house with a search warrant. Now everyone could get to work.

CHAPTER ELEVEN

Friday Night

As Gil and Joe arrived at the station with Geisler, the rest of the skeleton crew of officers stood in front of the TV in the conference room. They were watching the local news stations, all of which were doing a live feed from the Zozobra crime scene. Gil, who was putting Geisler in a holding cell, was too far away to hear the newscaster. Geisler had gone completely quiet during the car ride, not responding to even the most innocuous questions. Gil was worried he might go catatonic, which was known to happen in schizophrenic suspects.

Gil went over to his desk and pulled out his criminal law book. In the index, he looked up "mentally ill," then tracked down the appropriate case names. He had read *Colorado vs. Connelly* during his first few months of law school before dropping out after his dad died, but he couldn't recall the specifics of the argument at the moment.

Kline came to Gil's desk and asked, "When are you going to get in there and question him?"

"As soon as I can," Gil said. "I just want to make sure that any information we get won't be suppressed at trial. I need to reread *Colorado vs. Connelly* and then look over *Smith vs. Duckworth*. We have to stay within the guidelines of a voluntary confession so it will be admissible in court."

"Just because he's mentally ill doesn't mean any confession you get isn't voluntary," Kline said.

"That's true," Gil said, "but there are plenty of court cases that get thrown out because the defendant was mentally ill and the police interrogator took advantage of that to get them to confess."

"From my perspective the law is pretty clear on this," Kline said. "His schizophrenia isn't going to make him confess."

Joe came over and said, "Hey, did you guys see the news—" before realizing that they were involved in a conversation. "Oops. My bad."

"Look, I'm also not sure how I feel about this," Gil said. "My whole goal in interrogating that guy is to get a confession. I do that by manipulating him to hell and back. How ethical is it for me to do that to someone who is mentally ill? He doesn't stand a chance. He'll end up agreeing to whatever I say."

"Geez, Gil," Joe said with a laugh, "I didn't know you were that good—"

"I just would feel better if we could talk to the district attorney," Gil said, "to get their take on how to handle the interrogation—"

"I agree, sir," Joe said, surprising Gil. "This is a high-profile case. One of those cases that can make or break a department. Everything has got to be aboveboard or the press will kill us. Plus, this way we all get some sleep and come at it fresh in the morning. Geisler's not going anywhere."

"All right," Kline said, looking at his watch. "We have twelve hours before we need to legally figure out what to do with him. He'll be fine here. We'll consider it again tomorrow."

Kline walked off, and Joe started smiling, clapping Gil on the back, saying, "I might be a jackass, but at least I've got your back, brother."

"That's true," Gil said. "You are a jackass."

Gil opened the front door of his house as best he could in the dark. Susan had forgotten to keep the porch light on again. He walked quietly to the hallway closet and opened the door. On the top shelf, which only Gil could reach, was the gun safe. He opened it and put in his sidearm and BUG, then closed it and spun the lock.

He went to Joy's room but just stood in the doorway, watching her sleep. She was getting so old. She was almost thirteen. Probably the same age as Ashley when her father started abusing her. Gil closed his eyes, turned his head skyward, and breathed deeply, trying to release some of the tension he had been holding all day. Trying to banish the evil images that kept popping into his head.

He walked closer to Joy's bed and put his hand on her head, saying a prayer in Spanish that he had said over her every night since she was born. It was the same prayer his father had said over him. "May the angels watch over you as you sleep, and may God smile on you when you awake."

Gil went across the hall to Therese's room. She was, as usual, curled up in a ball with all the covers thrown off the bed. Susan called Therese their little fussbudget because she never could stay in one spot as she slept. Gil pulled the blankets over her and put his hand on her head, her skin soft and cool underneath, as he repeated the prayer again.

He went to his own room and opened the door, thinking Susan would be awake. Instead she was lying on her side, snoring. She'd probably had a long day trying to get ready for Aunt Yolanda's annual fiesta party tomorrow. Susan, with her natural organizational skills, somehow always ended up in charge of the party. A party that Gil might actually be able to go to, now that they had a suspect in custody.

He quietly kicked his shoes off into the closet and got changed into sweatpants, a T-shirt, and running shoes. Gil had always been religious about getting a run in every Monday, Wednesday, and Friday. It was something that had been drilled into him since his days on the basketball team.

He locked the front door behind him and slowly jogged the first block to warm up, then picked up the pace on the next. Gil rounded the corner and felt his mood improving, the crisp night air making his lungs ache slightly. He had agreed to meet Joe back at the office at 9:00 A.M., but Gil suddenly remembered that he also had promised Susan he would check out a house in Eldorado. Their current home was a three-bedroom that was cramped up next to his neighbors and was starting to need almost constant repairs. Whereas in Eldorado—which was referred to as a bedroom community—the houses were mostly new and were on lots that covered at least a half acre. Then they would have the breathing room Susan craved. If only they could sell the house they had now.

Gil jogged another fifteen minutes before turning around and going back the direction he came, down the cold streets. When he saw his porch light shining brightly in the distance, he picked up the pace in anticipation of getting a shower, a beer, some ESPN, and a warm bed.

Lucy was still at work when her EMS pager went off. At the same time, she could hear the scanner above her desk sending out tones for the same page. It was a 4-Delta call, which meant an assault with serious injury. Copydesk had just finished up their work on the skull story, so Lucy said her good nights quickly as she raced out the door. She called herself into service using the radio in her car and pulled out of the lot. She raced down the dark, mostly deserted streets while pulling off her work shirt and pulling on her navy blue EMS top. She always wore black pants to work in case she went out on a call. She kicked off her work shoes and pulled on her combat boots while driving, switching her feet between putting on a boot and the accelerator.

She was just tucking her shirt into her pants as she pulled up to the fire station and jumped into the ambulance with Gerald. She got on the radio, telling Dispatch they were en route, then took out the street map to help navigate. Behind them, the engine pulled out with three firefighters on board.

She and Gerald didn't talk while they hummed down the streets sirenless. There was no need to wake up the neighbors with shrieking noise when the roads were empty.

They arrived at the house—a sprawling ranch with an electronic front gate—but were stopped by a sheriff's deputy blocking their access.

Gerald opened the driver's window and leaned out, calling, "Hey, Jeanette. What's up?"

"Hi, Gerald," she said, smiling. "It's good to see you. So, we've got SWAT on the way." Which meant the scene wasn't secure and they couldn't go in.

Gerald backed the ambulance up and parked across the street, where they waited with the fire engine. The SWAT van arrived and pulled through the gate. Lucy could see nothing more than a dark street, the driveway, trees, and the sheriff's car blocking their path. People might think SWAT situations were all action, and they were. Just not for EMS. For them, SWAT meant waiting. And waiting. Lucy considered asking Gerald what she should do about Lopez's suggestion that she act as a reporter while on emergency scenes, but she knew what he would say. That it would be wrong. He would be disappointed that she even considered it.

Just then the cop blocking the driveway motioned them to drive the rig forward. Gerald said, "That was short," as they pulled up to the home. They got out and grabbed their gear bag, then walked through the mostly dark house, stuffed with heavy replicas of Spanish Colonial antiques. A woman sat on a deep brown couch, a light shining on her face while the shadows on the outskirts of the room crowded around. She was in her forties and dressed in khaki pants and a torn blue blouse. She had a welt on her cheek and a split lip that was already clotted. Gerald knelt down beside her while Lucy took notes. The woman talked about a fight with her husband, who had taken off before SWAT had even arrived. Apparently he had held his wife hostage at gunpoint for a few hours before running off into the night.

Domestic assaults made Lucy feel oddly detached, as if all she could do was observe the situation. She knew that if she let herself get more involved, she would beat up the husband, move the wife out, and then burn the house down for good measure. Her anger and aggression got worse when she was the one treating the patient.

Luckily, Gerald preferred to be the one doing the active care of female assault patients. He never said as much, but Lucy suspected it was because he wanted the woman to be cared for by a man who was gentle and kind. Maybe it was his way of standing up for the gentlemen of his gender.

Gerald said his usual spiel to the wife: Did she have anywhere else to stay? Was there a friend they could call? Did she need anything else? Her responses were the usual as well: No, no, and no. Gerald had the woman fill out a refusal-of-treatment form, and then they left.

Mai Bhago Kaur concentrated on emptying her monkey glands as she got ready for bed. She had cut her finger slightly as she chopped twenty-four cups of vegetables for dinner earlier, and now the cut hurt as she gripped her toothbrush. She wondered if she'd cut herself because she was still recovering from the trance state that she had spent hours in that afternoon. She had come out of it feeling foggier then usual. Perhaps she had inadvertently gone on a psychic path she hadn't meant to.

Or maybe she cut herself in her distraction over the new recipe she'd used for the vegetable curry and chapatis flatbread. It had been much harder than she'd thought it would be. Well, she would try it again tomorrow. She wanted to be able to make it perfectly for their welcoming feast day, which was only twenty-two days away, when Guru Sanjam Dev would finally be home again.

She wondered if this time he would tell them about the catastrophe that he had foreseen. She knew she would never ask him about it. God revealed these things only in due time. Nevertheless, since he had first told them about it during his last visit almost a year ago, they had spent hours each day reading the newspaper, looking at Web sites, and wondering if the next hurricane or global warming or Middle East war would bring the end to pass, and they concentrated on time training in the secret ways, both ancient and new. Only their prayers had kept them safe this long, and that was because their combined female energy was so powerful, it could save the world—but not indefinitely.

She finished brushing her teeth and went to her bed. She turned on her CD player and heard his voice. She relaxed even more. She turned off the light and fell asleep to him telling her that in God's love, they all were one soul.

Lucy was in the all-night grocery store, pretending to consider her shredded cheese choices, while in actuality she was watching a shopping cart that had food in it but no one nearby. It was about a quarter full. She could see a carton of chocolate mint ice cream that was surely melting. Any moment now, it would break through its cardboard container and—drop by drop—throw itself to the ground, making a mess. Then no one would ever want it.

She looked up and down the aisle one final time, certain the owner would come back. Who would leave a half-full shopping cart just sitting in a store? No, there was no one else around this time of night. She grabbed the cart and pushed it quickly down the row. She scanned the aisles looking for the frozen-desserts section. You would think that since she shopped here almost every night she would know where it was, but her trips here rarely involved food.

She came here for beer and the self-scanning checkout lanes. The anonymity of the place meant that she didn't have to have human contact and the judgment that would bring. She didn't have to pass under the all-seeing eyes of the cashier who would—after a week or so of seeing her every day—say a friendly "How are you tonight?" Which Lucy knew really meant, "Didn't I see you last night buying another twelve-pack?"

In the past, Lucy had a set schedule of convenience and liquor stores she would frequent after work. She would visit each of them randomly, but never on successive days. One night she hit a store that she hadn't been to in a week, yet as she walked in the cashier said, "You're in luck, we just have one twelve-pack left." Lucy was mortified.

She didn't face this trouble at the all-night grocery store, where everyone was weirder than she was. She was a misfit among misfits, none of whom got judged poorly by the self-scanning checkout computer.

She kept pushing the cart down the aisle and replacing items:

Kleenex, laundry detergent, fresh tomatoes. She thought fleetingly that stores should hire people with OCD to do nothing more than wander around. Their natural inclinations would force them to clean and straighten everything.

By the time she was done, her beer craving was at full tilt. She couldn't drink too much tonight, though, because she had agreed to meet Andrea at Starbucks at 10:00 A.M. They would formulate a plan and then go over to the apartment complex. At most, she would have two beers.

Lucy twisted the top off beer number five as she cleaned her kitchen sink, using a scrub brush to get under its rim to the ancient caulk underneath.

Lucy loved the little house she rented on Alto Street, with its mosaic of Our Lady of Guadalupe by the front door and the old-timey feel of the neighborhood. Her tiny casita was old itself, with a claw-foot tub and a kiva fireplace. One of the few things she hated about her house was the lack of a washing machine. Whenever she wanted to do her laundry, she had to go to a Laundromat about a mile away. It was an inconvenient process for someone who didn't tolerate inconvenience well.

At the moment, she had no clean underwear left and had worn the same socks the last three days. Her thought was to wash a few of her dainty things in the kitchen sink—but that would require that it be clean. She wiped the surface a few more times before she went to her room to figure out what she would wash.

She picked a few single socks that didn't match off the floor, and then some underwear. She also was half looking for Nathan's keys; his car was still in her driveway. She had come home from the grocery store expecting it to be long gone. Of course, she had expected Nathan to be long gone by that morning, and look how that had turned out. So he must have just pocketed the extra fifteen dollars she gave him for a cab back to her place. Classy.

After a few minutes of searching, and once again not finding his keys, she took her unmentionables out to the kitchen and threw them in the sink. She really didn't want to wash them. She grabbed her beer off the counter and took a swig. She looked at her dishwasher, considering.

As far as she knew, the dishwasher followed the same basic cleaning laws as a washing machine. She would just have to replace the dishwasher soap with laundry detergent and she'd be in business. She put her socks in the dishwasher's bowl rack and draped her underwear over the silverware tray. After a few squirts of laundry detergent, she turned it on and then took her beer into the living room.

She sat down in front of the TV and watched some old *Simpsons* episodes, but her mind was elsewhere.

She thought back to the budget meeting and how she was shut down. Why was it so hard for them to understand that what they were doing was wrong? She realized she was anxious, feeling the humiliation that she hadn't allowed herself to acknowledge during the meeting. She took another sip of beer to calm her nerves. Her co-workers had not only ignored her, they had mocked her for being some kind of police groupie because Gil simply stopped by to say hi. She cursed them all a few more times in her head. Maybe if she had explained to them about her friendship with Gil. Although "friendship" was too strong a word for it. Gil was more of her confessor. He knew why she punished herself. She took another sip of beer. If she had told him about her note in Zozobra, he would have understood that what she needed to be released from was her guilt. Guilt for causing someone else's death.

Lucy picked up her cell phone and went through her contacts list to find a number, one she hadn't looked up in six months. She dialed, listening to it ring four times before he picked up and said, "This is Detective Gil Montoya. Can I help you?" He sounded tired. Lucy looked at the clock. It said 1:45 A.M. Really? How did that happen?

"Listen," she said, not even identifying herself. "My boss is an asshole."

"Okay," Gil said hesitantly.

"I just wanted you to know that," she said. He needed to understand that she was not a party to her boss's misinterpretation of journalism ethics. She continued, "Okay, then, the thing is, those tapes you wanted, they aren't here. I mean, not here here, but at work here, and my boss thinks he's not being an asshole about this but he is, he just is." She stopped for a breath, realizing too late that she might sound drunk; on the other hand, she could usually handle her liquor, so he probably had no clue. "Then they all gang up on me. Anyway, the only thing for me to do is to just tell you that there are no tapes so you don't waste your time looking for them, you know."

"Are you saying there are no tapes from the security cameras in the newspaper lobby?"

"Correct."

"Thank you," he said. "That really helps us not waste our time."

"Cool. So what are you up to right now?"

"Sleeping."

"All right then," she said, before adding a quick good-bye and hanging up. She was suddenly intensely embarrassed that she had called him so late at night. She took another drink of beer, but it did nothing to help her anxiousness. She felt her hands go cold and numb. She took a few deep breaths to try to calm down, but that only made her dizzy—and more nervous. If she wasn't careful, she might end up in a full-blown panic attack. She knew that the only way to stop the feeling was to overtake it with another strong emotional response, possibly one that included a physical element.

She knew only one way to make that happen. She clicked her phone back open and dialed the next number by heart.

Gil hung up his cell phone and quietly put it on the nightstand, trying not to wake Susan. He turned off the bedside light but didn't close his eyes. He listened to his house settling down for the night, the floorboards sighing and creaking to bed.

Lucy had been drunk. She'd been talking fast and nonstop. Her words had been slightly unformed and indistinct, one almost banging into the next. He was glad she had called him about the tapes, but the conversation left him unsettled for reasons he couldn't quite pin down. It took him another forty-five minutes to finally fall asleep.

CHAPTER TWELVE

Saturday Morning

Gil woke up at 7:30 A.M., when he felt Susan roll out of bed next to him. He heard her running the water in the bathroom; she came back out and opened the bedroom curtains.

The sunshine cut a bright knife of light across the bed and onto Gil's face. He sighed and sat up. "What are you doing up? It's only seven thirty on a Saturday morning," he said.

"We have to be at the pet parade by nine," she said as she went out into the hallway. He heard her waking the girls. Gil couldn't remember if he and Susan had talked about going to the pet parade. It was the one part of fiesta they never missed. Last year they had watched from the curb, but Gil had only seen a few minutes of it before he was called off to investigate a hit-and-run.

Susan came back into the room and started getting her clothes together.

"So what's the plan?" he asked, trying to keep the question vague. He still couldn't remember discussing anything about the parade with her and wanted to avoid any sharp looks of disappointment when she realized he'd forgotten. He knew he'd be given one anyway when he told her he couldn't go because of the case.

"Me and the girls are going over to my sister's house to meet up with them, and then we're going downtown," she said as she tried to decide between a red and blue blouse.

"Oh," he said, slightly puzzled. Susan clearly had never assumed he was going to go. He wasn't sure if he was disappointed or relieved.

"I saw your mom and Aunt Yolanda downtown yesterday," Susan said.

Gil mumbled some sort of response as he got out of bed and went into the bathroom. He shaved and got a breakfast of cold Cheerios and milk as the girls swirled happily around him, chatting with Susan.

"Honey," Susan said to him as she packed up bottles of water and sunscreen, "don't forget to go by that house in Eldorado on your way to your mom's."

They were gone in a whirlwind of good-byes and smiles. He listened to Susan's car backing out of the driveway. He listened to the quiet house for a moment before getting into his own car and pulling away from the house.

Gil drove to Eldorado, looking at the stairstep homes that were cozied up to the interstate. Ten years ago, Santa Fe wasn't even visible from I-25. Now houses—all painted in the same species of beige—were fighting for space. The only variation in style was a red sloped roof here and there sticking out against the otherwise flat-topped homes.

Gil took the Eldorado exit and kept an eye out for the right street to turn on. There were long views of the Jemez, Ortiz, and Sandia mountains, but the Sangre de Cristos, the ones that dominated the view of Santa Fe, were hidden behind pyramid-shaped foothills. The biggest landmark that Gil had used all his life to orient himself in his hometown wasn't visible from here.

He turned down a dirt road, which was one of the ways Eldorado kept its country feel, and pulled up in front of a house with a FOR SALE sign. One of the draws of Eldorado was that there were no yards to tend to. The developers had left the wild desert alone and placed the homes among the cholla cactus and rabbit brush. There also were no fences, and the nearest neighbor was four house lengths away, leaving plenty of elbow room. Their old neighborhood had been built fifty years ago, when homes were built within ten feet of each other with a fence in between.

Even though homes in Eldorado were isolated, the community was governed by strict codes. The area was a haven for Anglo artists from back east, who brought with them the mentality of gated communities. They passed covenants and held lots of meetings about errant neighbors. Gil had heard of one man who had put up a playground set for his kids, but the slide was yellow, a color that was forbidden because it was "too distracting" to the neighbors. The man was forced to paint it forest green to make it—and his family—blend in. Gil was New Mexico born, and such intrusiveness by neighbors was completely unfamiliar to him. He wasn't sure he would handle it well. He had never told Susan his impression, not wanting to squash her dream.

There was another problem with Eldorado that Gil had never mentioned to Susan, but to him it was not a minor point—they would probably be one of the few Hispanic families in the town. Where they lived now, the mix was about 70 percent native New Mexico Hispanic and 30 percent Indian or Anglo. Here the mix was 95 percent Anglo and 5 percent a mix of other races.

Gil's grandfather, when he was alive, would have seen it as the only issue. He, like some other Hispanic descendants of the conquistadores, had thought of himself as white. They were European, his grandpa argued, just as white as any German or French person, and because their ancestors had spent most of the last four hundred years isolated from the rest of the world, they were the only ones of their kind. They were a special brand of white. A better brand. He had tried to drill this point into Gil in his authoritative voice, which he had polished over the years he sat on the bench as First District Court Judge Gilbert Nazario Estevan Montoya. Gil's namesake. A man who saw himself as the upholder of everything Castilian. The Judge would see a life in Eldorado as turning their back on their heritage.

Gil never bought into the Judge's own style of bigotry. Even so, he did admit that it would bother him if Therese and Joy went to a school where they would be considered a minority.

Gil walked around the house. It was a one-story with a small courtyard enclosed by a low curved wall. He peered in a few windows, into the interior with its new wood floors and Mexican tile. The house seemed fine. He would tell Susan to set up a time for a tour with the Realtor.

Gil got back in the car and headed to his mother's house, which was farther down the highway. He went south, toward Galisteo. Telephone poles made a low line of crosses along the road. The old wooden poles had glass transformers that shone blue and green in the sun. A red-tailed hawk was perched on a DO NOT PASS sign.

Gil drove into Galisteo, past the dirt cliffs leading to the arroyo. He turned off the highway and onto Avenida de Montoya, going slowly over the dirt and gravel road. Gil turned onto a smaller road, and drove past the Old House, which had been the family hacienda since the king of Spain granted it to them. The house was now mostly fallen down, its half-standing adobe walls looking forlorn. Gil parked in front of the new house, which had been built in the 1920s, and got out of the car. Instead of going into the house, though, he walked down toward the Galisteo River a few yards away. The river, which had been too wide to jump across when he was a kid, was now just a stream.

Gil walked close to the water's edge and up the side of the embankment. He pushed through a small path in the brush and came to a wire fence. He walked along the fence, checking the posts to make sure they were sturdy. One of the neighbor's goats had wandered onto their property last week, and Gil was still trying to determine how it had made it through the fence. The posts looked solid. A random goat was no real problem, but Gil wanted to be able to tell his mother that he checked the fence.

He walked back to the house and opened the front door, calling, "Mom, I'm here."

She was in the kitchen pulling a pan of carne adovada out of the oven.

"Hi, hito," she said, and she put the pan on the counter to cool. "How are you?"

"Fine, Mom," he said, kissing her on the cheek. He checked his watch as he sat down at the table. It was 8:40 A.M. He would have to get going in a minute if he wanted to meet Joe at the station at nine as promised.

His mom put a bowl out and scooped some carne adovada out for him. He didn't have time to eat, but he also knew it was useless to protest. Plus, his mother made the best carne adovada in the world.

He put a forkful in his mouth. The tender pork was infused with the slow burn of chile and garlic that hit the back of a throat. This was not the wildfire heat of green chile, but the ceaseless low fire of roasted red. The meat fell apart against his tongue, almost melting.

Carne adovada was a simple thing: pork, red chile sauce, garlic, and oregano. What made the difference was the cook. His mother never rushed it. She took a full two days to make it. She started by roasting her own chile instead of using chile powder, like Aunt Yolanda, and she didn't bother with cumin, which she dismissed as inauthentic since the spice wasn't found in New Mexico.

Gil put another forkful in his mouth. He did a few quick calculations in his head as he watched his mom move around the kitchen. Carne adovada takes four hours to cook. She must have been up since 5:00 A.M. if she was just taking it out of the oven now. Gil didn't say anything, though. His mother took such pride in her cooking he didn't want to scold her for being dedicated.

"Did you have fun with Aunt Yolanda yesterday?" he asked her as he took another bite.

"Oh, yes," she said, wiping her hands on her apron. "Did you check on the fence?" she asked.

"Yes, mom," Gil said, laughing slightly. He knew she would ask that. "It's fine."

"I just don't know how that goat got over here," she said in a tsk-ing voice.

"Hey, mom, what time is Elena getting here for the party?" His younger sister, who worked as a lawyer for the state attorney's office in Albuquerque, was supposed to play chauffeur for their mom.

"I think she said she'd be here at one," she said, still moving around the kitchen. Never sitting still.

Gil got up and pulled open one of the kitchen drawers. He took out a small blue canvas bag and said, "Okay, Mom, let's do this."

She finally stopped moving and sat down at the table, resting her left arm on the tabletop and extending her index finger. This was why he came over to his mother's house as much as possible—to check her blood sugar level.

Diabetes was a problem that hit native New Mexicans hard, both Hispanic and Indian. More than 17 percent of the adult population had it. His mother was just one of them. He only wished she would stay more on top of it.

Gil opened the bag and took out an alcohol pad. He wiped the side of her index finger with it and then pulled out a small glucose machine. He set up a test strip and then asked, "Ready?" She nodded, and he pricked her finger with a sharp lancet.

"Oooch," she said. "That stings." It always hurt her. No matter how often he checked her BGL. He held the machine up to her finger, waiting for a drop of blood to fall onto the test strip. They sat still like that, frozen. Waiting for the blood. The machine beeped when it had enough blood and they waited again until the digital display read 70. It was a little low.

"Mom, have you eaten yet?" he asked.

"I'll have something later," she said.

If he had time, he'd sit with her to make sure she ate. As it was, he'd be pushing it.

"Mom, you have to have something to eat soon," he said. "I mean within the next hour."

"Okay, hito," she said as she transferred some of the adovada into plastic containers.

Gil watched her for another moment before carefully storing the number in the machine's history and kissing her good-bye. As he headed out the door, he said, "Have fun at the party."

Lucy looked at her watch—8:30 A.M. She sat at a table at the Santa Fe Baking Company waiting for the waiter to deliver her breakfast burrito with extra green chile. The headache she had meant that she needed chile today. In Santa Fe, whenever you were hungover or sick—with anything from a cold to cancer—someone inevitably told you to eat green chile. Scientists all over the world studied its effects. The most recent report said if green chile was painted on the hull of a boat, barnacles wouldn't attach themselves to it. Such is the power of green chile.

She also was waiting for Del to get back from the bathroom. She had called him last night after talking to Gil. She and Del had been doing this every so often for the past few months. He was a recycled boyfriend. She was conserving energy by taking to bed a man she already knew well instead of investing her precious natural resources in a new relationship.

They would pretend that he was coming over in the middle of the night to watch a movie, but that had quickly become code for hookup sex. Last night, they had made an effort to watch part of *Superbad*. From there things got hazy. She was sure she had offered to make margaritas at some point, but she was also positive she didn't know how to make margaritas. They had woken up together in bed, twined in sheets that had wrapped around them during the previous night's action.

Lucy glanced at the nearby community bulletin board, trying to read the flyers pinned to it. They mostly advertised the same types of alternative healing as the one at Denny's. One flyer caught her eye. It was bright blue and said in bold black letters: THE MEDITATION OF RELEASE. Lucy thought of the prayer—actually, more of a plea—that she had put in Zozobra. The flyer went on to say, "So often in our lives we have old habits that hold us back. Meditation is one of the few methods that has been scientifically proven not only to reduce stress but also to help people overcome bad behaviors. We are a group of nurses who get together for the health benefits of this practice. Please join us for a class on Sunday, where we will teach you the basics of meditation with the promise that there will be no chanting." Lucy smiled when she read the last line. She thought for a second about going to the class, but her attention became quickly refocused on the waiter delivering her breakfast burrito. She barely looked up when Del came back from the bathroom, but did manage to snuffle an acknowledgment to him.

He said, "Thanks for waiting," as she smiled up at him. "So what have you been up to?" he asked. "I feel bad that we didn't get a chance to catch up last night."

She started laughing and said, "Yeah, I bet."

"Whose car was in the driveway?" he asked.

"Oh," she said, remembering that Nathan's car was at her house. "Now there's a story to make you laugh." She told Del about Nathan and the money, taking pride that he laughed in all the right places. That meant she had told the story right. For some reason she had taken to telling Del about her one-night stands and making them into a sort of comedic routine. Her love life as a punch line. She wondered how that had gotten started—and why she kept doing it.

"So that story you guys ran about the skull in Zozobra was pretty good, but I have to say ours was better," Del said mischievously.

She shook her head, smiling at how he teased her. They worked at competing papers, so ethically they shouldn't discuss their work, but it was a rule he liked to play with.

"I actually was at Zozobra," she said. "It was really fascinating."

"The whole thing is a little pedestrian for me," he said, taking a bite of his burrito.

"I liked it," Lucy said defensively. "I even wrote a note to put into the fire."

"Really?" he said, laughing a little with a mouth full of food. "What did it say?"

Lucy hesitated. She had told Del most of the story about what had happened in January, when she had first met Gil, and how one of her offhand remarks led to a woman being killed. Del had laughed then, too, calling the whole thing "a joke by a humorless universe." She wasn't sure she and her guilt could take his teasing now. So she said instead, "Oh, it was just some resolution to have more sex," thinking he would find that funny and let it drop. She didn't wait to see if he would laugh before adding, "So what about you? What's up at the *Santa Fe Times*?"

"I am so sick of it all," he said. "I can't stand the business anymore. The life has just been taken out of it with all the newspapers going under these days."

"Why not find another job if you hate it so much?" Lucy asked. "You always thought about going to law school."

"There's an ego there that disturbs me," he said.

"What does that mean?"

"If I say I want to be a lawyer, does that mean I want to be a lawyer or that my ego wants to be a lawyer?"

Talking with Del could get like this. When she first met him, every conversation was so deep and meaningful. It made him sexy. His word-based intelligence was as much a turn-on as any washboard abs.

It always intrigued Lucy that their intellectual talks were more enjoyable than the sex. Maybe that was because their sex life was more about individual performance instead of togetherness. Del believed that a person was responsible for his or her own orgasms. That meant she got no individual attention from him where it mattered most. Still, she gave him what he denied her in the hopes that it would foster generosity in him, causing him to reciprocate.

As she thought about their conversations, she realized they were exactly like their sex life. She was often left out of the equation while at the same time she was expected to pay tribute to him and his big words.

CHAPTER THIRTEEN

Saturday Morning

Gil started making calls as soon as he left his mom's house. His first was to the county detention center to check on both Rudy Rodriguez and David Geisler. He then asked to have them transported to the police station so they'd be there when he arrived. His next call was to Joe, but it went directly to voice mail. His third call also went to voice mail. It was to Chief Kline, telling him not to worry about getting the court order for the newspaper's security camera tapes. Gil would try to figure out later how to explain that without involving Lucy.

His fourth call was to Liz, who answered on the first ring and launched immediately into an explanation. "About the fingerprints you sent me," she said. "We're doing our best to try to match them against what we found at the Guadalupe crime scene, but it's going to take us a while to get everything analyzed. I'll call you as soon as that's finished."

"Sounds good," Gil said.

"Also, I did find out that the blood on the sword is human. Now, just try to stay with me while I explain the specifics," she said. Gil let her condescension slide by. "I won't know if it's definitely Brianna's blood until the DNA results come back, but if we look at blood typing I can determine in general if it might be hers. So, the blood on the sword is O positive."

"Which is fairly common," Gil said.

"Right. About forty percent of the population has it," she said. "Now, we don't know Brianna's blood type, but I still have both parents' blood samples and DNA that we took during the first investigation, so I did some more tests. It turns out her mom is O positive and her dad is O negative—"

"Oh, about that," Gil said, interrupting.

"What?"

"I forgot to call you, but the guy we thought was Brianna's dad—"

"Tony Herrera."

"Right. He says he's not," Gil said.

"God damn it, Gil," she said, clearly pissed. "Do you know how screwed we are now? I have to have both her parents' DNA to prove that the bones and the blood are hers. I can't do anything about a positive identification until we know who her dad is."

"Liz," Gil said hesitantly, trying not to make her any angrier, "I'm sorry."

"Whatever," she said. "I'll call you later." She hung up. Liz was prickly but always got the job done.

Gil next called Ashley's cell phone. He wanted to check in to see if she had been released from the hospital, but also to find out if she could come down to the station to see if she recognized David Geisler. Plus, it might give Gil a chance to ask the one question he had to have answered: Who was Brianna's father?

Mrs. Rodriguez answered, and she sounded exhausted as she explained that Ashley had started full labor. Gil knew this was bad news given how Dr. Santiago had explained the situation to them yesterday. He hesitated in asking Mrs. Rodriguez the next question but told her that they needed someone from the family to come down to the station. Mrs. Rodriguez's only answer was to say that they would talk it over. Gil wondered if the family's help was coming to a close once again. They hung up, and Gil tried to figure out how they could get Ashley to make an ID. Short of just going to the hospital and showing her a photo—which had a high incidence of misidentification—he was at a loss.

Gil arrived at the station before the detention center van showed up. Before Joe, too.

Gil was researching the court cases about mentally ill suspects when Joe walked in holding a twenty-two-ounce Mountain Dew. "Hiya, brother. What's up? How did you sleep? I think I actually had nightmares last night about those crime scenes."

Gil had slept badly after the call with Lucy, but he wasn't about to tell Joe that. He said instead, "The transport should be getting here soon with Rudy Rodriguez and David Geisler, so we need to get them set up in interview rooms."

"Cool," Joe said, taking a swig out of his Mountain Dew

"Oh, and one more thing," Gil said, trying to sound nonchalant. "I found out that the security tapes from the *Capital Tribune* won't do us any good. The cameras are broken."

"Seriously?" Joe asked. "Then what was that guy's whole crap fest about us needing a court order?"

"I don't know," Gil said, before changing the subject to his calls with Liz and Mrs. Rodriguez. He was just finishing updating Joe when three corrections officers came in with the prisoner transfers for the day, including Rudy Rodriguez, who was not handcuffed and looked disheveled but sober, and David Geisler, who was completely shackled and talking to himself in a low voice. Gil went over to them to sign the release paperwork while Joe got them both situated in interview rooms.

The two men met back up at Gil's desk, where Gil said, "So the plan is for me to do an assessment of Geisler. More to judge his mental state. Then I'll call the DA and see if we can legally interview him. After that, I'll interview Rodriguez." Gil sighed. He was going to have to get Rodriguez to confess to abusing Ashley in order to ask if he was Brianna's father.

"Sounds like a plan, man," Joe said.

Gil unclipped his paddle holster and locked it and his gun in his desk drawer, then grabbed a notebook and went into the interview room. Geisler sat in one of the two chairs in the room, rocking back and forth, constantly saying nonsensical words. He would occasionally laugh, always putting his hand up to his mouth and giggling.

"Hello, David, I'm Mr. Montoya," Gil said. "Do you remember me from last night?"

Geisler just kept talking. Among the mumblings, Gil could only hear a few distinct phrases. "A right wall no matter dumb, dumb."

Gil continued. "I need to get your age and address for the paperwork. Can you help me with that?"

Geisler looked up and said with an elfish smile, "Rarely heaven is dog symptom . . . move a consciousness my hip hip lock." Then he started giggling again.

Gil sighed and said, "David, can you understand what I'm saying?"

Geisler got up suddenly and walked to the wall, facing it. There he fluttered his arms and started saying, "Giraffe spoiled drum pink."

"Did you know Brianna Rodriguez?"

Geisler, still facing the wall, jumped on one foot and muttered.

Gil shook his head. He watched Geisler for another moment before getting up and leaving. He went to the room next door, which was the other side of the mirrored window. Joe stood in there, watching Geisler.

"I think he's worse," Gil said sadly.

"I agree with that," Joe said. "Now what?"

"Now we call the DA and try to figure out what to do."

Gil put a call in to the district attorney's answering service and asked that the lawyer on call get back to him about Geisler. In the meantime, he would interview Ashley's dad. They needed him to confirm two things: their suspicion that he had nothing to do with Brianna's disappearance and that he was—or wasn't—Brianna's father.

Gil wasn't looking forward to the interview. Sexual abuse was a delicate issue that needed lots and lots of interview time to even begin to break the suspect down and get at the truth. They just didn't have that kind of time right now, especially since they had no evidence to support the claim. In the end, the abuse charges would be turned over to the sexual offender detectives, who specialized in that kind of work. At the moment, it was the murder charges that concerned Gil. He had to know if Rodriguez had impregnated his daughter. Their blood evidence against Geisler now depended on finding Brianna's father.

The complexity of the situation meant that Gil would have to break the interview up into pieces. The first part would be easy. Gil would only ask Rodriguez about Brianna's disappearance and not mention Ashley's abuse. It was the second part that would get ugly.

Gil grabbed a general interview form and went into the room. He introduced himself again to Rodriguez before sitting down in one of the two chairs. The chairs were the only furniture in the room by design. They called it an interview room, but it was really an interrogation room, devoid of distraction.

Rodriguez was definitely sober now, his polo shirt and pants wrinkled from the overnight accommodations. Gil asked him to confirm his name and address, which he wrote on the interview form. The form served no actual informational purpose. Instead, it gave Gil a baseline from which to judge the way Rodriguez responded to questions. It allowed Gil to check the man's normal verbal and behavior patterns so that later, when asking the tough questions, Gil could determine if Rodriguez's answers fit the baseline. Anything outside the baseline could be a lie.

Gil leaned forward in his chair before saying, "Rudy, what is your understanding of the purpose for this interview with me here today?"

"I don't know," Rodriguez said, looking confused. "To talk about Brianna?"

Gil didn't respond to Rudy's question and instead said, "As you know, we have recently found evidence that leads us to believe that Brianna is dead." He stated this firmly with little intonation, following the basic interview script. It was the same method used by police across the country, and Gil found some comfort in staying within the rules of questioning someone. When it came to interviewing suspects, he rarely colored outside the lines. Gil continued, "If you know anything about Brianna's disappearance, our investigation will find that out. But if you had nothing to do with it, it will show that as well. If you know anything at all about it, you should tell me now."

"I don't know anything," Rodriguez said in a rush. "I swear."

Gil had been direct with his question on purpose. To throw Rodriguez off. Suspects rarely expected anyone to ask them directly if they committed a crime.

"Do you know who could have done this?" Gil asked.

"I've thought a lot about that, but I just can't think of anybody."

"Do you know anyone that you feel absolutely had nothing to do with it? Just your gut feeling?"

"Oh, there is no way Ashley or Rose had anything to do with it. Nobody in the family did," Rodriguez said. He stopped to think for a second and then said, "It had to be a stranger."

Gil nodded. Guilty suspects would usually be fast and furious when answering the question about who else could be to blame. They did not formulate thoughtful responses.

"You believe it was a stranger who took Brianna?" Gil asked.

"Yes, I do,"

Gil nodded again. It was a straightforward answer with no signs of deception. Rodriguez made no attempt to add on an improbable scenario, like Brianna had run away.

"When was the last time you saw Brianna?" Gil asked.

"About a month before she disappeared, when I moved out," he said as he started crying, his bloodshot eyes becoming even redder. At that moment, he was every inch a grandfather who'd lost his only grandchild.

"I'll get you some water," Gil said as he got up to leave. His mind was already on the next part of the interview, where he would find out if the grandfather was also the father.

Del was driving down Cerrillos Road as Lucy absentmindedly watched the buildings go by. Del was at the wheel of her car because just as they had been leaving Santa Fe Baking Company, Lucy's brain decided to spin the world a little more quickly. She thought it best to let him drive, but now it felt strange being a passenger in her own vehicle.

Neither of them spoke as Del slowed down for a traffic light. Lucy gazed out the window at a green street sign that stood on the corner. It read SECOND STREET in reflective white paint. Second Street, along with Third, Fourth, Fifth, and Sixth streets, seemed to be the city's one attempt at true grid planning, but the whole project included only five streets. There was no First Street. At some point, the industrious city planner who started the number system simply gave up. So where there should have been a Seventh Street, instead there was Llano Street.

The light turned, and the car ahead of them didn't move. Del lay on the horn.

"Stop it," Lucy said sharply without thinking, trying to pull his hands off the center of the steering wheel.

"What?" he laughed as the cars started to move. "Why?"

"People in Santa Fe don't honk," she said.

"Oh really?" he laughed again.

"It's completely rude."

"When did you become a Santa Fe expert?"

"I guess it was after I was forced to move here by my ex-boyfriend," she said meanly.

"I didn't force," he said just as cruelly. "I believed you begged."

Lucy snorted, shook her head, and looked out the window. She said nothing more until they got to Del's house. He got out and said his signature postcoital phrase, "Thanks for the sex," before closing the door. He had always thought it was so funny when he said it. Del could never get past the joke that only he appreciated.

Lucy got into the driver's seat and went home, still fuming at Del. Once in the house she jumped in the shower. She was reading the directions on the shampoo bottle—which she did before every use—when she remembered she was supposed to be meeting Andrea at 10:00 A.M. She had no idea what time it was. She rinsed off quickly and checked the clock: 9:49 A.M. Damn. She called Andrea's cell, hoping to catch her before she left the house.

"Hello?" said a male voice that answered Andrea's phone. He sounded familiar.

"Tommy? Is that you?"

"Hey, boss. How are you?" Tommy said, chuckling.

"I assume this means that you're with Andrea," Lucy said, laughing.

"In every way," he said.

"Eww, I don't want to hear about it," she said. "Can you ask Andrea if I can meet her at eleven instead? I totally lost track of time."

"Sure, hang on." She could hear Tommy saying something in the background before he got back on the phone. "She says that's fine. Hey, did you hear the news?"

"What's that?"

"They arrested somebody in the skull case. He's schizophrenic or something."

"What?" Lucy said, confused. She thought about all the planning it would take to put the skull in Zozobra. "That can't be right . . . there's just no way."

"What do you mean?" Tommy asked.

"I just don't see how that could be," she said. She knew she must sound like an idiot.

"I don't—" Tommy started to say. She could tell that now he was confused.

"You know what, Tommy? I'm not making much sense. Sorry. I'll see you later." She hung up before he could ask her more.

Lucy stood in her bedroom, with water dripping down her skin and onto the floor. She was too lost in thought to notice. They had arrested someone with schizophrenia in the skull case. It made no sense to her. The crime and the aftermath simply didn't match the medical manifestation of the disorder.

Lucy popped open her cell phone again and dialed.

Gil was about to go back into the interview room with Rodriguez when the front desk told him that Alex Stevens had arrived. Stevens came in looking tired with wrinkled clothes. Gil shook his hand and said, "I guess congratulations are in order."

"Not quite yet. Ashley's still got to get it out," Stevens said with a yawn.

"How's she doing?"

"Tired. She didn't sleep at all last night and the contractions . . . she's not handling it all too great." Joe came over to join them. "So," Stevens continued, "I hear you need some help with an identification."

Joe nodded. "We just want to know if you recognize the guy from anywhere."

"Who is he?" Stevens asked.

"We can't really get into that," Gil said quickly before Joe could answer. "We just want to know if you've ever seen him."

They went into the viewing room, which had a two-way mirror that looked into the interview room where Geisler was being held. Geisler was now sitting cross-legged in the corner, talking to himself. Stevens furrowed his brow before saying, "I think I know that guy."

"Really?" Joe said, surprised. "How?"

"I don't know. I think I've seen him on the street by the house," Stevens said. "Does he live in the neighborhood?"

Joe started to say, "Yeah, he—" but Gil interrupted with "Do you remember anything else?"

"I'm not sure," Stevens said, "but there was this one guy who would stop and talk with Brianna pretty often and sometimes play with her. I think that's the guy."

"What?" Joe said, clearly surprised. "What are you talking about? Dude, how many times did we ask you about strangers who talked to her? It's been a year and this is the first I've heard of it?" Joe shot Gil a worried look, like he expected to get reprimanded. Like it was his fault this had never come out before. Gil wasn't sure if it was or not.

"I told the police about it," Stevens said. "The other detective. The first one I met."

"Fisher?" Joe asked with a hint of disbelief.

"Yeah," Stevens said. "He said he'd check into it, but I never heard anything else about it."

"Hang on," Gil said, mostly to calm Joe. "This man you saw playing with Brianna. Is this him?" he asked, pointing at Geisler.

"I think so," Stevens said. "I can't be a hundred percent sure, but it sure looks like him."

"How long did he play with her?" Gil asked.

"I don't know," Stevens said. "I saw him one day with Brianna in the front yard when I pulled up in my truck."

"They were playing?" Gil asked.

"Yeah, it looked like they were playing with some dolls."

Joe turned to look at Gil. Gil guessed what he was thinking about. The doll-head necklace found on the first statue of Mary.

"Did you speak to him?" Gil asked.

"No, he got up and ran away," Stevens said. "I yelled after him, but then Ashley came out and said it was okay, that he was just a neighbor who sometimes stopped to say hi."

"Did Ashley say anything else?"

"Only that the guy seemed a little off."

"When was the last time you saw him?" Gil asked.

"About a month before Brianna disappeared."

"Alex, I have to admit that it concerns me that we're just hearing about this now," Gil said.

"Don't blame me," Stevens said, starting to get defensive. "I told that other detective. You're the ones who dropped the ball, not us."

Joe, looking furious, did the only right thing he could have done in the situation—he walked out of the room. Gil thanked Stevens and said they would stop by the hospital later to talk with Ashley and get a formal statement from him, after the baby was born. Gil knew Stevens would want to hurry back to the hospital and he hoped the gesture of goodwill would smooth over Joe's attitude issues.

Gil was about to go find Joe and try to calm him down when his cell phone rang. He answered, but before he could say anything, he heard Lucy's distinctive voice.

"You arrested someone in the skull case?"

"Lucy, I can't—"

"Gil, look, I'm not asking you as a reporter or even as a friend, or acquaintance or whatever it is that we are, I'm asking because I think you made a mistake."

"It's not—"

"Every news agency in the state, and maybe in the country, is going to be condemning this guy to death in a couple of hours. His life will be up on CNN, and then he'll have no life. Just let me talk to you."

"I don't have time—"

"Great. I'm coming to the station. I'll be there in ten minutes."

Gil wondered if she was still drunk.

CHAPTER FOURTEEN

Saturday Morning

Gil planned to explain to Lucy that under no circumstances could he discuss the case, and he was sorry, but he could not share any information. So when she was escorted over to his desk by a uniformed officer he started to say calmly, "Lucy, I can't—"

"Gil," she said, interrupting him and looking surprisingly composed. He had expected histrionics and possibly more alcohol at work, but she looked together and unruffled. She continued, "I'm sorry to barge into the station like this, and I know that you can't give me any details of the case, but I heard that you arrested a man with schizophrenia, and I wanted to discuss with you the possibility that, due to his condition, he would be unable to do what he's been charged with."

"First of all," Gil said, smiling. He could tell she had probably practiced that speech in the car. "I can neither confirm nor deny that we've arrested someone. Secondly, whether or not schizophrenia had a role in any crime would be up to the doctors to decide. Not you." He tried to add the last part gently.

She smiled and said, "Just consider me an expert on schizophrenia. Someone who can save you from making a potentially embarrassing mistake."

Gil heard a throat-clearing noise behind him and turned to see Joe. She stuck out her hand and said brightly, "Hi. I'm Lucy." Gil could see the wheels turning in Joe's head, and those wheels only turned in one direction. They shook hands as she said, "I was just discussing the case with Gil."

Gil quickly corrected her, saying, "We are not discussing the case."

"Jeez, Gil, lighten up," Joe said. "Let's hear what the lady has to say."

"So," she said with a smile at Joe. "I was just explaining to Gil that I know quite a lot about schizophrenia, and I thought before your investigation went any further it might do some good to look at your suspect's situation."

"His situation is that he's nuts," Joe said.

"Nuts how?" Lucy glanced at Gil and must have noticed his disapproving look. She put a hand on his arm and said, "I only want to hear a little about his behavior. I don't care about anything else. How is that going to hurt your case?"

"Yeah, Gil," Joe said. "How is that going to hurt our case?" Gil could feel himself relenting. He had to admit he was curious, mainly about how Lucy became a schizophrenia expert.

"Okay," Gil said, "but when I say any information is off-limits you have to respect that. Let's go sit in one of the interview rooms."

When they were all seated around the table, Gil asked, "What do you need to know?"

"Tell me what he's saying," she said. When she saw Gil's hackles go up, she added, "I don't mean tell me if he's confessed or said anything about the case. I mean how is he forming sentences? What kind of words is he using?"

"He's confused. His sentences don't make any sense," Gil said.

"No," she said. "I need to know exactly what he is saying."

Gil pulled his notebook out of his pocket and read, "Rarely heaven is dog symptom" and "Giraffe spoiled drum pink."

Lucy shook her head. "He's in word salad. It's the technical term. One of the hallmarks of schizophrenia is disorganized thinking, and word salad is about as disorganized as it gets. He's probably delusional, has hallucinations. What else is he doing?"

"He's constantly talking," Gil said.

"That's pressured speech," Lucy said.

"Oh, and Gil, man, don't forget the evil laughing thing," Joe said. "He laughs and giggles when you talk to him."

"Really?" she said, shaking her head. "No, see, this is the problem. This is why I wanted to come talk to you. People assume because schizophrenics act strangely that they are violent. A few might be, but the vast majority aren't. Like this poor guy. It sounds like he has hebephrenic schizophrenia. You've got to get ahold of his psychiatrist and find out."

"Why? What does that mean?"

"If he is hebephrenic, which I bet that he is, there is no way he could have had the ability to get all the stuff together that he needs, get downtown, get to Zozobra, put the skull in, and all that. That takes planning and purpose. Hebephrenics have no purpose."

"Yeah, but still, the guy is nuts—"

"He's out there, but he's not your killer," she said more strongly. "I mean, the way doctors diagnose hebephrenic schizophrenia is by two clear indicators: having no purpose to their movement and the laughing at inopportune moments. It's classic."

Gil shook his head. "Lucy, we have some fairly strong evidence against him."

"What evidence?" she asked.

"We have an ID from the family," Joe said, pretending not to notice Gil's disapproving look. "He has a history of approaching neighbor kids, and he used to stop and talk with Brianna and sometimes play—"

"Joe," Gil said sharply to make him stop.

"What, Gil? I didn't tell her who the family member was," Joe said, annoyed and whiny.

Lucy smiled and said to Joe, leaning over to touch his hand, "Gil is upset because you just confirmed to me that you think the skull is Brianna's, and what Gil thinks is that I will use that information. I won't. I promise."

"Gil is such a safety dog," Joe said to Lucy, shaking his head.

"I know exactly what you mean," she said, laughing. "He *is* a total safety dog. On my honor, Officer Gil, I swear I will look both ways before crossing the street." They were both laughing now.

"Anyway," Gil said.

"Sorry," Lucy said, as if she were apologizing to her dad or a teacher for acting up. "Anyway, there is no way a guy with hebephrenia would strike up a friendship with a two-year-old. Even on medication, he would barely to talk to anyone. At most, he would have possibly walked by her. Even then, he would have crossed the street to avoid her or anyone else. Your witness is wrong."

"We have no reason not to believe him," Gil said.

She shook her head again. "You guys have seen your suspect. Does he act like someone who just two days ago could get all the way downtown, put a skull in Zozobra, and then leave bones around town in the middle of the night? And yes, Gil, I know about the stuff at Our Lady of Guadalupe."

Gil looked at her for a minute, wondering how she had found out about the displays, before saying, "We have other evidence besides the ID, but not only that, he fits the profile."

"What you mean is, only a mentally ill person would make displays of Brianna's bones."

"Yes," Gil said, not trying to sugarcoat it. She nodded, but Gil was sure she was not agreeing with him.

"We've really appreciated your help," Gil said.

"Cut out the let's-patronize-the-crazy-lady tone, Montoya," she said, annoyed.

"Lucy," Gil said, feeling like he needed to explain the situation more, "we are looking for a person exactly like him. Now all we need from him is a confession."

She smiled bitterly and said, "It would be better for him and for you if you thought of him as a little green alien. Someone or something that doesn't even resemble us. Because that's what he is."

"That's harsh," Joe said.

"No, it's not," Lucy said, leaning forward in her effort to make them understand. "That's his disease. Look, if he ever gets out of the word salad stage and goes back to simple schizophrenia and then you ask him if he killed Brianna, he might say yes, but he has no concept of what he's saying yes to. If you asked him if the sky was pink, he'd say yes. None of this is real to him. His entire world is completely in his own brain. You have to accept that to him, only things in his world are real. Getting him to confess to a crime in our world means nothing to him."

"It's perfectly legal to interrogate a suspect who is mentally ill," Gil said.

"But is it morally acceptable?"

That was the crux of Gil's problem. It wasn't that he believed Geisler was incapable of the crime, as Lucy suggested. In fact, Gil was convinced he was guilty. It was the immorality of coaxing a mentally ill person into confession.

Joe said, "We could ask the judge to make him go on drugs—"

"Those will take weeks to work, if they ever do—and if they do work, he'll have no idea what he did while he was off them. Then after you ask your questions, he'll go right back off his meds."

"If he really wanted to get better he'd stay on his medication," Joe said.

"No, no. You don't get it. The meds are death to him. They take away everything he is. Everything in the world becomes the same color as beige," she said, adding with a tilt of her head. "Of course, we're in Santa Fe, so everything is already beige."

Gil stood up to signal that they were done, and Joe followed suit. Lucy stayed in her chair.

She asked sadly, "Could you at least dim the lights for him to decrease the stimuli? It'll make him calm down some."

"Sure, I can do that," Joe said as he went out the door, leaving Gil and Lucy alone.

She sighed deeply, then said, "The guy needs a case manager. Or maybe his parents know the deal. And maybe put him on suicide watch. Also, a lot of hebephrenics smoke. I don't know why. That might calm him down too. Honestly, he needs to be in the psych ward at the hospital."

Gil just nodded, then asked, "Is schizophrenia genetic?"

Now it was Lucy's turn to nod. She rested her head in her hands on the table.

"Does your mom or your dad have it?"

"My mom," she said, not even looking up. "My dad left when I was a kid when she was really bad."

"He left you alone with a schizophrenic mother?"

Lucy said nothing.

"Is your mother hebephrenic?"

"No. My brother is. She's a paranoid schizophrenic. Her delusions were about a CIA conspiracy. It's the paranoids who get violent."

"What about you? Have you ever heard voices?"

She smiled sadly and said, "Not yet. Still voice free. But as a child and sister of a schizophrenic, I have a thirty percent chance of developing it."

Now it was Gil's turn to say nothing. They stayed in silence for a minute until Lucy said, "Every day I think that today might be the day I go crazy. That today maybe the little bit of OCD I have will become voices in my head." She closed her eyes and took a deep, ragged breath.

Gil went to stand behind her. He was about to put his hand on her back in the only expression of comfort he could think of, but he let it fall back to his side when Joe opened the door.

Lucy, realizing she would be late to meet Andrea, said good-bye to Gil and was on her way out of the station when she heard someone say to her, "Leaving already?"

She turned, looking for the speaker, and had to peek into the conference room to see Joe sitting at the table, a mass of photos spread in front of him. On the wall behind him was a whiteboard with a list of motives and other case-related tidbits. She decided it was time to make small talk with Joe and maybe memorize the whiteboard in the process.

"So you're Gil's partner," she said with a smile as she walked around the table, taking a casual survey of the papers and photos while stealing glances at the board. "That must be fun times."

"I'm actually learning a lot," Joe said. "He's a really good guy."

"Is this your first case together?" she asked, picking up some photos in front of Joe and looking them over.

"Yep," he said. "We make a good team if I do say so myself."

"And what is it that you bring to the team that is so good?" she asked, teasing.

"I bring the heat, baby," he said. Lucy laughed, but her mind was on something else. She had realized that the photo she had in her hand was of the crime scene of Our Lady of Guadalupe Church. It showed the tower of the church in the background and the statue in the foreground, wearing a necklace that was hard to make out. She would really like to study the photo more.

"What do you do when you're not working?" Lucy asked.

"Hang out at the bar and drink," Joe said slyly.

"Actually, that is my favorite thing to do, too," she said. She leaned in closer. "How about this? How about as soon as this case is done, we go do our favorite thing together?"

Joe smiled. He actually was kind of cute with his red hair and blue eyes. "Sounds good to me."

"Why don't you write your number here," she said, flipping the photo over.

Joe wrote his information down on it and then said in a whisper, "I'll need that photo back."

She smiled. "Just call me and I'll rush right over to give it to you."

She walked away, holding on to the photo and knowing that Joe was watching her when she turned around to say, "Just one more thing. A kind of way to seal the deal, if you will. Just a small favor."

"What's that?" he asked.

"I was just wondering who made the ID of your suspect."

"Aren't you curious?"

"Yes, I am," she said, playfully. "About all things."

He smiled wickedly and said, "It was Alex Stevens, Ashley's boyfriend. Now you owe me."

"Yes I do," she said, laughing, with a sashay out the door of the police station.

"Lucy's really convincing," Joe said. He and Gil were back at the conference table, going over the case once again.

Gil smiled. "Yes, she is."

"Are you two knocking boots?"

Gil rolled his eyes. "I'm married."

"Hey, brother, that ain't no thing."

"Anyway," Gil said, annoyed, "as far as I'm concerned nothing Lucy said changes the fact that Geisler is our guy—but if Lucy was so convincing about his problems, then imagine what a defense attorney will do with it."

"Right."

"We have to nail down our evidence more," Gil said. "The most solid things we have are the ID from Alex Stevens, Geisler's past behavior with kids, and the blood on the sword."

"Yeah," Joe said. "We have to reinterview Geisler's neighbor who made the complaint and the guy's kids."

"First I have to finish the interview with Rodriguez," Gil said, not looking forward to it.

"Sounds good," Joe said, then added uncertainly, "I have to say that before Lucy showed up I was gung ho about Geisler. I mean, I still think he's our guy, but I kind of feel bad for him. I dunno. Everything is screwed up."

Gil smiled. When Lucy was involved, that was the way of things.

Lucy was just outside the doors of the police station when the tears started. She wasn't even sure why she was crying. She was just so frustrated. She fumbled with her car keys, trying to connect with the lock, but eventually got inside. She took a few deep breaths and then pulled out. She needed to meet Andrea in five minutes, but she needed something else more.

She had to have a beer. To calm her nerves. She pulled into an All-sup's and grabbed a Budweiser tallboy, taking a moment to straighten the remaining cans so all the labels would be facing the customer.

As she waited in line, she noticed that a man in front of her was buying a fifth of vodka and cigarettes. The woman behind her was buying three candy bars and a Coke. Lucy wondered if the convenience store clerks ever got depressed because they were the supplier for so many people's addictions. The sugar, the nicotine, the alcohol. Lucy showed her ID and bought the beer. In the car, she looked around to make sure no one was watching, then popped the top and took a big swig. The alcohol hit the back of her throat, and her tension level immediately dropped. She felt her mind slow down from revving its engine to quietly coasting.

She backed the car out and made it to Starbucks only a few minutes later. Andrea waited at the table.

Lucy ordered just plain black coffee and sat down. The two exchanged "good mornings," then got down to work. With Andrea taking notes, they formulated a few questions to ask the residents of the apartment complex. The questions started out innocuous but eventually got to the point. Andrea would start by knocking on some doors and telling whoever answered that she had just gotten to town and was thinking of renting. She would ask about rental prices, the neighbors, the parking, and then ease her way into the "What kind of problems could I expect?" question.

Lucy's suspicion was that one of the local gangs was shaking down other gang members who lived at the complex. She didn't tell Andrea that—she didn't want to scare her—but they did agree that Andrea wouldn't go inside anyone's apartment. She would stay where Lucy could see her. Just casually talking by the front door. If Lucy spotted trouble and honked the horn, Andrea would rush back to the car.

Lucy tried to teach Andrea how to do a cold undercover interview with people. How to smile, look slightly naive, generally be sweet. They sat for a few more minutes while Andrea talked at Lucy in Spanish. Lucy didn't understand a word, but that wasn't the point. Andrea was busy perfecting her cover.

They didn't want anyone to suspect that Andrea was Puerto Rican.

They might wonder why a legal U.S. citizen would live on their side of the tracks, and suspicious people were closed-mouth people.

Andrea was going to do her best to dodge the citizenship question by disguising the way she spoke Spanish. She practiced saying a word's final s, which wasn't pronounced in Puerto Rican Spanish, and tried to talk slower, enunciating each letter and emphasizing the r the way Mexican Spanish was spoken. She eventually started to feel more comfortable disguising her accent. Passing as Mexican.

They went out to Lucy's car, and Lucy panicked for a moment when she realized the beer can was still in the front seat. She got in but waited to unlock the passenger door for Andrea until she'd hidden the can in the backseat. She finally let Andrea in, and they set off toward the apartment complex.

Rodeo Road changed to Airport Road, and the signs changed from Applebee's and Bank of America to taquerías and carnicerías. This was the immigrant side of town, so unlike downtown in its crouched-over oldness. Here there were bright lights and sprawling strip malls. Here there were burrito trucks and ice cream vendors pushing their carts for miles. Most of the signs were now in Spanish, and piñatas filled the windows of the grocery store. This part of town was new, built up quickly over the past ten years. It seemed to be tacked onto Santa Fe's southern edge. Lucy pulled up in front of the Hacienda Linda apartment complex. It was a two-story bland beige structure with steel and cement exterior staircases and breezeways. The cars in front had license plates mainly from Chihuahua. Lucy pulled into an empty spot.

"You ready?" she asked Andrea.

"I think so." Andrea got out as easily as she could given her tight jeans and clicked her way up to the upper level.

Lucy watched Andrea approach the first apartment and knock on the door. A young woman with a toddler at her feet answered. Lucy couldn't hear what they were saying, but the woman smiled and scooped the toddler up into her arms. Lucy took it as a good sign that the woman hadn't slammed the door shut. She could hear Andrea and the woman laughing. Then Andrea, without a look back, stepped through the front door, which closed behind her.

"Oh hell," Lucy muttered to herself.

CHAPTER FIFTEEN

Saturday Morning

Gil's phone rang. It was Chief Kline. Gil let it go to voice mail; he didn't want to get in another conversation about interviewing Geisler until he had a chance to talk to the DA, but the district attorney on call had yet to get back to Gil.

He decided he had stalled as long as he could. It was time to finally interrogate Rudy Rodriguez—and it would be an actual interrogation.

So far, every conversation Gil had had with the various people surrounding this case had been an interview, generally casual and relaxed. Interviews had a script for Gil to follow, but they allowed for a lot of ad lib. In an interview, you mostly played fair, but in an interrogation, you made whatever play would get you a confession.

An interrogation was less malleable. It was much like the work of an expert jeweler who starts with a rough stone, but a hundred small cuts later, that stone has the crystal brilliance of a diamond. Gil would be the one making those hundred little cuts. And they would be painful.

He grabbed a manila file folder off his desk and wrote Rodriguez's name in the tab, then wrote the words CASE FILE followed by a random bunch of numbers. He grabbed some old police reports out of the recycling tray and then put the copier maintenance log and the printer manual in for good measure. When he was done, the folder looked packed full of incriminating information.

Holding the folder, Gil went back into the room with Rodriguez. "Are you ready for us to talk for a few more minutes?" Gil asked. Rodriguez nodded. This was part of the play. Ask the suspect's permission to speak to allow him to feel in charge. Gil, who according to the script had to remain standing for the next part, said, "If you don't mind, let's change the focus of the interview, okay?"

"Sure."

"Great. And thank you in advance for your cooperation," Gil said, smiling. This kindness was a ploy as well, but a necessary one. A person confessed when he felt understood and respected. "It's recently come to our attention that your daughter, Ashley, may have been touched inappropriately by someone close to her when she was younger." Rodriguez started to talk, but Gil interrupted him with a raised hand. "I can guarantee you, Rudy, that our investigation will uncover the truth. In light of that, if you know anything about it, you should tell me now."

"She's my daughter," Rodriguez said with a short laugh that was almost a bark. "Why would I do something like that?" He shifted in his chair and leaned back.

Gil sighed. Rodriguez had assumed that Gil was accusing him, and he had just given one of the most typical deceptive responses. If he hadn't abused Ashley, he would have been emphatic and firm in his denial, not indirect.

Still standing, Gil moved his chair directly in front of Rodriguez to the recommended distance of four feet. It was close enough to ensure intimate conversation but not close enough to make the suspect feel crowded. Gil sat down slowly, the manila folder in his lap. He opened the folder. The copier manual opened to a page about built-in networking operations. Gil looked at it for a ten count, taking a moment to read about the connections necessary for a secure network, then closed the folder. Rodriguez shifted in his chair, leaning back and folding his arms.

Gil took the opposite posture and leaned forward. He kept his facial features soft and sympathetic. "You know, Rudy, I just want to find the truth out about what happened to your granddaughter. I know you want that, too. I see how much you loved her, and I know you would have protected her if you could have . . . and I know you feel the same way about Ashley."

People always thought interrogation was fireworks of accusations and threats, when in fact it was a calm journey of a thousand lies.

Lucy sat in her car, staring at the apartment. It had been fifteen minutes, but Andrea still hadn't come out. Lucy had spent the first five minutes debating what to do, but she knew if a blond-haired Anglo suddenly knocked on the apartment door, it wouldn't help the situation.

A large sign hanging on the side of the building read: PARKING FOR RESIDENTS ONLY. ALL VIOLATORS WILL BE TOWED AT THEIR EXPENSE. Lucy laughed. The sign was a scare tactic. Nothing more. She had yet to meet anyone in Santa Fe who had had a car towed, even in the most egregious of situations.

Lucy looked again up at the apartment, but nothing had changed. She gave it another few minutes before texting Andrea. *R U All Right?* It took a minute, but the reply was a short *Yes* back. That relaxed Lucy a little, and she turned on the radio. The stations all had Western-sounding names, like the Range, the Peak, and the Coyote. She tuned in the public radio station that was playing its usual Northern New Mexico music of rancheros and mariachi. She flipped to the other public station, which was playing powwow music.

A man in a T-shirt and jeans walked past the car, and she quickly turned the station. She wasn't sure that as a white girl she had the right to listen to Indian music. They might think she was one of the many who came to Santa Fe in search of their own tribe—and did peyote and talked of the gift of the Great Spirit while sipping latte.

She watched the man go into the apartment complex office and close the door. He must be the manager. They would have to talk to him later, but only after they had secured a few interviews on the record. What Andrea was trying to get right now was simply information. They wouldn't reveal she was a reporter unless they had to. Instead, Tommy would come back next week and interview the people on the record, hoping that they would talk.

The man in the T-shirt came back out of the office and locked the door. He started walking up the stairs to the upper level just as Andrea, in her laughing way, began to come out the upstairs apartment door. The last thing they needed was for the manager to see her. If he did, and he challenged what she was doing there, they would have to tell the truth. Such was the journalism code of ethics. Lucy swore and got out of the car. In one motion, she pulled her hair out of its ponytail and pulled her blouse down lower.

"Excuse me," she called over to the man, who squinted at her in the sunlight. "I am so sorry to bother you, but are you the manager?"

"I am," he said, checking her out slightly.

"I was wondering if you have any places for rent?" she asked, still smiling.

"I do," he said hesitantly, "but I don't think this would be a good fit for you."

"Why not? What's the rent?" With her peripheral vision, she could see Andrea clicking her way down the stairs. She just needed to stall him a little longer.

"I don't think the element here would be your kind," he said.

"What do you mean?" she said. Andrea was on the ground floor, out of Lucy's peripheral sight, but Lucy could hear the clacking of the woman's heels on the pavement as she made her way to the car.

"This place can get a little rough," he said. Almost as a punctuation to his sentence, she heard Andrea slam the car door shut. They were in the clear.

"Well, okay," she said. "I appreciate the heads-up."

She joined Andrea in the car and said, "Well?"

"Okay," Andrea said excitedly, "so all the cars weren't stolen. They were actually taken away by a tow company."

"Then ended up getting burned?" Lucy said. "I didn't expect that. Maybe it's something against the tow company?"

"No, no," Andrea said quickly. "The tow company is the one burning them."

Gil sat on the metal chair in the interview room, leaning forward in a show of concern—but it was a show, plain and simple.

"Every father wants to protect his daughter," Gil said. "You know, I would kill anyone who ever touched my daughter. She's sixteen and just so beautiful." He would never mention his own daughters to this man. So he made up a fictitious daughter on the spot. "Being a father is all about love."

"I've loved Ashley since the day she was born," Rodriguez said.

"Sometimes," Gil said, "people don't respect how hard it is to be a dad. I think in a lot of ways that it's harder to be a father than it is to be a mother."

"They have it so much easier than us," Rodriguez said.

"Exactly. They don't have to put the food on the table," Gil said, as Rodriguez nodded vigorously. "They don't know about how a father always is thinking of his children, especially his daughters."

"I think of Ashley every second of every day," Rodriguez said.

"Right. I mean, sometimes I feel that my daughter is there for me more than my wife is. And my daughter is just there for me, not nagging, not wanting to know when I'm coming home. She is so easy to be with."

"Ashley and me are exactly like that," Rodriguez said with a satisfied smile.

"Like two peas in a pod," Gil said.

"Right, just like that," Rodriguez said.

Gil nodded. Inside, he was preparing for what came next.

There were levels to interrogation, and Gil rarely had to delve deep. Usually, he would just present the facts of the case in a certain order, tell a few small lies, and then explain that he understood why the suspect committed the crime, and he would have a confession. It was amazing how often that worked.

Gil had lines that he wouldn't cross during the interrogation process even when other investigators did. He wouldn't blame the victim to get a confession. He wouldn't tell a murderer, "I know why you shot your girlfriend. She deserved it." He wouldn't say that because he saw the danger it posed to himself. He worried that if he went to that place of blaming the victim one too many times, he would forget his own morals. He would lose his way. He would become indifferent. He would start to blame the victims as much as the suspects. That way led to burnout. He had seen too many cops hit that point, and Gil had steered well clear of it so far. The burnout rate for interrogators was high—higher than for regular police officers. Gil wondered if that was because interrogators lost a piece of their humanity every time they blamed an innocent victim just to get a confession.

Gil could keep working on Rodriguez, and later today, possibly tonight, he would finally admit what Gil already knew—that he had sexually abused Ashley and could be Brianna's father. Now, though, Gil didn't have time for the long, slow conversations that process would require. He needed that information fast.

The only way to get it was to step over the line he had rarely crossed before.

He would do it. Because it was the only way.

Gil took a deep breath. "You know, I talk to a lot of men in my job, and it's really helped me to see that a relationship with a daughter is special, but there is part of it that no one talks about," Gil said, lowering his voice to a conspiratorial whisper. "When a girl becomes a woman, it is such a beautiful thing. A lot of dads feel that way. You know what I mean?"

Rodriguez nodded but said nothing, forcing Gil to continue. "The girls know that you are looking. They are just tempting you, with their bodies. They want you to look."

"Ashley had this little tank top that really showed off her figure, and I thought about all the boys looking at her, but then I realized that she was wearing it for me, because she wanted me to look."

"I think it's only natural for a man to look," Gil said, "and you know that they want you to do more than look."

Rodriguez just nodded, so Gil went on, "This one time, I was walking past my daughter when she was about twelve and I brushed her breast with my arm. I felt so alive because she was right there and everything was so new and sensitive. And I knew she liked it." Gil thought his insides at that moment might be mistaken for dead if anyone had bothered to look.

"Ashley's breasts got so big. It was like overnight she was a woman," Rodriguez said, shaking his head in wonder.

"What were they like when you touched them?" Gil said. It no longer mattered what he said. He had gone so far over the line that he wasn't even horrified by the words coming out of his mouth.

"So soft and sweet," Rodriguez said.

Gil was so close now; he just needed an answer to the next question, and then he could be out of this cold, dead place. "And when you made love for the first time, what was it like?"

"So good," Rodriguez said, clearly caught up in nothing but the memory, not realizing that he had just given Gil what he needed.

Gil almost breathed a sigh of relief. He had his confession. It would be useless for Rodriguez to protest now that he had never touched Ashley.

Gil knew that a part of him was now gone. He had offered it up as a sacrifice. To get to the truth. He hoped it wasn't a part he might need later.

He wanted to get out of the room. He looked at Rodriguez, who didn't seem human now. More a caricature of a human. Gil felt exhausted, but he pressed on. He didn't want this nonhuman to get back out into the world.

"How old was Ashley when you started spending time together that way?" Gil asked, all business now, purposely being vague about the abuse so as not to spook him.

"She was just turning into a woman," Rodriguez said, not noticing the change in Gil's voice from thoughtful friend to interrogator.

"So about when she was eleven or twelve?" Gil asked. Rodriguez nodded. "And how often did this happen?" Gil asked.

"A few times a month."

"Did you have intercourse with her or just oral sex?"

"We had both—" Rodriguez stopped, finally sensing the change in tone. He looked up at Gil, who stared flatly at him and tried very hard not to let the hatred seep out of his eyes.

Rodriguez just looked defeated now. His lies were gone.

Gil had no sympathy.

The man was a moral coward like all sex offenders. They blamed the victim, while they themselves were guiltless. They believed they had done no wrong, even as those they abused went from happy people to decimated husks. To Gil, sex offenders were almost worse than murderers. A killer stole a life once. A molester stole a life over and over again. Gil agreed with the Catholic Church about the death penalty, except when it came to child molesters. The quicker they were dead, the better for everyone.

"Are you Brianna's father?" Gil asked.

"No," Rodriguez said. The first strong objection he'd made during the entire interrogation. "I'm fixed."

"You had a vasectomy? When?"

"About ten years ago." If it was true, then he wasn't Brianna's father.

"Do you know who Brianna's father is?" Gil asked.

"Tony Herrera," Rodriguez said, giving the same answer as everyone else. Gil could see that Rodriguez didn't have much more information to offer.

"When was the last time you had intercourse with Ashley?" Gil asked.

"Last year when she wanted me to sign the papers."

"Which papers were those?" Gil asked, thinking less about the question and more about getting out of the room so he could finally breathe.

"The papers about Brianna, you know," he said.

"I'm not sure what you are talking about," Gil said, his mind coming back to the conversation.

"The adoption papers that lawyer had us sign," Rodriguez said.

CHAPTER SIXTEEN

Saturday Morning

Lucy zipped down streets and through traffic lights on her way back to Starbucks to drop off Andrea, who swayed and jostled in her seat, although she didn't seem to notice as she told her story.

The woman Andrea had interviewed was Gladys Soliz Portilla. She had been the owner of the second car that had gotten torched. It had only taken a few questions to get Gladys to open up about it. The woman, who had come from Mexico with her young son a few months ago, had her Dodge Neon towed from the apartment parking lot. When she went to get it from the tow company, they told her she had to produce a lease showing she lived at the complex. Because of her undocumented status, she hadn't signed a lease.

"Then," Andrea said, getting into the story, "a man comes to her house and tells her that if she pays him eight hundred dollars, she can have her car back, but that's like almost a month's salary. She tells him that she'll call the police. That's when her car was torched.

I guess when the people couldn't pay, their cars were burned to send a message."

"This towing company sounds lovely," Lucy said.

"It just pisses me off that anyone would take advantage of people like this," Andrea said. Lucy smiled. Andrea was still too young to understand that it was human nature to pick on the weakest among us, and who is weaker than undocumented single mothers? The whole scam relied on the victim not feeling like she could go to the police. When the woman went outside her role as the victim and threatened to call the cops, they proved to her that they were untouchable by torching her car.

"She says that it's happened to at least three of her neighbors," Andrea said, speaking fast.

"What's the name of the tow company?" Lucy asked.

Andrea checked her notes and said, "Ultimate Towing, but I bet you all the tow companies in town are in on it."

"Wait a minute," Lucy said. "We have no proof of that. Let's not get ahead of ourselves." She found it strange to be the one urging restraint.

"Okay, so we need some proof," Andrea said. "We can go over to Ultimate Towing, and I can pretend that they took my car—"

"Hell, no," Lucy said.

"Fine, then, we can stake them out—"

"No way," Lucy said. "Listen to me. That's not how it's done. There is a bunch of documentation we need to get on them first—"

"I'll be careful, I swear—"

"I don't care about that. You'll ruin the investigation," Lucy said, not realizing how cold she sounded until the words were out of her mouth.

Andrea looked a little stung and a whole lot young. The girl was just excited about doing real journalism, and now Lucy was crushing her.

"Okay, look," Lucy said, trying to make amends. "How about we go over to the county impound lot? That's where they would have taken all the burned cars."

Andrea clapped her hands, which Lucy took to mean that she was up for it. What Lucy didn't tell her was that they wouldn't be going into the lot. It was a Saturday, so it was unlikely that anyone would be there to open the gate. Even if someone was, Lucy and Andrea were not official county personnel. They would never be let in. At best, they would be able to peek through the fence before they were scared away by a security guard.

Lucy drove out toward the grassy plains on the highway and turned down a dirt road where an orange sign full of bullet holes read: ROAD PERMANENTLY CLOSED. That never meant anything out here. There would be side roads and dirt paths that meandered out to nowhere. A bird squawked on a telephone line as they drove by.

They turned into the county impound lot, which was fenced with eight-foot-tall razor wire. They pulled up to the closed gate, and Lucy was about to explain to Andrea that they would have to just look through the fence when a little man in overalls wandered out of a small shack and opened the gate. He came over to them, looking at Lucy flatly, then over to Andrea.

"Hi," Lucy said. She wasn't sure what else to add. She hadn't been prepared to make up anything about what her business there was.

He looked over the interior of her car and seemed to see something that made sense to him, because he said, "I'll keep the gate open until you leave." Then he walked away, never asking Lucy who she was or under what authority she was looking at the cars.

Mystified, Lucy glanced around the inside of her car, wondering what had made him decide she belonged there. It took a moment for her to realize that the man had seen her EMS radio firmly mounted on the dashboard and the large sticker on its side that read PIÑON FIRE AND RESCUE. Damn it. She had just inadvertently used her EMS credentials to get info on a story. Lopez would be so proud.

She maneuvered around the dirt lot, which was packed with county maintenance vehicles and cars that had been seized by the sheriff's office during criminal investigations. Lucy drove slowly as they looked at the rows of cars, trucks, and vans. Andrea let out a squeal when she saw a burned car among some weeds. Lucy took it as her cue to stop.

"Okay," Andrea said, getting out, her high-heeled shoes crunching on the dirt. "The woman said her car was a red Dodge Neon."

"Do we know what kind of cars her neighbors drove?"

"Yeah, a Ford F-150. She said it was black. And then a blue Accord."

They walked over to the burned-out car, but it didn't match any of the descriptions. They kept walking in the maze of cars through what was all but a junkyard.

Behind a school bus, near some outer buildings, Lucy found one of the three. This was the blue Accord. Andrea clapped her hands in excitement.

They walked around it. The interior of the car was burned black, with jagged metal plates where the upholstery used to be, and the roof was charred a bright white. The back of the car was surprisingly untouched, and its cobalt blue paint glinted in the sun. The smell of burned plastic still hung around the area. Lucy took a few pictures of the car with her cell phone, then walked to the back of it to write down the plate. She was just starting to note the numbers when she saw a slash of red spray paint on the body of the car. She stared at the uneven paint, which had drip marks along its edges. Even with the bad application, it was possible to make out a few letters that hadn't been eaten up in the fire. Actually, it was possibly a word. Maybe in Spanish, but all she could clearly make out was the beginning letters, EL TIE. The rest was lost to the fire.

Andrea came and stood next to Lucy, looking at the writing.

"What could that say?" Lucy asked.

"Maybe it's 'el tiempecillo' or 'tiempo.' I don't know."

They walked farther into the lot. This time it was Andrea who found the next vehicle. It was the F-150. Or what was left of it. The windows had all splintered, and the dashboard had melted into the floor. The truck hadn't been as lucky as the Accord—it was nothing more than a charred heap of metal.

"Two down, one to go," Andrea said.

When they found the red Dodge Neon, it was sitting in remarkable condition at the edge of the lot. The windows were charred but

intact. Only the hood had been bent up in the fire. Whoever had set
this fire hadn't done as good a job. The red spray paint was easily
visible on the side of the car, even over the endemic red paint. It read
EL TIEMPO DE PAGAR.

"What does that mean?" Lucy asked.

"Time to pay."

Gil left the interrogation room as quickly as possible. He went to the
room next door, which was the other side of the mirrored window,
where Joe was waiting for him.

Before Joe could start on his rant, Gil began one of his own.

"How the hell had we missed this? Ashley tried to have Brianna
adopted?" Gil said loudly and uncharacteristically. "What is going
on?"

He cursed Detective Fisher in his head. Maybe Fisher took his
own life because he knew how badly he had botched the case from
the beginning. Gil took a deep breath. He was starting to get crueler
as this case went on. Maybe that piece of himself he lost was his
compassion.

"No one ever said a word about this," Joe said. "Not Ashley, not
Mrs. Rodriguez. No one." Joe paced to the edge of the room, then
came back more urgently, saying, "I think this guy is full of shit. There
is no way. He's a lying alcoholic pervert who doesn't know what
the fuck he's talking about."

Gil attempted to calm himself but let Joe go on and on until he
was worn out. Gil tried to think of how they missed it. They had
checked all court records and every other conceivable type of official
document. Maybe Joe was right. Maybe Rodriguez was lying.

Gil wanted so badly to be done with Rodriguez. The man was
so far out of the realm of fatherhood. He was nothing more than a
narcissist. He wanted something and he took it. The world owed
him.

Gil knew he had to talk with Rodriguez again, though. He was
the one who had the answers. He was also the only one who had ever
mentioned an adoption. He hadn't gotten whatever family memo
had been sent around telling everyone not to talk about it.

Gil opened the door and went back in. He sat heavily back down in his chair and said as calmly as he could, "Tell me more about these adoption papers."

"The lawyer said I had to sign them as a witness," Rodriguez said, "but the whole thing must not have worked out."

"What makes you say that?"

"Well, because Brianna came back," Rodriguez said. "I guess if it had worked out my baby might still be alive . . ." His eyes got watery, making Gil want to get as far away from him as possible, but he needed Rodriguez to keep talking.

"Do you remember any names that were on the documents?"

"I know the lawyer's name was Anna Maria, because that's my sister's name, but her last name was Roybal."

Gil was confused. "Whose last name was Roybal?"

"The lawyer's. I remember because she had pictures of her kids on her desk. A little boy and a girl. They looked so sweet."

Gil got up and left before his revulsion finally got the better of him.

Ashley Rodriguez had tried to sleep during the night, but the contractions made it hard. At some point around 3:00 A.M., they decided that she was finally in real labor. Then the craziness began. They did more tests and gave her shots for the baby's lungs. They talked about the chances of a vaginal birth since Ashley had already gone through a C-section. She heard the doctor say that Ashley should go through labor as long as possible so her body would release a hormone that was good for the baby. Ashley paid no attention. She was too busy just trying to make it though the contractions, which now made her yell in pain. Her mom was there, strangely quiet and asking lots of questions. Ashley even saw her take a few notes. She couldn't even remember where her mom was when Brianna was born. Well, it had happened so fast. Her dad had been there, though. The thought made her dig her fingernails into the palm of her hand, the pain giving her a moment of relief. She brushed her fingers over the scars on her arms, where she had cut herself. A few were still fresh. She had told a nurse that they were from her cat.

Ashley had been twelve when she tried suicide for the first time. She was going to hang herself like she'd seen in a *CSI* episode. She had made the rope out of her clothes and thrown it around the bar in her closet. She cried for an hour before she finally decided that she wouldn't kill herself then. Maybe tomorrow. She had been telling herself "Maybe tomorrow" for years. Her plan had changed over time, from hanging to a drug overdose to shooting herself with one of Alex's guns. She never talked about it with anyone. She had always heard that people who threaten suicide are just doing it to get attention, but the last thing she wanted was attention. She just had a plan that she knew she would carry out one day. Then she would be free and safe.

She looked at the door of her room, scared and at the same time hopeful that it might open. That her father would be there. She hadn't seen him since just before Brianna disappeared. She wondered if her mom had even called him now. She hoped she had. Because Ashley was feeling alone, and scared, and she knew her father would make her feel better. Like she was the only one he wanted or needed. That she was so special and beautiful. She felt suddenly nauseous. She needed to cut herself. To make it stop. But there were so many people standing around her. So she dug her fingernails into her hand until she felt the skin pop and the warm blood. The thoughts didn't stop, though. They only got louder. Then, blessedly, the next contraction began, searing its way through her abdomen and allowing her to finally smile in relief.

Joe met Gil in the hallway outside the interrogation room.

"Okay," Joe started. "Here's my idea. I say we send this guy back to County because I'm sick of looking at him and then go talk to Ashley and her mom some more."

"Do you think that'll get us anywhere?" Gil asked.

"No. I honestly think at this point pretty much the only thing that's going to get us anywhere is kicking that guy's ass."

"Anything more constructive?" Gil asked.

"I think that would be really constructive for me."

"Well, thankfully," Gil said, "I have another idea. Give me a second." Joe wandered off down the hallway toward the vending machines as Gil flipped open his phone and dialed. His sister, Elena, answered, saying, "Hi, Gil. What's up?"

"Do you know an Anna Maria Roybal? She does adoption law?"

"Hmm . . . maybe. There was an Anna Maria a year ahead of me in law school. Hang on a second, I'll have to go look for my New Mexico Bar Association directory." He heard her making noises in the background as she searched for the book. Knowing Elena, it was likely under a pile of legal papers. He heard her thumping around for another couple of minutes before she said, "Okay, here it is." She gave him the number.

"What time are you coming up?" Gil asked her. Elena would be making the hour drive up from Albuquerque later in the day to go to his aunt's fiesta party.

"I told mom I'd be there at one."

"Oh, hey, by the way, Mom made her adovada," Gil said.

"Fantastic," she said. "I'll bring some empty Tupperware."

They hung up, but Gil didn't put away his phone. He dialed the answering service for the district attorney's office again, and left another message for the on-call lawyer to contact him. Nothing had changed with Geisler. Gil still had to interrogate him, but if the DA didn't return his calls, he'd have to do it without the benefit of legal counsel.

Joe came back, sipping a Mountain Dew. "So what next?"

"A conversation with Anna Maria Roybal."

Lucy made sure to compliment Andrea on her great investigative work as they drove back to Starbucks, where they had left her car. As Andrea was getting out, she was still buzzing about the story, talking about leads to follow and who to interview next.

Lucy finally said, "I promise you, we will get to it next week, when Tommy can help, okay? Just go have a good day off, and I'll see you on Monday."

Andrea said good-bye and closed the door. The car became blissfully silent, and Lucy took a minute to appreciate it. She decided to go on a drive. She took New Mexico 14 away from the city and into the flat plains of the valley, which was ringed by mountains and old volcanoes gone silent. The ground was covered in low, straight grasses that were drying into a haystack yellow in the late summer heat. The flatness gave way to a few roller-coaster hills.

She topped a rise and saw the desert change from a flat plain to rolling hills of piñon and juniper. Below her, at least two miles away, a crease of green cut the ground. She knew there had to be a river there. The entire state of New Mexico was shades of brown and beige that were occasionally struck through by a line of bright shocking green that held the blood of life—water.

In Florida, she had never thought about water, about what it meant. There was just so much of it. Here it was precious. People had been killed over it. The Pueblo Indians and original colonists had built extensive acequia systems that brought the water from the rivers to the farmlands. They had created a complex system of water rights and inheritance laws around it. Each acequia had its own water board and mayordomo. Often, the water boards held as much power as a city government. All for simple irrigation ditches.

As she got closer, she saw that the river actually had water flowing in it, which was unusual. Most rivers were usually just dry arroyos until a fresh rain filled one up to the brim. The water would churn its way downstream until it petered out, and then the riverbed would be dry again. The arroyos varied widely according to landscape. Some had six-foot-tall cliff banks made of sand, while others were as wide as an eight-lane interstate.

Whatever its size, where there was once an arroyo, there will always be an arroyo. That's why native New Mexicans shake their heads at newcomers who build their huge houses on an arroyo plain. That arroyo might not fill up with water for several years, but when it did—because it eventually would—that house would be gone.

As Lucy drove over the bridge that crossed the arroyo-turned-river, she saw that this one had a soft sand cliff for its riverbank, its jagged edge stretching off into the distance like a pink puzzle piece.

She thought about the man Gil had in custody, who was stuck in prison simply because of his mental illness. She wondered which prison was she was referring to—his brain or his cell. Just like her mother's prison, and her brother's. A family history of incarceration because of a simple problem of genetics. Lucy wondered if either of her grandparents had it. Or was it some long-lost ancestor who cursed them with it?

She had never met her grandparents. They had disowned her mother when she was in her early twenties over some money issue. Lucy never knew the specifics. They said it was because she was selfish and immature. They never knew that she was already hearing the voices then. The people in her mom's head told her things. Strange things. They told her that the CIA was watching her and that the government would come for her. She was able to ignore them when she was a teenager. So much so that she finished nursing school and got married.

The people in her head never left her, though. They whispered and yelled and demanded. By the time Lucy was four, the voices started to win. Both her brothers were old enough to go to school, leaving Lucy home alone with a mother who would talk to herself in whispers and write endlessly on newspapers. When her father and brothers came home at night, her mother would pull it together and make a meal, looking drawn and worn, but sane.

By the time Lucy was in first grade, her mother could no longer pretend. That's when the doctors first showed up. A parade of them with a brass band of various diagnoses, eventually settling on schizophrenia. Her mom was put into a psychiatric hospital to get her started on medication.

A week later, her mom came home looking blank, but no longer talking about the commandos. She would stay on the meds for about three months—three blissful months—then decide she was cured and no longer needed them. It was a cycle that would last until Lucy was eleven. Her dad was long gone by then, having left when Lucy was eight. She, her mother, and her brothers had moved without him to L.A., Atlanta, and then Tampa. Once in Tampa they had moved again and again, with the shifts of her mother's mind. So often that Lucy had stopped unpacking. Or making new friends at school.

One day the police came to the house. Her oldest brother, Jason, who was fourteen, had stolen a car. In the middle of a chase with police, he had rolled the car four times. He was in the ICU on a ventilator. Lucy didn't know it then, but that was the day her life would start. When things would go from the daily drone of almost unbearable to almost bearable.

At the time, Lucy and her brothers had been on what they called "mom watch." Their mom was taking her medication, but they knew any day she would go off it. Before she did, they would make a plan of which of them would buy the food, which would cook, and which would make sure their mother didn't try to kill herself—or them— yet again.

By chance, when Jason rolled the car, their mother was fully medicated—and something inside her clicked. She realized that if she went off her medication, she wouldn't be able to care for her son. Soon the usual three months had passed, but her mom didn't start complaining about the way the meds made her feel. Jason was moved to rehab, and her mother stayed with him, going in daily to help him with physical therapy. Eventually the rehab facility offered her a nursing job. Her mom had lost so many nursing jobs over the years, and Lucy knew it was only a matter of time until this one fizzled or exploded . . . but it didn't.

When winter rolled around, they didn't move to a new house, either. They stayed where they were. It took Lucy another two years to believe that her mother might stay on her medication. By then, though, Jason was starting to hear the voices, and it began again, only this time with a different main character. Her mother became a supporting actor where she had once been the star. It might seem ironic that a sick patient—now better—would be forced to care for another patient with the same disease, but it never seemed that way to Lucy. All she could think was that they would never be free.

She turned around near the Turquoise Trail volunteer fire department and headed back toward town. This time she was so caught up in her thoughts, she saw little of the scenery.

She thought of Alex Stevens. She knew nothing about him, but she hated him just the same. She hated him for preying on someone because the person was mentally ill. For lying and not caring that he had just ruined another person's life. And he did lie. Of that Lucy was sure. She just couldn't understand why. She didn't know the ins and outs of the Brianna case well enough to make an educated guess, but she was happy to make an uneducated one—Alex Stevens was lying because he'd killed Brianna. This was his crude way of pointing the finger at someone who had no way to defend himself.

Lucy had no problem with this assumption, because the police had assumed much the same way that a mentally ill person must be the killer. She hadn't realized until that moment that she was mad at Gil. In fact, she was furious. She had thought better of him. She had thought he wouldn't assume that just because someone was insane the person was guilty. She wasn't sure why she had granted Gil such lofty characteristics in her own mind. Maybe it was because in the past—their past—he had been so impeccably honest. And good. And kind. And cute. Lucy sighed. She knew how she sounded—like an infatuated girl. Now she was an infatuated girl who had just discovered her handsome prince was only human.

She got onto the interstate and took the exit toward downtown. She kept to the back roads to save time. She took Paseo de Peralta around downtown and headed toward Fort Marcy Park.

She pulled into the parking lot where Zozobra had stood two nights earlier. The ash from the fire had been cleaned up, as had the field that the hill overlooked. It had been carefully turned back into the baseball diamond that it was. Lucy walked over to the concrete slab holding the metal pole that served as Zozobra's backbone, where a makeshift memorial had been erected overnight for the victim. There was a mass of candles on the ground, some still lit, others long gone out. A rainbow of plastic rosaries twined around the pole. Vases held flowers, some fake, some real, some handpicked from the roadside. There was a large poster that read HEAVEN HAS A NEW ANGEL and a fair number of stuffed animals—unicorns, teddy bears, and dolphins. Two women were at the memorial, standing off to the side. They prayed quietly on their rosary. This was typical of how New Mexicans reacted when a child was killed. A few years ago, when the body of an anonymous little boy was found buried in the sand of an Albuquerque playground, the neighbors of the park held daily rosary services and candlelight vigils. The playground was overtaken by a memorial much like this one. The neighbors said they prayed for the boy because his own family had left him unclaimed and abandoned.

Lucy thought again about Alex Stevens. Had he killed the little girl? Maybe. Probably. She had no proof, though, and she knew Gil would need proof and not just her word that Stevens was lying.

For that, Lucy would have to make use of some of her old-fashioned reporting tricks—and they were called tricks for a reason.

CHAPTER SEVENTEEN

Saturday Afternoon

The front desk called to tell Gil that the lawyer had arrived. He went out to greet her. Anna Maria Roybal had brought her two children with her, a boy about eight and a girl a year or two younger.

"I hope it's all right that they came with," she said. "We were on our way down to fiesta when you called."

"No problem," Gil said as she escorted them through the office and into an interview room.

They all sat down, and the boy immediately started kicking the underside of the table. "Honey, stop that," Anna Maria said, putting her hand on his leg. The little girl squished down in her seat, clearly intimidated by the whole situation. Joe popped his head in and said, "Hey, Gil, if you wouldn't mind, could I take the kids on a tour of the station?"

Gil's response was drowned out by the chorus of "Cool" and "Can we, Mom?" Anna Maria smiled as the kids went off with Joe.

"Well, that was nice of him," Anna Maria said.

"That's Detective Phillips," Gil said with a smile and a hint of sarcasm. "He's just a nice guy."

"So you wanted to talk to me about an adoption?"

"Yes. The one involving Brianna Rodriguez," Gil said.

Anna Maria closed her eyes, as if she were in pain, and put her head in her hands. She stayed that way for a few moments, then said, raising her head, "Before we start this, I want to clear something up. Are you telling me that if I don't answer your questions you will consider it an obstruction of justice and will subpoena my testimony?"

Gil knew what she was asking him to do. It was her way of getting around the strict rules of attorney-client privilege. Anna Maria could not disclose any conversation she had with Ashley. Not even if Ashley died. One of the few exceptions was if Anna Maria was forced to do so by the courts via a subpoena. She was asking Gil to threaten her with the only thing that could potentially free her to speak.

"Anna Maria Roybal," Gil said firmly, "if you do not answer my questions regarding this matter it will be considered an obstruction of justice and a subpoena will be issued forcing your testimony."

Anna Maria nodded, but she looked defeated. She knew what she was about to do—break the very rules that made her profession what it was—and she clearly didn't do it lightly.

She breathed deeply and said, "Then I guess I'll have to answer your questions."

"Tell me about Brianna Rodriguez's adoption," Gil said.

"It was an independent adoption that was structured more like a foster parent arrangement in that either party could terminate the agreement at any time," she said. "It was on a trial basis."

"Who tried to adopt her?"

"Donna Henshaw."

"Who is she?"

"You know, the actress from the seventies. The one with all the self-help books about finding your inner female warrior."

"When did Donna Henshaw contact you?" Gil asked, trying to remember what he knew about the actress.

"When Brianna was eighteen months old, which was about eight months before she disappeared," she said. "Ms. Henshaw didn't want Brianna to come live with her before January for tax reasons. If she had claimed her as a dependent in December that would have hurt her financially."

"Then what happened?"

"Brianna went to go live with Ms. Henshaw at the beginning of the year. I got a call six months later that the adoption had been terminated on the request of Ms. Henshaw, and Brianna got sent home."

"That would have been in June, only a month before Brianna disappeared," Gil said. Anna Maria said nothing. This was why she was talking to him. Because the coincidence was just too coincidental.

"Do you know why the adoption didn't work out?"

"No."

"Do you still have the placement reports?"

"I only have the preplacement report," she said. "The postplacement report was never filed because the adoption was terminated before the trial period was over."

"So it's like it didn't happen?"

"In the eyes of the court, yes."

"How did this work out? I'm confused."

"As I understand it, Judge Victor Otero set it up."

"Judge Otero? He's a municipal judge," Gil said. The municipal judges in Santa Fe were not required to have a law degree. They decided the sentences for parking tickets and barking dog violations. They were elected officials who often played to the masses. Judge Otero was known for his Turkey Fine during the holidays. If the suspect donated a turkey to one of the area shelters, he would waive the ticket. He was also known for less than ethical practices. He was currently under investigation for sentencing driving offenders to a traffic school run by his clerk.

"Apparently he was the presiding judge over some of Ashley's many speeding tickets. I assume she told him about the pregnancy and her desire to find adoptive parents. I guess he knew Ms. Henshaw professionally and that was that."

"Do you know who the father is?"

She looked momentarily confused. "Tony Herrera signed the papers. He's not the father?" Gil should have known that Herrera had held something back during the jailhouse interview. Most inmates did. The idea was to keep a piece of information handy in case you needed a free pass on another crime.

"He says he's not," Gil said. "Why did Ashley's father sign the forms?"

"Just as a witness."

"How did Brianna end up back with Ashley?"

"Again, that I don't know," she said. "My involvement was pretty much over after the paperwork was signed and all the payments were made to Ashley."

"I'm sorry," Gil said, "did you say that Ashley got paid?"

"Yes. Which is a completely normal practice. She was given ten thousand dollars to pay for housing, transportation expenses, post-adoption counseling, and my legal fees."

"Did Ashley ever say why she wanted to do the adoption?"

"You'd have to ask her that." Her answer made Gil curious. It was the first evasive response she had given him. It made Gil think there was something there. He considered it again: Why would Ashley give Brianna up for adoption?

Joe came back in with the kids. The boy was on Joe's back, and the girl was holding his hand, dragging him toward the conference room. They were all laughing.

"Mom, Mom," the boy was saying as Joe eased him off his back, "we got locked in a holding cell. It was so cool."

Anna Maria got up and hugged her kids tight, then kissed the tops of their heads. The boy wiggled away as soon as he could, not understanding how badly his mother needed to be near him right now. To know he was safe. To make sure he knew he was loved. She needed the confirmation that she was not Ashley and her children were not Brianna.

Gil asked Anna Maria to e-mail him all the adoption paperwork, then thanked her and watched the family leave. Joe still had a smile on his face when Gil said to him, "You sure were good with those kids."

"I couldn't wait for those brats to leave," Joe said. Gil doubted him but said nothing about it. He told Joe everything that Anna Maria had passed along.

As they were talking, one of the assistant DAs finally called back. She sounded annoyed. He explained the situation with Geisler to her, but before he could get to the meat of the problem she said, "Send him to the hospital for a mental evaluation. Then on Monday we can get working on making the guy take his meds." She then hung up. Gil got the impression the mental evaluation was more because she didn't want her weekend interrupted and less because of the merits of the case.

He next called the hospital and asked for the psychiatric unit. He and the nurse in charge of the floor discussed how to best get Geisler there. In the end, they decided to have him go in the back of a police cruiser instead of an ambulance. Before they hung up, Gil asked if she could look over Geisler's medical chart and see if there was a phone number for his next of kin. She found it and gave it to Gil. They hung up, and he dialed the number for Geisler's parents. The area code was in Denver. No one answered, and the robo voice on the automated answering messages only said "No one is at home," so Gil left a message asking them to call him back. He didn't give any details.

Next he had Rudy Rodriguez transferred to a holding cell and called the sex offender detective on duty. It took Gil about five minutes to get him up to speed and officially have his unit take over custody. Gil hung up the phone and Joe, who was waiting nearby, asked, "Now what?"

"Let's go talk to Judge Otero."

Joe hadn't enjoyed the time it had taken them to get to the Plaza, where the fiesta was in full swing. Gil had been able to park the

Crown Vic nearby, using his lights to break up the crowd. Even so, they still had to walk at least five blocks through the river of people, which churned this way and that. Gil could only walk a few steps before another cousin, high school friend, or someone from church greeted him. This was what fiesta was all about. Catching up with people. The concept was lost on Joe, who was exasperated by the slow progress. Joe had only lived in Santa Fe for a few years, and his life consisted of the police department. There was no one in the crowd who would push over to greet him because he was an outsider.

They finally made it to the Plaza, its block-sized area of green grass playing picnic grounds for what seemed to be hundreds of people. Food booths selling funnel cake, tamales, and Navajo tacos ringed the edges.

"We are totally getting some of that action," Joe said, watching a young woman walking by eating a funnel cake. Gil hoped he was talking about the food.

"Well, if it isn't little Gilbertito Montoya," Gil heard someone nearby say, using the diminutive form of his first name. Something his own parents had never done.

"Although I guess you're not so little now," said Judge Victor Otero, walking toward Gil with his hand outstretched. He was dressed in the yellow and red satin shirt of the Protectores de la Fiesta. "I bet you no one calls you Gilbertito anymore." Next to him Gil could feel, rather than see, Joe laughing.

"No one ever really did call me that, sir," Gil said, shaking Judge Otero's hand, then introducing Joe.

"I haven't seen you since you were a teenager at your grandpa's funeral," Judge Otero said.

"Yes, sir," Gil said, using "sir" less out of respect than because Judge Otero would expect it.

"You know," Otero said, clapping Gil on the back and turning to Joe, "I knew this boy's grandfather. He was a hell of a judge and one hell of a drinker." Gil said nothing. Otero added, "I even knew his father. Best district attorney I ever met." Otero seemed to expect Gil to thank him for the compliments to his relatives, but Gil felt no sense of obligation. Judge Otero had been one of many local officials that had been over to his parents' and grandparents' houses when he was little. They had been among the movers and shakers of the day. Gil hadn't seen Judge Otero in more than a decade, though. They had no friendship, only an acquaintanceship now well past its peak.

"So when are you going to start coming to the Protectores' meetings?" Judge Otero asked Gil. "Your father and grandfather were some of our most dependable members."

"We have a few questions to ask you, sir," Gil said, still keeping the honorific in order to smooth over the conversation's rough edges, and ignoring the judge's question.

"Yes, I know. Chief Kline already called and told me," Judge Otero said. Gil wished that the chief had told him about his plan to call the judge when they had talked earlier. Gil had decided he had finally avoided his boss long enough and called to give him an update on the case. Kline was disappointed about Geisler being sent to the hospital but didn't blame Gil, instead heaping his scorn on the DA. Gil also wanted Kline's blessing to talk to Judge Otero. Gil didn't really need it, but he thought it was a good idea to give the chief a heads-up. Now he wished he hadn't. The interview might have been more telling if Judge Otero were surprised to see them.

"Do you know Ashley Rodriguez?" Gil asked, seeing if it would throw the judge off his game.

"Of course," Judge Otero said as he shook the hand of an elderly woman as she walked by and murmured a greeting. "She came to my court over a speeding ticket, and I helped her with a personal matter."

"What kind of relationship did you have with her?" Gil asked, thinking he might get an emotional response of some kind.

"Purely professional," the judge said. "Actually, I take that back. I did feel a little fatherly toward the girl the one time I met her. She came into my courtroom and told me she was three months pregnant. I think at the time she was using her condition to try to get leniency on a speeding ticket, and I admit, it worked. She reminded me so much of my own daughters."

"What did you do to help her?" Gil asked.

"Well, while she was testifying, I asked her what her plans with the baby were. I just wanted to make sure she was a fit mother, and she said she was going to give it up for adoption."

"What happened?" Gil asked.

"I had her stay after court was over, and I told her I knew some-one who was hoping to adopt. I gave her a phone number of a friend of a friend."

"You mean Donna Henshaw," Gil said.

"Yes. I simply introduced them," the judge said as he shook the hand of a young man and murmured, "So good to see you."

"That's the only involvement you had with Ashley?" Joe asked.

"That is all," he said.

"Why didn't you come forward when you saw Brianna was miss-ing? It must have occurred to you that the adoption hadn't worked out."

"Of course, if I had been a normal citizen I would have come to you right away," Judge Otero said, "but I'm not. I take my oath of office very seriously. It would not have been within the law for me to tell you about it. I even checked with my attorney to see if there was a way around it." Gil had to admit that he had no idea of the legali-ties of the oath for municipal judge. It could be there was a clause that forbade him from discussing court proceedings.

"Plus," Judge Otero added, "I simply passed a phone number between two people I barely know. For all I knew, Ashley never even called Ms. Henshaw."

"I was told by Ashley's lawyer that you set up the adoption," Gil said, keeping the insinuation out of his voice. He was simply stating a fact.

"The only thing I did was give Ashley a phone number of an ac-quaintance," the judge said without seeming defensive. "I didn't 'set up' anything. All I did was help two people who were in difficult situ-ations."

"And you don't know why Ashley waited until Brianna was eighteen months old to have her adopted?"

"I have no idea," the judge said, smiling as a group of people eating funnel cake and ice cream approached them. Clearly, this was his family. "My guess would be that she found that motherhood was too much for her."

Lucy sat at her computer in the newsroom. It was Saturday afternoon, so no one was around. Copydesk would be arriving in a little while, as would a single reporter. There was no city editor on weekends anymore. That had been one of the first things to go during a round of cutbacks and layoffs. Her fellow editors spent many an hour bemoaning the death of newspapers, but they were old school. They hadn't grown up using the Internet, as she had. Lucy had made her peace with the fact that one day, after most print newspapers closed, she would probably work as a blogger or as an editor for an Internet news company.

She looked at her computer screen as she typed "Alex Stevens" into Google.

She found a MySpace page for an Alex Stevens from the Czech Republic, who, judging from his shirtless photo, was a gay porn star and had apparently just finished filming *The Empire Strokes Back II*.

She tried the search again. This time she added "Santa Fe" next to his name on the query line, yet still came up with only porn-related entries.

She was just getting started. Some people made the mistake of thinking that a journalism degree was the same as an English degree and assumed that Lucy had spent all her time in college writing compositions. In fact, a journalism degree is more like one in criminology. She was taught to read upside down and backward, just in case someone she was interviewing had a file folder on the desk she would have to read surreptitiously. She learned surveillance techniques and the legalities of secretly recording conversations. Her professor had once given her a list of ten names of elected officials. Her job: to track down their Social Security number, describe the interior of their home, get their police record, and find out if they drank coffee. All of that required hours of stakeouts and undercover interviews.

Lucy, still in front of her computer, next went to the newspaper's digital archives. Here she found actual information about Santa Fe's Alex Stevens. He had his own tow truck company, called Alex's Towing, which Lucy found mildly interesting. Her second run-in of the day with a tow company. There was mention in the police notes about a break-in at the tow yard a few years ago and some tools being taken. She read all this as she was actually scanning for the oldest entry under his name, hoping to find a birth announcement. She finally saw it under the year 1979. It told her he was an Aries and had been eight pounds six ounces at birth—and it gave her his birth date.

"Gotcha," she said, smiling in satisfaction at the computer screen.

She got up and walked to the end of the newsroom and went through heavy steel double doors. They were designed to keep the sound of the press and its churning gears restricted to the back of the building. She walked through the dark machine room past the huge two-story press, which was silent at the moment. In the corner, she went toward another room and, using her editor's key, unlocked the door. Inside were a chair, a desk, and a computer. This computer was old and clunky. She turned it on and, several minutes after a start-up that involved lots of whirring and pinging, the screen flashed to life. The computer was locked in here because the information on it was sensitive. The computer's only job was to connect remotely to the Motor Vehicle Division. The connection would give her not only Alex Stevens's driving record but all of his personal information, thanks to the computer's ancientness. This was why it would never be upgraded to a new improved model. The 1997 Driver's Privacy Protection Act restricted access to the personal information in someone's MVD record, but the computer predated 1997, as did its connection. They had been grandfathered in, but it wasn't something the *Tribune* staffers liked to brag about. They weren't even sure if the MVD had ever bothered to check if its back door was still open. She typed in Alex Stevens's name and birth date and was rewarded with his Social Security number, current address, driver's license number, and arrest report.

He had been arrested for two DWIs five years ago, but nothing since then. She wondered how he could run a tow business with a DWI record. She wrote everything down and turned off the computer, which winked out. She left, relocking the door, and went back to her desk.

She had everything she needed to find out about Stevens's life. Now she would use it to get him to tell the truth.

CHAPTER EIGHTEEN

Saturday Afternoon

Gil got Donna Henshaw's address from the MVD and headed toward that part of town. It was in the mountains above the city, where new homes of the rich and famous were starting to encroach on national forest land.

They stopped at a gas station to fill up. Gil stayed in the car but could hear Joe outside beeping at the pump as it beeped at him. Gil called Susan, who picked up on the third ring. There was the sound of a band in the background as she was yelling hello.

"Hey, my mom made carne adovada," he said. Susan and the girls would be going over to Aunt Yolanda's party in a few hours.

"Thank God," Susan said. He heard her yell to the girls, "Grandma made carne adovada," then heard Therese's shriek of excitement.

"Where are you?" he asked. The noise coming from her side was unending.

"We're on the Plaza," she shouted, and Gil heard the girls laughing in the background.

"Really?" he said. "I was just there. I didn't think you were going to go over there after the pet parade or I would have looked for you."

"Oh, the girls talked me into it," she shouted over the noise. "How about you?"

"I don't think I can make it to the party, but—" Gil was interrupted by Susan yelling, "Damn it . . . Joy just spilled her Coke all over herself. I've got to go. I'll call you later." Then she hung up.

Joe came back into the car drinking a Mountain Dew and chomping on some Cheetos. Gil pulled out and headed away from downtown.

"I wonder why Donna Henshaw would adopt a kid?" Joe said, not really asking. "She must be in her sixties, but, boy, back in the day she had some truly outstanding knockers. I mean, like real ones. She put the boob in boob tube."

"How old were you when her shows were on?" Gil asked.

"Oh, hell, I wasn't even born," Joe said, "but they still show her stuff on late night TV. Like her first sitcom, *Can You Dig It?* About her and her two black roommates. That stuff was groundbreaking back in the day, you know. Like when one of the guys accidentally joined the Black Panthers? That was hysterical."

"I don't think groundbreaking is the way to describe it," Gil said. "It was just stupid."

"No way, dude. Now her second sitcom, in the eighties, that one was stupid," Joe said, then took a large drink of his Mountain Dew. "She was, like, this single divorced mom who had a kid, but when the kid wasn't cute anymore they did a *Cosby Show* and brought in a younger kid for the cute factor."

"What was the name of that show?"

"It was called *Word to Your Mother*, like from the Vanilla Ice song," Joe said. "She did some movies, too. I think she was in one of the Conan movies with Arnold Schwarzenegger." Joe's voice went down an octave, and he said with a fake German accent, "What is best in life? To crush your enemies, see them driven before you, and to hear the lamentation of their women."

"Is that from the movie?"

"Dude, that's like a classic line," Joe said.

"Oh please, a classic movie line is like 'What is your major malfunction?'" Gil said.

"You pull out a *Full Metal Jacket* line on me? Well, I'll take some of that action, 'Only steers and queers come from Texas.' What do you say to that?"

"A day without blood is like a day without sunshine," Gil said, smiling.

"Damn, Montoya, I never had you figured for a war movie guy," Joe said, actually impressed. "What about having a wife and kids? You can't watch *Full Metal Jacket* with your little girls around."

"I can when they go to bed," Gil said.

"Oh, I am finally learning all about the secret life of Detective Gilbertito Montoya," Joe said, laughing. "What else do you do when your family is in bed? Make crank phone calls? Or maybe you call up that pretty girl from the newspaper?"

Gil said nothing but was annoyed. "Oh, dude," Joe said as he saw Gil's look. "It was a joke. I don't really think you're porking her. I can't even joke about it?"

Gil said nothing and hoped that, for once, Joe would do the same.

Gil turned onto a dirt road and drove another quarter mile. He expected to see a mansion covered in huge windows that would allow the occupants to admire the beautiful vistas of the valley below. Instead, they came upon a large gate set in an eight-foot-tall razor-wire fence. At the gate was a guard shack painted white. There was nothing to be seen but woods. No house. No cars. No nothing.

A woman came out of the shack and headed toward their car. She was dressed in a cobalt blue turban and pajama-like shirt and pants in the same color. Around her waist was a burnt orange cummerbund with a small jeweled dagger tucked into it.

Gil heard Joe say next to him, "Well, what the hell is this?"

The woman came up to the driver's side of the car, and Gil rolled down the window. The woman, who was Anglo and looked to be about forty, smiled and said, "Blessings and victory upon you."

"Umm . . . thanks," Joe said.

"We're here to see Donna Henshaw," Gil said, showing his badge. The woman smiled again and went back to the guard shack, where she got on a walkie-talkie. They were too far away for Gil to hear what she was saying.

"Is that an AR-15 on the wall?" Joe whispered just as Gil noticed a black rifle with a collapsing stock, laser sight, and pistol grip hanging in the shack.

"I think it's an FAR-15, not an AR-15," Gil said. He unsnapped his paddle holster but didn't take out his .45 caliber Smith & Wesson. Joe hit the release of the shotgun bolted to the dashboard but left it sitting in its mount, then pulled out his own sidearm and held it down by his right side, where it couldn't be seen. Gil watched the woman on the walkie-talkie, ready to unholster his gun the second she made a move toward the FAR-15.

Joe, staring intently at the rifle, said, "I think you're right. My guess is it's a clone. That would mean it has a ten-round magazine and fixed muzzle. I'm also going to guess it has a forward assist, which personally I'm not a fan of."

Gil was watching, but also thinking of where he would put the seven rounds he had in his Smith & Wesson and whether the car door would stop the high-velocity rounds from the FAR-15. If the rifle was fully automatic, and there was no way to tell from this distance if it was, she could get off eight hundred rounds a minute.

The woman finally put down the walkie-talkie and walked back toward them—away from the rifle. She pulled open the gate and motioned Gil through with a wave of her hand. Gil didn't put the car in drive. He didn't want that FAR-15 behind him, where it could be used to shoot at them after she closed the gate and blocked their only exit. She looked back at them, but Gil still didn't move the car forward, forcing her to come back to the car to see what the problem was.

"I just have a few questions for you," Gil said, his hand staying on his gun. "For instance, why do you have that rifle?" He nodded his head toward the shack. Gil could feel Joe next to him, hard with tension, ready to move if things went badly.

"We get bears up here sometimes," the woman said, smiling.

"That's a lot of firepower for a bear," Gil said.

"It's not even loaded," the woman said. "Let me show you." Before Gil could stop her, she turned back toward the shack. Joe was out his door in an instant, standing up next to the car and using it as a shield. Gil saw Joe's gun hand come up and rest on the roof. Gil followed suit, opening his car door, dropping to one knee behind it, and pointing his gun out the open window.

The woman, her back still to them, started to reach inside the shack.

"Ma'am," Gil said firmly and almost quietly, "I need you to step away from the building."

The woman turned. Gil saw her register the guns aimed at her, and she looked surprised. Then scared. She whispered a high-pitched "Oh my" before putting her hands up.

Gil kept his gun pointed at the woman while Joe went to the shack and found what the woman had been reaching for: a fully loaded magazine that could be slapped into the FAR-15.

The woman looked at them with big eyes. Gil reholstered his gun, and Joe took the FAR-15 off the wall, checking to see if it was loaded. It wasn't. They had no right to seize it since they were on private property, but they could hold on to it until they left.

"Who are you?" Gil asked.

"I'm Jind Kaur. I do security here," the woman said.

"How many more weapons like that can we expect up at the house?" Gil asked.

"Umm . . . I don't . . . I'm not sure," the woman said.

"Well, call up there and tell them that if we see even one weapon we are going to have to call the ATF," Gil said. "We are going to take the rifle with us for now, but we'll give it back to you before we leave." Joe put the rifle across the backseat, and then they got back into the car, settling into their seats.

"Are we really going up there?" Joe asked. "Can we call for backup? I really don't want to get killed by a security guard."

"Then it'll be all over the news how we raided the house of a famous actress," Gil said, "and we can forget about getting any information on Brianna."

Gil pulled the car through the gate and down the dirt road.

"What was the deal with the turban?" Joe asked. "What was she? Like Muslim?"

"No, she's a Sikh," Gil said. "You've probably seen them around town. Most of them wear white. I'm not sure why she was in blue. A few thousand live in Santa Fe and Española. Like Adam Granger. He and his parents are Sikh."

"But he's a white guy."

"Yeah, they pretty much all are," Gil said as he drove into a sprawling compound. The road changed from dirt to pavement and became a circular driveway. The main house was multistoried, with light brown vigas jutting out from its sides and a curved entranceway decorated in multicolored tiles. The forest had been cleared away around the mansion for several smaller buildings, all painted an ocher brown and surrounded by neat gardens of late-blooming summer flowers. In front of the main house was a carved wooden sign with GOLDEN MOUNTAIN ASHRAM written on it.

"Where the hell are we?" Joe muttered.

CHAPTER NINETEEN

Saturday Afternoon

Rose Rodriguez sat in her chair, just trying to feel the solid metal frame that was holding her up. She had her feet planted on the ground in front of her and her hands folded tightly in her lap. She was praying hard.

She didn't like speaking to groups of people, but she knew her turn was next. They had started with the usual reading of the preamble and the traditions, before moving on to the testimonials and open discussion. The leader of the group had shared his story first. His life sounded full of adventure and travel, even after he started drinking. Rose was jealous. Of his ability to talk so happily and calmly to the group. Like he enjoyed it. Of course, he had been sober for five years. She had been sober for all of three months.

She'd had her last drink the day after what would have been Brianna's third birthday. Rose had been in the convenience store getting some vodka when she saw the front page of the newspaper in the rack. There was a large photo that showed her and Ashley surrounded by cake, balloons, and people—all there for Brianna. All there praying that she would be found. Rose looked at herself in the photo. She looked like one of the wizened apple-head dolls her grandfather used to make. The caption said the photo was taken the day before. Rose would have to take their word for it because she couldn't remember. Her drinking and her blackouts had gotten worse after Brianna disappeared. Now here was a picture of her, supposedly crying hysterically over her lost grandchild, and she couldn't remember any of it. She had gotten her angel of a sponsor that same day.

She said a quick prayer to her higher power in thanksgiving. She knew that gratitude to her higher power and relinquishing control were part of the journey. Because it was when she thought she was in control that she was actually out of it. Only her higher power was ever in control.

She looked around the meeting room to distract herself from her anxiety. It was a conference room in the cancer clinic next to the hospital, which was why she was able to make it. Ashley was still in labor. Rose had debated not going to a meeting today, but her sponsor convinced her, saying, "That's the committee in your head making decisions instead of you standing back and letting your higher power make them." So she had Alex and Justin stay with Ashley as she went to the meeting. Now she was glad she had gone, but still nervous. She took a deep breath and tried to calm herself. Her sponsor's voice kept running through her head. "You can't do it on your own. You can only do it in these rooms."

The leader finished his testimonial, saying, "If I'd never given up alcohol and drugs, I would have jumped off the Taos Gorge Bridge by now."

The group turned to her. She tried to speak, then had to clear her throat so she could be heard as she said, "My name is Rose and I'm an alcoholic."

Gil parked the car next to a sign that said VISITOR PARKING, and they got out. They stood and looked around for a moment, deciding which way to go. Gil noticed a sign that said GIFT SHOP. They went inside.

The floors were finished in Mexican tiles. The walls were painted gold and lined with carved wooden shelves that held bottles and pots, boxes and bags. The room smelled heavily of incense. Gil's police brain instantly thought that they must be trying to cover up the smell of marijuana, until he realized that this probably was one of the few times in his career that he was around incense being used for its intended purpose. Purification. Music came from speakers mounted on the walls. The sound of a string instrument that Gil didn't recognize rose and fell as drums nodded off and on in the background.

Gil walked over to the nearest shelf and looked closer. Tea, massage oil, DVDs, potpourri, and books. Gil moved toward a circular table in the center of the store. Here was a large framed photo of Donna Henshaw herself that must have been taken at least twenty years ago. It showed the short red hair and crystal green eyes for which she had been famous. Her books surrounded her picture in a loving display. The titles—*The Woman Warrior Within You* and *She Not He*—had been popular back in their day. Susan had even read one of them about ten years ago. It had been about women's empowerment. Susan had made sure Gil knew all the tools needed for a woman to "take back her life." Gil had even gotten her to laugh a little at Tool Four, titled "The One Tool You Need for Satisfaction." Gil had made the obvious sexual joke. That had been a long time ago. When the girls were little. When he and Susan still talked about the books they read. When they still had time to read books.

Gil moved toward another shelf just as a woman came out from the back room. She was young. Maybe in her early twenties. Her bright blue eyes matched the cobalt blue of her turban. The effect was almost disconcerting. She was tiny, no more than five feet tall, but her turban gave her at least an extra foot. It also looked like it might crush her at any moment. In her orange sash was tucked a curved dagger.

Before Gil could speak, Joe said from behind him, "Well, hello." The woman smiled and said, "Blessings and victory be upon you."

"We're here to see Donna Henshaw," Gil said before Joe could start in on anything.

"She is in a conference but should be out shortly," the woman said, still smiling. Her teeth were perfect, and her skin was a soft dusky white. Gil could see why Joe was suddenly next to him, standing straighter and smiling up a storm.

"Can I help you with anything?" she asked.

"We need to discuss a personal matter with Ms. Henshaw," Gil said.

"Of course," she said, eminently serene. "Please let me know if I can be of any assistance. I'm the general manager." The title surprised Gil. He had expected something more in keeping with a religious group—like yogi or acolyte.

"Is the ashram a business?" he asked.

She smiled. "By the grace of the Wonderful Teacher, we have been blessed. We sell mostly online, although the initiates who come here for yoga retreats do buy a fair amount as well."

"So what's your whole thing here?" Joe asked. Gil had to admire his straightforward attitude.

"We are a group of Sikhs who run a center for teaching kundalini yoga, and, of course, we all are still students ourselves of the Guru, victory be upon him."

"Okay, so I didn't understand a lot of that," Joe said, "but I'm going to pretend I did."

She laughed, which was what Joe had wanted, and he asked, "How did you end up here?"

"I was studying at the University of Connecticut when I heard my yoga teacher speak of the Guru—victory be upon him—and his belief in the woman warrior, so I moved here to further my studies," she said.

"Is the Guru here?" Gil asked, thinking that he might be a longshot candidate for Brianna's father.

"No. He will arrive here in a few weeks for his yearly visit," she said.

"What were you getting your degree in?" Joe asked, moving closer to her.

"I was studying for a master's in business finance," she said, "but I realized that the material instincts of the world were not conducive to my path of light. Here I am free to embody the saint-soldier that is written about in the sacred scripture."

"Are you like . . . I mean, do you consider yourself a member of the Sikh religion, like, from India?" Joe asked.

"Yes, I am of the Pure Ones, the chosen who began their fraternity in the 1700s," she said, proudly. By that time, Gil thought, his family had already been living in Santa Fe for almost a hundred years.

"So by 'pure one' do you mean virgin?" Joe asked.

"You know what?" Gil said quickly. "We are going to wait outside for Ms. Henshaw. I'm sorry for the trouble. Please just let us know when she can see us."

Gil sat in the driver's seat of the car with the door open. The fresh mountain air was crisp and light. A yellow swallowtail butterfly floated past, catching a ride on a slight wind.

Gil was on his cell phone with Adam Granger, who was saying adamantly, "They're not Sikh. They came with the rest of the Sikhs in the 1970s when my parents came, but they split off from the ashram in Española at least twenty years ago when I was still a kid. I remember that was a really hard time at the compound. My mom cried a lot."

Sitting in the passenger seat next to Gil, Joe typed away on his smartphone, where he was supposed to be looking up everything he could find about the Golden Mountain Ashram.

Gil asked Adam, "How are they different?"

"They have some Sikh traditions, like they do meditation and yoga and they've all taken Sikh names, but they're a straight-up cult," Adam said. "I had a couple of friends who went in, and they were just gone. They were so swept up in it."

"So they are a fundamentalist Sikh group?"

"Sort of. Sikhs believe in a universal God and equality between the genders, but those guys at Golden Mountain have taken the whole female warrior concept to the extreme."

"How do you mean?"

"Like they only allow women to join their ashram, but their guru is a guy, which I think just sounds weird. Like he has his own harem or something. On top of that, they do hard-core weapons training. They are told that if they sleep more than six hours a night, they are committing evil. They have to get up at 3:00 A.M. to meditate and chant for four hours, then take a cold shower and eat only certain raw foods. Stuff like that."

"It sounds almost like brainwashing," Gil said.

"It is. They really try to stress the 'us versus them' concept, where they are the chosen ones and everyone else is an idiot," Adam said. "Honestly, they're just a bunch of white people who know nothing about Sikh religion. They're just making stuff up."

"Thanks," Gil said, getting ready to hang up. Then Adam said, "I'd be careful up there, though."

"Why?"

"They really believe in the warrior tradition of the Sikh, so they're probably armed to the teeth. Sikhs are famous for their use of weapons."

Gil laughed. "I really wish I'd called you before I came up here."

They hung up, and Gil looked toward Joe, who was watching a yoga video on his phone. Gil told him what Adam had said, but Joe didn't seem to be listening. He was too intent on his video, which he kept his eyes on while saying, "There's instructions for kundalini yoga online . . . looks like lots of turning back and forth with your arms up and some squatting . . . pretty much it's slow motion Jazzercise. I could totally do this." Joe said, turning his torso back and forth in the car, mimicking the movements on the tiny screen.

"What else did you find out?" Gil asked.

"Okay," Joe said, finally putting down his phone and picking up his notebook. "So there are no complaints or arrests or anything that involves the ashram or Donna Henshaw or the property. They seem to not cause any trouble. They don't have any concealed-carry gun permits, but as for nonconcealed guns, who knows." That meant they had no way of knowing how many guns might be at the compound since New Mexico only requires a permit for concealed guns.

The women at the ashram could legally buy as many as they wanted to stockpile.

"Oh, here's one for the Did You Know category," Joe said. "Did you know that Sikhism is the fifth largest religion in the world? It's even ahead of Judaism, which is number six."

"I did not know that," Gil said. "What else?"

"As far as cults go, these guys hit on every mark," Joe said, reading off his notebook. "They do mind-altering stuff, like meditation. They follow a strict diet. They believe they are the chosen ones. They create their own words for their practices. Basically, they believe all you have to do is humbly follow the Guru and all the bad things will disappear. Which sounds really nice. There also are several blogs and chatrooms from people who have left the cult. They say that the Guru claims the right to initiate all of them into the sect, which I guess includes taking illegal drugs. Another woman says that members are expected to take part in lesbian activities with other members. This is my kind of cult."

"Anything else?" Gil asked.

"Yep. Here's a little-known fact—this ashram is one of seven in Santa Fe, including one in Lamy that has horses. I'm not sure if that means the people meditate with the horses or if the horses are the ones doing the meditating," Joe said, closing his notebook. "What is it about Santa Fe that attracts these people? And why does it always involve movie stars? We have more celebrities around here than fake tans at a porno convention. Like Ali MacGraw, Shirley MacLaine, Julia Roberts, Jane Fonda."

"They claim there's vortexes around the city that open up to another universe," Gil said, "and then there's an alien landing pad up here in the mountains somewhere."

"Cool, dude. Can we go look for that?"

"Just as soon as we find out what happened to Brianna."

Gil heard someone walking behind the car and turned to see the young woman from the gift shop, who said, "She will see you now."

Joe and Gil followed the woman to the main house.

"So are you related to the Sikhs in Española?" Gil asked, wondering how she would describe them.

"They are the White Sikhs," she said firmly. Dismissively. "They are from the outside and they will always be from the outside."

"You aren't?" Gil asked, trying not to sound too challenging.

"Yes, because I follow Guru Sanjam Dev, victory be upon him. He is the first and only true Guru since the writing of the sacred scripture."

The path beneath Gil's feet crunched, and he looked down, stopping. The ground was littered with spent cartridges. A few were clearly .22 caliber from a rifle, while another was a .50 caliber, possibly from a machine gun.

"You've got shell casings here from some really diverse weaponry," Gil said.

"The Guru likes us to honor the traditional Sikh warrior code," she said. "As the scripture says, we accept death, and give up any hope of life."

"That's really dark," Joe said.

"Many of our most famous warriors were women," she continued. "My own name, Rajindar, comes from Princess Rajindar, who led three thousand warriors to save her cousin after he was captured."

"So what you're saying is, don't mess with Sikh women," Joe said.

"One of my favorite prayers is 'May I die fighting with limitless courage,'" she said. "Of course, you are warriors, too. I'm sure you understand this."

"Yeah, I'm not so much about the die fighting part," Joe said. "I'm more about death by old age."

"Is the .50 caliber from a rifle or a machine gun?" Gil asked.

"Actually a handgun, the Desert Eagle," she said.

"That's a whole lot of recoil to deal with," Gil said, trying to gauge her knowledge about weapons.

"Yeah, and not much of a magazine," Joe added. "It has like, what, seven rounds?"

"That's the same that your Smith & Wesson has," she said, nodding at the gun at Gil's waist. Clearly, she knew her guns.

They entered the house through a glass sliding door, and she told them to take off their shoes. Inside was a white room with gold carpets. On a dais covered in heavy red brocade fabric and surrounded by gold pillars was a large book covered in gold cloth. Rajindar clasped her hands together in prayer, then bowed to the dais. Gil wondered if the book was the sacred scripture she had talked about.

They followed her up a flight of stairs to a loft with sweeping windows that overlooked the valley. In the center of the room, a woman in a blue turban kneeled next to a small, low table that held a steaming teapot and cookies covered in sugar crystals. The woman looked athletic and had obviously had plastic surgery. Her cheeks were shiny and tight. Her eyes shone bright green even from this far away. This had to be Donna Henshaw.

"Blessings and victory be upon you," Rajindar said to Ms. Henshaw, then bowed low.

"Victory belongs to God alone," Ms. Henshaw said, bowing low in return.

"Hello, Ms. Henshaw, I'm Gil Montoya with the Santa Fe police, and this is Joe Phillips," Gil said. He normally would have offered his hand to shake, but he thought better of it here.

"Please, I prefer the use of my spiritual name—Mai Bhago Kaur," she said, smiling. Unlike Rajindar's, her smile seemed fake. Perhaps it was a side effect of the plastic surgery and Botox.

"Should I call you Mai?" Gil asked as he sat on the floor cross-legged.

"Of course," she said, "and thank you for honoring me by using my spiritual name. Such a name is a vibrating blessing that summarizes our journey of intent here on earth and strengthens our journey to a higher destiny."

"Oh, interesting," Gil said, not quite following. He was about to move on to the next question when Joe interrupted. "Who gives you your name? Can you just pick one? Can I be Lancelot Skywalker?"

She smiled dimly at his attempted humor. "Because of my spiritual path, Guru Sanjam Dev, victory be upon him, gave me my name, but for others you can go to our Web site and for a small offering have your name selected."

"Seriously?" Joe said, laughing. "You get people to pay for a random spiritual name generator?"

"May I inquire as to why you are here?" she said, looking at Gil, clearly done humoring Joe.

"We were hoping to talk to you about Brianna Rodriguez," he said.

She nodded. "Of course. Before we get to that, I would like to present you with a small gift for taking the time to visit me in my home."

"Of course," Gil said, purposely mimicking her words, thinking she was going to offer him tea and cookies.

Instead, she said, "Detective, I am honored to be the acharya, the meditation teacher, here at our humble ashram. In order to gain this honor, I had to share my gift of purpose with the world, and it is this gift that I now focus on you."

"Thank you," Gil said.

"My gift tells me that you are not in harmony with your own subjective reality," she said, smiling kindly. As a teacher would at a slow child.

"You know, I tell him that all the time," Joe said.

"We all follow a path of spiritual enfoldment, which at its core reveals that we all are of the same divine essence," she said serenely. "Detective, I assume you're Catholic, with all your wonderful saints, who were seekers of the unequivocal truth, as well as your Holy Trinity, which are all located within your own body. We worship not only the sacred light but also the sound, and through this we will find our own personal God realization. Look inside your sacred temple and visit the inner planes to see that this is true."

"Yes, of course," Gil murmured, not sure where she was going with this. He added, "Thank you," when she seemed to be expecting him to say more.

"I am fortunate to have a tincture of ginkgo, saffron, and rose that was placed in darkness and then allowed to absorb the vibratory force of an amethyst over seven days. It will increase your biological energies and encourages the cohesion of cells, organs, and glands. I will give this to you."

She got up easily, her limbs supple and her muscles taut, probably the effect of decades of yoga. She opened a cupboard and took out a small, dark bottle with an eyedropper stopper. She sat back down and handed it to Gil, who took it. It had no instruction label of any kind. Gil wasn't sure if he was supposed to drink it, rinse with it, or rub it on.

He set it down next to him and said, "Thank you," again, realizing that it was the third time he'd used the phrase in roughly two minutes of conversation.

CHAPTER TWENTY

Saturday Afternoon

Lucy was just finishing up her research at the office when one of the copy editors came over to her desk.

"Oh, hey," he said to her. "I'm glad you're here. I know it's your day off, but I was going to call you about the SWAT thing last night. We need a brief about it."

"What SWAT thing?" she said innocently.

"I don't know," he said. "All I know is that Lopez told me to ask if you were there, and if you were, to tell you that you should get a brief in."

"Umm . . . no, I wasn't," she said, lying.

"I could have sworn I heard your voice on the police scanner."

She just smiled, hoping he couldn't see the deception in her eyes, and said, "Nope." She kept smiling until he walked away.

As fast as she could, she jotted down all the information she had on Alex Stevens. Then she pulled the crime scene photo she had gotten from Joe out of her purse and went to the Xerox machine to make a color copy. The machine took a minute to wake up, and Lucy tapped her foot, hoping to get out of the building before someone challenged her about the SWAT call again. She would have gladly forgone making the copy, but she knew Joe could call her and ask for the photo back at any time. Remembering the wolfish look on his face, she guessed it would be soon.

She stared at the bulletin board over the copier, which held a conglomeration of photos, memos, articles, and a single earring looking for its owner. There was also a bright blue flyer with the headline THE MEDITATION OF RELEASE. It was the same flyer that she had seen that morning at Santa Fe Baking Company advertising a meditation class tomorrow night. It was stalking her. She read it over again and smiled once more as she read the final words that promised "there will be no chanting."

The copier finally sprang into action and spit out a single copy. She pulled it out of the machine's tray, went back to her desk, and quickly shoved it in her purse. She hurried out the back door before anyone else could stop her. Out in her car, she sighed in relief and put her head on the steering wheel. She wouldn't be able to keep dodging questions about her life at the fire station. She would have to tell Lopez that she simply wouldn't do it. She wouldn't be a frontline spy for him.

She drove home and pulled into her driveway. Nathan's car still was sitting in front of her house, which was exactly what she wanted. She went inside and put on a low-cut shirt with sequins. It was a bit much for this time of day, but it would do the job. Especially when put over a push-up bra, which in her case had to be a push-up, pull-forward, and thrust-out bra in order for her to have any kind of cleavage. She then put on dark jeans with cowboy boots. She spent the next forty-five minutes doing her makeup and her hair. She was still sporting hot curlers when she called Alex's Towing.

A man she assumed to be Alex Stevens answered, and she said, "Hi. My boyfriend's car, I mean my ex-boyfriend's car, is in front of my house, and I need to get it towed." She laughed and said, "You know how it is."

"Yes, I do," the man said, then asked for her address. She gave it to him and hung up.

She went to her closet and got out her black purse, which she had bought when she was a cops reporter in Orlando. The purse had perfect pockets for holding all of her investigative equipment. She transferred her wallet to the new purse and added a small makeup kit in case her face needed retouching later. She slid a voice-activated tape recorder into one of the side pockets. She said the word "sibilance" a few times, then rewound the tape and listened to make sure it was working. Next, she put a reporter's notebook and three pens in another side pocket. Then she transferred over all her notes about Alex Stevens and the copy of the crime scene photo. It was only then that she realized she had left the original photo lying facedown on the glass of the copier at work.

She swore fast. The words ran together, tripping over each other into a continuous sound. She sounded like a singing cicada on a dark night. The photo was part of an official investigation, and to take it, she had flirted up a storm with a man who expected to get it back. Now it sat in the Xerox machine, just waiting for the next person to hit COPY.

She had no time to go get the photo now. The tow truck would be there in just a few minutes. Her only hope was that no one would try to make copies. That was possible, given that it was the weekend and the newsroom was dead. She sent up a little prayer, then finished packing her purse, adding a flashlight, camera, Mace, and a pocketknife.

You never knew where an investigation might lead you.

"What can you tell us about Brianna?" Gil asked, massaging his leg as it started to cramp from sitting on the floor.

"Actually, we changed her name to Bibi during her time with us," Ms. Henshaw said.

"Okay," Gil said slowly, "and what can you tell us about Bibi's life here?"

"She was unable to enjoy our simple ways," she said.

"How do you mean?" Gil asked.

"As you would expect, we conduct satsang to discuss our dreams—"

"What's a santag?" Joe asked. Gil wasn't sure if he was mispronouncing it on purpose.

"It is in satsang where we join each other and listen to a discussion of light," Ms. Henshaw said.

"So, it's a lecture," Joe said.

"Yes, where we use hu to seek out our divine essence—"

"Use what?" Joe asked.

"Hu. It's how we connect through uplifted voices with our divine self and thus our own—"

"So hu is a song," Joe said.

"Yes, of devotion."

"Why can't you just say that—"

Gil interrupted. "When you were doing the hu, what happened with Brianna?"

"She was unable to concentrate on her inner path and found the only way to express herself was through crying."

"She was two," Joe said slowly, his tone implying that Donna Henshaw was a bizarre new breed that had never interacted with humans before. "No two-year-old can sit still through church."

"Detective, we are not a church—"

"That much I got—" Joe said.

"So Brianna was crying during the satsang," Gil said over Joe, trying to get her to continue.

"The Guru concluded that she had too much tamas."

"I'm not sure what that means," Gil said.

"A person who is tamasic has a force inside that is overwhelmed with shadows and resistance. It is the most negative of the three gunas, which refers to someone's tendency. It is marked by destruction and darkness."

"And you thought Brianna had this?"

"Yes."

"Is there no cure?"

"We tried many remedies, but to no avail," she said, still almost monotone. "We even held an eternal waters healing rite."

"Yeah," Joe snorted. "When the eternal waters healing rite fails, you are just screwed."

Gil finally had enough. "Detective Phillips, you need to go outside."

Joe stomped out.

"I'm sorry for that," Gil said, trying to make his voice calm.

"I'll say a prayer for him," she said calmly.

"I'm sure he'll appreciate that."

Lucy was sitting outside on the curb next to Nathan's car, when the tow truck with ALEX'S TOW written in red on the side pulled up. She got up and smoothed her hair.

A stocky man got out of the truck. His gray T-shirt was pulled tight over his chest and only partially tucked into his pants. The jeans were slick in places with oil and dirt. Like so many other Santa Fe men, he sported a small, thin mustache that followed the curve of his upper lip.

Lucy went over to shake his hand, saying, "Hi, I'm Tina. You must be Alex."

"Nope," the man said as he wiped his hand on his jeans before reaching out for hers and shaking it. "I'm Manny."

Lucy smiled as her insides crumbled. She had assumed that Alex Stevens would be the driver. She never considered that he'd send someone else. Especially after she had been so charming and cute and happy and chirpy on the phone.

"Where's Alex?" she asked, no longer trying to be cute or happy.

"His girlfriend is having a baby," Manny said. "I'm just helping him out by driving his truck."

It was a good excuse, but it didn't make Lucy feel any less crushed. She had done so much research. She knew all of Alex Stevens's information. She knew the names of his brothers and sisters. She knew what position he played on his high school football team. She knew the address of the house he grew up in as a kid. Damn.

Her plan had been to get Alex talking. She was going to pretend that she knew him. Hence the need for all the personal information. She was going to tell him things about his past that only someone you grew up with would know. He'd inevitably try to hide his ignorance by insisting that he did remember her from high school. As any old friend would, she would ask him about his life. The story about Brianna would come up. Then Lucy, in all her innocence, would say, "Hey, didn't I see you at Zozobra on Thursday?" Then she would sit back and see what happened. He would have probably denied that he was there, but the man had killed Brianna. He would have had to be at Zozobra to watch the skull burn up in the fire. Or he put it in one of the public boxes. Either way, his face would tell her all she needed to know.

Now her little fantasy was over. Instead of getting the chance to feel smug and righteous as she exposed a killer, she would have to watch Manny and his greasy pants while he hooked up Nathan's car.

"We did try to make it work," Ms. Henshaw was saying. For the life of him, Gil couldn't remember her new name. "I even bought Bibi this gorgeous handmade lace from Ireland to use as her turban, but she refused to wear it, or any turban for that matter."

Gil thought of Joy and Therese at two years old. They had always refused to wear their sunhats, although Joy did become strangely attached to hers after she found out it worked better as a purse that she could fill with rocks and leaves. It always made Gil smile to think of Joy, barely able to walk, wandering around the house and the grocery store carrying her purse full of dirt.

"Do you know anything about Brianna's, I mean, Bibi's father?" he asked, wanting to get into the meat of the interview.

"Nothing," she said.

"How were your interactions with Ashley?"

"There were none," she said, pouring some tea for herself but not offering him any. "We never even talked on the phone. It was all handled by the lawyer and Judge Otero."

"Judge Otero said he introduced you two."

"I believe he meant that he introduced the idea to Ashley, and she contacted a lawyer," she said. Gil found it interesting that she would so readily put words in Judge Otero's mouth.

"How do you know Judge Otero?"

"We've been close friends for a while," she said with a smile. "We share some common beliefs." Gil found it hard to imagine that a local politician and this woman would ever even find themselves in the same room together.

"Do you think it's a coincidence that Bibi disappeared just a month after you sent her back home?"

"No, it's clear to me that she ran away."

"Really?" Gil said, having a hard time not using the same tone that Joe had earlier. The more Gil talked to this woman, the happier he was that she never ended up adopting a child. She had no concept of children. A two-year-old could never form the intent it took to run away.

"Of course, it would not have been Bibi's fault," she said. "It would have been part of her tamas."

"Do you know anyone here who has a particular interest in or dislike of the Catholic Church or the Virgin Mary?" Gil asked, not wanting to get back into the tamas discussion.

"No," she said. "We stress the inclusivity of all faiths. Any talk against another religion would hurt God and therefore hurt ourselves. The path of all is the path of one."

Gil seemed to have gotten all the answers he needed, so he stood up to leave, his legs creaking. He asked her if she had copies of the adoption papers, and she promised to e-mail them to him. The second such promise he'd gotten today. He thanked her and headed toward the stairs but stopped short.

He turned to ask one last question.

"Do you ever worry that you are creating a cult here?" he asked.

She smiled slightly, but it didn't reach her eyes. Doubtless, she had heard the question before, although likely it had been phrased as an accusation. "All we are creating is a community," came the automatic-sounding reply.

Lucy was sullen as Manny hooked up Nathan's car. The large tow truck had a hard time maneuvering in the narrow street.

"This old part of town sure is tricky," Manny said good-naturedly as he dropped the tow bar and eased it under the car. He latched a tie around the driver's-side tire and got in the truck.

Lucy wavered. Her plan had been to say she needed to tag along with Alex Stevens on the pretense that when they dropped the car off, she would have to give Nathan his keys, which she still hadn't found. That story was necessary just to get her into the confines of the tow truck with Alex Stevens and get him to answer questions. Now that was moot. She could just let Manny take the car over to the Cowgirl, and she wouldn't have to get involved, but thinking of the Cowgirl made Lucy crave a beer. She decided to get into the cab. She was paying for Nathan's car to get towed, after all; she might as well get a ride to a bar out of it. She told Manny she was coming along, and he shrugged.

She stepped up the side stairs to the truck's cab and, using one of the hand hooks in the ceiling, hauled herself bodily inside, just like a little kid would, and got settled in her seat. Manny pulled away from her house, and Lucy surveyed the inside of the truck. The floor was covered in various papers, which were getting crushed under her feet. The center console had more papers, a stun gun, a crowbar, and several wire hangers.

"Where to?" he asked.

"The Cowgirl," she said. "It's where he works."

"I hope you don't mind if I smoke," Manny said as he lit up a cigarette. She wondered how he could hold the slender cigarette tightly while wearing heavy work gloves. He looked to be in his late twenties, probably about the same age as Lucy.

"So have you been a tow truck driver for long?" she asked, trying to be friendly.

"About ten years," he said, exhaling smoke. "I started when I was eighteen."

"Have you always worked for Alex?" she asked, starting to warm up to the conversation. She could at least pump him for information about Stevens.

"Nah," he said. "I only help him out sometimes, like when we have a really tough repo or like now when he's gotta be over at St. Vincent's."

"What do you do when you're not working for him?" Lucy said, only intending to make small talk about Manny himself before she started in on the questions about his boss.

"I work for a couple other companies in town, you know, just when they need me," he said. The tow truck jostled over a pothole, and Nathan's car behind them jumped. "So what do you do?" he asked, smiling. Clearly, her makeup and push-up bra were still doing their work, not realizing that Alex the big fish had gotten away.

"Oh, I'm an editor," she said, not bothering with her cover ID.

"Huh," he said. She could tell by his response that he didn't know what an editor did.

So she said, "I work at the newspaper, and I just read over stories that the reporters write."

"That sounds interesting," Manny said, taking another puff.

"I used to be a reporter, though," she added lamely, as if that were the more respectable of the two jobs.

They sat in silence for a moment. Something suddenly occurred to Lucy and she said, "Do you ever work for Ultimate Towing?"

"Yeah," he said. "All the time."

"Really," she said, smiling at him. "I think you might know one of my friends. Her name is Gladys. She lives over on Airport Road at Hacienda Linda."

Manny sat still. He didn't seem to notice when a clump of cigarette ash fell onto his leg.

Gil walked back to the car. Joe sat in the front seat, texting on his phone. Gil got in and headed back toward the gate, where Gil returned the rifle to the woman in the guard shack. He drove out onto the main road before he said, "Joe, I'm not sure what to do with you sometimes. Your temper is getting to be a problem."

For a few seconds Joe said nothing, then, looking out the passenger window, he said, "They dumped Brianna because she cried."

Gil didn't answer him.

Joe shifted in his seat to look at Gil. "You know, after Brianna went missing, I was trying to think of all kinds of stuff I could do to help. Like I would go out on my days off and walk the arroyo. Or I'd bring the guys watching the house coffee or whatever. Stuff like that. So this one night I looked up stuff about preemie babies, 'cause, you know, Brianna was a preemie. I was thinking, like, maybe if someone was, like, holding her and we could say she was a preemie with special needs . . . whatever. Anyway, I was reading these chats from all these moms who were just at their wits' ends because their preemie babies cried like all the time. It's this really common thing."

"So you're thinking maybe Donna Henshaw was right about Brianna crying all the time?"

"No, what I'm saying is if that bitch had spent ten minutes on the Internet and saw that preemies outgrow that stuff, that she might not have sent Brianna back to her house to get killed."

They didn't say another word until they reached the station.

Manny said nothing. So Lucy waited. She thought it was a good sign that he didn't deny knowing Gladys. That meant that he was probably part of the scheme to rip off the immigrants.

She waited a little longer before saying, "Her little boy is just so cute. It must be hard for her to come here to a foreign country and start over. And you know why she did? So her kid would have a better life. You know, I don't think my mom would have done that for me." She silently sent an "I'm sorry" to her mom. "Would your mom have done that for you?"

They pulled up in front of the Cowgirl. It was late in the afternoon on Saturday, so the patio was full of people eating dinner and having a few beers. Lucy was worried that she had waited too long to say anything to Manny. Or that she had used the wrong approach. She had to keep the conversation casual, though. She couldn't let him know the newspaper was investigating. He might tip off the other players. All he had right now was Lucy seemingly asking about her "friend." Nothing more.

He got out of the cab without saying anything as he dropped the car slowly down to the ground. He unlashed the tire and put the tow cables back under the truck. The whole time, Lucy stood nearby. She tried to radiate friendliness and understanding so he might open up. He was climbing back into the cab when Lucy said, "How much do I owe you?" He stopped, half hanging out the door, looking at the floor of the cab. Lucy put her hand on his arm. "Let me buy you a beer," she said. He surprised her by nodding.

They sat away from the bar at a small table. She saw Nathan at the bar chatting up a blond girl. Tonight he was wearing black jeans with a black T-shirt and a different pair of combat boots but the same spiked collar.

Across the table from her, Manny took off his gloves. His hands were callused and cut. It was probably an occupational hazard when you worked with metal and steel and horsepower.

"So tell me about your work" was all that Lucy said. The first rule of journalism was to start with open-ended questions. Nothing yes or no.

"It's fine," he said. "Usually . . . it's fine."

"And what about it isn't fine?" she said, her voice going up at the end of the sentence to make it a question. The waitress came by, and Lucy ordered two Coronas.

"Just some stuff," he said, staring at the table.

Lucy sat back and looked at him. He wanted to confess. He wanted to tell her about how he was preying on people. She just needed a way to tell him it was okay without actually saying anything. She needed him to trust her.

"Are you married?" she asked.

"I was, but she cheated on me," he said. Lucy quickly saw the minefield there and took another path.

"Do you have any kids?" she asked, hoping the question wouldn't blow up in her face.

"Yeah, two," he said, still downcast.

"Really?" she said with lots of enthusiasm. She would have to carry all the emotion of the conversation until he took up his part. "How old are they?"

"One is five and the other is seven months," he said, ever so slightly showing signs of coming back to life.

"Those are such great ages. Are they boys or girls?"

"I got one of both," he said, almost expressing some interest in the conversation.

"That is fabulous. Do you have pictures?"

He reached into his back pocket and took out a leather wallet slick with grease. He pulled out two pictures, both showing the same tiny girl, who looked about ready to start kindergarten, and a little smiling baby.

"They are beautiful," Lucy said, looking up at him. He nodded slightly. "He has your eyes."

Manny smiled a little and asked, "You think so?"

"Absolutely," she said as their cold beers arrived.

They were out of the conversational woods and headed into more open territory. All she needed to do was ask a few more questions about his family. Maybe a couple about his mom and where he went to high school. Then, maybe, if the time was right, she would ask him again about Gladys.

CHAPTER TWENTY-ONE

Saturday Night

Gil stood by himself in front of the whiteboard in the conference room. On it, he had started to write a timeline of Brianna's adoption. So far, all he had written was Brianna's birth date—May 5—and the day she disappeared, July 18, two years later. His goal this morning had been to find Brianna's father so he could prove the blood on David Geisler's samurai sword belonged to the little girl. Now it was almost 6:00 P.M., and he was no closer to figuring out who her dad was.

He had called Dr. Santiago on the way back to the station to check if Ashley had delivered the baby. He left a message for the doctor, who called him right back, saying, "I am sorry, but you won't be able to talk to Ashley until after she delivers. She can't even form a sentence right now . . ." Dr. Santiago didn't finish the statement. Instead, she said, "Look, I can't give you any additional patient information, except to say that that Ashley is completely effaced. She should be delivering soon."

He had to talk to Ashley. It could not be put off any longer. He thought about interviewing her over the phone, between contractions, but whereas that might have been possible yesterday, today they simply had too many blanks for her to fill in. Plus, how do you ask a woman who is giving birth to identify the father of her first baby, a baby who is now dead? There was no proper etiquette for that conversation. Besides, if Ashley was anything like Susan, all she was doing between contractions was praying for them to stop.

Next Gil called another department in the hospital to get an update on David Geisler. The nurse on duty told Gil that Geisler was safely in his room, but he wouldn't get a mental evaluation until tomorrow.

Officer Kristen Valdez, dressed in street clothes, popped her head in the door and said, "Hi, Gil. I just got off shift and wanted to see if you needed some help."

"Thanks, Kristen," Gil said. "Actually, I do need something that is fairly simple. That way you can get out of here and still make it down to fiesta." He asked her to put together a folder of anything she could find out about Donna Henshaw and the Golden Mountain Ashram. She took a few notes as he talked, then went back out to the main room to work.

That left Gil to stare at the timeline on the whiteboard. He was wondering about the exact date Donna Henshaw had adopted Brianna when Joe came in saying, "Dude, I wanted you to be the first to know. My new spiritual name is Mr. Ram Inder Singh."

"You went to their Web site and paid to get a name?" Gil asked.

"Hell, yeah. This shit is too funny to pass up. I got you a new name, too."

"Really?" Gil said.

"Yep. You are now Mr. Baba Singh, which, in case you can't tell, is a dork name. I have the cool name—I'm Ram."

"How much did all of this cost you?"

"Twenty-five bucks each."

"You spent fifty dollars to get us new names because it was funny?"

"Hell, yeah."

"You clearly don't have any wife or kids to support."

"That's exactly why I'm never getting married again. It takes all the fun out of life, doesn't it, Mr. Baba Singh?"

Gil ignored him and looked back at the whiteboard, trying to fill in information on the timeline.

"Hey, Joe—" Gil said.

"Hey, who? You talking to me?"

"Okay, Ram. Do you remember how old Brianna was when Donna Henshaw adopted her?"

"She was twenty months old," Joe said, "and twenty-five months when she went back to her mom. Then later she disappeared at twenty-six months on July 18." Gil added all that information to the timeline.

"I don't know about you," Joe said, "but I've got even odds that Donna Henshaw or one of the women from the Vigilante Vagina League up there in the mountains has something to do with this."

Gil, intent on the timeline, ignored Joe, instead thinking he should include the date Ashley met Judge Otero, who was in essence her adoption broker.

"Hey, Ram, do you have the court dates for Ashley's speeding ticket?" Gil asked.

Joe pushed a few papers around on the table. "Okay, here it is. It looks like the first one was September third."

"Her first one?" Gil asked. "How many times did she appear in Judge Otero's court?"

"Umm . . . it looks like four times."

"I thought Judge Otero said he only met her once," Gil said. "Do you have your notes from his interview?"

"Hang on a second," Joe said as he fumbled for his notebook, then read, "'I did feel a little fatherly toward the girl the one time I met her. She came in my courtroom and told me she was three months pregnant.'" Joe added, "I guess the judge meant to say 'one of the times I met her.'"

"Maybe," Gil said, putting the dry-erase marker down. "Or maybe Judge Otero meant to lie to us."

Lucy would never have guessed that Manny was a lightweight. They were only three beers into the night, and he was already sloshing drunk, telling her everything she wanted to know. Lucy, on the other hand, who had been matching him drink for drink, wasn't even buzzed. Maybe she had discovered her superpower: drinking men under the table.

She had already gotten the names of the ringleaders out of Manny, as well as how much money they were taking in. After beer two, she had started to write everything down since Manny was beyond caring, and she checked to make sure the tape player was still recording, just in case.

"You know the worst part," Manny was saying, "these are my people. My grandparents came here from Mexico in the 1950s. I'm taking advantage of my own people."

Lucy didn't even need to ask prodding questions anymore. He just kept talking. At one point, while Manny was cursing out his bosses, Nathan came over; he had finally noticed her from the bar. He had the decency to look ashamed.

"Hey" was all he said as he stood by the table with a white bar apron tied around his waist.

"Hello," Lucy said. "Your car is out front. I had it towed here."

"You are the best," he said soberly. Sincerely.

"Thanks. So I'll see you later," she said, turning back toward Manny, who was still swearing about his boss.

"Can I, you know, buy you a drink?" Nathan said. Lucy wanted to turn him down. It would have been best for everyone. Then again, it was a free drink, and he did owe her.

"You could get me another beer," she said. He smiled like a hound dog and went back toward the bar.

"Me, too," Manny yelled after him.

Lucy looked at the time on her cell phone. It was 6:13 P.M. They had been sitting here for almost two hours. She wondered how much more information Manny had to offer. What he had already told her had been great but limited, since he was nothing more than an underling, not a key player. He admitted towing two of the cars from the apartment complex to the tow yard, but he hadn't asked any of the tenants for money and didn't even know that the cars of those who wouldn't pay had been burned.

She really just wanted to leave, but she would need to get Manny home safely.

She heard a cell phone ring nearby. It was a fast hip-hop song. It wasn't hers.

"Manny," she said to him, nudging his elbow. "That's your phone."

"Oh man," he said, looking at the caller ID. "It's Alex. He's probably calling to see what his cut of the tow was, that chingada madre." Manny didn't answer it and turned off the ringer.

"I thought he was your buddy."

"Yeah, right," Manny said. "He's nothing but a liar."

"Why do you say that?" Lucy asked. Suddenly something occurred to her. "You mean that Alex Stevens is mixed up in the immigrant thing?"

"Him? No," Manny said, scoffing. "He's worse."

"Really?" Lucy asked, leaning in closer. She had almost given up hope of pinning something on Stevens.

"Yeah, we do all these repos together that are five hundred dollars each, and he never pays up," he said, shaking his head.

Lucy leaned back, disappointed. "Is that all?"

"What do you mean, 'Is that all?' He owes me almost a thousand dollars. Plus, he's always bragging that he owns the tow truck and I'm just his driver, but I'm going to get my own truck some day. I just have to save up . . ."

"Then why are you still working for him?" she asked, back to wondering if it was possible for Nathan to take any longer with her beer.

"I don't know," Manny said. He turned his head slowly toward his phone and said, "I'm going to call him and tell him I quit."

"That's a great idea," Lucy said, mostly out of annoyance at Alex Stevens. She knew encouraging one of his employees to quit was a petty way to get back at him, but then that was who she was.

Ashley Rodriguez wondered why someone had put a copy of that day's *Capital Tribune* in her room. Maybe a nurse thought she would want to read about the bones found in Zozobra. The bones that might be her daughter.

The doctors had told Ashley that Brianna might have developmental problems because she was a preemie, but she had been perfect for the first four months. They had been happy then. Brianna was all smiles.

Then one day she stopped eating and started crying, screaming and gagging. It wasn't just once in a while, either. It was every day. For hours and hours.

Her parents didn't help much. Her mother called Brianna spoiled and would ignore her when she cried. Her father would jostle Brianna too roughly. Ashley would have to make up little excuses to get Brianna away from him, especially when he was drunk.

Her father reminded her of Judge Otero, whom she had met just before she found out she was pregnant with Brianna. He had helped her with a speeding ticket. He hadn't asked for much in return.

A few weeks later, she was in his court again, on another speeding ticket. By then, she was pregnant and Tony was in jail. She was only seventeen, had no job, and had just dropped out of high school. She broke down in tears as she told the judge. He had a clerk show her back to his office after the session. He sat behind his big wooden desk and gave her a way out that she had never considered—adoption. He even gave her the name of someone who wanted to adopt. She recognized it. It was the name of someone famous. It was something she couldn't consider, though. She still thought that Tony would get out of jail and that they would live together in a trailer on his parents' property. One big happy family. Still, she kept the phone number tucked away in a drawer, just in case.

Of course, by the time Brianna was born, she knew Tony would never get out. She found herself in the middle of the night trying to soothe Brianna, wondering what it would be like to be free and childless again. She had thought that as Brianna got older, things would get easier, but they didn't. When Ashley started feeding her baby cereal, Brianna choked her way through the first few bites, then threw the rest. Ashley, in tears, would plead with her baby to eat, but Brianna wouldn't, and she would only sleep two or three hours at a time. Ashley took Brianna to the doctor, who said that there was nothing wrong. He told Ashley that she just needed to be more patient. Ashley tried.

One night, though, when Brianna was nine months old and lay screaming on Ashley's bed, all Ashley could do was to yell "Shut up" over and over. She knew her parents wouldn't wake up. They never did. Ashley threw her clothes around her room and smashed a ceramic bear. Brianna kept crying. Ashley grabbed a pillow and pushed it down hard on her daughter's face. She only held it there for a moment, but after realizing what she had almost done, she grabbed her daughter and held her tight. Ashley swore she'd try harder.

By the time Brianna turned a year old, her father was getting more insistent. More needy. He called Brianna his little angel and kissed her constantly, even though his scruffy beard scratched her soft baby skin. For her first birthday, he bought Brianna some Bonne Bell lip gloss, "to make her look sexy," he said.

That was when Ashley called the phone number Judge Otero had given her. It took a few more months, but suddenly Brianna was gone. Ashley had her life back.

And her daughter was safe.

Lucy was helping Manny get out of his chair, so they could leave, when Nathan came over to them.

"So, are you taking off?" he asked solemnly.

"Yeah, we got places to go, people to see," she said, trying to brush past him.

"Here's the thing," Nathan said slowly. "I can't let you drive. I've seen you drink four beers."

"I'm not driving," she said. "Manny here is." He swayed slightly at the mention of his name. She realized just how ridiculous that sounded as she looked at Manny in his drunken stupor. She clearly hadn't thought this through.

"Okay, I see your point. I guess we need to call a cab," she said.

"Well, if you want to wait, I'll get off in fifteen minutes," he said. "I can take you both home."

Lucy sighed. She sat Manny back down in his chair as she retook her own.

Twenty-five minutes later, Nathan appeared, sans apron, and the trio of them walked outside to his car.

"So, can I get my car keys?" Nathan asked, looking at Lucy expectantly as Manny leaned against the car for support.

"I don't have them," she said, confused. "I never found them. I thought you'd have your extra set with you."

"Why would I carry around my spare keys when my car was at your house?" Nathan said.

"All right, fine. Whatever," she said, getting annoyed. Nothing with Nathan was simple. "We'll just get a cab, unless you can drive a tow truck."

"Yeah, of course I can," Nathan said. "I worked one summer as a heavy equipment operator for the Forest Service, remember?"

Nathan got the keys from Manny and opened the truck up. Lucy climbed into the passenger seat and started clearing out the papers and other junk so all three of them could sit in the cab. She threw the stun gun, crowbar, and wire hangers on the floor, but her OCD took over when it came to the mess of papers, which looked to be mostly invoices and other towing-related documents. She gathered them up into a bundle and then straightened them into a neat pile, which she held on her lap as she sat in the middle of the seat. Nathan helped Manny into the passenger side, then got into the driver's seat, saying, "Where are we going?"

"Well," Lucy said, "I guess we'll take Manny home, and then you can drop me off at my house—"

"We can't do that," Manny said. "Alex will kill me if I let someone else drive his truck when I'm not there."

"How about we go to my house and get my car keys," Nathan said. "Then we can come back to get my car, leave the tow truck here, and then I can drop you both off at home."

"This is making my head hurt," Lucy said. "I guess that's the best plan. Then Manny will have to get a ride tomorrow to pick up the tow truck."

That settled, they pulled away from the bar. Manny fell asleep during the ten-minute drive, while all Nathan wanted to do was make small talk. She tried to keep her answers to one or two words until they pulled up in front of a house that seemed slightly run-down, although it was hard for Lucy to make anything out in the darkness without the punctuation of streetlights.

"I'm not really sure where my extra set of car keys is," Nathan said, as he started to get out. "This might take a minute."

Lucy sighed as she watched Nathan go into his house. She looked over at Manny, who was happily passed out leaning against the glass of the passenger-side window. She switched on the overhead light and dug around in her purse for her cell phone, to see if she had any messages. No one had called. Bored, she started to look over the stack of papers in her lap. Most of them were invoices and other records for work Alex Stevens had done with banks, which were trying to recoup their losses on defaulted loans by repossessing their cars.

She flipped through the records and realized some went back two or three years. Did Alex never clean out his truck? She started looking at the pages, thinking maybe she'd find something devious, like some evidence of fraud against one of the banks. As she searched, she checked the dates closely. She found some from last year and a few from the month of July. The month Brianna went missing. That made her stop. Maybe the papers might reveal some suspicious behavior patterns in the days after Brianna disappeared. Maybe they would show that Alex was back at work the next day, making him seem nonchalant about the lost little girl.

She didn't expect to find what she did.

A paper from New Mexico Savings Bank confirming the delivery of a Chevy Tahoe to Socorro on July 18 at 1:43 P.M. The day Brianna disappeared.

Lucy's brain worked as fast as it could under the influence of four beers. Socorro, in the southern part of New Mexico, was at least two hours away. If Alex Stevens was in Socorro at 1:43 P.M., he would have had to leave Santa Fe at noon and would have arrived back at 4:00 P.M. Lucy tried to remember what time of day Brianna went missing, but it wouldn't come to her. She slid out of the truck through the driver's door, still holding the document. She went up to Nathan's house, his dark yard now haphazardly illuminated by the chunky pieces of light that came through the large front windows. She walked in without knocking and quickly took in the shabby furniture before yelling to him, "Hey, do you have today's newspaper?"

"No," he said, coming into the living room, "but go check the neighbors' recycling bin on their porch. I just steal it from there."

She went back outside without asking him how his search for the keys was going, then realized he hadn't told her which neighbor to steal from. She surveyed the nearest houses as best she could using just the light thrown from Nathan's house, looking for one with a porch. The next-door neighbor had a small porch with the dark lump of what could have been a couch on it. She went back to the tow truck, grabbed her purse off the seat, and fished out her flashlight. She glanced over at Manny, who was still sleeping, then closed the driver's-side door quietly. She switched on her flashlight and crept up to the neighbor's porch. On it was a green recycling bin. She pushed past a few empty cans of cat food and pulled out that day's *Capital Tribune*. She scanned the front page quickly by the light of her flashlight. She knew Tommy had mentioned in his story what time of day Brianna disappeared. She opened the newspaper to the jump page. There in black and white it said, "It was 2:00 P.M. when the family said they first noticed Brianna was missing." Lucy felt a surge of vindication. She said, "Gotcha," to no one.

The light from Nathan's house flashed off, and the street was in the dark once more. She tucked the newspaper under her arm, along with the bank document, as Nathan came out of the house. Turning off her flashlight, she made her way over to him in the dark.

"We're going to the police station," she said to him as they met at the truck door.

Gil was still in front of his computer, looking over the adoption paperwork he'd gotten from Donna Henshaw, when three people walked in the side door with a patrol officer, who said, "I met these guys in the parking lot looking for you."

The tallest one, an Anglo man, had on a spiked collar and was dressed in black; the only skin visible that was not covered in tattoos was his face. A smaller man who was darker and looked Latino had a mustache and was wearing a dirty gray T-shirt and jeans. It was Lucy who stood out. She sparkled in a sequined top and tight jeans. Her hair and face were done up as Gil had never seen them.

"Hey, Montoya," Lucy said, coming over to his desk. "This is Manny. He sometimes works for Alex Stevens as a tow truck driver. I got a ride with him tonight and found this in Alex's truck." She slapped a piece of paper down on the desk in front of Gil. "This is solid proof that Alex Stevens is a liar. Now, as a bonus prize, Manny here will tell you all about another crime involving Ultimate Towing. Just give him a ride home when you're done."

With an angry look at Gil, she started to walk out, but turned back to them and said, "Oh, and one more thing . . . I fucking told you so." She smiled smugly and left with the man in the studs following her, while Manny stared fearfully at Gil and Joe.

CHAPTER TWENTY-TWO

Sunday Morning

Gil, his shirtsleeves rolled up, was at his desk early. He had already checked in with everyone. Ashley was still in labor. David Geisler still hadn't had his medical evaluation. Liz and Adam had no new information. Liz asked, "When are you going to give me DNA from Brianna's dad?" Gil had no answer for her. He then called his mom, who immediately started talking about Aunt Yolanda's party yesterday.

He had stayed at the office until 11:00 P.M. last night interviewing Manny, whose full name was Manny Luis Reyes. It had taken a while for Manny to open up, mainly because it appeared that Lucy hadn't asked him if he wanted to talk to the police. Instead, she had technically kidnapped him and brought him to the station. He finally got Manny to talk about Ultimate Towing, but quickly realized it was a case for the major crimes division. Gil turned the investigation and Manny over to the detective in charge of that unit.

Gil had called Alex Stevens last night, politely asking

him to come to the station, without telling him what it was about. At first, Stevens protested, saying that Ashley was still in labor, but Gil insisted. Finally, Stevens said he would meet them at the office at 8:45 A.M. the next morning. Not that night. Gil relented. Stevens would be easier to interview if he came in on his own terms.

Gil was using the last few minutes before Stevens arrived to take a look over the paper in his hand. It was the one Lucy had slammed down on his desk. He had a call in to the New Mexico Savings Bank to see if they had any more information about the situation surrounding the car Stevens had repossessed. Gil had already talked to the car's former owner, waking him up. The man confirmed that a tow truck driver who matched Alex Stevens's general description had been at his house about noon on July 18 of last year and taken his Chevy Tahoe.

Now they were just waiting for Stevens. Joe sat across from Gil, texting away on his phone.

Gil pulled down his shirtsleeves and put his suit jacket back on. He took a bolo tie out of his desk drawer. It had been his father's tie and was made of a large piece of turquoise and some coral set in silver. In New Mexico, a bolo tie was considered as formal as a necktie; it was even the state's official neckwear.

Joe, who had been watching Gil, said, "What's the deal?"

"We have to get ready for the interrogation," Gil said, taking his paddle holster off and putting it in his desk drawer.

"Wait, you said, 'We have to get ready.' That implies that we're both doing the interrogation. Not just that you're doing the interrogation."

"That's right," Gil said.

Joe nodded to himself, looking pleased. "You think if you look all professional this guy is going to be more convinced to talk? Is that what all your books tell you?"

"Pretty much."

"Cool." Joe stood up, tucked his T-shirt into his pants, and locked his gun in his desk drawer. "I guess I need to start leaving a tie and dress shirt here, huh? This T-shirt just makes me look like your schlubby sidekick."

Gil ignored the comment and asked, "So what should we think about before we get started with the interrogation?"

"That we are cool as shit?"

"Besides that," Gil said. "Remember to always look for the good qualities in the person. Everyone has something decent in them."

"So you find that decent thing and then exploit it?"

"Pretty much."

"Anything to get a confession, huh, Gil?"

"Almost anything," Gil said, thinking back to his interrogation of Rudy Rodriguez. The decent thing he had exploited in Rodriguez was his love of Ashley, even though it was love that was twisted beyond recognition. He sighed and then tried to get his head back into teaching mode. He wanted Joe to be able to get some experience out of all this mess. "So what should we take into account before we go in there?"

"The guy's got no real experience with the system, which gives us a much better chance."

"Why?" Gil asked.

"Because he won't know our games," Joe said. "He won't know what to expect. If he's had a lot of priors and been interrogated about other crimes, he'd know exactly what to say and not say."

"Exactly," Gil said.

"However, I do want to point out that Fisher interviewed the guy a dozen times," Joe said.

"That could definitely impact this interrogation," Gil said. "Do you have a baseline on him? I've only met him twice, and I wasn't really concentrating on gauging his responses." Gil kicked himself for that now. Maybe if he had been paying more attention yesterday during Alex Stevens's ID of David Geisler, he might have caught something. Getting a baseline was really one of the fundamental rules of interrogation. The idea was to just talk to suspects about inconsequential things and see how they respond. Judge their eye movements and posture. Then, when you are interrogating them later and they deviate from their baseline, you know that you just asked a question that was not inconsequential to them.

Joe thought for a second before shaking his head. "Nah. Fisher handled all that kind of stuff the first time around. Plus, I wasn't thinking like a detective back then."

"Okay," Gil said. "So we need to get a baseline. How should we go about doing that?" He was purposely asking straightforward questions to get Joe's head into the right mindset. Make him think like an interrogator.

"Umm . . . I could take in an interview form and just ask him basic questions like his name and address and see how he responds," Joe said.

Gil smiled. "That is exactly why the interview form was created. Just to make it easy for the interrogator to get the baseline." The side door to the station opened, and Alex Stevens was escorted in by an officer.

"So, Joe," Gil said quietly, "grab the interrogation form, and why don't you get started? I'll watch from the other side of the mirror and then come in when it's time to move to the next part."

Joe smiled but looked nervous. "Let's rock and roll."

A blast of noise from the pager woke Lucy up from a dead sleep for the second time in three days, but this time she was alone in bed, having had the good sense to let Nathan only drop her off and not sex her up.

She listened to the dispatcher call out an MVA with injuries on the interstate as she jumped out of bed. She ran naked around the room trying to find some clothes. She found two socks that actually were crunchy with foot sweat and no underwear. She suddenly remembered the laundry she had done in the dishwasher. She ran to the kitchen and opened the dishwasher door. She was greeted by the smell of mold. Or maybe it was mildew. Or maybe she didn't care, because she was naked and didn't have any underwear or socks. She ran back to her room and pulled on her work pants, minus underwear, and then pulled on her work boots, minus socks. The only underwear she did have was a bra, which, truth be told, didn't have all that much work to do. She pulled on her EMS T-shirt, grabbed her handheld radio, and ran out the door. She was in her car and down the street before she realized she hadn't done the Breathalyzer test. She'd had just the four beers with Manny, so that should put her blood alcohol level around .02. She hoped.

She and Nathan had left the tow truck in front of the Cowgirl, and then Nathan had taken her home in his car, which, she noted, actually did have gas in it. More than half a tank, in fact. That had made it quite easy to turn down his advances the night before, since he had clearly lied.

Gerald was already in the ambulance as usual when she arrived and jumped in. They didn't say much as he drove, instead listening to the sheriff's deputies on the radio who called in as they arrived on the scene. All of a sudden, she heard one of them yell into the radio, "Expedite, expedite, EMS, expedite," basically a mayday. Gerald hit the gas, the sirens, and the lights in one motion, and Lucy called in on the radio. "Santa Fe, this is Piñon Rescue One, we are expediting. I repeat, we are expediting."

She looked over at the speedometer as Gerald nosed the heavy ambulance past 80 mph. They were on a straight open street with little traffic. An "expedite" call was bad. It meant that everything was going to hell in a handbasket.

Lucy braced herself as Gerald turned onto the interstate on-ramp and gunned it up the hill. On the radio, several deputies at once started calling out mile marker numbers to identify their location. Lucy tried to make sense of what they were saying. They kept talking on top of each other until the Santa Fe dispatcher said firmly, "This is Dispatch to all units. Clear the channel. I repeat, clear the channel." There was silence for a moment until Dispatch said, "Piñon Rescue One, what is your ETA to scene?" She heard Gerald next to her mumble a swear word, something she had never heard him do before. He did so now out of frustration. He could not get the ambulance to go any faster, and whoever was on scene needed medical help. Now. The deputies would not be freaking out unless they were desperate.

Lucy checked the map book and made a guesstimate. "Santa Fe, this is Piñon Rescue One, ETA is approximately five minutes." The dispatcher responded, "Copy that, Rescue One. All units, traffic can resume on this channel." Gerald topped the speedometer out at 95 mph as the ambulance flew down the interstate. There was little traffic out this morning, so there were fewer drivers to frighten as a huge ambulance came hurtling toward them. Finally, in the distance, Lucy could see the strobing lights of the sheriff's cars. She picked up the radio and said into the mike, "Santa Fe, Piñon Rescue One on scene."

Now for the horror, she thought.

While Gil waited for Joe and Stevens to get situated in the interview room, he picked up a file folder on his desk and started to flip through it. It was all the information Kristen Valdez could find on Donna Henshaw, the Golden Mountain Ashram, and Guru Sanjam Dev, from property records to background checks. It turned out that the exalted guru, who was Anglo, had had a run-in with the law when he was in India. He was accused of defrauding female believers by charging them hundreds of dollars for an audience. Gil only had time to read a few pages of the file before he had to go observe the beginning of the interview.

He went into the room with the two-way mirror, which was kept darker than the room on the other side. He sat at the table and took notes while Joe asked his baseline questions. Alex Stevens seemed fairly relaxed but tired. Gil wondered how much sleep he'd had in the last few days. Gil remembered when Susan was in labor, he didn't sleep at all. Stevens's tiredness might work in their favor. It would be harder for him to mask his reactions.

Joe was finishing up, so Gil grabbed some blank paper and a pen, put the paper in the manila file folder with Stevens's name written on it, and went to the interview room. He knocked before he entered, to give Joe the ability to say "Come in," thus cementing his authority. Joe would need all the help he could get in that department since he was dressed in a T-shirt and jeans.

Gil went in, but instead of sitting down he kept standing and said, "Alex, do you know why you are here today?"

"Umm . . ." Stevens said, "I guess to talk about the guy you arrested?"

What Gil said next was basically the same introductory statement he'd made to Rudy Rodriguez the day before. "It's recently come to our attention that we have been misled regarding some things about the day Brianna disappeared. I can guarantee you, Alex, that our investigation will uncover the truth. In light of that, if you know anything about it, you should tell me now."

Stevens went suddenly pale. Which made Gil glad. It meant this interview might be easy.

Gil picked up his metal chair and positioned it exactly four feet in front of Stevens. Joe, who was watching Gil intently, did the same, putting his chair next to Gil. There was no table in the room and therefore no intervening furniture to make it easier for Stevens to feel protected. That was the point.

Gil sat down purposefully and leaned forward in his chair, saying, "Alex, I know you lied to us."

"I only did it to protect my family," Stevens said defensively.

"Sure," Joe said, jumping in smoothly for a change. "I get that. I would have done the same thing."

"It's not like I did anything wrong," Stevens said. "I only did what I had to."

"I totally get that," Joe said, almost in a murmur.

"Besides, that guy really needs to be locked up," Stevens said.

"I completely agree," Joe said.

"I mean," said Stevens. "You guys said he was crazy."

Alex Stevens was admitting not to being in Socorro when Brianna disappeared but to lying about David Geisler. Gil decided to jump in. There was a series of questions that had to be asked now, and Joe might not be able to pull them off.

"He is," Gil said, continuing to agree with Stevens. "He's in the hospital right now being evaluated. One thing you can help us with is just telling us what you know about David Geisler."

"Who?" Stevens asked. Gil felt Joe take in a short breath. This was why Gil had jumped in. Why Joe couldn't do this part of the interview. His anger might get the best of him, especially when faced with a subject who didn't even know the name of the man he almost sent to prison.

"David Geisler is the man you saw in here yesterday," Gil said with a knowing smile. He was almost relieved to be doing this interrogation. It was so clean. So simple. It brought him back to what he loved about the process—the control, the rules, and the self-discipline. Maybe it would banish from his mind the role he had played yesterday with Rodriguez.

"Oh," Stevens said. "The crazy guy."

Gil smiled. "Right. So how well do you know him?"

"I've never met him, just seen him walking around a few times," Stevens said matter-of-factly, not even showing the least bit of remorse for what he had done.

"And you'd never seen him with Brianna?" Gil asked gently.

"No," Stevens said, "but when I saw him in here yesterday, I knew he was crazy and that he might hurt other kids, so I did what was right."

"What makes you think he's hurt any kids?" Gil asked, trying to sound relaxed.

"Oh, I just assumed," Stevens said. "I mean, the guy is seriously off. He needs to be locked up."

Gil could have asked so many other questions, such as why Stevens would derail the investigation so completely or who he was trying to protect by identifying an innocent man. To ask those questions, though, Gil would have to pull out evidence of Stevens's other lie. He wasn't ready to do that. Yet.

The woman lay on the pavement of the interstate like a wrung-out rag. The force of the impact had twisted her torso and her lower body in opposite directions. The car that had crashed into her must have impacted at her femur, turning her body to the right. Then she hit the pavement as the car made its long, agonizing attempt to stop, turning her body to the left.

Lucy had no idea why the woman was walking in the middle of the interstate. Was she trying to cross it? Had she simply been walking along the side of the road and the driver didn't see her?

It really didn't matter. What mattered was that the woman wasn't dead. She was as good as dead, but not dead yet. Likely she had no idea of what was going on around her. Lucy went and knelt down next to her anyway, touching her shoulder in the only place that wasn't broken. Gerald started his physical assessment, but they both knew it was useless. People often think that when medics see an obviously dying patient, they will make every heroic effort to save her, that EMS workers will cut open the patient's chest and clamp the aorta as she lies in the middle of the street—but that is fiction. In reality, when a woman has been struck full on by a car going 75 mph on the interstate, the laws of physics and rules of medicine are clear—she will die. Even if she is still breathing when the medics get on scene, protocol dictates that they do not start CPR. Because it will not work. They are required to do nothing. Lucy, though, was unaccustomed to doing nothing. So she put her hand more firmly on the woman's shoulder as her breathing slowed to silence.

Because it was better than nothing.

"So we have another problem that we were hoping you could help us with," Gil said to Stevens. "It's about what happened the day Brianna disappeared."

Stevens looked nervous. "What do you mean?"

"Well," Joe said, jumping in, "we just wanted you to go through the events of the day one more time. Just to walk us through it."

"Sure," Stevens said. "So Ashley and I got up about nine o'clock that morning, and Brianna woke up a little bit later. Ashley changed Brianna's diaper while I went to the store to get stuff for the cookout . . ."

Gil's job at the moment was to judge Stevens's level of detail. Usually the amount of specificity someone gives about a scenario says a lot. The more detail, the more likely the story is true. However, Stevens—like the rest of the family—had already been interviewed multiple times. He would have repeated over and over the day's events. He would have said numerous times that he and Ashley got up by 9:00 A.M. Even if that was initially a lie, it was now one that he had told so many times that his emotions and body language had become used to it. His face would no longer provide the telltale signs that it was a false statement, and the baseline that Joe had so carefully noted would be useless. So, Gil planned to ask Stevens questions about that day he'd never been asked before. If Stevens did tell a lie, it would be a new one that the baseline would accurately define.

"What did you buy?" Gil asked.

"I got buns for the burgers, meat, and then some beer. Oh, and I think we were out of mustard, so I got some of that, too." Stevens's answer had been quick. This part of the story he had told before. Gil could see that Joe was watching Stevens intently, trying to judge his response.

"What did you do next?" Gil asked.

"I bought some gas, went home, and turned the grill on," Stevens said neatly.

"Then what?" Gil asked.

"I put the TV on while the grill heated up, I opened a beer, then put the burgers on . . ." Stevens was well into territory that he had already talked about during previous interviews. It was where Gil wanted him. On familiar ground. Now he would throw him off that ground.

Gil interrupted Stevens, asking, "When did Mrs. Rodriguez wake up?"

"Umm . . . I guess about eleven or so . . ."

"And when did Justin come over?" Gil asked.

"At, like, noon—" Stevens said.

"And was Laura with him?"

"Yeah, she was—"

"And did they walk or get a ride?"

"They walked—"

"From where?"

"If you would let me finish talking I would tell you," Stevens said, annoyed, but that was what Gil wanted. It was a version of electroshock therapy. To reset everything. If he was going to undo all of the badly handled previous interrogations, he had to throw Stevens severely off his game, so all of his rote responses no longer worked. Within that little exchange, they had traveled outside of the realm of what had come before.

THE BONE FIRE 251

"I'm sorry," Gil said, sounding sincere. "Maybe we should start at the beginning again. Now, when you were at the store, how much did everything cost?"

"Ahh . . ." Stevens said. That simple hesitation told Gil that he had just asked a question Stevens hadn't answered before.

"It's okay if you don't remember," Gil said. "Let's move on. You mentioned you bought gas. How much was the price per gallon?"

"I . . . I'm not . . ." Stevens said, fumbling.

Gil didn't expect Stevens to actually remember any of this. It was more than a year ago. What Gil wanted was Stevens's actual memories, not ones he had created over time.

"When you were back at home, what did you do with your keys?" Gil asked.

"I'm sorry?" Stevens said, looking confused.

"Your car keys," Gil said. "Did you put them in your pocket? On the kitchen counter?"

"Umm . . . I guess I don't know," Stevens said. It was that statement that Gil had been waiting for.

"Are you sure?" Gil asked, having Stevens repeat it so the uncertainty of his answers would stay put.

"No," Stevens said. "I don't know."

Gil nodded. He had one more question to ask as a test to see if Stevens would lapse back into his recitation. "When did you start to eat lunch?"

"I don't . . . I think we started just after Justin and Laura got there," he said, sounding unsure.

"Good, good," Gil said. "And you were eating in the backyard?" Stevens nodded.

"Great," Gil said. He took one of the sheets of paper he had brought in and handed it and a pen to Stevens, saying. "Draw the backyard at the time Brianna disappeared."

"What?" Stevens asked.

"Draw the backyard," Gil said.

"Like a sketch of it," Joe added.

They waited while he awkwardly drew while holding the paper on his lap. Gil made no effort to make the task easier for him, wanting to keep him right where he had him—off his game. Gil had sized up Stevens in the few minutes that Joe was getting a baseline. What Gil saw was a man who would flatly lie if confronted directly with the fact that he wasn't present when Brianna disappeared. Stevens was the kind of person who would stick to his lie even when faced with proof of the truth. The only way to break down that kind of man was to shake him up. So Gil's questioning technique had actually served a dual purpose—it washed the interview slate clean and broke down the man's stubbornness.

Gil watched Stevens draw the arroyo, the house, the gas grill, the outside table and chairs. After he was done Gil said, "Now, if I understand correctly, it started to rain, and you were all about to go inside when you noticed Brianna missing. So show me on your map where Ashley was standing just before you noticed Brianna was gone."

"Umm . . ." Stevens said, "I don't know . . ."

"You have to know," Gil said. "You were there. Was Ashley sitting, standing, what?"

"I guess she was sitting . . ."

"And where were Justin and Laura?"

"I guess they were sitting, too," he said.

"And Mrs. Rodriguez?"

"Sitting," he said, now more sure of his lie.

"And where were you?"

"By the grill," Stevens said, assuredly.

"And when I leave here and go to the hospital and ask Ashley if she was sitting or standing when Brianna disappeared, what will she say?" Gil asked.

"Uh . . . I . . . umm . . ." Stevens said.

Gil leaned forward. "Look, Alex. It's okay. I understand. You had a chance to make some money that day, and you took it. Like you said before, you were taking care of your family." Joe was nodding in agreement. Gil purposely didn't call Stevens a liar. He kept everything vague to soften his crimes. Gil continued, saying, "Now it's time to stop. You have done an excellent job taking care of Ashley and the new baby on the way. Now it's time to step up to the plate and tell us what happened. For your family."

Stevens took a deep breath and said, "Okay, I wasn't there . . . I had a repo job in Socorro."

Gil should have been happy that Stevens admitted the truth, but instead he felt empty. Because Stevens's confession meant that the family was lying about everything. It made Gil think about something he didn't want to consider—that the family knew who the killer was and was protecting him.

CHAPTER TWENTY-THREE

Sunday Morning

Gerald pronounced the woman dead, as Lucy went to get a sheet to cover her. They had to wait for the medical investigator to show up before they could leave.

Lucy draped the woman's body and maneuvered the sheet so it also covered up a pool of blood nearby. Deputy Segura, who had been with her on the car fire two days ago, approached her and said, "I need your help." He looked overwhelmed and tired, so Lucy agreed. She followed him over to a minivan parked on the side of the road, a few yards beyond the crash scene. In the back sat a woman and a child.

"Hi," Lucy said softly. "How are you doing?" She assumed this was the dead woman's family, who had been called to the scene by the police. Lucy had been asked once or twice before to check out a family who had just been given the news that a loved one had died, to make sure they were not suicidal or homicidal. The woman was just looking off into space, holding the little boy, who looked to be six.

"Ma'am," Lucy said, "I just want to talk to you for a moment and see how you are."

The woman said nothing. Lucy wondered if this was the dead woman's sister.

Deputy Segura, standing next to Lucy, said, "This is Karen and Max." Lucy smiled at the little boy and said, "Hi, Max." He said nothing.

"Karen, I just want to say that I can't imagine how difficult this is for you," Lucy said. She was glad that she had thrown the sheet over the body. The accident scene was a few yards behind them, and the body wasn't visible from the van, but Lucy wouldn't want Karen to inadvertently see her dead sister just lying on the road.

"Is there anything I can do to help?" Lucy asked.

Karen cleared her throat and said, "The officer mentioned that he could arrange for someone to take us home."

"Of course," Lucy murmured as she turned to look for Deputy Segura, who suddenly was nowhere to be seen.

"We can have your car towed to your house," Lucy said.

"No," Karen said strongly as she started to cry. "I never want to see this car again. Never."

Max had started to cry as well now, but Lucy couldn't tell if that was fear or grief.

Something in Max's eyes made Lucy stop. He looked so scared. So petrified. She got out of the van slowly and walked to the front. It was dented in two feet from the impact. The bumper was painted red with blood. Lucy looked back at Karen and Max inside the van.

Lucy needn't have bothered to cover the body for their sakes, because they had already seen much worse.

Joe was sitting silently next to Gil, not jumping in as much as usual. It concerned Gil slightly as he went on with Stevens's interrogation.

"So I admit I'm a little confused," Gil said. "Why didn't you say from the beginning that you were in Socorro when Brianna disappeared?"

"Okay, well, here's the thing," Stevens said. "I had been drinking on the drive back to town, and then I got Ashley's call that Brianna's missing, and I didn't know what to do. I mean, I can't go home because there are cops all over the house. So Ashley said that I should keep driving around to sober up and she'd say I'm out looking for Brianna."

"So that's what you did?" Gil asked. It wasn't much of a master plan to avoid a DWI. It also wasn't much of a reason to lie.

"Yeah," he said. "I stopped and got some coffee and just sat in my truck until I was sober enough to go home."

"Wait a minute," Joe said. "Why not just tell the police that you were in Socorro and then when you got back to town you went to look for Brianna? Why lie about where you were? The only thing you really needed to lie about was driving while drunk." Gil winced a little every time Joe used the word "lie," but Stevens didn't seem to notice.

"I don't know," Stevens said. Gil thought Joe made a good point. The lie Ashley came up with was overkill. It was too complicated.

"How long were you and Ashley dating before Brianna disappeared?" Gil asked.

"Like two months."

"So you started dating while Brianna was still living with Donna Henshaw," Gil said. Stevens squirmed a little in his seat at the mention of the adoption. Clearly, he had been told not to talk about it.

"It must have been hard when Brianna came back," Joe said. "A little kid sure does put a damper on your love life."

"That's for sure," Stevens said.

"I know I would have been mad as hell," Joe said. "It was like being tricked. You didn't sign up for no little kid."

"It was messed up," he agreed.

"You must have told Ashley how hard it was with Brianna around," Gil said. "We know Brianna cried all the time. That must have really got on your nerves."

"I did tell her, but she said there was nothing she could do," Stevens said. "That kid was so spoiled and just screamed whenever she didn't get what she wanted." Gil looked over at Joe, knowing that he was protective of Brianna, but he showed no sign of his usual anger.

"I mean," Stevens continued without prompting, "she was supposed to be fucking adopted, but all of the sudden, she's back again, like nothing happened. What was I supposed to do?"

"I know what I would do," Joe said. "I'd tell Ashley it's either the kid or me."

"Exactly."

"So what did Ashley do?" Gil asked a little more quietly, maybe because he was afraid of the answer.

"I dunno," Stevens said, looking down.

"Do you think it's possible that Ashley did something to Brianna?" Gil asked.

"I dunno."

Gil thought of Ashley, only twenty. No job, no money, no education—and the man she loves threatening to leave.

"Alex, do you think it's possible that Ashley made sure Brianna was gone so you would stay?" Gil asked.

"Yeah," he said. "Maybe."

Lucy found a deputy who offered to take the woman and her son home while she went in search of Gerald. She hoped he was doing the paperwork so they could get out of there soon. She found him talking to Deputy Segura, who asked, "How are they?" Lucy just shook her head, not knowing how to answer. Instead she asked, "So what's the deal? How did this happen?"

"Suicide by car," Segura said.

"What?" Lucy asked. "How is that a good suicide plan?"

"I didn't know there was such a thing as a good suicide plan," Gerald said.

"I'm not sure on the details," Segura said, "but it sounds like she and her boyfriend were up all night drinking and then they got in some big fight. I guess she was always telling him about how she was just going to walk into traffic if he ever left her. Tonight she said something like 'You'll be sorry when I'm gone.' They live in a trailer just down the embankment there." He gestured over to the left. "She went out for a walk and never came back."

Joe, starting to get the feel for the interview, said to Alex Stevens, "It takes a lot of love for a woman to choose her man the way Ashley chose you."

"Yeah," Stevens said, not sounding convinced.

"You don't think Ashley loves you?" Gil asked.

"I dunno," he said. "Sometimes, I know she does. Other times . . . who knows."

"What makes you think she doesn't love you?" Joe asked. "She must love you if she's having your baby."

"I'm not even sure it's my kid," Stevens said, then instantly seemed to regret he'd said anything.

"What do you mean?" Gil asked.

Stevens stopped and leaned his head back and looked up at the ceiling, as if he were imploring God to deliver him from this interrogation. He rubbed his eyes and then said suddenly, "Okay, look. I love Ashley, man, but she's a trip. She's got issues." He started bouncing his leg. Gil said nothing. He would let Stevens's tension do the talking for him. With that much nervous energy, he would eventually have to talk it out. A moment or two later, after some deep breaths, Stevens said, "Just so you know, I'm, like, a normal guy. I like sex and everything."

"Yeah, I can tell," Gil said, because it seemed important to Stevens that he be seen as normal.

"Okay, so, things sex-wise with Ashley were always kind of different," Stevens said, not looking at Gil or Joe. "She just has problems, you know. I try to be understanding of that."

"What kind of problems?"

"Just, you know . . . okay, like for instance she can't have sex unless she's had a few beers," Stevens said, as if he had just laid something out on the table. Just given up his king of hearts. It was an important card, but it wasn't the most telling. He was still holding an ace.

"I get that," Gil said as a filler response to show that he wasn't judging the man.

"You know, if she's drinking and then I'm drinking . . ."

"So you've only ever had sex when you were both drunk?" Gil

asked. Stevens shifted in his seat uncomfortably, but there was nothing strange about the conversation yet. It was common for women who had been sexually abused to need alcohol to overcome their fears in bed.

"Yeah," Stevens said. He was still bouncing his leg. There was something else.

Gil said, "When both people are drunk it gets complicated." It was almost a nonstatement, but it might move the conversation along.

"Yeah, like, okay, so we haven't had regular sex for a really long time," Stevens said, leaning in closer and talking quietly.

"You mean intercourse?"

"Yeah, I mean, we've done other stuff . . . you know, but not that," Stevens said.

"When was the last time you had regular sex?" Gil asked, thankful that Joe wasn't jumping in to ask questions about his favorite subject.

"We got drunk one night about eight months ago, and then later Ashley said we had sex, but I can't remember it. Plus, like a guy can tell, you know." This was Stevens's ace of spades. The card that would break him. Gil quickly realized why this fact, this one instance, was so important. "So you're not sure you're the new baby's father?" he asked.

Stevens leaned back and said, "It's not that . . . maybe . . . I don't know." His leg started jumping again. He let out a few more slow breaths before saying, "I have to be the dad, you know? Ashley would never cheat on me. And then plus, with all of her hangups . . . we were dating for four months before she could even have drunk sex. So, like, who would she have sex with?"

That had been the question from the beginning.

Gil stood outside the interview room with Joe, who rolled his neck and said, "I have no idea where this leaves us."

Gil wasn't sure either. He had one of the uniformed officers bring Alex Stevens a soda and a bag of chips so he wouldn't get too nervous and ask for a lawyer while they considered filing false statement charges against him for fingering David Geisler.

Gil and Joe went back to the conference room and looked at the whiteboard, which still displayed Brianna's timeline, as well as all the lists and the phrase *I was dead and buried.*

They stared at the board in silence until Joe said, "I know the family is lying to us, but I can't see any of them putting Brianna's bones up in those displays. It's just too evil."

"That's my issue with it, too," Gil said.

"I wonder about the David Geisler thing," Joe said. "I know he could still be our guy . . ."

"Although it seems less likely since Stevens lied about seeing him with Brianna."

"But he fits the profile perfectly." Joe got up and stood next to the board. "I don't know. Maybe the profile is wrong."

"Our profile is solid," Gil said. "I know it is. Whoever killed Brianna and left her bones fits this profile."

"The profile that describes David Geisler," Joe said, exasperated.

Gil's head was starting to hurt again. "So let's change tacks here," he said. "Alex Stevens seems pretty convinced that Ashley got rid of Brianna, but you and I both know that no one in the family put up the displays of Brianna's bones. So let's assume both things are true. How would Ashley get rid of Brianna in a way that explains how we found her bones?"

"The only thing I can think of is that Ashley sold Brianna to a psychopath," Joe said, "and now we are back to creepy land."

They kept looking at the board until Joe said hesitantly, "Could Ashley have sold Brianna to David Geisler?"

It was a measure of how much of a toll the investigation was taking on Gil that he actually considered it.

CHAPTER TWENTY-FOUR

Sunday Morning

Having no other ideas, Gil and Joe went back to old-school detective work—looking through documents. Gil had spent the last half hour going over Ashley's financial statements from a year before Brianna went missing up to a month after. The statements had been part of the original investigation and the warrant that went with that. Gil knew it was unlikely they'd get a court order for her most recent financial information, given the lawsuit, but he thought he'd satisfy his curiosity about the money Ashley was paid for the adoption. Anna Maria Roybal said that payments to the birth mother from the adoptive parents were normal, but it still rubbed Gil the wrong way. He could understand that there were expenses, but it felt like a payoff.

Joe, of course, had his own agenda, which was proving his most recent theory. He was looking over David Geisler's bank statements, which they had found during the search of his house. Unfortunately, Geisler's statements were incomplete, with many months missing.

Joe sighed and said, "What kind of mom sells her kid to a crazy guy?"

"I really don't think she did," Gil said, already regretting that he hadn't stopped Joe when he first started to tug on this crazy thread.

"It fits nicely, though," Joe said. "We've got the blood on the sword, the prior complaint by the neighbor that Geisler approached some kids. Plus, the guy is nuts, but he really wasn't that messed up when we first went to his house. He started that thing . . . What did Lucy call it? Word salad? He started the word salad thing only after he was in custody."

Gil said nothing, and the two worked quietly until Joe said, "Gil, can I ask you a question?"

"Sure."

"How would you have done the initial investigation differently?" Joe asked, looking at Gil intently. "Like instead of how Fisher did it?"

"Joe, I don't—"

"Look, Fisher is dead, and he was a good guy, but he was no genius."

"Why do you ask?" Gil said, purposely deflecting the question.

"It's just," Joe said hesitantly, "when we were sitting there asking Stevens all those questions, like really manipulating the hell out of the guy, he didn't even realize it. That's when I saw how an interrogation is supposed to look, and it occurred to me that I never saw Fisher come close to doing what you do."

"What is it I do exactly?" Gil asked. He did not want to get into a conversation about Fisher. Joe had seemed to worship the man. If there was one rule Gil had learned when he was a teenager, it was don't talk bad about your buddy's ex-girlfriend, because when they get back together, you won't be friends anymore. Gil felt the same thing was true in this case. Fisher was dead, but Joe's hero worship wasn't.

"Gil, man, don't take this the wrong way, because I mean it as a compliment, but you are one cold motherfucker," Joe said. "You lie better than my ex-wife, and she lies for breakfast, lunch, and dinner." Gil didn't take it as a compliment. Instead, it only made him feel vacant.

They spent the next few minutes in silence while they continued to go over the financials. Gil finally tracked down the ten thousand dollars. It was paid to Ashley in January when Brianna was adopted. He flipped through the papers and found what he was looking for toward the back of the file. It was a personal check, and the signature on it was clearly written, without flair or flourish. Victor Otero.

"Interesting," Gil said, showing the check to Joe.

"Why would Judge Otero give Ashley a check as part of the adoption?" Joe asked. "Why wouldn't Donna Henshaw just write it?"

"I don't know," Gil said. "First he lies about only meeting Ashley once and now this. I think Judge Otero is much more involved then we thought." Gil stared at the check, writing down the account number and the judge's other information. Joe was unusually quiet.

"Uh, Gil," Joe said. Gil looked up to see him looking at the whiteboard. "I don't think the only thing the judge lied about was meeting Ashley once."

"What do you mean?" Gil asked, joining him to stare at the board. All he saw was Brianna's adoption timeline and then the lists and that ominous phrase—*I was dead and buried*. There was nothing new written on the board.

"Do you remember me telling you that Brianna was a preemie?" Joe asked. "She was born in May and was thirty-three weeks old instead of the normal forty weeks."

"Okay," Gil said.

"That would put her conception at around mid-September," Joe said.

"Okay," Gil said, staring at the board.

"You don't see it?" Joe asked.

"I have no idea what you are talking about," Gil said.

Joe stepped up to point at the adoption timeline on the board. The first date on it was when Ashley met Judge Otero. The next mark was for Brianna's birth date on May 5.

"If you work backwards thirty-three weeks from Brianna's birth date . . ." Joe said. Instead of finishing his sentence, he wrote the word "conception" in big letters, then drew a mark to September 16, the same day Ashley met with Judge Otero.

Lucy was pulling up to her house when she remembered that she had to go rescue the crime scene photo from the copier at work. The thought made her weary. She just wanted to go to back to bed. She turned the car around and headed to the newspaper. She had a hard time finding space in the parking lot, which struck her as odd for a Sunday morning. Then she remembered that it was fiesta, so everyone at the paper was making use of their work parking permits. She was getting out of her car when she heard someone call out to her. She turned to look. It was John Lopez with his family. Lucy had met his wife and two children several times but couldn't remember their names. She would have to wing it.

"Hi," she called to them. "How was fiesta?"

"Wonderful," the nameless wife said. "We always come for the green chile enchiladas." The nameless children, who looked to be twin girls of about eight, just ignored the grown-ups.

"Great," said Lucy, falling back on the one expression she seemed to automatically use around Lopez. She really just wanted to get inside, get the photo, and leave. She was always so bad at chitchat. *What's boring with your life?* Please, let me tell you about it for ten minutes.

"I'm glad I ran into you," Lopez said. "I have two things I wanted to bring up."

She suddenly remembered last night, when she avoided the questions on the SWAT situation. She figured that was what he was about to mention.

Instead, he said, "We never finished your review."

She smiled. Having dodged the SWAT bullet, so to speak, she was more than happy to talk about continuing her painful yearly review. "Oh, yeah," she said. "When do you want to reschedule it?"

"I was thinking that before we do that, I want to have you fill out a self-evaluation."

"Umm . . . sure? But wouldn't I just evaluate myself as great?

'Cause I am, you know," she said. The nameless children, bored with the conversation, went to play near a wrought-iron fence that surrounded the parking lot.

"Well, let's see what happens," he said, always in the patient dad voice. "When you write your self-evaluation there are a few things I want you to keep in mind and maybe write about."

"Okay," she said slowly. Nameless wife left them, going over to her nameless children, while inside Lucy was pleading with her to stay.

"So one of the things I want you to think about is what you see as your future, not only with the *Capital Tribune* but wherever you think you want to go with your life," he said, smiling gently. "I also would like you to address your future with the company."

"Okay," she said, then added as a joke, "Just to be clear, do you think I have a future with the company?"

He smiled. "I think, as with any employee, there are considerations." The answer did nothing to make her less nervous.

"Like what?" she asked, but not really wanting to know.

"For instance, I'm curious why the police haven't served us with a court order for the security tapes."

Her stomach fell five stories during that one sentence. She started to say, "I don't—"

"It's almost like someone told them that trying to get the tapes was useless."

Lucy said nothing. There was nothing to say. No excuses to be made.

Lopez shook his head and said, "Lucy, you have to decide where your loyalties lie. I think this needs to be a major part of your self-evaluation. For example, look at what you're wearing." She glanced down at her EMS uniform and combat boots. "Yet here you are at work," he said.

"I have thought about that, a lot. Basically, when I'm here, my loyalties are to the newspaper, and when I'm on call, they're with the fire department."

"You don't see a problem with that?" he asked.

"No. It's everyone else who has a problem with it."

"Do you at least see why?" he said with a slight smile that she really wished didn't look so condescending.

"Frankly, no," she said, trying not to sound defensive. "I do a good job when I'm here and a good job when I'm there."

"That's true—but every once in a while your two worlds collide, and suddenly the police know more than they should and we know less than we should. For instance, there's the car fire story that Tommy and Andrea are working on, which is based on information that you got while working for the fire department," he said. In her head, Lucy cursed out Andrea, knowing that she had to be the one who talked too much about the story. Lopez continued, "Then, of course, there is that SWAT situation."

Lucy said a thousand little swear words to herself.

Gil stood in the bright morning sun, watching the exits of the cathedral. He could have gone inside—in fact, probably should have—but he couldn't bring himself to go into this holy place when he knew the questions he had to ask would involve immoral answers. The statues in front of the church were alone at the moment, with no tourists to take pictures of them. The sightseers probably all had been drawn to the spectacle inside the cathedral, where the closing Mass of fiesta was taking place.

Gil wondered if the tourists understood why there were grown men dressed in conquistador helmets and pantaloons at Mass. He wondered if the tourists would giggle at their simple, quaint tradition of having a fiesta queen dressed in a white gown and cape. They would probably go back home and tell their friends about Santa Fe's backward ways. How they had an archbishop—the most senior representative of the Catholic Church—preside over a service that included city councilors and people in costume carrying swords. Gil knew the tourists would never understand what fiesta was to Santa Fe. To him. They wouldn't understand that this was not an amusing celebration of a historic moment long past. This wasn't their version of a medieval-days festival or a Civil War reenactment. To Santa Feans, celebrating fiesta meant celebrating their ancestors.

Gil had convinced Joe to let him come down to the cathedral by

himself while Joe stayed at the office and tied up loose ends—
making calls, processing paper, and looking over reports. Joe was
unhappy, but Gil needed to do this next interview alone. It required
a certain touch.

The bells started ringing in the cathedral towers, and the front
doors opened. Out came the archbishop, followed by a gush of priests,
as well as Don Diego de Vargas, La Reina, and a crowd of people in a
riot of colors. They were in their fiesta best—ribbon shirts for the men
and multicolored broom skirts for the women. They stood in front of
the cathedral, chatting, waiting for the procession to start. Gil scanned
the crowd. He saw the huge cluster of the Protectores de la Fiesta, their
yellow satin shirts shining in the sun. A mariachi band started playing
as four men came out of the church, carrying a huge wooden platform
on which was a carpet of flowers and the two-foot-tall statue of La
Conquistadora.

The band started to proceed down the street, and the four Protectores carrying the padded litter followed, with the wooden bars
that supported the platform on their shoulders. The platform had
its own white awning, embroidered with gold roses. Underneath,
safely away from the sun's harmful rays, was La Conquistadora.
The real one. This was the only time of year she ever left the safety
of one of her chapels. Today, La Conquistadora was dressed in a
cape of deep blue with gold stars. On her head was a crown of
flowers. Around her neck was a tiny silver filigree crucifix made with
real pearls and rubies that matched her earrings. Behind her litter, a
trail of priests, dressed in green vestments, walked with the archbishop. Next came La Reina and Don Diego, along with the fiesta
royalty. They were followed by the religious organizations, holding
banners and flags showing different appearances of the Virgin Mary.
Last was the crowd. They marched down the street as the band began to play.

Within a block, all of the careful groupings had been destroyed
as wives went to go walk with husbands and city councilors stopped
to shake hands with constituents. Gil stayed on the outside of the
procession, trying to catch a glimpse of Judge Otero. He finally saw
him praying the rosary aloud among one of the religious groups.

Gil was trying to get as close as he could to the judge when his phone buzzed in his pocket. It was Joe, sending him a text that read: *Henshaw gave $10,000 to Judge O's last campaign.* Gil knew that was the legal limit for campaign contributions. He wondered why it was also the exact amount that Ashley had been paid.

He started looking for the judge in the crowd once again. He spotted him and walked quickly toward him, skirting people and musicians.

Gil could hear the rises and the falls of the Hail Mary as he approached the praying group. Gil slowly came up next to Judge Otero, just as he was finishing an Our Father.

The judge turned his head and saw Gil next to him, exclaiming, "Gilbertito. How are you?" Before Gil could say anything, the judge said, "You need a rosary. Who has an extra rosary?" he yelled to his fellow faithful. A plastic yellow rosary was passed from hand to hand across the processing crowd. Judge Otero grabbed it and put it into Gil's hands.

"Look, we just finished the Second Mystery, so we are right here," Judge Otero said, pointing to the correct bead on the rosary. They were making good time, having already gotten through thirteen Hail Marys and three Our Fathers. Gil clicked off the beads as the crowd went through the prayers. He could wait until they were done, which would be about twenty minutes, but then they would just start again and keep it up until they reached their destination—the Rosario Chapel, La Conquistadora's second home, which was about three-quarters of a mile away.

"Sir," Gil said almost in a whisper, "I need to talk to you about Brianna."

"This is the perfect time to talk about her," Judge Otero said, making no effort to lower his voice. "What better time to talk about that poor girl than when you are praying?"

"Well then, sir," Gil said, "I wanted to clarify a few things with you."

"Of course," the judge said in the middle of a Hail Mary. Gil tripped slightly on the pavement and had to steady himself as they walked.

"I wanted to ask you how many times you and Ashley talked over the adoption," Gil said, trying not to let the crowd, the band, and the praying distract him.

"I told you," he said. "It was just the one time."

"The court records show that she was in your courtroom multiple times," Gil said.

The judge didn't respond, but he stopped praying the rosary as they walked. Gil had never really considered asking the judge to come down to the station so they could do a formal interview. The judge's position meant that Gil would have had to wade through the mayor, city attorneys, and even his own chief if he wanted to talk with him officially. That left Gil with one option—a surprise attack. Of course, Gil knew that as a good member of the Protectores, the only place the judge would be this morning—on the last day of fiesta—was at the procession for La Conquistadora.

"I can think of several reasons you wouldn't want to tell us that you knew Ashley better than you let on," Gil said. "The first one, of course, is that you are Brianna's father." Once Gil saw the look on the judge's face, he knew the surprise attack had been the right way to go. That look of guilt.

The mariachi band started a different tune while the crowd near them moved on to the Third Mystery.

Gil said, "I know she was seventeen, so she was past the age of consent, so there is no problem as far as statutory rape goes."

"However, statutory rape has a second part that makes it illegal for people in a position of authority to use their office for certain favors," Judge Otero said. He turned and looked at Gil. "I never touched that girl."

There had never been a chance that the judge would admit to anything. He had too much to lose. Gil had actually gotten further with the interview than he had expected to. He had thought the judge would tell him to talk to his lawyer almost immediately. Now it didn't matter if he did. Gil had already gotten what he came for— the guilt drawn tight across the judge's face. He finally knew who Brianna's father was. He had started to suspect it was the judge when he saw the personal check to Ashley. Gil might never have proof, but the knowledge would be enough. Now he was just curious about a few more pieces of information.

"Can I ask about your relationship with Donna Henshaw?" Gil asked.

"As I said, she was just a friend of a friend," Judge Otero said, exasperated.

"She must be a good friend of a friend since she gave your last campaign ten thousand dollars," Gil said. "That's an awful lot of money for a municipal election."

Judge Otero said nothing.

"I'm confused, sir," Gil said, "so I'm just going to ask flat out, did Donna Henshaw give you campaign money for you to give to Ashley? Then Ashley gave Brianna to Donna Henshaw?"

Judge Otero still said nothing, and any guilt that had been on his face was long gone. Gil could keep asking him questions that he wouldn't answer. Like if he was the father of Ashley's new baby. The man knew when to shut up. The judge might not be a lawyer, but he did know the law. He knew Gil couldn't prove any of it. Gil probably didn't even have enough evidence to compel the judge to take a paternity test to see if he was Brianna's father. When all was said and done, they could do nothing more than prove the judge was improperly involved with an adoption.

The procession was leaving the crowded buildings of downtown now and was going toward an area more populated with businesses. Gil decided to give it one more try.

"Was Ashley blackmailing you about being Brianna's father?" Gil asked.

"You can ask my lawyer," Judge Otero said. He started saying the next prayer. "Hail Mary, full of grace . . ."

Lucy used her keycard to let herself in the side door of the newspaper building. No one was around, and all the lights were off. There was enough sunlight creeping through a few of the painted-over windows for her to see her way to the copier.

She opened the lid, and there, lying facedown, was the photo.

"Hallelujah," she whispered to herself as she clutched the picture to her chest.

As she closed the cover of the copier, she saw the bright blue flyer hanging on the bulletin board in front of her. THE MEDITATION OF RELEASE. It sounded so peaceful. She read the first line of the flyer once again. "So often in our lives we have old emotions and habits that hold us back and try to tear us down." She smiled. Bitterly.

She heard a noise from down the hallway and saw a form appear from the shadows. She flipped the light switch nearest to her and saw Peter Littlefield.

"Jesus, Peter," she said. "You scared me to death. What are you doing here?"

"I had that special opera review to write," he said.

"Right," she said, nodding, wondering how many Santa Feans really read the paper for its up-to-date opera news.

"You're here early," he said, peering over his glasses.

"I forgot something," she said, still clutching the photo to her chest.

"Oh, you mean the picture of the Tamara," he said, nodding. "I saw that in the copier. I knew she was working on a new piece, but I had no idea it was so intricate."

"I'm sorry, what?"

"The photo," he said. "I assume it's of her new work."

"Whose new work?"

"Tamara. She's a fabulous naturalist. I mean, look at her use of color," Peter said, reaching for the photo. Lucy turned it over to him, and he pointed out the sunflowers and the doll's heads.

"Tamara is an artist?"

"Well, yes," Peter said, frowning at Lucy. "She did the statues in front of the new judicial complex, and she has a few pieces hanging in the permanent collection at the capitol."

"How do you know she did this?" Lucy asked, waving her hand at the photo.

"Are you kidding? This is classic Tamara," he said. "Look, here and here, at these bones that are strung together in that delicate star shape? That's one of her signature motifs. She did a whole piece using star bones last year at SITE Santa Fe."

"You're positive she did this?" Lucy asked.

"Absolutely," he said. "Her themes always include religion, death, and innocence."

"How do you get all of that from this photo?" she asked, peering at it.

"Look at the interpretation," he said. "You have the inherent religious image of the statue, and death, of course, is represented by the bones. And see how she mixes it with the classic pop-culture symbols of innocence, the flowers and dolls?"

"She works with bones?" Lucy asked, still not understanding. Not believing. "Why?"

"Because you have to have death in order to have life, and art is all about life."

CHAPTER TWENTY-FIVE

Sunday Afternoon

Ashley lay on the hospital bed motionless, waiting, tense. She heard a nurse telling her to relax, but Ashley knew that was impossible. How could she relax when she only had a few minutes before the worst pain in the world started again? The pain was in control of her body. Ashley had no thoughts left that were her own. They all belonged to the pain. She whimpered as she felt the next contraction start to rise, then let out a high-pitched yell that seemed to go on for hours. She panicked, thinking the pain wouldn't end this time. This felt like death. Like there was no going back.

She heard a nurse say, "Don't fight the pain. Work with it." Ashley just wanted it over. She wanted it out of her. The contraction started to fall off, and Ashley lay back. She wondered momentarily why Alex wasn't there, but it hardly mattered. There was no need for him to be there. Her mother stood in the corner looking pale. Ashley had a wild thought that maybe her father had come in during the contraction. She looked around the room, peering at the faces of the two nurses and the doctor. She tried to study them; she had to make sure he hadn't slipped in. The contraction started again before she could be sure, and the pain rose fast. She tried to fight it, but it was too strong. She couldn't control it. She felt like her stomach was being crushed into a tight ball. She kept yelling until the pain stopped and she was panting on the bed.

Ashley tried again to look at the faces in the room. Her father wasn't there. He wouldn't be there. Thank God. She hadn't seen her father since he moved out, always making excuses to her mother so she wouldn't have to visit him.

The last time they were in the same room together was a few days after the actress's lawyer had brought Brianna back. Ashley hadn't missed Brianna as much as she thought she would. Of course, she missed the cuddles and the kisses, and every night Ashley would wake up because she thought she heard Brianna crying. There had been no real crying while Brianna was gone, though, and in the blissful silence, she could think.

Ashley had started dating Alex. She was thinking about getting her GED. She even thought about taking some college classes with the money she had gotten from the adoption. Then, five months after she left, Brianna was back. It was immediate. They called and twenty minutes later dropped her off. The lawyer said they didn't want the money back. And that was that.

Alex was angry. She had told him about Brianna, but he hadn't counted on ever meeting her. Her mother seemed fine with it, but then it was so hard to tell. It was her father who was the happiest. Ashley watched as he bounced the little girl on his knee and kissed her tiny face with his rough lips.

Ashley knew she had to do something. She would rather that Brianna die than go through what she had.

Ashley finally decided the best thing to do was write a note. She had taken a piece of paper and written, *If you don't move out, I will cut your balls off while you sleep.* Then she tucked it under the windshield wiper of his car.

She was surprised how well it worked. He was gone the next day. Maybe he thought Alex had written the note. Or that Tony Herrera had ordered it done from jail. Either way, he left. For the first time, Ashley felt a glimmer of safety in her own home.

That vanished along with Brianna.

The next contraction came on faster than she expected, and suddenly she was in a pool of water. The nurses laughed and said, "Your water broke," as if it were something to celebrate. The doctor looked down between her legs, and suddenly everything changed. The doctor said something about a prolapsed cord. One nurse helped Ashley get on all fours on the bed as the other nurse called out to someone that they needed an OR. The baby was in trouble.

Lucy parked her car near an old adobe house with an attached sunroom that had a lovely garden clinging to the shady areas. Two dogs came running up to her as she got out. One was a black Lab mix, and the other was a three-legged collie who really needed to get her hair brushed.

Lucy walked closer to the house and yelled, "Hello?" No one answered, so she stepped through the open door of the sunroom and called, "Hello?"

It took her eyes a moment to take in her surroundings, and suddenly she thought she had entered hell. There were bones everywhere on the rough wooden tables. They were being bleached in the sunlight. A large glass aquarium held no water or fish. Instead it was filled with what looked to be beetles and the severed head of some large creature that still had most of its flesh. It could have been a cow. Or a deer. A large stone pestle and mortar sat on a bench, clearly being used to crush bone into dust. If she hadn't known better, she'd have sworn that she'd just walked into a serial killer's house.

She did know better, though. She had gotten Tamara's address from Peter, then done some research on the woman before she left the office. It had been easy enough to do. She was a world-renowned naturalist artist. Her work had been featured at the UN building in New York City. She had a master's degree in biology from Stanford, but after graduating she found herself drawn more to art that represented the real, living world. She started with sculptures of the interior of the intestines. She taught herself how to skin animals and process the tissues. She would make articulated puppet skeletons of bones from several different animals as a way to show how all of nature fits together. Her idol was Georgia O'Keeffe, who was famous for her paintings of bones. Tamara said in one article Lucy found, "Where Georgia O'Keeffe painted pictures of bones, I cut out the middle part and just use the bones as art." The articles only referred to Tamara using animal bones. Never human.

"Hello," called a female voice back to Lucy. A woman stepped out into the sunroom and smiled. She looked to be in her late fifties, with yellow curly hair. She was dressed in jeans and a tan linen vest over a white T-shirt. Around her neck, reading glasses hung from a red-beaded chain. She looked fit and happy. Like one of those older women who needed no makeup to help their beauty. She held paintbrushes in her hand and was wiping them with a rag.

"Hi," Lucy said.

"Are you bringing me a dead cat?" the woman asked, smiling.

"Was I supposed to?" Lucy asked.

"Oh, no," she said. "I was just teasing. A lot of times when strangers come to visit my studio they bring me roadkill for me to use in my work. Instead of flowers."

"Sorry," Lucy said. "No dead cats or flowers."

"Why are you wearing an ambulance uniform?" the woman asked.

Lucy had completely forgotten once again that she was wearing her EMT clothes. "Umm . . . no reason," she said, hoping that the subject would be dropped. "I actually just want to ask you a few questions. I'm with the newspaper."

The woman's face lit up, and her hands went up in the air in an expression of relief as she said, "Finally. I was beginning to think it didn't work and I had spent all those hours for nothing."

"What didn't work?" Lucy asked.

"The publicity," she said. "Here, come inside. Let's sit down." Lucy followed her though the sunroom and into the house, which had low viga-lined ceilings and Mexican tile floors. Out a huge picture window was a sweeping view of the plains. "Do you want any tea? Or water?" the woman asked.

Lucy said no, and they sat in comfy light green chairs by a low coffee table painted with sea blue streaks. On the table was a sculpture of a face, but it was made completely out of small bones. Another example of her work.

"Now," Tamara said. "Tell me everything. How were they found?"

"Umm . . . I'm not sure exactly what you mean," Lucy said. "Can I just clarify a few things?" Lucy pulled the photo of the crime scene out of her purse and handed it to Tamara, who put on her glasses and looked at the photo, smiling.

"So," Lucy said, "is this your work?"

"Yes," Tamara said, before adding, "Oh shoot, it looks like the balloons I put on there are gone. I guess the wind took them away. There's five dollars down the drain."

"And this was publicity?" Lucy asked.

"Yes. It's guerrilla art. Like my version of graffiti or flash mobbing," Tamara said. "My publicist and I figured that I would do these outdoor installations as underground promotion. The only way to make it work was to do it anonymously. I thought you all from the media would have contacted me about them on Friday, and we would get some free publicity for the show I'm doing at the Clear River Gallery on Canyon Road." Tamara reached over to the coffee table, picked up a slick brochure, and handed it to Lucy. On its sand beige cover was a cross made of two long bones with the words I WAS DEAD AND BURIED. Lucy guessed that was the name of the show. Catchy.

"You can imagine how nervous I've been since I set the installations up," Tamara said, still smiling. "I've been pulling my hair out wondering how they were being received. Of course, the artist in me decided that the reviewers simply hated the work and that's why no one was calling me for an interview."

"You realize that you used human bones?" Lucy asked. She had been struggling with the idea that a respected artist like Tamara would use Brianna's remains.

"Of course," Tamara said, scooting forward in her seat in her eagerness. "That was the point. I wanted it to be shocking to show how our society's physical treatment of people's bones is hypocritical. We spend millions of dollars a year to put bodies into the ground and another million dollars digging up ancient bodies that have been deemed museum worthy. I consider myself an anti-archaeologist."

"What's an anti-archaeologist?" Lucy asked.

"I believe that archaeology itself is no longer a science," Tamara said. "Think about it. Why do archaeologists dig up our ancestors and their homes when they have computer programs that can virtually do it for them? It's because they want to be the next person to find King Tut's tomb. It's about glory for them."

"Okay," Lucy said. "I sort of get that. So why did you use the Mary statues?"

"Because the Catholic Church is one of the worst archaeological offenders," she said. "Most churches, even our cathedral here, have human bones on display. Every church in Europe has a body part of a saint that it's known for. A church in Siena, Italy, has the head of St. Catherine in a box, while her right thumb and a foot are in other churches. It's like entertainment or a circus sideshow."

"Where did you get the bones?" Lucy said, still confused and trying to speak slowly. She hoped Tamara's answer wouldn't include the use of any form of the phrase "I killed."

"Where I get all my bones," Tamara said, then looked back at the photo and asked, "Why is there crime scene tape around my installation?"

Gil's phone rang as he was driving back to the station. He saw on the caller ID that it was Lucy and almost didn't answer it, but picked up on the fifth ring.

"So, listen, Montoya," she said loudly. He could tell she was outside by the wind whistling through the phone's mouthpiece. "I figured out why all those bones were left around town."

"What?" he said. "How?"

"You know, I don't want to say too much about that at the moment," she said. He said nothing, so she filled the space. "I take that silence to mean that you think I'm crazy, but I swear I haven't started to hear the voices yet. I really do know why the bones were left. I actually can tell you quite a lot about them now. For instance, I know that all of them were left before three different statues of Mary and that the skull in Zozobra had a lovely hat with plastic bottle caps attached to it."

"It did?" he asked.

"Well, I was told it did," Lucy said. "Maybe it came off in the fire." Gil thought of the swirled plastic on the back of the skull that melted in the blaze.

"Where are you?" he asked. "Are you in any danger?" She must be with the killer. That would be just like her.

"Oh, it's so sweet how you worry about me," she said. "I'm fine. I just have someone that I want you to meet." He heard her say to someone in the background, "Say hi to the nice policeman." He thought he heard someone say "Hi," but it was lost in the wind.

"So are you coming?" she asked. Gil agreed, and she gave him directions. As she was hanging up she said, "By the way, you might want to release the schizophrenic guy you're holding, and you don't need to bring any backup. It's not what you think."

Gil shook his head. With Lucy it never was.

They stood in the sunroom waiting for Gil, as Lucy nervously eyed the glass aquarium that held the beetles and the skull.

"I'm sorry," Lucy said, "but can I ask what this is?"

"Those are my Beetle Boys," she said. "They're my little helpers. They clean my bones for me. They're carpet beetles. They'll have that deer skull cleaned for me in two days."

Lucy poked at some fur on one of the tables and asked Tamara innocently, "Where do you get your bones from?"

"Oh, all over," Tamara said. "I find them or people bring them to me."

"Where did you get the bones used for your recent installations?" Lucy asked. She was trying very hard not to step into interview territory that Gil would want to cover, so she was fishing around the edges.

"Those of course came from the archaeological dig," Tamara said.

"That's where you got them?"

"Well, sort of. I found them pretty close to the dig, plus the bones had weathering on the surface that continued into the bone tissue. You wouldn't see that on a more recent bone."

"Really?" Lucy said doubtfully. "Is there any way bone that is, say, a year old could be mistaken for bone that's a hundred years old?"

"I don't see how. Bone weathering is pretty consistent when it's buried underground, especially around here where the soil isn't acidic. I'm pretty familiar with the concepts."

"But it sounds like you didn't find these bones underground."

"Only because they washed down the arroyo from the site up on the hill," Tamara said as she peered into the Beetle Boys' aquarium. "Before that they were buried. The state has only been digging up there a few weeks."

The woman had made an assumption. It was as simple as that. She had assumed that when she found pieces of a human skeleton, the only place they could have come from was the archaeological dig. She never considered that the body could be fresh. Any other person who had found the bones would have called the police.

Lucy saw a large freezer in the corner and opened it. She poked around, seeing if any human body parts poked back. She pushed aside a frozen ziplock bag full of tamales. Underneath was a plastic bag holding a foot-long fuzzy stick. Huh. A furry stick in a freezer. Weird. She pulled the bag out of the freezer and looked at it closer. At one end of the stick was something lumpy she couldn't make out through the ice crystals. She mashed the bag around until she got a better look. The lump turned out to be a paw. She said, "Oh God," without thinking. "Umm . . . Tamara? Can I ask what this is?"

"That's Esperanza's leg."

"Wait," Lucy said aloud. "You mean the three-legged dog outside? This is her leg? Really? Why do you have your dog's leg in the freezer?"

"I'm thinking about using it in a sculpture," Tamara said.

"Okay," Lucy said, the idea disturbing her. "How long ago did Esperanza lose her leg?"

"About four years ago, after she was hit by a car," Tamara said.

"Hmm . . . Well, just FYI, I think Esperanza's leg has seen better days, so you'll have to figure out some way to incorporate a little freezer burn into your artwork."

Gil stopped at the station to get Joe and then followed the directions Lucy had given him. Joe spent the drive asking questions that Gil couldn't answer, like how Lucy had found the killer and why they weren't calling in backup. A few minutes later Gil parked the car in front of a big house set well away from any main road and got out.

Lucy and another woman came out to the front of the house, followed closely by two dogs—or as closely as the three-legged one could manage with a hobble. The woman called hello to them and said, "I am so happy to see you. I'm Tamara."

Gil looked over at Lucy and then back at Tamara, observing the entire situation before saying a word.

"Why are you happy to see us?" Gil asked carefully. He hadn't known what to expect. He still wasn't sure, but it was not this nice woman. Not this nice house.

"I'm so excited about being arrested," she said.

"You think you're getting arrested?" Joe asked.

"Of course," Tamara said, all smiles. "I fully expect to be charged with desecration of a grave. I admit I did it. I even have my bail money ready to go."

"Why did you do it?" Joe asked slowly.

"To show the hypocrisy of our archaeological system," she said firmly. "We allow people who claim to be scientists to dig up people's ancestors and display them, yet when I do the same thing, I get arrested. It was a part of my plan."

Lucy interrupted, "It was for publicity." She showed them the brochure of Tamara's upcoming show. They read the line I WAS DEAD AND BURIED.

"Publicity?" Joe asked. "Seriously?" He turned and looked at Gil for what seemed like a full minute before he walked off a ways.

"He seems upset," Tamara said.

"He's always that way," Gil said as he looked over the brochure.

"She got the bones from an archaeological dig," Lucy said, trying to bring them back to the subject.

"Actually I found them in an arroyo just a few minutes' walk away," Tamara said. "They washed down from a new dig the state started. I guess they're excavating another old pueblo or something. It's just up on that hill over there." She pointed at a mound off in the distance, about a quarter of a mile to the north.

"So, Officer," Tamara said to Gil tentatively, "have you seen the art installations I did?"

Gil must have looked confused, so Lucy offered, "That's what she calls the displays."

"Yes, I have," Gil said.

"Can I ask for a layperson's point of view?" she asked, then, without waiting for an answer, said, "Did you get the symbolism of the jars I put in the cemetery installation? My idea was that I was speaking for the dead who are on display in our museums by printing on the cards the phrase 'I was dead and buried.' I meant the card to be like one of those explainer plaques you see at an exhibit but from the dead person's point of view. Did that come across?"

"You know, I don't think I got that," Gil said.

"Please tell me that the coat of watches I made for the statue of Mary indicated our different measures of time," Tamara said. "It was the idea that we all will be bones in the ground and ancient one day, and then we might end up in a museum."

"I can't say that I really understood that precise meaning," Gil said, "but I am curious why you did the installations this weekend."

"Because it's fiesta," Tamara replied. "Your Hispanic and Pueblo Indian ancestors have been some of the most exploited people when it comes to these digs. They are taking your grandparents out of their graves and putting them in glass cases. Did you know that there are more than a hundred and forty thousand archaeological sites identified in New Mexico and that the state has millions of stolen artifacts in its warehouses? It's a disgrace."

Joe strode back over to them and stood directly in front of Tamara and asked, "So you're telling me that you had no idea that those bones you used belonged to Brianna Rodriguez?"

"Who's Brianna Rodriguez?" Tamara asked.

Hobbit piñon pine were everywhere as they walked, looking more like fluffy bushes than majestic trees. Cholla cactus lined the edges of the path, all spikes and tall, chubby arms.

Tamara turned off a fork of the main trail, and they walked until they were no longer following a path, more a suggestion of one. The sand between the clumps of vegetation made a patchwork maze where pink flower clusters and yellow star grasses grew unobtrusively. Ahead Lucy saw the dark green of arroyo trees.

They topped a rise, and the arroyo spread out below. It was at least three car lengths across with a drop-off that was a slope in some areas and a cliff in others. The arroyo bottom was gray-beige sand pocked with stones, driftwood, and nonnatural debris—plastic bottles, a lawn chair. It was mostly all trash that had gone downstream in the summer floods and ended up here when the river meandered out.

They stood looking over the riverbed as Tamara tried to find a way down. They could see the archaeological site just to the north, across the arroyo and off in the distance. Gil could see why Tamara thought the bones had come from there. The summer rains had created rivulets in the sand that led straight from the hill to the riverbed. The erosion patterns had misled her.

They walked slowly down to the bottom of the arroyo, picking their way carefully so as not to slide in the sand. Joe reached the bottom first, then put a hand out to help Lucy down. Tamara walked over to the other side and crouched down in the shade of a piñon tree. As they approached, she took a stick and pointed to the small bones. Gil saw ribs and a few vertebrae. Tamara dug a little with her stick and revealed other small bones beneath the film of sand. The water runoff from the summer storms had probably tumbled and turned the bones many times, leaving them here to be buried by the desert.

The arroyo, which had been filled with nothing more than the sound of a meadowlark that morning, was now buzzing with activity.

Lucy had called Gerald Trujillo, who had been at the fire station, and asked him to look up the nearest dirt roads in their one-of-a-kind back-road map book. Gerald found an easy access road just a few yards down, and then people started to show up quickly.

The first had been Liz, who had been driving back up to Santa Fe to get a change of clothes and give her family a kiss. She got the call while she was on the interstate and was able to hit the right exit.

At the moment, Liz was bent over the bones with Tamara, saying, "The problem is that you didn't account for the smaller bone size and density, which makes the weathering process happen more quickly. Bone weathering is all about the surface-to-volume ratio. The smaller the bone, the higher the surface-to-volume ratio and—"

"The quicker the weathering," Tamara said, finishing her sentence. "I get it. Of course, I see where I made the mistake . . ."

Lucy sat in the shade of a cottonwood tree, just looking at the sky.

Joe came over to Gil, who was still watching Liz and Tamara. The two women had just shared a laugh about some concept of bone aging.

"So," Joe said, in a low voice. "There never was any crazy person who was a serial killer pedophile with a mental illness and a guilty conscience."

Gil said nothing. Their profile of the killer had been right, but they had created that profile based on an assumption—that the man who killed Brianna kept her bones in order to set up the elaborate displays. The problem had not been with the profile. The problem had been in that assumption. They never looked at the killing and the displays as separate events. David Geisler had suffered for it.

Gil looked down again at the map book in his hand. He had gotten it out of Liz's car. It was the same book that all police and firefighters used to get around town. It had page after page of detailed maps. If you leafed through the pages fast enough, it was almost like a flipbook, showing the heart of the city, then the residential areas, and finally the rural lands. Where they were now. Gil had used that continuity to check a theory he had.

"I guess Ashley didn't sell Brianna to a psychopath, either," Joe said. "Now we just have to figure out how the body ended up here."

When Gil had looked though the map book, he had been following a dotted line. One single line. From page to page, he used his finger to trace that dotted line. He followed that line from behind the Rodriguez house to right where they were standing now. In the map's legend, a dotted line indicated an arroyo.

"The answer to that is easy," Gil said. "Brianna did go into the arroyo behind the house the day she disappeared—but she didn't fall in and drown. Someone stabbed her and threw her in. The water carried her here."

Gil looked up at the sky as a crow flew overhead, then said, "We just narrowed our suspect list down to the four people who were in that house."

CHAPTER TWENTY-SIX

Sunday Afternoon

Rose Rodriguez sat in the hospital waiting room trying to will her sponsor to arrive. She had called the woman in a panic.

Rose wanted a drink. Badly. Painfully. In her head, she had already gone to her car and driven to the gas station down the road to get the vodka she knew they had behind the counter.

She started to cry. She wasn't sure if it was the pain of the wanting or because her daughter had just gone into emergency surgery. That was why she wanted the vodka. Because Ashley was having such a hard time in labor, they had to do an emergency C-section.

The doctors said that the baby's heartbeat had started to fade. Then, as a nurse looked between Ashley's legs and said something about the cord, it seemed that everyone was suddenly in such an angry hurry. Rose was told to leave. Ashley started crying. Alex was nowhere to be found, and Justin and Laura were probably somewhere making out.

Rose now sat. Alone. Alex wasn't answering his phone. She had yet to see Justin and Laura, and she honestly didn't want to see them. What she wanted was killing her. She wanted alcohol. God help her, at the moment, she wanted alcohol almost more than she wanted Ashley to be okay.

She started to say the Serenity Prayer in her head. "God grant me the serenity to accept the things I cannot change." She couldn't change what was happening to Ashley. That was all in the hands of her higher power. So how could she accept it? Rose was at a loss. Maybe it was through acknowledging that she had no control over the situation that she could accept it. She wasn't sure.

She said the next line of the prayer, "the courage to change the things I can." What could she change? She could change nothing about Ashley's situation. But could she change how badly she wanted alcohol? If her sponsor didn't arrive soon to hold her down, she would be in the car and on her way to the vodka. She said the last line in desperation, "and wisdom to know the difference." She tried to consider that one. The wisdom to know the difference between the things she couldn't change and the things she could.

When Rose had first entered AA, it had been out of guilt because of Brianna. That had been the very first thing she had to accept that she couldn't change. Now, as she thought again of the day Brianna disappeared, Rose suddenly realized that there was something she could do to change that day. On the heels of that realization came dread. Intense and horrible. She prayed once again for her sponsor to arrive, because her desire to drink had now become unbearable.

As Lucy drove back to town from Tamara's, she could see from horizon to horizon.

She had stayed on the scene with the bones for about a half hour until a uniformed officer gave them all a lift back to the house, with Gil in the front passenger seat and Lucy crammed in the back between Tamara and Joe. During the ten-minute ride, Joe had leaned over and whispered into Lucy's ear, "I'll need that photo back." She looked up in time to see Gil glance at them in the rearview mirror. They got back to the house, and while everyone else stood around debating whether Tamara should get arrested, Lucy went to her car to fetch the photo. She was able to slip the picture into Joe's hand while Gil was busy explaining to Tamara how it would not be in anyone's best interest to arrest her for desecration of remains. Lucy waved a merry good-bye to the group and went on her way before anyone could stop her, feeling the need to be alone.

Now she watched the clouds as she drove. As always, they were fabulously diverse. Towers of froth and masses of meringue. Off to the south, a thunderstorm dropped a sheet of gray down to the earth, but where she was, the sun was bright, the sky a robin's egg blue. The shifting sun sent shadows scattering over the mountains, whose curves looked like a sheet draped over a woman.

The last thought made Lucy grip the steering wheel tightly. She had seen a woman die today. So far she had been able to keep it out of her mind.

It had been the first dead body she'd seen since January. Since she'd killed a woman. Since the guilt started to overwhelm her.

Lucy's eyes became hot, and she felt the first few tears well up.

Joe was driving for a change as Gil made phone calls in quick succession. The first was to the hospital. He told the nurse on duty at the psych ward to expect paperwork from the DA later in the day that would order the release of David Geisler. Next, he paged the DA, who this time called him right back. He briefly told her the situation with Geisler. Her only response was "I'll take care of it."

The next call was to Chief Kline. Gil gave him an update in as few words as possible, mostly because of shame. His guilt over David Geisler was apparent in his voice. Kline said, "Look, I know you feel bad about Geisler, but some good came out of this. At least the guy will be evaluated and on medication." What Gil didn't say was that he wasn't sure that was a good thing. He clicked off the phone as they were just a block from the hospital.

"I guess the good news," Joe said, "is that now we have only a few suspects."

Gil nodded. "We just have to narrow it down."

"Is it sexist of me to say that I can't see a woman doing this?"

"I think it's naive," Gil said.

"It makes it easy, though. It leaves us with Justin, who we honestly don't know much about," Joe said.

"You must have profiled the family members back during the original investigation."

"Yeah, but Justin was only fourteen when Brianna disappeared," Joe said. "He still needed Ashley to babysit him. We never looked at him because of his age." *That was another mistake,* Gil thought.

They pulled up to the hospital and went inside, up to the maternity ward. They were about to pass by the waiting room when they saw Mrs. Rodriguez sitting next to another woman, deep in conversation.

She stood up as she saw them, saying, "Where's Alex? Ashley finally delivered the baby."

Gil and Joe awkwardly murmured congratulations to the new grandmother before Gil said, "Alex needs to stay at the station a little longer, but we wanted to come see how Ashley was doing."

"She had a really rough time," Mrs. Rodriguez said. "There was some problem with the cord, and she had to have an emergency C-section. It was bad."

"Is she all right?" Joe asked.

"She's doing better now. They got the baby out, and he's fine. He's so cute, and he has a full head of hair," she said, beaming.

"Is Ashley able to talk to us?" Gil asked. Dr. Santiago had said they could interview her once she was out of the woods.

Before she could answer, the woman Mrs. Rodriguez had been talking to stood up and said, "Hi. I'm Carla." She shook both of their hands.

Joe looked at her curiously, as if he should know who she was. "Are you a friend of the family?" he asked her.

"In a way," Carla said smiling.

"She's my AA sponsor," Mrs. Rodriguez said, slightly nervously. "She came here to make sure I was doing okay. The past few days have been pretty stressful."

Joe nodded. "I noticed your three-month pin. Congratulations."

Gil hadn't even noticed that on Mrs. Rodriguez's white blouse there was a gold pin. It was a triangle with the letter *G* inside the top and then the sun between two capital *A*'s.

"What step are you on?" he asked.

"I just started Step Eight," she said, smiling and looking toward her sponsor for approval.

"Oh, so that means you're making the list of people you have harmed," Joe said. "That can be a hard one." Gil wondered where Joe's information about alcoholism came from.

"I'm getting there," Mrs. Rodriguez said.

"Have you thought about Step Nine at all?" Joe asked. "About making amends?"

Mrs. Rodriguez looked down at the ground, her eyes suddenly overwhelmed by tears. "Just breathe," her sponsor said, putting her hand on Mrs. Rodriguez's shoulder. "In this moment you are fine. You are among people who care." Mrs. Rodriguez nodded and tried to smile, but failed.

"It seems like that might be a hard step for you," Joe said, more sympathetic than Gil had ever heard him.

Mrs. Rodriguez looked up at Joe, then over at her sponsor, who said, "It's okay. We only move forward when we want to. This is a process, and it takes time." Gil felt himself waiting, almost holding his breath, while Joe seemed relaxed and accepting. Gil wondered at the change.

Mrs. Rodriguez kept nodding, as if she were building up courage through the affirmative action. She looked back up at Joe, let out a deep breath, and said, "I wrote a letter to Brianna last week." Those seemed to be the only words she could manage as tears flowed down her face. Her sponsor gave Mrs. Rodriguez a tissue.

Joe said, "Of course. Just because she's no longer with us doesn't mean you can't make amends. I'm sure your sponsor helped you with the letter. They can be hard."

Mrs. Rodriguez said, "I told Brianna that I was sorry, and I asked for her forgiveness."

"What were you sorry for?" Joe asked tenderly.

"I was never there for her, because of the drinking. Even on the day she needed me the most . . ." Mrs. Rodriguez paused, and Carla put a hand on her shoulder. Mrs. Rodriguez stood straighter in resolve and continued. "The day . . . the day she went missing, I was passed out drunk in my room. Ashley had to wake me to tell me she was gone."

Joe just nodded and said nothing. After a moment he looked up at her and said, "You are not to blame for this. You did nothing wrong." Mrs. Rodriguez nodded. Joe smiled. "I know this has been hard for you, but I just have one more question for right now, okay? What do you remember from that day?"

"I got up in the morning and then in my head I said, 'It's Saturday, why not make it a party?' So I had some vodka . . . I don't remember anything else until Ashley woke me up."

"So you were out of it from around 10:00 A.M. until right before the police arrived at 2:00 P.M.?"

"Yes," she said.

Joe said, "Thank you so much, Mrs. Rodriguez. I think we need to go talk to Ashley now, but I'll try to come back and visit with you some more." She nodded gratefully. "Just keep working those steps," Joe said.

They walked away toward the nurses' station. Once out of earshot Gil asked, "Do you really believe that Mrs. Rodriguez isn't to blame and did nothing wrong?"

Joe snorted. "Hell, no. She was an absent mother who let her own child get molested and her granddaughter get killed. She's as guilty as anyone, and I hope she rots in hell." Gil smiled. The old Joe was back.

"How do you know so much about AA?" Gil asked.

"My mom," Joe said. Gil didn't press the issue. They stood at the nurses' station and told the woman in charge that they wanted permission from Dr. Santiago to interview Ashley.

"Our suspects are dropping off the list like flies," Joe said.

The nurse came back, saying Dr. Santiago had approved their visit, but warned them that Ashley might be groggy. She led them into the ward, which was very secure due to baby theft concerns. They went down the hallway, where they heard a tiny baby's cries interspersed with grunting sounds coming from another room. The music of labor and delivery.

They went into the next room on the left. Ashley looked tired but strangely awake for someone who had just had a C-section. She was sitting up in the hospital bed, holding a tightly swaddled baby. She was cooing at him as Justin leaned over her shoulder, smiling. Joe and Gil watched them for a moment before Joe cleared his throat and said, "Hi, Ashley. Congratulations." She looked up at them, surprised but happy. As if this were her first time being a new mom.

"Thank you," she said, looking back down at the baby, who stared at her intently without making a sound. "Isn't he beautiful?"

"He sure is," said Joe. "I heard the labor was pretty hard."

"Yeah," she said. "It was bad."

"Where's Laura?" Gil asked. "Is she here?"

"Yeah," Justin said as he played with the baby's fingers. "She went to the cafeteria to get a Coke."

"You know, Ashley," Joe said, "we do need to ask you a few questions."

"Actually, Joe," Gil said, "why I don't take Justin here outside while you two talk?"

"Sure," Joe said, confused. *He must be,* Gil thought. They had been waiting to interview Ashley for three days, chomping at the bit. Ashley was the one who held the answers, although she had proven capable of lying to them and everyone else. She held the key to everything. Now when they finally had her, Gil wanted to leave.

In fact, as soon as Gil walked into the hospital room, he realized talking to Ashley wasn't the only way to get to the truth. Because what Gil saw in that room was Justin and Ashley framing the new baby in their arms. It was the picture of happiness. The picture of a family.

Joe had been right. They knew nothing about Justin. At that moment, though, Gil saw Justin for who he was. Because a father can recognize another father.

Lucy walked into the yoga studio and immediately felt like a hippo in a lily patch. Everyone else was wearing tight cropped shirts and pants. She was in sweatpants and an oversized T-shirt. She didn't know there was a dress code for meditation.

She had swung by home, glad to be finally kicking her way out of her EMS uniform. She had decided on the road back from Tamara's that a meditation class might do her good. She tried to keep herself from questioning it too much, knowing her tendency for wanting to avoid uncomfortable situations. Meditation definitely sounded uncomfortable. Just yourself, sitting.

On the walls of the yoga studio were taped handwritten signs that read: NO SHOES PLEASE. Lucy panicked. She still wasn't wearing socks and hadn't done her toenails in weeks. Her polish was chipped and worn. She didn't want to be judged by her feet. She leaned against a wall and casually watched a few shoeless people come in. There were some manicured toenails and some that needed a date with a hedge clipper. She relaxed and slipped off her shoes, as she wondered if this was how the fantasy of a foot fetishist might play out.

A woman in clingy workout clothes went to the front of the class and said, "Okay, let's have everyone take their seats." Only there were no seats. Just a hardwood floor. Lucy sat down cross-legged and eyed the other people in the room. It was actually a diverse group. She had assumed it would be all entitled white people, since meditation was their favorite pastime, but there were several people who had real color in their skin, unlike Lucy's palest shade of white.

The teacher told them to close their eyes while she put on a CD of soft classical music.

"Now breathe deep," she said, "and feel it leaving your airways as you exhale."

The woman talked in a voice that was almost as calm as John Lopez's. That thought immediately made Lucy remember the talk with her boss. She wasn't exactly sure what Lopez had been getting at with the self-evaluation form—and why did he want her to write about her future plans? She would have to make some up because, at the moment, there were none. Maybe that was his point—she needed to stop thinking of just today and start thinking of tomorrow. Which made her think she had just quoted a Fleetwood Mac song.

Maybe that had been her problem in approaching her dual life of newspapers and EMS. She never looked past the moment.

She thought back to what Lopez had said. Was he asking her to choose in his no-pressure, nice-guy way? Was she going to have to quit one thing or the other? If that was the case, she had no idea which she would choose. Either way, she would be only half of herself.

Gil and Justin sat in the chairs in the hospital hallway as nurses rushed by and the sound of crying babies ebbed and flowed. Smiling families walked by, loaded with stuffed animals and flowers, eager to see their newest member. Gil sighed. Yet another interrogation. This time he only felt sad. He knew this one would not have the horror of the Rudy Rodriguez interview, or the simple, long, dramatic movements of the one with Alex Stevens. This one would be quiet and grief stricken.

He knew he needed to get started.

"You and Ashley have been together a long time," Gil said. Justin nodded; he didn't protest or try to deflect the truth. Gil wondered why. Maybe the boy wanted to tell someone about the abuse? Or maybe he thought that Ashley had done nothing wrong?

"You make a good couple," Gil said, "and now you have this beautiful baby together."

The boy smiled, looking upbeat, looking too young. Gil smiled, too, but his was more sad than sincere.

"Alex never found out?" Gil asked.

The boy shook his head and said, "He was gone a lot, and he just acted . . . you know."

"That must have been hard for Ashley. She must really love you." Inside Gil was just a shade of gray. Not angry. Not understanding. Resigned. He needed to get solid facts from Justin. So much of Gil's job in this case had been about manipulation.

"Ashley always loved me," Justin said.

"How old were you when she started babysitting for you?"

"About seven, I think," the boy said, his young face looking thoughtful.

Gil looked at the floor as he did some calculations in his head. Ashley would have been twelve at the time. Just when her own father had started abusing her and she was powerless to stop it. So she abused the only person who had less power than she did.

"It must have been hard for you when Brianna was born," Gil said.

"Yeah. They wouldn't even let me in to see her . . ."

"Because you were too young." Gil finished the sentence for him. Actually it had probably been more than that. A nurse just couldn't let an adolescent boy drop in on the maternity ward. He might see secret female things he shouldn't and get ideas. Because teenaged boys were the perpetrators of things vulgar and perverse. Not always, though. Sometimes they were the victims.

"Ashley probably thought it was a bad idea for you to tell anyone that you were Brianna's father. They wouldn't understand that kind of love," Gil said.

The boy nodded vigorously and said, "They would think, like, it was gross about me and Ashley, you know." Justin would have been twelve years old when Brianna was born, while Ashley was seventeen.

"It must have been hard for you when Brianna disappeared." Gil purposely didn't say "murdered" or "killed."

"Yeah, it was," the boy said. "I couldn't even tell people she was my daughter."

"When did Laura find out?" Gil asked. This was a guess on his part, but he decided to throw it out there to see what happened.

"I don't know. She seemed to kind of just know one day."

"And Laura was okay with it?"

"I tried to be a gentleman about it. I, like, didn't throw it in her face or anything," Justin said.

"What about Ashley? What did she think of Laura?"

"Ashley knew that Laura and I . . . that it was no big deal," Justin said. Gil had to keep himself from reacting to that. There is no such thing as "no big deal" when it comes to how girls feel about boys. That was one thing he had learned from his own preteen daughters.

"Did Laura and Ashley get along?"

"I dunno. I guess."

Gil felt the boy starting to close up, so he started at the beginning. The newest new beginning—the baby.

"Do you have any names picked out?" Gil asked, smiling, patting the boy on the shoulder like he would a proud father.

"Ashley wants to name him Tristan, but I think he'll get beat up a lot."

Gil laughed. "I have to say, I agree with you on that. What about a family name?"

"Maybe Levi for my grandfather," Justin said.

"What about Justin Junior?" Gil said. The boy smiled proudly.

"I guess you won't name him after Ashley's dad," Gil said in an understanding, understated tone.

"That's for sure."

"So you don't like him?" Gil asked.

"Nah. He's a jerk."

"I guess it was good he wasn't around much anymore, especially the day Brianna disappeared," Gil said. Justin nodded. Gil was finally back to where he wanted to be—the day Brianna disappeared. This was where he would get his answers.

"It must have been weird being in the backyard that day with just Laura and Ashley. I mean, two girls like that . . ." Gil said.

"Tell me about it."

"And everybody was probably drinking . . ."

"Yeah."

"Then the rain starts up. Did you all just run inside?"

"Yeah, but I had to carry Ashley into the bedroom, she was so wasted."

"And you guys were probably soaking wet . . ."

"Totally . . ."

"What'd you do?"

"I tried to get Ashley out of her wet clothes . . ."

"I bet one thing led to another . . ." Gil put in seamlessly.

"Yeah . . ."

"Where was Laura?" Gil asked.

"She was knocking on the bedroom door like crazy, but I'd locked it . . ."

"That was good thinking . . ."

"I told her Ashley was sick and throwing up."

"And she didn't suspect anything?" Gil asked.

"Yeah. Can you believe it?" Justin said, shaking his head at his good luck and smiling.

"When you and Ashley were done, what did you do?"

"We got up and went to get some food. Laura was in the kitchen. That's when we all noticed that Brianna was missing."

CHAPTER TWENTY-SEVEN

Sunday Night

Ashley wished Justin would hurry up with the police officer. She wanted to show him what the baby had done; he had blown the cutest little bubble of spit. Then the bubble popped, and the baby closed his eyes again.

The baby looked like Justin, just as Brianna had. They both had his eyes.

Justin had been a pretty child. So sweet. So alone. His own mother, her aunt, had two jobs and a boyfriend. So, ever since Justin was little, he'd been coming over to Ashley's house every day so she could watch him after school and on weekends. He would sleep over most nights. They had fun together, playing and being silly. She felt so free with him. She had never had any brothers or sisters to play with, so she felt like a child for the first time.

He was like an angel with his blond hair, but he also was so mature for his age. They would talk about the meaning of life and sneak drinks off her mother's vodka bottles. Ashley often thought that he was the only man who had never used her.

One night, when her father was drunk, Ashley snuck into Justin's bed so her dad couldn't find her. They cuddled together in the night, protecting each other. They had slept together like that for many nights since. They would wake up together and tease each other, both laughing at the same things.

Ashley knew that people would think it was wrong. They would think that she had somehow hurt Justin, as if she ever could. He wanted the togetherness as much as she did. Even though she was twelve and he was seven on that first night they were together, the difference in their ages was only five years.

In a few years, when she was twenty-three and he was eighteen, those five years would mean nothing.

Gil and Joe sat in the police station. It was quiet. Fiesta was over, so all the overtime officers had gone home. They were looking at the photos of the Rodriguezes' backyard taken just after Brianna disappeared. Everything was a muddy mess because of the rain that day. In the background of the photos, the arroyo was almost overflowing as water rushed through it with violence. It was so different from the quiet arroyo that Gil saw behind the Rodriguezes' house when he first visited them.

Gil and Joe were looking over the pictures to try to spot the knife that might have been used to stab Brianna. Chances were it had been thrown into the river, washed downstream until the water petered out, and left on some sandy bank. Just like Brianna.

They didn't need the knife. It would have been a nice additional piece of information, but they had something that would work just as well—the last person who saw Brianna alive. Laura Gutierrez sat in the interview room, waiting for them. They were making her wait on purpose. To keep her off balance. Her parents had given them permission to interview her without them being present and declined to come down to the station, even after Gil explained the situation briefly.

As Gil looked absentmindedly at the photos, he thought about the Rodriguez family. They had all lied from the beginning about where they were the day Brianna disappeared. Each one thought that telling the truth of where they really were would be worse than the lie. Alex Stevens was drinking and driving. Mrs. Rodriguez was passed out. Ashley and Justin were intertwined in bed. Laura was alone with Brianna. In the end, they cared more about their lies than about that little girl.

Gil looked at Laura Gutierrez as he and Joe entered the interview room. She sat with one leg crossed over the other, leaning back. She didn't look nervous. She was smiling slightly. Gil, who was holding the usual manila folder with Laura's name on it, kept standing and started the usual speech. "Laura, do you know why you are here today?" He was tired. He thought about all the people in the case who were sexual abusers—Ashley, her father, Judge Otero. Gil wondered how many of them would ever be charged. That was a decision for the sexual offender division and the DA. Gil would be happy to be left out of it.

"The hell if I know," Laura said, still smiling, bringing him back to the interrogation.

Gil just looked at her, not reacting to her disdain. Because that was what she wanted. Instead, he rattled off the introductory statement. "It's recently come to our attention that we have been misled regarding some things about Brianna's disappearance. I can guarantee you, Laura, that our investigation will uncover the truth. In light of that, if you know anything about it, you should tell me now."

She looked at Gil flatly and said nothing. For the first time, Gil actually wished Joe would say something. He wasn't sure he had the energy for this. For her. Because she was going to take a lot of energy to interrogate. Nevertheless, she wouldn't be hard to get a confession out of, because her motive to kill was so primal—jealousy. That was usually a hard emotion to cover up.

"How long have you been dating Justin?" Gil asked, sitting down. Joe pulled up a chair next to him.

"Three years, two months," she said. "We hooked up when we started middle school."

"What did you think about his relationship with Ashley?" Gil asked.

"It wasn't a relationship," she said scornfully. "She was just using him."

"How so?" Joe asked. Gil felt grateful to him for jumping in.

"She would just have him when Alex wasn't around," she said. "It was disgusting for a woman her age to be doing that."

"That made you angry?" Gil asked. He actually wanted her angry. It would make the confession easier.

"It made me pissed," she said, as if pissed were a different emotion than anger. As if the word "anger" didn't describe the height of her emotion to the right degree.

"Were you pissed at Justin?" Joe asked.

"No. It wasn't his fault. She was abusing him. Sexually abusing him," she said, deliberately enunciating every word, as if it would come as a surprise to them.

"Did you talk to Ashley about it?" Joe asked.

"That bitch? She just laughed at me."

There was nothing new to this story. He had heard it many times. The woman, scorned by her lover, with nowhere to turn, takes her anger out on something else. Sometimes she might shred his clothes. Or run over his golf clubs. Or crash his car. Or kill his daughter.

"We know you were alone that night with Brianna," Gil said. He was rushing to the end because he was tired of playing games with this child. She had no remorse. She somehow believed in her mind that killing Brianna was necessary to get back at Ashley.

"So?" she said.

"You were the only person alone with her that day," Gil said.

"So?" she said again.

Gil almost rolled his eyes at her. "We know you killed her." It was too blunt, but he wanted to shake the attitude out of her.

She finally looked nervous but was trying to hide it. Gil knew he should tell her that he understood why she killed Brianna, that it was the only way to make sure Justin didn't leave her for Ashley, but he just didn't have the energy. He was thankful Joe spoke up.

"My guess is that you didn't even think before you did it," Joe said. She was finally listening a little and seemed less concerned with keeping up her bravado. "It was just such a quick response, and you were just so angry. Then before you knew it, there you were, and there she was, and you had to do something . . ."

"It wasn't like that at all," she said.

"Well, then, what was it like?" Joe asked.

"Yeah, I was pissed," she said, "but all I did was make a phone call."

"To who?" Gil asked.

She didn't answer.

"To who?" Gil asked again, too loudly.

Joe said, "I can go on my computer and get your phone records in just a few minutes, but it would be better if you told us yourself."

"Fine. Whatever," she said, all attitude again. "I called Tony."

"Tony who?" Gil asked without thinking.

"Tony Herrera."

An hour after her meditation class, Lucy found herself standing on the labyrinth in front of the cathedral, still dressed in her comfy sweatpants. She took the first step of the cobbled maze and started to follow its twisting path. She had left the class feeling energetic but pensive, so she drove to the cathedral and started on the labyrinth without really knowing why. The meditation class had been interesting, but the teacher had talked in a monotone voice incessantly about "following your breath," which was an instruction that Lucy didn't understand. The teacher did say one thing that made Lucy listen a little more carefully—she had said, "Quiet your mind." That wasn't something Lucy did too often. In fact, she usually did the opposite. She numbed her mind, distracted it and inundated it.

She wondered why she avoided the quiet so much. Was it because it seemed so boring as she ran toward the chaos?

The teacher had said something else. "Rid yourself of anything that disturbs the quiet of your mind." The teacher had been talking about stray thoughts and images that came up during the meditation, but all Lucy could think of was the guilt. The old distraction that she kept going back to.

She took one of the twists of the path and thought about Del. Why hadn't she told him what she'd really written on her note in

Zozobra? Why should she care if he teased her? She *did* care—the guilt had somehow become important to her, and she didn't want him mocking it. It took her a moment to realize that she was angry at him. Furious, in fact. She listened to all of his incessant blather, and he made fun of her for having real emotions? Lucy started to walk faster as she cursed Del in her head. She felt guilty about the dead woman because she was responsible. She was to blame. In truth, though, Lucy had done nothing wrong. Nothing at all. She had only done the best that she could. Just like she had done nothing to make Del break up with her. Nothing at all. Lucy stopped short as the final thought hit her. It was the first time she realized that she blamed herself for the collapse of their relationship. She only absently saw that she had reached the center of the labyrinth. Her mind was suddenly quiet.

Death. Del. Guilt. Quiet. It was all a little too much for a Sunday afternoon, and where did it leave her? She looked up at the trees above her, then at the church towers. It left her in the center of a maze that she had no idea how to get out of.

At least she knew one thing—she did want to get out. She wanted to be released. She deserved it. Because she had done nothing wrong.

Gil drove the Crown Victoria back toward the adult detention center on the outskirts of town. Joe sat in the passenger seat. Silent.

They had left Laura in a holding cell at the station while they went to check on her story. After her act of annoyance dropped away, she told them, piece by piece, about the day Brianna disappeared. About Tony Herrera.

Laura had gotten jumped into the West Side gang when she was ten. The same gang that Herrera once ran in. The girls who jumped her in had been nice, probably because she was so young, only giving her a black eye and a few scrapes. It was because of West Side that she met Justin.

As a little sister in the gang, she was only expected to do small things, every once in a while. One of those things had been to hold some drugs for Tony Herrera, who was dealing out of the food court in the mall. Laura had stood next to the Gap waiting for him, the little bag of heroin in her pocket. Tony had just gone to buy a shirt at Sears, where the security guards were a tad too quick to arrest gang members.

When Tony came back, he was with Ashley. His girlfriend. Next to Ashley was Justin, the cousin she was babysitting. For Laura, it was love at first sight. She didn't realize until later how much of a hold Ashley had over Justin.

Laura explained to Justin that it was wrong. That Ashley was just taking advantage. A year ago, Justin finally agreed to stop seeing Ashley. Or so he told Laura. She didn't find out the truth until the afternoon Brianna disappeared, when she heard Justin and Ashley in the bedroom. It was too much. She saw Brianna outside, playing alone in the backyard, and thought about what Tony would do if he knew Brianna wasn't his kid.

"But Herrera couldn't have cared less that Brianna wasn't his," Joe said to her.

Laura snorted in response, saying, "Yeah, right. As soon as Ashley delivered the baby he went and tried to cut off his West Side tattoo. He was always talking about how he had to be a good father and all that shit. He tried to get a real job over at Home Depot and swore that as soon as he got enough money he'd buy Brianna all these toys. But he never paid a cent in child support and barely saw the kid."

Gil parked the car, and he and Joe walked into the detention center. They went through the procedure once again of signing the visitors' log and putting their sidearms in the gun locker.

This time they went to a different beige room and waited for Tony Herrera to be escorted in.

Gil felt tired as he thought of all the mistakes they had all made in the case. Sure, Fisher had committed a lot of them, but Gil was not blameless. He had interviewed Herrera two days ago, and he forgot to double-check whether the man had been in jail when Brianna disappeared. Fisher had written in his notes that Herrera had been in custody. In fact, Gil found out with a little checking, Herrera had been released the week before due to overcrowding. He was just a low-level drug dealer, after all. A minimum security prisoner. No real danger to the community.

Gil also had missed something crucial. Something he had seen with his own eyes. He thought back to the interview with Herrera. Gil had known Herrera was lying when he said he left the gang because of the lifestyle, but he had been so focused on finding out if Herrera was Brianna's father that he hadn't asked any follow-up questions. He never asked if Herrera left the gang for Brianna. Fisher wasn't the only one who had made mistakes, and David Geisler had paid for them all.

Herrera came in in his orange jumpsuit, his shaved head glinting in the fluorescent light as he sat down.

"Hey, man," Herrera said to Joe, but as soon as he noticed that Joe's friendliness had evaporated, he leaned back in his chair, tattooed arms crossed in front of him.

Gil looked at Herrera and felt strangely relaxed. Maybe it was because he wouldn't have to lie in this interview. Maybe because there were no games left to play.

"We talked to Laura Gutierrez," Gil said.

Herrera said nothing. He just stared at Gil. Hard.

"She told us about the day Brianna disappeared," Gil said.

Gil wasn't asking questions. He was just making statements. Because he knew Herrera wouldn't talk to them. Even if he did, he certainly wouldn't tell them the truth. Because they had nothing to trade for it. The only bargaining chip might be a reduced sentence for a confession, but that would be up to the district attorney. Right now, they had nothing valuable to offer. So Herrera would stay silent. Gil guessed that the man wouldn't ask for his lawyer right away, though. Mainly because prison is boring. Joe and Gil offered a distraction. They were like a television program to Herrera; they were entertaining to watch.

Gil still hoped to get something out of the interview, despite Herrera's silence. It wouldn't be evidence. It might only be the knowledge that Gil did everything he could to seal up the case.

"Laura says she called you and told you something shocking," Joe said. "She told you that Brianna wasn't your baby."

Herrera didn't move, but he was listening.

"You know what else she told us?" Joe said. "She said she had to explain to you about babies because you actually thought a kid who was due in July could have been conceived by you almost a year earlier."

Herrera didn't react to Joe's mocking.

"Dude, did you even listen in sex ed class?" Joe asked. "It's nine months, man. Nine. Not ten. Not twelve."

Still no response from Herrera.

"Then Laura tells you that Justin is Brianna's real father," Joe said, "and you lost it, because here Ashley wouldn't have sex with you, this tough guy, but she was doing this kid?"

Herrera was stone still.

"And this was after you had gone and left everything—the gang, your friends—to take care of your little girl," Joe said. "Man, you even tried to cut off your own tattoo."

Gil interrupted, saying, "Laura told us that you showed up just a few minutes after she called. She said you tried to break down the front door, but it was locked, and she was too scared to open it. She thought you might try to kill them all."

"When you couldn't open the front door, you went around back, where you saw Brianna playing in the backyard."

Herrera was trying to look disinterested.

"It's so nice when you have an eyewitness," Joe said. He leaned forward and added in a low voice, "Laura saw everything you did through the kitchen window."

Herrera's jaw tightened.

Gil and Joe left Tony Herrera sitting in the beige room. He had never spoken, not even to ask for his lawyer. The DA would be charging him in the morning, which would bring stacks of paperwork on the case. Tomorrow they also would sort out if the rest of the family knew about Herrera's involvement. For now, they walked across the parking lot of the detention center. Gil took a few deep breaths of fresh air. The coming night would be beautiful. Clear and crisp. He popped open his cell phone and dialed. All he said to the person who answered was "Can we go some place and get dinner?"

Lucy wondered if God had made greens and browns dominate the desert so the sunset—like the one she was watching now out the restaurant window—could be painted across a noncompeting muted canvas. The colors changed from yellows and oranges to reds and fuchsias, every color more molten than the last. The sunsets in New Mexico stopped her in her tracks. Always. Daily.

She looked up as Del slid into the booth. He looked good, wearing faded-just-right jeans and a light blue T-shirt. She could see why she had fallen for him all those years ago. He looked rakish and confident. She had called him just after walking the labyrinth to see if he wanted to get dinner, knowing that he'd think it was a prelude to sex.

They wouldn't be having sex this time.

Something had shifted. She was finally starting to see Del—who was so witty and who she'd thought was so much smarter than she was—for what he was. Suddenly, after the day she'd had, that mattered. She and Del had been languishing in a place between being a couple and being broken up, and Lucy had allowed it, thinking that it was better than nothing. It wasn't. It was worse. For her.

"What's up?" Del said to her as the waitress came over to get his drink order.

Lucy waited until he'd asked for coffee before she said, with what she hoped was a sincere smile, "We need to talk."

They were already at the table when Gil arrived. Joy and Therese were coloring on their place mats even though the crayons were meant for children much younger. Joy seemed to be drawing a rainbow, while Therese was making hearts and stars. They were both too old to get the same kind of pleasure a two-year-old might out of making bright streaks across a white page, but the girls were still smiling as they drew.

Susan was chatting on her cell phone and only noticed Gil as he leaned over to give her a kiss on her cheek. She looked at him, surprised, then smiled. The girls both said, "Hi, Dad," as they kept coloring.

He sat down across the table. Watching them. They were so intent on their drawings. He didn't expect them or Susan to ask him about the case. Nor would he want them to. Even if they did, he wouldn't tell them anything. It was his way of protecting them—and himself. They were a refuge from work. Their little family problems gave him something other than death to deal with.

Susan hung up her phone and said, "I was just talking to the Realtor, and I realized I forgot to ask you if you'd looked at that house in Eldorado."

"Yeah, I did," Gil said.

"And?" she asked, taking a sip of her iced tea.

Gil said nothing. Susan knew him well enough to know that he would answer eventually. A full minute went by as the girls kept drawing and Susan looked at him. He wasn't sure what he wanted to say. Gil thought about the house he'd seen, about its open space. It was beautiful, but he knew it would never be home to him. He needed to be able to see the Sangre de Cristo Mountains. They were his compass. He needed a place where there was more history to the land—his history.

He said carefully, "I don't want to live in Eldorado."

"Gil," Susan said, annoyed, "We've been over this . . ."

"I think we should move to Galisteo." The idea had come to him when he was walking across the parking lot of the detention center. Out of the blue, crisp air.

"And live with your mother?" Susan said. The girls watched them, ignoring their drawings. "You know I love your mom, but there is no way—"

"No, we could build our own house on their property." Gil saw her hesitation, so he added, "We'd still be in the Eldorado school district, so the girls could go to the good school."

Now it was Susan's turn to consider in silence.

"And you could get your dream house," Gil said, surprising himself with how much he wanted to do this.

"What would you get?" she asked.

"To go home."

ACKNOWLEDGMENTS

I would like to thank Annice Barber, Angela Barber, Kristen Davenport, Pat West-Barker, and Tasha Rath for their constant support—which never wavered even when I was writing while sleep deprived and started seeing invisible bugs. The horrible invisible bugs. Special thanks to Dr. Rex Baker for doing emergency surgery on my computer. And to Barbara Ferry for all the Spanish consults. Muchas gracias. And to Linda, Deborah, and Tania, who gave me great insight into their worlds.

I also wish to thank, as always, Anne Hillerman, Jean Schaumberg, the Tony Hillerman Mystery Writing Contest, Peter Joseph, Thomas Dunne Books, and everyone at St. Martin's Press for giving me my start in this business.

Finally, to the Santa Fe Police Department, the Santa Fe Fire Department, the Santa Fe County Sheriff's Department, the Santa Fe County Fire Department, and *The Santa Fe New Mexican* newspaper—thank you for being champions of the public, each in your own way.